RELEASING LISA

RELEASING LISA

RICHARD R. ROACH, MD, FACP

RELEASING LISA

iUniverse books may be ordered through booksellers or by contacting:

iUniverse
1663 Liberty Drive
Bloomington, IN 47403
www.iuniverse.com
1-800-Authors (1-800-288-4677)

ISBN: 978-1-4917-6085-7 (sc)
ISBN: 978-1-4917-6086-4 (e)

Library of Congress Control Number: 2015902248

Print information available on the last page.

iUniverse rev. date: 3/24/2015

To Temujin Jonathan Roach,
master of political science and economics,
who taught his parents how to succeed despite the barriers

ACKNOWLEDGMENTS

I wish to thank my wife, Priscilla, for encouraging me to write this book. She wanted to know how Lisa became such a strong character. An acknowledgment is due to our son, Temujin, who taught his parents so much about personal value. Without his strength of character, this novel could never have been written. Our daughter, Tirzah, did a great job on the basketball court and is responsible for the insight into Lisa's athletic prowess. Thanks to Martha Hull for her vivid description of guiding a football team on a canoe trip. Her insights as to how to make their trip enjoyable and meaningful were invaluable to the composition of those chapters. A special thanks to Mark Loehrke, MD, for editing the chapter on the basketball game. He and his children have played competitive basketball through college, and at present, he is the basketball announcer for the high school his children attended. His daughter even set up a basketball court in Benin where she was assigned in the Peace Corps. She made a profound impact on the people in her community. I want to thank Mr. Kumshaw, my high school art teacher, who explained to me how the Louvre was heated during the Nazi occupation and shared his personal struggles as a displaced person trying to stay alive during the Second World War. He knew every brushstroke on the canvases in the museum by personal experience. Thanks to Judith A. Johnson for the frontispiece illustration inspired by one of the first drafts of my novel. I want to thank iUniverse for their marvelous help in editing this book and preparing it for my expectant readers who wanted to know what happened to Heidi after *Saving Skunk*.

Richard R. Roach, MD, FACP

CHAPTER 1

Nobody realizes that some people expend
tremendous energy merely to be normal.
—*Southern Living*, May 2006

Mr. Rasmussen, the principal, welcomed everyone to the graduation ceremony. "Thank you all for coming to the 1991 graduation of Duluth East High School."

Everyone cheered except Lisa, who stopped listening to all the speeches that followed. She was anxious about whether she really graduated. She recalled the conversation she had with her father that morning. He told her that the school board met in special session to decide whether she would graduate. "Did I?" she asked.

He replied that he didn't know yet, that it was complicated. "Because of your dyslexia, they may overrule Mrs. Burns, but if they agree with her, you may have to take English in summer school. At least you can walk in the ceremony with your classmates."

Her English teacher, Mrs. Burns, had told her that she would flunk senior English and would have to take the class over in summer school. *Just because I can't spell*, Lisa thought. *But then it probably didn't help that I refused to write my whole name on my paper from the first day of class.* She remembered the incident that started the conflict with Mrs. Burns.

"Mrs. Burns," Lisa had said, raising her hand. "Why did I get an F on my assignment? I did all the work."

"Elizabeth, the first rule is to put your name on your paper."

"But I did."

1

"Elizabeth, why do you insist on being argumentative?" Mrs. Burns had spat. "Your name is not Lisa Zuc; it is Elizabeth Zuccerelli."

Lisa struggled to spell her name correctly. The school had refused to have her tested, but her father had sent her to a special psychologist who had diagnosed some dyslexia. However, her English teacher had refused to accommodate her disability. Lisa would stare at words and couldn't tell the difference between her name spelled correctly or incorrectly. In the past, teachers had laughed at her. She had not wanted to give Mrs. Burns that opportunity, so she had yelled, "It's a registered trademark." Her classmates had snickered. Her father, who was the largest employer in the county, owned Zuc Industries Inc. Besides, most of the girls on the basketball team just called her Zuc. Her best friends called her Lisa, but those were few.

"That won't do, young lady. I will crush that pertinacious attitude you have. Go to Mr. Rasmussen's office till you can be civil."

Everything had gotten worse after that day. Lisa had tried, but her relationship with Mrs. Burns had just deteriorated. Now, at the end of the school year, she had the distinction for the most detentions in the history of the school. Her parents had met with the school counselor, but Mrs. Burns had screamed that she was the captain of her ship and Elizabeth would conform or flunk.

I will just have to wait and see what is in that leather folder, she thought. *I hate school; the sooner I am out of here the better.*

"Elizabeth Rebecca Zuccerelli," the principal announced from the platform. Lisa was the last student to be called to the platform. She was always last, as her name started with the last consonant and last vowel of the alphabet. She stood and stretched to her full six-foot lanky frame in her black gown. She was taller than any other girl in the school and even taller than most of the boys. Underneath her gown her illegal shorts and T-shirt felt peculiar but comfortable. As she marched to the platform, she looked carefully at what the principal had in his hand. *Was it really a diploma? Had she graduated?*

She climbed the last step. The diploma was only inches away. *Once I have it, no more school.* She gave a quick glance to the side. *Everyone's looking at me. Probably because their butts are sore and they can't wait to get out of this auditorium.*

She searched the audience to find her parents. Her father looked handsome and distinguished in the shiny, black suit he'd bought in Italy. He had wavy, black hair and an Italian complexion that he'd passed on to her. Her mother was Finnish. With her straight, blonde hair that she worked so hard to curl and an ivory complexion, she looked stunning next to her father. The bright-blue satin dress she'd gotten in Paris accentuated her statuesque figure. Lisa had always thought that her mother was as pretty as any model on a magazine cover. She wanted to wave to them.

Mr. Rasmussen handed her the gray-and-red diploma folder in the school colors. She thanked him courteously and then picked up her pace. The repetitious music stopped as he headed for the podium for the closing remarks.

Lisa opened the folder. It read: This is not a diploma. Please present this certificate at room 105 to receive what you have merited. Lisa panicked. *Does this mean I didn't graduate? Do I have to take English all over again? I will never pass it.*

Her vision blurred with tears as she walked down the aisle. Her father was sitting on the end of the row, so rather than return to her assigned seat, she walked past him and tossed the diploma cover into his lap. He turned, startled, and stretched his arm toward her, but she ran. No one would catch her. She was the fastest runner on the track team. Besides, everyone was turned to listen to Mr. Rasmussen's speech about how this was the best class ever. "Except for me," she said as she slammed through the auditorium door. She went straight to the cloak room. She tore off her gown and slammed it on the table in front of the woman from the rental agency.

"Is the graduation over?" she asked.

"For me it is."

The lady handed her the mortarboard and tassel. "You can keep these. You earned them."

"No, I didn't." Lisa tossed them back at the table with such force that they ricocheted right onto the woman's lap. In her shorts and T-shirt, she ran out the door to the parking lot, jumped in her Jeep, and drove home.

She rapidly tapped out the code on the security gate. She drove down the curving driveway and screeched to a stop, jumped out of the

Jeep, and ran upstairs to her room. Her camping clothes were already packed. Running down the stairs with her bundle, she noticed that the dining room table was set with all the leaves added for the many guests invited to the graduation party. The table was decorated with red and gray ribbons in her school colors. The best china was out. There were a myriad of forks and even a fish knife beside each plate.

"Have fun," she said to the empty room as she penciled a note. She spoke the words out loud as she wrote them: "I don't deserve a party. I'm going canoeing till I get my head on straight. I am not running away. Don't worry; you taught me to be a good paddler. Please don't be too disappointed in me. I love you. Elizabeth." She looked at what she had written, especially at her name. *I think I misspelled … I'm not sure. Oh, they'll figure it out.*

Tears dripped from her eyes as she folded the note and put it on her father's plate. Her father had been her camping partner; he'd taught her how to paddle a canoe, start a fire after a rainstorm, and make an emergency shelter from pine boughs, but since he'd became CEO, after Grandfather Zuccerelli had retired, he had been too busy.

She rushed out to the garage. For days she had been putting oatmeal and soup mixes into her hidden food pack. Beef jerky and a bag of nuts mixed with M&M's completed her menu. She loaded her two weeks' worth of rations and then hoisted her fifteen-foot, lightweight Grumman canoe onto her Jeep's roof rack, tying it securely. She squealed her tires as she drove back down the driveway. She looked both ways. No sign of her parents' car.

"To Canada," she whispered.

After an all-night drive and an inconsequential border crossing into Canada, she arrived at her designated landing outside Atikokan. She parked the Jeep, locked it up, and launched her canoe. She put on her life jacket and crawled into the stern of the canoe, balancing her gear in the bow. She paddled toward the first portage around a waterfall at the north end of the lake. Peace and calm pervaded her spirit. No tests, no papers to write, and no Mrs. Burns to yell at her. She felt confident.

That confidence slowly dissipated as a fog quickly rolled in. Lisa dipped her paddle in the still Canadian water. She cinched her life vest as she slid her canoe forward with trepidation. *This fog came out of* nowhere. *This morning it was so clear. I must have been distracted with my thoughts and not paying attention. And where is the map? In my pack in the bow, how stupid. Now what am I going to do?*

She could see nothing, but she heard a waterfall. *I must be paddling downstream,* she thought. *I'm sure I'm traveling north. I crossed the Laurentian Divide, and I know that all water flows to Hudson Bay. But the waterfall sounds like it is coming toward me.*

Her father had taught her to study the water below the canoe to discern the current. But a careful search for motion in the water plants under her canoe did not reveal any current at all. She approached the sound of the falls as timid as a fawn approaches an open field. Neither shore nor trees were visible. A continuous gray blanket of fog surrounded her. Even the water she dipped her paddle into was gray. Each stroke was silent in the hush of the heavy air.

A shrill scratch made her jump. She gave an agile stroke to spin the canoe sideways. She spotted the culprit of the scratch: a branch of a submerged cedar tree. Her eye followed the branch to the shore. She balanced her paddle on the gunnels and relaxed her muscles to listen. *I'm safe,* she thought. *The falls must be to my right. I'll just follow this shore to the left.*

Dense cedars dipped into the water like the scraggly hair of an ancient hag. The mist prevented any perception beyond. She followed the shore, ready to turn her canoe if necessary but unwilling to lose contact with the land. Several times she paddled around a fallen tree but then followed the windfall back to the shoreline. Her bow hit a boulder left by glaciers millenniums ago, and she made a defensive turn. As she skirted the rock, a small channel just wide enough to maneuver her canoe appeared. She followed the channel into a bay. Her canoe slithered through without a scratch. The roar of the falls diminished.

With wide eyes, she peered at nothing but gray. *I suppose this leads into a swamp.* She stopped paddling. The canoe remained motionless. *No current.* She turned right, and after a few quick strokes, the shoreline disappeared. "Now what?" she shrieked with frustration. She realized that there was nobody for three days' paddle in any direction to hear her.

"What the hell!" With abandoned caution she jetted the canoe ahead and scraped aground on sand. Fear melted to relief. Her muscles quivered. She climbed out of the canoe and scouted the beach. It was pristine with only tracks of shorebirds marking the smooth shore. *Is this an island?* The sand abruptly ended, interfacing with solid granite. "I found the Canadian Shield," she yelled as if that made her safe. She climbed up the rock face and found a pile of rocks blackened with soot. "And a fire pit. I found a home." She jumped for joy.

She pulled the map out of her pack from the bow of the canoe and squatted on the rock shelf to ponder her position. She chided herself, *Next time I keep the map in my pocket.* Her finger followed the lakes north of the last portage she had taken. There was nothing around her that correlated with any marked campsite. She spanned out the distance that she thought she had traveled, but there was no waterfall marked at the northern end of the huge lake she had traversed.

She collapsed on her back. *Why did I come on this solo trip anyway? My parents would have helped me work out my problems. They're reasonable people, aren't they?* But she knew why. *Life is confusing. I failed English, and therefore I did not graduate from high school and now have to go to stupid summer school. I need this break.* She sat up and yelled, "I'm such a loser." Her voice echoed off into the mist. She took a deep breath and looked at the map again. *Let's see, a wise person would at least have been using a compass.* She'd considered crawling up the center of the canoe to reach her pack and get the compass, but she'd been unwilling to chance tipping the canoe. So she'd left the compass where it was and had kept paddling. The fog had become opaque as the sun had shifted in the sky. She'd lost all sense of direction, and now here she was, hours later, at a site that did not match anything on the map.

A squirrel approached her, begging for a snack. "You don't get anything till I'm done eating, you scrounge." She pulled her pack out of the canoe and hauled it to the fire pit. She gathered tinder, careful not to venture too far in the fog. *The last thing I need is to be lost in the woods away from my gear,* she thought. A small pile of split logs grayed with age greeted her under a protective shelf of granite. *Someone knew I was coming.* She laughed at her logic, turning the logs over in her hand. They were at least a year old judging by their dry, gray sheen. She placed the split logs in the fire pit, and kneeling beside the tinder, she lit a match. Despite the humidity, the tinder burst into flame. She added wood from the split supply. The dancing flames made her feel at home. She soaped the outside of her only pot and added water. When it came to a boil, she added a soup mix and waited.

I'm safe. I have food. I have a canoe and a warm sleeping bag. What more could I want? I have most of Maslow's pyramid, she thought, recalling her psychology test questions.

The soup started to boil, so she pulled the larger sticks out of the fire and snuffed them out in the sand, saving them for the next meal. A quick spoonful of soup burned her tongue. She set it aside to cool and walked back to the shore to haul her canoe to a level area. She draped a tarp under one edge of the canoe, then over it, and spread it out across the moss in front. She put a few rocks down to hold the tarp in place for her shelter. Her father had offered to buy her a tent, but she considered the comforts of a tent a weakness. She preferred to sleep under her canoe.

Now her soup was a perfect temperature. She watched the few remaining embers dance and snap as she slurped her nourishment. She picked up a stick that had a burning ember on the tip and blew on it until it glowed. Fascinated by the fiery patterns, she contemplated, *Am I burned out?* She ground the stick into the ashes. *I'm not meant for school. What's left? Work for my parents? But Mother wants me to be a lawyer. That will never happen.* As the fire burned down, she drank the last of her soup and kicked dirt on the remaining embers.

Down at the beach, she used sand to scour her pot to a shiny brilliance. Rinsing it, she noticed how warm the water was. Her eyes searched in vain for the perimeters of the bay. She climbed the rock shelf and packed her mess kit and then tucked the pack under the bow of her overturned canoe. "My home," she said, patting the canoe. She took off her boots, sheltering them under the canoe. It was time for a swim.

She took off her shirt, folded it, and laid it on the canoe. She had taken off her bra at the first highway rest stop. It was somewhere in the backseat of the Jeep. She hated bras. She unzipped her jeans and slid them off with her underwear and wool hiking socks. She took a deep breath.

She loved being naked. The one thing she liked about herself was her body. She was strong, had long legs that responded quickly, agile arms, good balance, and strong abdominal muscles. Her breasts were two nice handfuls, and she had an unblemished caramel complexion thanks to her Italian heritage.

She'd dreamed about being a model after getting a Barbie doll one Christmas. But Barbie had a nice, plain face, and Lisa's was covered with freckles in odd places. Barbie also had long, wavy, blonde hair while hers was auburn and unruly. She'd given up the model notion one night while washing the dishes. Her father had made saffron rice with curry beef sauce. Standing over the sink cleaning the pots, she'd realized her hair was the same color as the dishwater. She'd laughed so hard her mother had come to check on her. Her mother hadn't understood the humor.

After that Lisa hadn't even tried to curl her hair; instead she combed it straight and wore it in a ponytail. She liked ponytails because then she could pull her hair through the hole in the back of a baseball cap. That had become her trademark at school. There was no rule against girls wearing hats; she'd checked and explained it in detail to the principal.

Jumping, running, doing layups, kicking soccer balls, spinning, and twisting—anything that was active—thrilled her. And swimming, she loved water. Her mother often told stories about Lisa's escapades at her dinner parties. The story that always got the most laughs was when three-year-old Lisa had plugged the bathtub and filled it to overflowing. Then she'd jumped in, splashing and spinning till the water had poured out from under the door. "We had some ceiling repairs to attend to after that incident," her mother would say to finish the story.

Lisa walked down the granite surface to the sand, feeling the contrast of textures with her toes. The cool evening air danced across her skin, so free without clothes. She spun and danced in the sand. The water was smooth as a mirror. She dipped in her foot to test the temperature. It felt warm despite being spring-fed. She surface-dived, and the water wrapped around her nakedness like frozen silk. The thermocline was only a foot deep, and below it the water was ice cold. Her skin tightened; her nipples became hard as stones. She celebrated the sensation.

Twilight added ink to the fog. The long day was over. She listened for the waterfall, oriented her position to the faint sound, and swam for shore until her feet felt the sand. She spun out of the water rejoicing in the security of her camp.

She added a few twigs to the remaining embers, and a small fire burst into flames, licking the wood she had banked against the rock. She turned to its warmth, shaking her head above the flames to dry her hair. *I better save this gift wood for morning,* she thought as she kicked dirt to smother the fire.

Walking just far enough from camp to be sanitary, she squatted to urinate. A multitude of mushrooms crawling out from under the rotted leaves greeted her. Fluorescent orange and pearly white contrasted with the foggy tan of the hubris. She wondered which ones were poisonous and which were safe to eat. She finished her toilet and returned to camp. She pulled out her sleeping bag, stretched it out under the canoe, and crawled in, squirming in its warmth. *Tomorrow I'll find myself.*

CHAPTER 2

Bright sunshine streaked around the edge of the tarp, and Lisa opened her eyes. Refreshed and mellow, she stretched in the warm morning air. The fog was gone. Rich greens of the forest and volcanic black of the granite contrasted in the brilliant sunlight. Pulling toilet paper out of her pack, she searched for a better latrine. Up over a massive rock and down through a mossy area, she found a perfect spot. Tiny pine trees paraded through the moss at her feet. They were no taller than her outstretched hand. "Which of you will become great trees, and which will die?" she asked them. After wiping and then burying her excrement, she headed back to her canoe-shelter. *This is sure a nice place.*

A level, mossy area invited her to do her morning routine: fifty push-ups followed by fifty sit-ups. Hands on her belly, she loved the sensation of her abdominal muscles contracting and relaxing. Sweat beaded on her brow as she finished.

"Now for a swim." Almost circular, the bay's only interruption was the narrow channel she had discovered. The west showed evidence of a once-ancient stream cascading into the bay. Her eye followed the cedar trees hugging the eastern shore, which abruptly turned to white pines on the knoll that was her camp. *If I only knew where I was, I could come back.* She laughed, jumped into the water, and swam laps until hunger growled in her stomach.

Climbing out of the water, she met a frog eying her from the safety of the cattails. "Good morning, Mr. Frog. How are you this morning? Make sure you eat lots of mosquitoes." She squatted, not daring to move closer, fascinated with the frog's iridescent skin and copper-colored eyes. In a giant leap, it disappeared in the tall grass.

Lisa climbed back to her campfire, unsheathed her hunting knife, and scraped dry kindling from the half-burnt log she had removed from the fire after supper. She lit the shavings and placed small sticks on her fire, soon adding the split logs to the blaze. She soaped the outside of her pot so that she could wash off the smoky black streaks later. Then she added water. She sat on a log waiting for the water to boil. *Nice bench. I wonder who camped here before.*

Restless, she fetched her map and compass and made herself comfortable. *I know I came across this portage.* She put her finger on the red dotted line marking the portage trail on the map. *I paddled about four hours, and I had to be going mostly north, at least till I got lost.* She drew a circle with her thumb about the distance she thought she could have paddled. The lake was huge. The northern shore had a myriad of bays. It would take at least a day to paddle east to west without wind. *Lots of bays in which to get lost. Which one has a waterfall?* She scrutinized several different bays. Two had waterfalls marked, but neither had a bay to the west with a marked campsite.

Her water started boiling. She added oatmeal and a handful of raisins, took the pot off the fire, and stirred it. She returned to the map. A third bay had a river flowing into it, but no waterfall was marked. There was no listed campsite, but there was a single symbol of a swamp to the west. *This might be it. And it is about the right distance.* Setting the map on a smooth rock and holding the edges with her toes she spooned oatmeal into her mouth. The warmth matched her need for nutrition, and the raisins were plump and juicy. *Hunger is an excellent spice, but how long can I live on oatmeal and soup?* she wondered.

A sudden poke in her upper lip startled her. She pulled a pine needle off her spoon, scanned the pot, and pulled out part of a pinecone. She looked up in the tree, searching for whatever had knocked the pinecone into her oatmeal.

Just then a squirrel chirped up in the tree. She focused her gaze on it. It jumped to the lower branches and then scurried to the end. The branch bent to its weight. "You're probably mad because I didn't leave you anything last night." She covered her bowl. "You're not getting my oatmeal." It jumped off the branch, scooted across a bed of pine needles, and climbed up on a rock beside her. Standing on its back legs, it begged.

"All right. You win." She set a small spoonful of oatmeal on the rock beside it. It bowed like a Japanese ninja, instead of the petty thief that it was, and started eating its gift.

Lisa turned her attention to the map and searched other bays for possibilities. *This has to be the place. But why is there no campsite marked?* She brushed the bark off her bare butt and went down to the beach to wash her pot. As she scoured out the oatmeal with sand, minnows rushed in to enjoy the remains. She squatted, clutching her knees to her chest, to watch their antics.

She cinched the food pack as tight as she could. *I hope that keeps Mr. Squirrel out of my food.* She'd seen no bear scat around the trails leading from the camp, so she decided not to hang a bear bag.

No one has been here for at least a year, judging by the dry wood under the rock. She spun in the air, feeling refreshed and free. *I'm surprised there are no mosquitoes or black flies here; the bats and frogs must be doing their jobs.*

But I suppose if I'm going to the waterfall there might be people. I better put some clothes on. She pulled out a T-shirt and a pair of shorts from her personal pack and slipped them on. The folded map and compass went in her shorts pocket. She flipped the canoe on her shoulders and walked it into the water. She climbed in and squatted in the middle of the canoe to lower the center of gravity. She paddled out through the narrows and followed the roar to the falls.

The cascade fell over twenty feet through a jumble of rocks and then plateaued before cascading in a torrent, divided in half by a boulder the size of a garage at the base. It was spectacular. Canoeing up the eddy current on the near side, she discovered a portage trail. She examined the map; of the three potential bays for her location, only one had a portage. Focusing on the details, she noticed the symbol for the swamp was exactly where her camp was. She checked the date; the map was published last year. *I'll bet they forgot my campsite. That means no one with a new map knows it exists.* She screamed, "I have my own private camp!"

"Now that I know where I am, how do I get to my Jeep?" With her finger she followed the chain of lakes on the other side of the portage, making a circle tour of the area. Several large lakes brought her within a portage of the landing where she'd parked. "That circuit should take no more than three days to make, two if I work at it. But I have plenty of food."

The sound of the water cascading over rocks made her pensive. *What difference does it make? I didn't tell anyone when I was coming back, and they don't know where I am.* She laughed. *I didn't even know where I was till just now.*

She sat on a rock and put her feet in the swirls of the current. *I suppose they're worried about me. Right now I'm not sure I care. But I'll run out of food sometime.* The rapids massaged her feet. The crisp smell of pine accented the rhythm of the falls. The sun snuck out from behind a cloud and warmed her skin.

She went back to the canoe and pulled her fishing rod out of the gunnels. A small box tied under the seat held lures. She cast her lure just short of the large rock at the base of the falls. She was ready to exchange her pole for her paddle when she got a strike. The fish pulled so hard that it yanked the stern of the canoe into the current. The bow caught in the eddy current and spun her around. She maintained the tension on her line and pulled in a thrashing walleye.

The hook was clear through the upper lip. "Looks like supper," she said as she pulled the fish out of the water and plopped it into the canoe. *I guess there is no need to worry about food.* She put her fish on a stringer and smelled her hands. "Yuck, I need a bath."

Her canoe had drifted east of the main current while she had been fussing with the fish. A sheer cliff of white rock was to the right. A small beach formed of alluvial sand invited her. She edged the canoe into the eddy current and paddled upstream behind the cliff. A few strong strokes wedged the canoe between the rocks. She stripped off her T-shirt and shorts and danced on the rocks, rejoicing that no one was around. *Oh, this is great. I wish I never had to wear clothes ever again. At least till winter.* She laughed as loud as she could. The sound echoed from the cliff.

Out on a rock shelf, she jumped into the foam at the base of the falls. Her body splayed chaotically in the complex current. Out of breath, she surfaced, spun her head, and gasped. She was way past the white cliff. "That was a roller-coaster ride."

She swam with her strongest stroke toward the shore, but the current thrust her farther out into the lake. In a panic, she felt a rock underfoot. Balancing, she managed to rest. Fighting the current was exhausting.

Now this is a fine mess, she thought as she shivered. *Even if I make it to shore, there is no path back to the canoe.* Between her and the shore were boulders, slippery with algae, and beyond that a heavy growth of cedar trees.

That wasn't very smart. She swam to another rock closer to the shore as her eyes searched for a trail. The dense undergrowth was impenetrable. Hungry, tired, shivering, wet, and naked, she climbed onto a rock. The granite felt warm from the sun, but within a short time she would be in the shade. She crouched, holding her knees, her bare back absorbing as much sun warmth as possible.

I am just going to have to swim back. There is no other way. After absorbing the sunshine, the water felt colder. "Do or die," she yelled as she plunged in the water and swam along the shore, trying to maintain an efficient form. When she got near the stronger current of the falls, the eddy current whisked her upstream. But near the white cliff, the current became turbulent. Even using every ounce of her strength, she made no progress. She gave up and landed on the beach. The sand felt warm from the noon sun, and she rolled in its comfort.

How am I going to get past that cliff? As she brushed the sticky sand off her chest and belly, she spotted a path. *Is that an animal trail or human?* She followed it. The branches of jack pine and balsam scratched and scraped her skin, raising welts on her legs. A branch snapped against her breast. Pinecone remnants discarded by squirrels bit her feet. But when she broke into the clearing, there was her canoe.

A splash beside the canoe made her jump. She pulled up her stringer. A turtle had eaten half of her fish. She dropped what remained in her canoe and shoved off.

"Enough adventures for today; I'm going home," she called to the waterfall. She paddled downstream, crossed the current, and headed for the entrance to her cove. She felt a sense of calm in the bay and collapsed on her back. Breathing in gasps, she watched the afternoon sun turn the wisps of clouds orange and red. The rough skin of her hands turned purple with cold. She warmed her hands against her belly. Her stomach ached. *Am I sick?* She panicked. *No, I'm hungry. This is the hungriest I've ever been in my whole life.* Her thoughts drifted to the spicy sauces and rich, creamy desserts her father often made. She could hear her father say, "Tough luck, kid; you have to cook for yourself tonight."

Her stomach gnawed at her as she assembled twigs and shavings to start the campfire. Her fingers trembled as she dressed in warm clothes. She took the bag of nuts from the food pack but smelled her fishy hands and decided not to contaminate her snack.

Once the fire was blazing and she'd warmed her hands, she headed back to the shore to check what was left of her fish. The turtle had eaten all the intestines; then, starting at the tail, had eaten the best parts of the fillets, but there was still meat around the head and on the dorsal spine. She flayed off the skin and added what was left to her soup. It smelled good, and the first taste was very satisfying.

Pensive, she poked the fire with a stick. *I don't mean to upset my parents. I love them, well, most of the time. I just don't fit into their world.*

Her father had inherited her grandfather's factory, which employed almost a thousand people. She and her father had had so much fun together when she was growing up—camping, fishing, and canoeing. Then Grandfather had decided to retire. Lisa's father had become CEO and, with that, had gained a lot of responsibilities. Their time together had vanished.

She had been the leading scorer for her basketball team and the most valuable player. Yet neither of her parents had come to a single game. It had been board meeting or tax time or always something.

Lisa remembered one morning after a game. While reading the newspaper, her father had scooped broiled grapefruit into his mouth and said, "I see you made most valuable player last night, Elizabeth. That's good."

"Thanks, Dad." She'd fidgeted with her spoon in her cereal. "You want to see me play next Thursday? It's a big game."

"Sorry, I have a corporation meeting that night." He'd returned to his paper.

Her mother was a corporate lawyer, part-time with the factory and part-time on her own. It seemed to Lisa that her mother had two full-time jobs. Other people were impressed, but Lisa just felt intimidated. And just try to win an argument! Lisa had tried when she was younger, but it had always ended in disaster. Whenever she got in trouble at school, which lately had been fairly often, her mother always took the teacher's side. In the end, even Lisa had been convinced that she was wrong, always.

And Linden, her smart, talented older brother, was planning on taking over the family business after he finished at Harvard. He could play the piano and even played violin when he decided it was important. He'd gotten straight As all through high school and would probably get all As at Harvard too.

"I just don't fit into this family," she yelled. She jabbed the campfire with a stick, and sparks flew upward. She watched them till they were lost in the stars above.

When she'd started dating, the problems had multiplied. If her brother didn't know the family or a sibling of the guy she wanted to date, her parents did. "We just want you to make wise decisions," her mother would say. That usually meant she did not approve of Lisa's choice.

"That guy's a bum, sis," Linden had said of one guy. "I know his older sister."

"Did you date her?" Lisa had asked, trying to mount a defense.

"No way," he'd said, and that had been the end of the conversation.

Lisa admitted that she had trouble picking boyfriends. She wanted to date other athletes, but if she played one-on-one in basketball or tennis with them and won, they never asked her out afterward.

One of the receivers on the football team, Roger, had asked her out once. She didn't play football, but only because it wasn't available for girls; otherwise she would have. He had taken her to a greasy-spoon restaurant, gulped his food down, and then driven past her driveway on the way home and parked in the woods.

"You're definitely hot," he said.

"This has been fun," she lied.

He turned on the radio to the hard rock channel and turned up the volume. "I just got new speakers. What do you think?"

Lisa yelled, "Pretty wild!" as she turned down the volume. He turned it halfway back up. They sat silent, gazing out the windshield at trees that were slowly becoming shrouded in darkness with the setting sun.

"I like you, Lisa. Do you like me?"

"I guess so."

"Great." He scooted close to her and put his right arm around her shoulder, resting his left hand on her thigh. "I love this music." He started playing with her dangling earrings and kissing her neck.

Her neck muscles tightened, and she pushed him away, but he persisted.

"You're great," he said. "I love your muscles."

"Roger." Her voice was drowned out by the blaring music.

"Yes," he said as he unbuttoned her blouse and drifted his hand across her breasts. "You're so firm. I like that." His hand slipped down to her lap and inside her panties. "You got the best abs ever. None of the other girls got abs like you."

"Roger," she said more insistent.

"Yes, baby?" He unclasped the latch on the front of her bra and started fondling her breasts.

"That's it; I'm out of here. Get your hands off me." She pushed him away.

"You're nice looking too." His eyes fixed on her nipples as he scratched at her breasts.

She fumbled to reclasp her bra and button her blouse. His paw marks turned red on her tender breasts, making her nauseated. A sudden need to vomit gnawed at her belly. She swallowed hard and glanced out the window. Diverting her focus to the woods, she realized where Roger had parked. This was the city park that adjoined her parents' property. She often went for walks here to clear her mind.

Unlucky Roger, she thought as she grabbed her purse and sprang out of the car. Recognizing one of the trails, she jumped a hedge and ran down the bank. He started the car and spun it around. Through the open car window, he yelled in her direction, "Was I going too fast? I'm sorry. A little petting is good for you. It stimulates your hormones."

Standing still behind a large white pine tree, she watched Roger slam the brakes to a stop and run in the direction he had seen her go. But he didn't know the trails, and in the dark lit by a half moon, she saw him hesitate. Silence would give him no clue as to where she'd gone.

"Last time I date you, bitch. I hope you get fucking lost." As he walked backward up the bank to his car, he fell. He got up, ran to his car, screeched his tires as he left, and disappeared.

"A lot of fun that was," Lisa said as she walked the moonlit trail. She found the low place in the fence that separated Chester Park from her parents' property and vaulted over it. The hiking trail on the other side led to the tennis court behind their garage.

She paused in the driveway. *Now what should I do? Linden told me not to date him.* She straightened and tucked in her blouse, then waited till she was no longer sweating and her breathing returned to normal. She went through the back door into the kitchen and poured a glass of milk.

"How was your date, honey?" her mother asked as Lisa came out of the kitchen.

"Pretty bad. I left him and ran home."

"He didn't have the decency to bring you home?"

"Oh, he would have, but he wanted to stay out later, so I left."

"Was he a nice boy?"

"Nope, I don't think I like him. He doesn't seem to know too much about anything. He's a dull conversationalist."

"I'm sorry, Lisa."

"Thanks, Mom." Lisa gulped down her milk, put her glass in the dishwasher, and bounded up the stairs.

"Good night, sweetheart."

"Good night, Mother." She had run the rest of the way to her room, shut the door, and stripped off her blouse and bra to examine her breasts in the mirror. She'd applied aloe lotion to the irritated scratches. "Well, at least his claw marks should heal without scars."

That had been the end of dating Roger. She'd asked Ted Knickerbeck, the smartest kid in math class, to take her to the prom, but he'd said that he wasn't even going.

She'd told her mother that her date was meeting her at the dance. She'd planned to sit out the dances and talk to the girls on the basketball team. When she'd gotten there, all her friends had been occupied with their dates. So she'd sat alone, drinking a Diet Coke.

Then Hank Singer had asked her to dance. He was the best tennis player in school. When they played together, he usually beat her but not by much. When she was into her game and he was tired, she could beat him. He was a fast and adroit dancer. They'd looked so good together that the other dancers had stopped to watch, applauding afterward.

Hank was dating Angel. She was a thin, petite blonde with wavy hair and a pug nose that set off her cute, dimpled face. She was much prettier than Lisa and wore expensive clothes that set off her figure, but she couldn't dance well. She also didn't play any sports. Lisa thought of her as a flower in a vase, but she did get good grades and always got 100 percent on spelling tests.

Lisa knew Hank had asked her to dance to make him look good, not that he cared about her. After they'd danced, he'd thanked her with the same tone of voice as when he would say, "Good game," after they played tennis. He then had returned to Angel.

Lisa jumped as a spark landed on her arm. *I'm tired. Enough of this musing by the campfire. Tomorrow will be better.*

CHAPTER 3

As she got cozy in her sleeping bag, the mosquitoes came out with a vengeance for her blood. Lisa crawled deeper in her sleeping bag to cover up, but a flapping sound made her poke her head out. Bats were flying around her camp in large arcs. Suddenly, the mosquitoes disappeared. "I am so thankful for bats." She unzipped her sleeping bag and crawled out from under the canoe to lay still in the tepid air and listen to the loons sing their haunting melodies. She decided that she loved loons, frogs, and bats and maybe even squirrels.

A shooting star with a bright tail stretched across the sky. Shooting stars fascinated her. Astronomy had been a two-week unit in her science class, and Lisa had aced the test. "What a show, and it's free," she cheered. "And nobody matches the music of loons." During the light show with operatic chorus she fell asleep.

• • •

The next morning was warm and sunny. After morning toilet, exercises, swimming, and oatmeal, she was ready to explore. Dressed in shorts, faded T-shirt, and sandals, she searched the campsite and found a trail that seemed human. It led right to the portage trail but was blocked by a fallen tree. *Good; no one will inadvertently wander into my camp.* A squirrel followed her, its raucous call announcing her progress. She walked to the end of the northern end of the portage and looked out across the lake. A multitude of islands fit the configuration of the map. "Now I am sure of where I am," she said.

On the way back, she followed the river instead of the portage trail. Pushing aside the thick undergrowth, she blazed her way through the brush to the top of the cliff that overlooked the falls. She climbed down the cliff bank and stood at the very edge of the cascade. A jumble of rocks led to an oval pool in the middle of the falls. Curious, she charted her way. *That must be just like a whirlpool,* she reasoned.

She snaked her way down the west bank till she was at the plateau of the falls. Remembering the topography from above, she jumped from rock to rock, then waded through some fast-moving water that threatened her footing. "Careful, girl, or you'll plummet to your death," she muttered to herself. She jumped. She landed on a rock covered with lichens and slipped but caught herself on all fours. The map was still in her pocket. She checked for blood on her hands; there was none. She secured her footing and found a long, flat, submerged rock that led straight into the pool.

The falls flowed in from each side, swirling around before spilling over the edge. She looked out over the lake. She could see way down the bay. With no one approaching, she took off her clothes, folded them, and placed them on a flat rock to stay dry. Slipping into the pool, she gasped for joy. She plunged her head in and then out of the water and spun, whipping the water out of her hair. She slipped deep into the swirl down to her chin. Her nipples ached in the cold water. She arched her back so they broke the surface. The water tickled as she watched her pubic hair waft like seaweed in the current.

Lisa's thoughts turned to home and her lack of friends. *Why do I have so much trouble with relationships? People choose me for their team, but when the game is over, they leave me.* She thought about Sherilyn, who used to be her best friend. *We played basketball, practiced together. We won division, and then she was done with me.* She recalled the incident.

"Let's go to a restaurant," Sherilyn had suggested. "Coach says we don't have to stay for the final game."

"Great, where do you want to go?" Lisa had asked.

"There's a French restaurant in our hotel. I saw it when we came in."

They'd checked with Coach, and she'd said, "Return to your rooms by curfew; that's all I ask."

Lisa and Sherilyn had met in first-year French class. Lisa had barely passed, and the teacher had not encouraged her to continue. Sherilyn had aced the next two years and was fairly fluent, by high school standards.

"Maybe we can speak French to the waiters," Sherilyn said. "There should be some cute ones. Maybe the menu will even be in French."

"You might have to translate for me."

"No problem."

They went back to their rooms, dressed in their banquet clothes, and tripped off to the restaurant. They requested French menus, and the maître d' answered in French when Sherilyn said, "A *table pour deux, s'il vous plaît.*"

Lisa understood what meat the dishes were, but her pronunciation was not good enough to order. Sherilyn ordered for her. They tasted their foie gras.

"Wow, this is excellent, isn't it?" Sherilyn said.

"Best I have ever had."

"These little knives are sure cute. We don't have anything like this in our silverware drawer."

"They are neat." Lisa's parents did have such knives. They were fish knives. Sherilyn obviously did not know what they were used for, as she used hers to smear butter on her baguette. "What did we order next?" Lisa asked, unsure of the translation.

"Some kind of fish in a sauce I didn't understand. I hope we like it."

The presentation was spectacular, and the sauce had a touch of tarragon. Sherilyn scooped her fish up with her spoon. "This food just stimulates my taste buds. What do you think?"

"It's really good." Lisa used her fish knife and fork to eat her portion, just as her mother had instructed her when they were in Paris.

"Too bad we lost that last game. I wish we could have won, but their center was just too good."

"We were down eleven points and came back to tie the game. That's pretty good."

"I was exhausted," said Sherilyn, "and the last two minutes seemed an eternity."

"I know what you mean." In those last two minutes they had just needed two points to tie the game, and then they could have tried to win in overtime. "I felt so sorry for you when I passed you the ball and then you missed your shot. I could tell you were tired. I just wanted to hug you; I felt so bad."

"It was a good pass. I just didn't set well before I shot."

"We almost won."

"If we had, we wouldn't be having this great French meal on your parents."

"Right." Lisa had tried to sound enthusiastic as she put the last morsel of fish in her mouth. Not only did Sherilyn not know what a fish knife was for (that could be excused), but she also always assumed Lisa was going to pay for everything. It wasn't that Lisa couldn't afford it or that her parents would say anything; it was the presumption Lisa resented. After that the rest of the meal had tasted flat. Doing anything with Sherilyn after that meal had made Lisa feel manipulated, so Lisa had avoided her, and that had been the end of their friendship.

"I'm looking like a giant prune," Lisa said as she edged out of the whirlpool and climbed onto the flat rock to dry. She slipped on her sandals and clothes to make her way back. *Imagine a whirlpool in the middle of a waterfall.* Back at the portage trail she climbed over the fallen tree to head back to camp.

She held up her fingers to the horizon as her father had shown her to estimate sunset. "About two, maybe three, hours of daylight, and I'm hungry." She launched her canoe and returned to the base of the falls. Sliding up the eddy current, she threw her lure at the base of the massive rock and let the current pull her canoe downstream. A few casts later she had another walleye.

"I'm eating this one before you take your turn, Mr. Turtle, you thief," she yelled toward the shore. She paddled back, flayed the fish, and threw the guts to curious gulls circling overhead. *It's curious that gulls are so far inland. Maybe they are a different species from the ones near the ocean.* She settled in for fish dinner with soup. For the first time since leaving home, her stomach felt satisfied.

That night as she watched the sky from her sleeping bag, the stars disappeared. "That means rain," she said and jumped up to secure her camp for the coming storm. Content that everything was safe, she crawled back into her sleeping bag and fell asleep.

A flash of lightning and thunder like an explosion overhead awakened her. She glanced at her watch. Three o'clock in the morning. Ten minutes later a deluge poured down. It rained so hard that the raindrops pelting the lake surface produced a roaring sound. Lisa found her flashlight and checked her nest under the canoe. The water was flowing away from her tarp on all sides. It wasn't that comfortable, but at least no rivulets were threatening her dry sleeping bag.

She thought about a night in August when one of her junior-high soccer games had been rained out. One of the coaches had dropped her off at her house's security gate. By the time she had walked the driveway to her house, she'd been soaked. She had taken off her clothes in the laundry room and turned to go up to her room. That's when a crazy idea had hit her: *I can't get any wetter. I'm already soaked to the skin, and nobody's home.*

She had run outside naked, danced, and sung, rejoicing in the rain. The raindrops on her skin had excited her, and the shadows she'd cast from the security light on the garage had been enchanting. When she'd heard the security gate open, she'd run for the house, ducking in through the back door just as her parents turned the corner to the garage. She had bounded up the stairs to her room and jumped in the shower. Later her mother had thanked her for putting her wet clothes in the laundry basket instead of leaving them in a pile on her bedroom floor, apparently unaware of Lisa's escapade.

"No one's here but me!" Lisa yelled as she climbed out of her sleeping bag and ran in the rain. She loved the sensation. *I can't do this at home, at least not very often.* Her eyes adjusted to the darkness as she splashed and danced in the rain until she was exhausted. She collapsed in a puddle and was covered in mud. Jumping up, she dove into the lake. It was still raining when she crawled under her tarp to dry off. She was shaking with chills and was sure that her skin was blue. Once she was dry, the chills stopped, and she nestled into her warm, dry sleeping bag. Content.

$$\cdots$$

The morning sun reflected off the puddles like hundreds of mirrors. Everything was wet, but it had stopped raining. Only the wood stuffed under the rock shelf was dry. She dressed in her rain gear and ventured out behind camp to urinate and bring back some spruce boughs. Snapping them in small pieces, she started her fire with the protected wood and then added the spruce. Oatmeal was soon boiling in her pot.

She packed her gear and loaded her canoe. "I wish I could just stay here forever," she said, scanning the site, "but I must say good-bye. You are the best campsite ever." She swung her canoe around and paddled out of the bay. "See you next year," she said over her shoulder. As she turned toward the portage, ducks were fishing by the big rock. *I guess I'm not the only one who got a good meal at this place.*

Pack on her back, canoe on her shoulders, she hiked the trail, casting a last glance at the whirlpool. At the end of the portage she set down the canoe and pack and took a compass sighting, just as her father had taught her. In the direction she wanted to go according to the map, a large island was her first focus. Then she needed to turn east. From the shore the island looked intriguing. She reviewed the map and noticed a marked campsite on the eastern shore. "I'll stay there for a day or so, and from that island I'm just a good day's paddle from the landing. Good plan," she congratulated herself.

However, the lake clearly had other ideas. As she paddled toward her landmark island, the wind became fierce. Halfway to the island, whitecaps formed, and the wind came from the direction she needed to go. With considerable effort she reached the island and then stayed in the wind shadow to rest. It was peaceful. The water was calm as a mirror, but the wind roared through the trees, whipping their branches. In the calm created by the island she balanced in the canoe and stretched her arms and back. *Now I'm ready to tackle the wind.*

Paddling around the island, she was hit with gale-force winds. She could not hold the canoe in position. She tried to point the bow into the wind, angled enough so the resultant vector would send her in the right direction, but the wind was too strong. After a couple of hours of paddling she had made no forward progress. She paddled into the wind shadow of another island, pulled her canoe on shore, and climbed out on a rock to rest. The island was too small for a campsite, but she crouched behind a large boulder to get out of the wind. Her back and arm muscles screamed with exhaustion. She stretched and massaged her arms. She stood and rubbed her sore back against the sheltering rock.

Her hands smelled clean, so she pulled out her nuts and M&M's. "What a treat." She sat behind the rock and munched her snack. Her shoulders felt hot. "This should be good exercise for basketball," she said, "if I survive." In the solitude of howling wind, with a full belly, she fell asleep.

She awoke with a start, wondering how long she'd been asleep. The wind was roaring louder than before. The whitecaps were so peaked that they sprayed into the air. *I can't stay here. There's no place to turn over the canoe, and there's no wood for a fire. No shelter and no warmth could be lethal. I can't just wait out the storm here; I have to keep going.* She climbed into the canoe, fastened everything down, and cinched her life vest. Paddling on the left side, she thought she could keep the right angle.

She was wrong. Powerless, she was blown northwest with such force that paddling was futile. Her muscles raw from her wasted effort, she let the wind blow her and paddled hard to keep her canoe aligned with the wind. If she got crosswise to the wind, she would capsize for sure. The cold water would be her grave. With periodic gusts she grabbed the gunnels to keep from capsizing. She fought for her life. Then the rain came blasting with the wind.

The canoe rocketed out of control. She used every paddle stroke she knew to keep some stability. Large waves buffeted her as she searched for any refuge. Every island seemed out of reach. *Tolerate the pain, or flip the canoe,* raged through her mind. Waves crested over the gunnels. Crosswinds whipped the spray into her face, searing her cheeks. Twice large waves crested her canoe, partially filling it with water. At least she knew it wouldn't sink, because of the floats in bow and stern.

Hours later she found her peace as the wind blew her into a northern bay. She was way off course, unsure again where she was. Out of the wind she sought shelter behind a peninsula. The canoe handled like a soaked log. Her strained muscles screamed for rest. Each stroke felt like a punishment. Winded and depleted, she slumped in the canoe. Her shoulder muscles seemed torn from her bones. Unable to maintain her concentration, she gasped as the gentle rocking of the canoe tried to put her to sleep. If not for the pain, she would have fallen asleep. Shaking her head, she took a deep breath, focused once more, and headed the canoe to the shore. On shore she tipped the canoe to empty the storm's excess water and collapsed beside it. The rain stopped.

Sitting on a rock, she unfolded the map to reconnoiter. The bay where she found herself fed into a river system. Following the chain of lakes, she found a different route to the landing. She put her finger on one of the portages she would have to take. "The Wickstead portage is four hundred rods." She gasped. "That's over a mile long. But then I can paddle across this chain of small lakes, and I'm back. It looks easy, except for that portage, and from here it'll be a lot faster than my original route."

There was no place to camp on this shore, so she launched her canoe into the still bay, then flopped back, too tired to paddle. She watched the clouds zip across the sky. Then the roar of rapids ahead caught her attention. Sitting up, she realized that she was caught in current. She forced her unwilling muscles to give a few determined strokes to escape into an eddy. In a moment she was at a portage. It was a short twenty rods, twenty lengths of a canoe. There was a campsite to the side. Tall white pines provided excellent wind cover, and years of fallen pine needles made a soft orange carpet. The needles under the tree were amazingly dry due to the direction of the wind.

This is home tonight. I'm too tired to take any more portages, much less four hundred rods. She flipped the canoe over and set up her tarp for a shelter. She found a stack of wood; some of it had gotten wet, but a few sticks still had bark. With some scraping and slicing with her knife she made dry pieces for kindling. She pulled out the beef jerky from her food pack. *Should I add it tonight or save it? I better save it since I still have quite a ways to go.*

Sitting on a log by the water's edge, she made a few casts while waiting for her soup to boil. Her line became heavy like a snag. The rocky bank slopped gradually to the water so she pulled her line downstream to dislodge it. It gave, so she reeled against the resistance, dragging something. Close to shore, what she thought was a log jumped into the air.

The reel screamed as she tried to maintain tension on the line. The fish headed downstream, using the current to its advantage. Hunger forced her to be patient, winning back more line. When the fish fatigued, she reeled it back up the stream. Near the shallows it fought again. With slow and deliberate determination she worked the fish into a rocky crevice. When it jumped, she heaved it up on the granite shelf. A three-foot northern pike lay stunned on the rocks. It would not taste as good as a walleye, but, under the circumstances, it didn't matter.

"Sorry, fish, but I am very hungry tonight, and I am so thankful you gave your life for me." She felt uncomfortable talking to a dead fish but didn't know any other way to be grateful. Skinned and flayed, the fillets sizzled in the grease. The Y bones slowed her eating, but the meat was delicious and satisfied her hunger.

A sharp squawk caught her attention. A waiting gull scooped up the guts and skin. "Everyone wins, right, Mr. Gull? Well, except for the fish."

The wind died down, and the maelstrom of a few hours earlier calmed to mirror stillness as she sat on a rock to watch the sunset. She licked her fingers, savoring the fishy flavor. She had second thoughts about her decision. *Should I paddle back to where I was? The question is whether I can follow a compass in the dark.* The Milky Way spread overhead. "I'm too tired," she said with a deep sigh. She undressed, feeling the soothing of the cool night air against her skin. Her muscles fasciculated as she squatted at the water's edge and let the water tickle her toes. "Too tired to even swim."

The night air smelled of pine, cedar, and the humus of rotting leaves. *That scent should be made into a perfume. I might wear a perfume like that.* She seldom wore perfume. The sweet candy smells her friends wore sickened her. She much preferred the scent of the forest—pine, cedar, marsh marigolds in spring, rotting leaves in fall, and even the winter forest. Everything frozen had a scent, though it was more subtle.

The silhouette of the trees against the night sky provided backdrop as the loons started their chorus. A good canoe, a full stomach, and an inviting sleeping bag made her happy. A continuous breeze kept the mosquitoes at bay. She rolled out her sleeping bag.

What if someone portages here? I can't crawl out naked. I'll just have to greet them from my sleeping bag. That's what I'll do.

. . .

The sound of the rapids played sweet music to her ears as the sun danced across the water the next morning. No one had crossed the portage. Her bladder was screaming for release. She crawled out of her bag, scanned the portage for visitors, and made a quick dash to the latrine. That resolved, she jumped into the water below the falls, careful to swim in the eddy so the current wouldn't thrust her downstream.

Refreshed by a morning swim, she cooked her oatmeal. *It's going to take longer to get back to the landing than I planned. I'll just have to catch fish and ration my oatmeal. The problem is this next portage.*

She dressed in shorts and a T-shirt. *I better hit it early. I can rest this afternoon in one of those next lakes.* The campsite looked tidy after packing her canoe. All set and feeling a refreshed confidence, she headed downstream.

She almost missed the portage but swung into the eddy current just in time. The portage lay at the far end of a small cove sheltered by a steep hill. Poplar trees two and three feet high grew in the middle of the path. "No one has used this portage for a long time," she said. But the notch of an ancient axman, clearly visible on a gnarled cedar, pointed to the path. As she reached the shore, the stench of rotting fish and bubbling muck struck her nose. Black slime solidified around her canoe. She stepped on a slippery rock and jumped to drier ground before pulling the canoe to where she could flip it on her shoulders.

This place is horrible. It smells like a sewer. Should I go back? She thought about the strong current. What had just taken twenty minutes could take hours. *I'll do the portage.*

CHAPTER 4

Experience is the best teacher, but often
a cruel teacher. Experiences that have no
precedent are forever ambushing you.
—C. Albert Snyder

Pack on her back, canoe on her shoulders, her feet sank in the
muck to her boot tops. Out of the mud her footing was better, but
the trail became steep. Footholds were hard to come by. Once,
her knee jarred her chin as she braced herself to jump to the next rock
up the hill. She held the canoe almost vertical to avoid hitting rocks
with the bow, but this put all the strain on her neck. By the time the trail
leveled, she was panting for breath, her vision was blurred with sweat,
her leg muscles were strained, and her shoulders were rubbed raw. She
gazed ahead. "Finally a level trail," she said. "You are one bad portage."

Around a corner a huge white pine had fallen across the trail,
making a barrier higher than her six-foot frame. She looked both ways,
but the forest was so dense on either side that she could see no way to
hike around it. Exhausted, she rested the canoe on the tree. Dried prickly
branches stuck out in all directions.

She set her pack down and pulled out her hatchet. Chopping off
limbs, she made a three-foot clearance between the tree and the ground
by removing some of the branches. One branch was under such tension
that as she cut it free, it snapped her in the face. There was no blood,
but the abrasion stung.

With the canoe on the ground and a rope tied to the bow, she crawled through her tunnel and pulled. The screeching of the branches on the aluminum sounded like screams of harpies, but the canoe came through unscathed.

"That was a challenge," she said, sitting on the canoe gasping for breath. The raw area on her cheek throbbed, and she wondered what it looked like in a mirror. *The nearest mirror is my car's rearview mirror. No chance of that.* After she caught her breath, she shouldered her pack and flipped the canoe, refreshed. She tried to reason whether the next lake was at a higher or lower elevation. *Will the trail be progressively uphill, or will it go down toward the end?*

White pine and jack pine shifted to scrub cedar. By the time she realized the change she could not find a tree on which to prop the canoe. Her shoulder muscles cramped, and her raw skin on her shoulders burned. *I've got to rest. This portage goes on forever. If it wasn't for my faith in that map, I'd believe this trail goes all the way to hell.*

The trail turned to mud, if there was a trail. Wet, slimy, sticky swamp engulfed her. Turning between two cedars that scraped the canoe, she lost her direction. Ahead was dark, putrid-smelling water, arrow plants, and low bush cranberries enmeshed in an impenetrable jumble of plants and lots of mud.

A cloud of mosquitoes discovered her fresh source of blood. She screamed as they became black fur on her exposed skin. Frantic, she laid the canoe in the mud, opened her pack, and yanked out a long-sleeved shirt and jeans. The mosquitoes flew up the legs of her pants and her shirtsleeves. She buttoned her sleeves, put on doeskin gloves, and tucked her pants into her stockings, and then with frantic precision she ran her hands up and down her arms and legs to squash the insects underneath the fabric. Buttoned to her neck, she brushed her face to keep the insects from her eyes. She pulled a stocking cap down over her forehead till she could just see.

Brushing the mosquitoes out of her eyes, she yelled, "Now where is that stupid path? I can't troop around with the canoe trying to find it. Not with these mosquitoes." She yelled at the insects, "Remind me to come back after frost when you're all dead." She macerated three mosquitoes with her tongue as she gulped air.

To the left the swamp was deep in water but too shallow to paddle across. *Is this the end of the portage?* But she knew she had gone no more than a half mile. Off to the right she saw an opening in the trees and matted ground. Leaving the canoe, she ran right through the twisted cedars. Fifty yards later, up an incline, she found the trail. She followed it until she found high ground on the other side of the swamp. A slight breeze blew away her attackers. She collapsed and brushed off the remaining mosquitoes.

"Now where did I leave that canoe?" With regained composure, she backtracked, following broken branches and her boot prints in the mud. Finding the canoe, she realized where she had veered off the trail and stumbled into the mud.

Loaded up and brushing away mosquitoes, she managed to find her way back to the high point of the trail. She held the canoe with one hand and swatted mosquitoes with the other. Once on high ground, she paused. The trail turned steep and rocky, but the jack pines greeted her as friends. A brisk breeze through the trees blew away the blood-sucking horde. She rested the canoe in the notch of a tree and pulled off her stocking cap, long-sleeved shirt and pants. Her body was drenched in sweat. Her arms and legs had huge welts from hundreds of bites. Her thirst was tremendous, but the water in her bottle was stale and almost empty. *That was poor planning. I can't wait to get to the lake on the other side. A swim will feel so good.*

"Time to go. I won't get through this standing around." She swatted the last few hitchhiking mosquitoes out of the canoe, forcing them into the forest breeze. The trail became a series of rocks. "How can it still be going up?" Over the next steep hill she was relieved to find the trail headed down. *I must be almost there.* But as she turned another corner, rocky steps led into a muddy basin with a sharp rise on the other side. There was no sign of a lake or an end to the portage.

She stood at the edge of the mud, wondering how deep it was going to be, when she noticed rocks to step on to avoid the mud. She shifted the canoe on her shoulders but had to lift the bow to climb the steep bank on the other side. It was too narrow. So she walked sideways out of the gully.

The trail leveled off again. Aspen trees lined the path, and a breeze cooled her and blew away the last of the mosquitoes. *I must be near the lake.* A few hills later she saw water.

Her emotions plummeted as she stood at the edge of a forty-foot cliff. The water below was brackish, dark, and muddy. Her dream of a crystal-blue lake where she could swim and have a drink was shattered. The water looked dead. This gruesome portage ended, but the lake below the cliff was not inviting. She set down the canoe and pack and flopped on the ground. "Steep hills, swamps, mud, millions of mosquitoes, and now the end of the portage is down there. How am I supposed to get down this cliff?"

Thankful for the breeze, she searched the sky between the aspen branches. *No one would ever find me here. No one's taken this portage in a long time,* she thought.

She pulled out the map. What she had thought was a printing smudge of blue in the middle of the portage she now understood was the swamp. "Clearly marked," she yelled.

She rolled on her stomach and looked over the cliff. "I can probably climb down this, but how do I get my canoe down?" The cliff was too steep to the left, but as she searched to the right, she noticed what seemed to be a human trail through the trees. Or was it just an animal track? It was steep, but there were strategic trees that could be used as handholds. She followed the course with her eyes, contemplating each step.

I'll take the pack down first. She put on her pack and climbed down the trail. Scuffed leaves suggested that whatever creature had made the trail had done so recently. It gave her confidence to think someone had traversed this portage, but it took all her focus to place her feet where they wouldn't slip, and she had to use both hands to keep from falling. When she reached the bottom, the water was dark and brooding, but following the course of the black muck, she saw an opening through the trees that she assumed was a portage. Consulting her map, she identified the mudhole as a small lake; it was not honored with a name, but on the far end there was a five-rod portage to a substantial lake on the other side. "It better be pretty," she said, shaking her fist at the sky.

She set down her pack. "I'm so thirsty," she said, but the water was covered with black slime.

The canoe's next. As she climbed the steep trail, she made a mental note of where to put her feet, where to find handholds, and where the gravel was loose. She rested at the top, then shouldered the canoe. As she headed down the steep trail, the canoe slipped forward, and the strut bit into the back of her raw neck. She pulled the bow level with her feet to keep the stern from knocking the rocks above. One handhold at a time, first the right, then the left, she inched down the hill. *Don't rush it*, she told herself. The weight of the canoe on the back of her neck felt like a knife stabbing her cervical spine. The stern hit a rock, and a bolt of electricity shot down both her arms, zinging her hold on a tree.

She paused. *This is not going well. I'm not even halfway, and there is no place to rest.* Her thoughts were prophetic. The next step, she slipped. The canoe crashed over her head. She lost hold on the tree as the stern of the canoe smashed into the back of her head, and the boat plummeted down the cliff. She tumbled down after it, spinning and somersaulting through the air. She jerked to a stop. A sharp pain seared her butt like a branding iron. Her vision went black.

• • •

It was twilight when she regained consciousness. She tried to focus. Her canoe was stuck in the mud at the bottom of the cliff. Her pack lay half submerged in mud next to the canoe, wedged in slime. But everything was upside down. She was stopped in the middle of the cliff, headfirst. Something was holding her. The severe pain in her right buttocks intensified as she attempted to move. She looked at her hands. Her gloves were crusted with gravel. She spit gravel out of her mouth onto the roots in front of her face and noticed blood. She took off her right glove and wiped her mouth. Blood. She inspected the rest of her body. Chest seemed all right, other than a few bruises, but taking a deep breath filled her lungs with fire. Her ribs were tender on the right. She felt a click and a searing pain with each inspiration. A rib must have broken. Her stomach wasn't tender. But the fiery pain in her butt was unrelenting. She slid her hand up the hill to her thigh. She was hanging from a broken sapling that had pierced through her jeans. *That's what stopped my fall*, she reasoned. *Am I going to die here? No one will ever find me. But it is no use going into a panic and screaming. There is no one for miles.*

She replaced her glove and tried to get a handhold, but every position

34

shift made the pain more intense. Her pants felt wet. *Did I pee myself?* She touched the dampness and looked at her glove. More blood. She ground her teeth to ease the pain and grabbed at rocks and roots to try to get upright. There was a loud snap.

She catapulted down the cliff. She covered her face with her hands, hitting rocks and smashing into trees as she fell, grinding through a cloud of gravel that cascaded with her. Her body slammed into the side of her canoe.

She shrieked. Her voice echoed against the cliff. Reaching back she found part of the sapling still stuck in her jeans and into her flesh. She grabbed it. Intense pain ripped through her thigh as she jerked the stick. It was stuck in her muscle. She gritted her teeth, and with an intense, primordial scream, "Oh, God," she jerked it out. In that instant, her jeans became soaked with blood. "Oh, shit!" she screamed, but that only increased the pain in her chest.

"It hurts so bad," she whispered as she squirmed in the mud. *Calm down; control your fear,* she commanded herself. *It won't do any good to scream, a waste of energy.* Frustration, desperation, and disappointment flashed through her mind.

She looked up through the matrix of trees at the wisp of sky. The setting sun blazed orange. "God, look at me. Do you love me?" Her strained vocal chords produced but a whisper. "I'm sorry to be selfish, God. I'm not going to ask you for anything or promise you anything. I'm not exactly in a position to be demanding." A sardonic smile crossed her face at the ridiculousness of her prayer. "But I don't want to die in this muck hole."

She slowed her breathing and tried to sit up. Scorching pain made her grab at the canoe. She pulled with both hands and collapsed to her left. Any pressure on her right buttocks sent electric shocks down her leg.

She scanned the canoe for damage. *If the canoe isn't seaworthy, I'm dead,* she reasoned. A dent in the bow seemed minor, and there were no cracks in the aluminum. All the rivets appeared intact.

Grabbing the canoe, and with another scream, she forced herself to her feet. She could bear weight on her right leg. "Our bones aren't broken," she told her canoe. She wiggled her toes and bent her knee, and there was no pain. But motion at her hip was searing. Bracing herself on the canoe, she pulled her pack out of the muck and flung it into the canoe. In minute stages she edged the canoe around till it was pointing toward the portage. She breathed a prayer of thanks to find the paddles still locked into the gunwales. She pulled them out, dropped them to the bottom, and slid the canoe into the muddy water. Climbing in at the last moment, she collapsed in the bottom.

I was so arrogant to come on this solo trip. Who do I think I am? She pulled herself up and pushed the canoe with the paddle toward the portage. She found a position on her left knee, with her right leg extended behind her that she could tolerate. She pushed, inching along with each painful thrust. *What am I going to do when I get to the portage? Will I be able to carry the canoe?* Despite the pain, the horror of dying in muck was worse. The sky was black as ink as the canoe hit gravel. "I made it. Thank God."

She pulled the pack up on the bow. Squatting on her left leg, she managed to sling one strap of the pack over her left shoulder. She stood and grabbed a paddle to use as a crutch. Step by painful step, she inched across the portage. When she got to the other side, she was dazzled by a full moon, the bright Milky Way, and a lake with such clear water starlight danced on the ripples. She took a deep sigh. "Beautiful. I'll be back in a moment, by God's grace."

She went back for the canoe. There was a rock shelf a few yards up the portage. She dragged the canoe, apologizing to it for any damage she was causing, and lifted the bow first on one rock and then another till the canoe was upside down on top of the rock shelf. She crawled underneath, and then with a scream that she was sure scared loons and wolves for three lakes in every direction, she stood up with the canoe on her shoulders. With her crutch-paddle in her right hand and balancing the canoe with her left she hobbled across the portage. She could not swing her right leg past neutral, so it was slow going. She tripped but caught herself with one hand, grabbing at a balsam as she started to fall. Luckily the canoe stayed balanced on her shoulders. The moonlight glinting off the surface of the lake gave her the adrenaline to finish.

"I made it," she exclaimed when water came into view. The stars sparkled on the near mirror surface of the water. *Could heaven be any more beautiful than this?* "Now you can let me die, God. I wouldn't mind dying here, and I promise not to complain." She crutched her way into the lake. A smooth, sandy shore continued out into deeper water. Waist-deep, she flipped the canoe into the water and gently edged it back to shore. Her pack felt heavier than usual, but she managed to slip it in the bow. Cautious not to stress her right hip, she climbed into the stern and sat on her left gluteal muscles to paddle. An island silhouetted against the starry sky seemed an obvious campsite.

A small, sandy cove allowed her to beach the canoe. The triumphal orchestra of loons singing and the frogs croaking in chorus elated her spirit. Pulling the canoe up and turning it over for a shelter, she calmed herself enough to take out the food pack and eat some beef jerky. She needed protein.

Now, to check the damage. She took off her gloves and T-shirt, putting them in the plastic bag in her pack even thought they were soaked in mud. The bottom of the pack was dry. She gnawed her jerky as she took off her boots and socks. Pain shot through her hip as she tried to take off her right boot. She couldn't sit, and it was too painful to pull her right leg up, so she caught her boot in the cleft of a rock and pulled. She fell over as the boot came off. Lying flat, she gasped until the pain abated.

Next she held on to a rock and took off the left pants leg first. Then she slid her left foot up the right leg until she could pull off her pants with her toes. She was free. A huge rip was drenched in crusted blood. She tried to slip off her panties. Ripping pain told her that the material was stuck in the wound. She bit her lip and yanked the underwear off.

"The moment of truth," she said as she retrieved her flashlight and some soap from her pack. Still clutching the rock, she turned the flashlight on her wound. She could see that she was still bleeding but couldn't twist into a position to see the wound.

Time for a swim, the only solution. She tossed her floating soap into the water and used her paddle to crutch her way to the water's edge. She set the crutch securely on the beach and then edged into the water. There was a sudden drop-off. Swimming was almost painless unless she tried to kick too hard with her right leg. Suspended, treading water by kicking with her left leg, she felt almost normal. The water felt warm and cleansing even though she knew it was cold. She swam a few strokes to retrieve her soap and washed her face and hair, diving to rinse. Then she soaped her arms, breasts, and belly. *So much sweat and sticky slime to wash off.* The cool water took away the itching of her mosquito bites.

"Here goes, God. Help me." She felt her wound. It seemed deep enough to put her fist into the gapping laceration. If she had been standing, she would have fainted. She forced her fingers inside the wound, feeling the torn muscle. She pulled out bits of stick and gravel and even part of her pants. She twisted the soap into the crevices. That provoked instant nausea, so she paused. Grinding her teeth, she swished out foreign material, repeating the process till it felt clean. It was so painful, but she was screamed out. *I need stitches. Where's the nearest emergency department?* She laughed at the absurd thought. Kicking with her left leg and breaststroking with her arms, she swam like a wounded frog. *It's a good thing this is freshwater, or I'd be attracting sharks. But bears are attracted to blood. I hope this island is too far for the lazy creatures to swim for a tasty meal of me.*

The stars dazzled her as she swam weightless, the beauty mesmerizing her pain. "Maybe I should swim home." But she started to chill. The evening air was warmer than the water as she crawled out. She grabbed her paddle-crutch and limped back to the canoe. There was dribbling down her leg and with the flashlight she saw a trail of fresh blood on the rocks. She grabbed her towel out of the plastic bag. She hadn't used it yet, so it was still clean. She tore off a third of it lengthwise and stuffed it into the wound. She tied another towel strip as tight as she could around her buttocks. *Good thing I'm blessed with narrow hips.* She put on her tightest underwear and crawled belly-down on top of her sleeping bag. She covered herself with a long-sleeved, flannel shirt. *I guess I'm sleeping on my stomach tonight. I hate sleeping on my stomach.*

Exhausted, she prayed, "Dear God, I'm still alive. So I guess you still want me around. I'm yours to do with as you please. Thanks that there are no mosquitoes on this island. And thanks for the nice clean lake and the bright stars and warm weather and soap and …"

. . .

Lisa awoke to throbbing pain. *How amazing; I can count my pulse in my butt.* As she tried to move, her stiff right hip refused. She did a one-leg pushup. A cramp made her extend her right leg. She arched her back and neck as her paraspinal muscles convulsed, but she managed to get upright.

The campsite was idyllic in the morning sun. Wood squirreled away under a rock, including kindling, a rock ledge for a table, and the sandy beach completed the amenities. A dried, blood-crusted trail up the rocks was the only detraction. *That portage was really difficult, and there are many ahead. I think I should just stay on this island until I heal enough to make those portages without so much pain.*

Despite nausea, she decided she needed to eat. She pulled her pot and oatmeal out of her pack and retrieved the matches stowed in double plastic bags. The kindling was tinder dry, and the fire started without coaxing. She fetched water and soaped the pan. Her trusty paddle functioned well to keep her ambulating. Since it was too painful to sit, she leaned against a rock shelf until her water come to a boil. The oatmeal quenched her nausea, and her hunger abated.

Now, do I go swimming again or keep it dry? I wonder. She took off her underwear and untied the piece of towel around her hips. Fingering her wound, she pulled the blood-encrusted wad of towel out with intense pain, but on inspection, the bleeding seemed to have subsided. She tied the dressing around her hips again, only tighter. It seemed to throb less the tighter she cinched it. *I feel like a porno star with this rag tied around my hips, not covering much of anything else, with a cute little knot dangling over my groin. Some fashion statement I am.* As much as she wanted to swim, she decided that she would heal faster if she kept it dry. She lay in the warm sun on her stomach on top of her sleeping bag. She rubbed sunscreen on her exposed skin and put on her long-sleeved shirt. *This is going to make weird tan lines,* she thought as she fell asleep.

CHAPTER 5

Toilet functions caused intense pain, but they had to be done. She also knew that she had to eat to heal. She threw in her lure in the evening and within five casts had a nice walleye for supper. As long as she kept her binder tight, she functioned fairly well. She took it off to inspect her wound and realized her mistake. With the binder off, the wound throbbed, and the pain increased. She tied it up again. It was hard to gaze at the stars lying on her stomach, and with the bleeding stopped, she rolled to her left side to watch for shooting stars. That night she slept inside her sleeping bag. The stars shining brightly overhead meant no rain. *Good. I need to stay dry.*

The next day was better. The scab felt dry, but if she flexed her hip, the wound gaped, so she kept her leg straight. She took out the blood-soaked rag, rinsed it in boiling water, dried it in the sun on a bare rock, and stuffed it back into her wound. After a liberal application of sunscreen, she lay her wound bare to the sun. *Most of the time I want to be naked; this time I'm forced to be naked.* Dry air and sunshine seemed to shrink the gap, and it gave her time to think.

What am I going to do if I ever get out of here? She laughed. *Why am I worrying about what I'm going to do when I get out of here? I have no idea if I'm going to make it out of here. But if I do, I guess I'll go to the university. My parents will be pleased, if they forgive me for disappearing.* Her thoughts rambled. *Maybe I could major in sports. Will the hole in my butt prevent me from playing sports? I could marry some rich guy. But I don't even have a boyfriend. The guys hot on me are such crud. I don't want to marry any of them. Besides, why do I need money? I can live my whole life on my inheritance. Oh, God, what are you going to do with me?*

By the third day she was walking better. The wound was dry and gaped only if she flexed her hip more than halfway. Out of curiosity she retrieved her map. *The portage out of here is a third of a mile. That's my goal.* She tried to flip the canoe on her shoulders to practice walking around her island, but it was too painful. *Maybe tomorrow.*

The next morning she stripped and slipped off her binder. Palpating her wound as she flexed her hip, the scab seemed to hold. *It's amazing how things heal. But I really want to go swimming.* She pulled some grease out of her food pack and smeared it across her right backside, thinking that the oil would protect her wound.

She slipped into the lake. The sensation was incredible. She felt weightless in the water, free to move in ways that weren't possible on land and comfortable swathed in cold water. She swam, stretching and exercising her legs and arms with minimal pain in her wounded leg. Unsure how long the grease would protect, after a circular excursion in front of her camp, she climbed out of the water. There was instant pain as she battled gravity up onto the shore. "Back to thinking in the sun," she said as she stretched out. The warmth of the unclouded sun soothed her skin. She reapplied her binder and her tightest underwear and tried again to flip the canoe. She couldn't do it.

"I need a new approach," she said as she lifted the bow, the stern resting on the ground. She turned around and slid backward into position. The yoke in place, the canoe felt good on her shoulders. *I can leave tomorrow,* she decided. *What a wonderful hospital this campsite has been. I will have to come back someday when I'm not injured.*

In the morning, she discovered that she was almost out of oatmeal. There was one serving left. *I am at least three days from the landing, and I can't paddle efficiently,* she thought, *so it will probably take me longer.* "God, I need something to eat," she said. She cast her fishing lure several times into the area where she had gotten the walleye but caught nothing. She ate raisins and a few nuts but decided to save her last meal of oatmeal for later. *This could become a hungry adventure. But staying here, as nice as it is, will not get me home.* For the first time since starting this trip, she wanted to go home. *I have to go. I've got to* … She couldn't finish the thought. *Just take one portage at a time.*

She cinched her binder as tight as possible without ripping the towel, packed her gear, and dressed in shorts and a T-shirt. Using her new technique, she shouldered the canoe, limped out to thigh-deep water, flipped the canoe, and loaded it. She took one last look at the map and paddled off.

She found a comfortable position by kneeling while resting her left buttock on the seat behind her. It was too painful to put pressure on her right side. She used her fleece to pad her knees and wore her life jacket, not quite sure of her balance.

The portage was exactly where she expected. Her technique of lifting the bow and backing into position worked, but walking was more painful with the added weight of the pack and the canoe. *Going over the portage twice seems like twice the pain,* she thought as she put the pack on her back, gritted her teeth, and lifted the canoe in place. There was no wind, and the next lake was easy to cross. Two portages and two more lakes exhausted her endurance. *I've got to rest. This has taken all morning. Before, I could have done this in a couple of hours.*

Checking the map, she was encouraged to see that she was more than halfway through the chain of lakes. *Another day and I'll be in the big water, and then it's just a long, painful paddle south to the landing.*

She found a campsite where a fast-moving stream flowed into the lake and camped. There was no evidence that anyone had camped here all season. The grass was knee-high. She pulled out her fishing gear.

Her lure plopped nicely into the current of the stream. She let it drift out into the lake. When it stopped moving, she reeled in. A sudden splash made her jump. Her line spun off the reel. She set the hook and reeled in a pound-size bass. She tied it to a stringer and tried again. Nothing. She cast into the middle of the stream, precisely where she had before. The lure drifted and then stopped. She started to reel: another strike, another bass. Each time she cast her lure in the same place in the middle of the stream and let it drift, she caught another bass. She kept the biggest ones on her stringer and let the others go.

She was delighted with her success, and her stomach growled. Her mind recreated the smell of cooking fish, which intensified her craving. Then, as if someone rang a bell, the fish stopped biting. Six casts produced nothing. *I guess they're tired. But I have a great supper.* Four big bass made eight nice fillets. She built a fire, added grease to her pot, and fried the fish.

The sizzling sound of the frying fillets lifted her spirit. She fried four, turning them over with her fork till they were golden brown. *Sure would be nice with a squirt of lime and some spicy tartar sauce. I'll have to bring that next time.* After gobbling down her fish feast, she was content. She put the uncooked fillets in the cooking pot, submerged it in the cold water near her landing, and put a large rock on top to keep it secure from marauding turtles.

"Now for the hard part," she said. She took a deep breath and loosened the knot on her binder. The pain increased. *I guess that proves that it's helping.* She palpated the scab and checked her hand for drainage. It was dry. It only felt warm at the edges.

Powerless to the siren call to swim in the lake, she stripped off her clothes, smeared grease on her wound, and dove into the water. *I just can't skip this part.* She jumped into the current, then swam into the eddy, unsure of her endurance. Her leg felt good, so she kicked as much as pain would allow. Treading water was comfortable. Floating on her back in the safety of the eddy current was even more comfortable. She watched the clouds float across the sky as the current spun her around like a rubber duck in a bathtub drain. She closed her eyes and drifted in peace.

When she opened her eyes, dense clouds were forming on the western horizon. She stood on a submerged rock. *Rain's coming. I better make sure everything is secure.* Out of the water she patted her laceration dry, then tied her binder in place and put on her panties for support. Slipping on a T-shirt and long-sleeved shirt gave her a sense of security.

It took a lot longer to get her tarp in position and secure the camp. Several times she stopped, gasping for breath because of intense pain, but persisted because the storm approaching appeared violent on the horizon. The sky churned with surreal black-green clouds. Bent over a rock, exhausted, her arms hung limp in front of her, her sore butt protruding skyward. She could no longer bear weight on her right leg. She caressed a boulder to watch the violet sunset.

The loons sang early and sounded frenzied. The frogs remained silent even though she observed several in the reeds frantic in their breathing. She put more rocks on top of her pot of fish fillets to secure her food for morning. She smelled the ozone before the storm hit. No longer placid, the water crashed the shore in wind-blasted waves.

Back in the woods, clinging to a small pine tree, she gasped to defecate. *Why now, oh bowels!* As the sky darkened, no stars appeared. Back at her camp she wedged herself under the canoe, slipping into her sleeping bag to avoid pressure on her laceration. Balancing on her left hip and elbow, she took off her shirts. She zipped up her sleeping bag and fell asleep, safe in her cocoon.

Lightning, thunder, and the deafening roar of rain crashed together, waking her. Thunder blasted the instant the lightning struck. Wherever she focused, the flash image imprinted on her retina as darkness resumed. Then the downpour commenced. Cuddled in her sleeping bag, she wondered if the rocks holding the tarp were heavy enough. The wind whipped across her shelter, but the tarp held. She felt cozy, watching the Wagnerian symphony surround her. She stayed awake to witness the turmoil and then fell asleep as the storm abated.

In the morning, soaked wood made starting a fire difficult. Despite lots of smoke, the fire kept going out. She started over. With choice pieces from under the canoe, she whittled kindling. The drizzling gray sky frustrated her efforts. Her hip was stiff, but the possibility of fried fish for breakfast encouraged her to keep trying. More careful, she slivered some dry pine and started the fire under the canoe, adding birch bark. When it seemed healthy, she transferred the fire with two sticks to the fire pit. Despite the constant spit of lingering raindrops, it kept going. She stacked a pile of the wet wood around the fire to dry. Split sticks of sappy pine kept it going. With prayer and constant attention the fire eventually burned with confidence.

The pot of fish with the rock on top had survived the turmoil undisturbed. She greased her skillet and added the fillets. Raindrops sizzled on the hot griddle. But her investment in the fire was paid with delicious, crispy dividends. She gobbled down all four fillets, frantic to get the warmth in her belly. *What a perfect breakfast for a miserable morning.*

Icy blasts of wind and intermittent squalls forced efficient packing. The portage to the next lake was around the point. Despite the intense pain with each step, the effort to portage her pack and canoe warmed her.

Constant drizzle made it difficult to keep her wound dry even with her rain suit tucked underneath her butt. By midday she paused to change into her last pair of dry underwear before attempting the portage to the next lake. "I want to be dry," she yelled. The scream, which echoed from rock cliffs surrounding the lake, calmed her frustration.

The next lake appeared huge on the map. The landing and her car were on the southern shore; she was on the north. She ate a few mouthfuls of nuts and dried fruit. Hope filled her like fire in a boiler. The dread of dying and no one ever finding her evaporated. This was a popular lake with multiple campsites, even some resorts on the southern shore.

But she camped, too miserable and exhausted to continue. She wanted to fish, but the task of casting seemed insurmountable, so she ate the last of her jerky, cut up into the last of her soup. *Oatmeal in the morning, and then I am out of food, so I better make it tomorrow, or my stomach will eat me alive.*

The wind started blowing from the south, clearing away the clouds. By the time she curled up in her sleeping bag, she could see stars on the horizon. *Dry at last, but I still have to face the wind, again.*

During the night she dreamed of fighting the wind. She fought with all her strength, but the wind just laughed at her. Exhausted, she could fight no longer; she admitted defeat, ready to die. That's when the wind picked her up, and her canoe started to fly. Her spirit felt free as she soared over the trees and skimmed the whitecaps. The wind set her down and sheltered her behind a massive rock.

"You're working too hard, Lisa. I'll carry you where I want you. You can't fight me. I'm too strong."

Tears burned her face. "Can I trust you?"

"You can."

"I'm afraid. I can't do stuff. I'm hurting."

"I love you the way you are. I'm not the wind. I'm the one who made you."

Bright sun without a cloud in the sky greeted Lisa the next morning, but the wind flew in her face as she stood on the shore enjoying the last of her oatmeal. As she started to launch her canoe, the whitecaps smashed her bow and sprayed her face. But she remembered her dream, and it gave her courage.

I could stay here and wait for the wind to die down. But if I stay, I have nothing to eat unless I catch another fish. What should I do? If I swamp the canoe, I'll die. If I stay here without food, I'll be too weak to paddle. And what if my wound gets infected? I'll die. The spray of the waves did not make her decision any easier. She said out loud to convince herself, "I'll try it. If the wind is too strong, I'll turn back before I get too far from shore."

She put the pack low in the bow of the canoe and tightened the straps on her life jacket. Her forehead burned as she faced the gusts of wind off the lake. She held the canoe so the bow went directly into the wind and shoved off.

It took every muscle in her arms and shoulders to keep the canoe headed in the right direction, and she made no progress. A few yards from shore a gust of wind spun the canoe completely around. She was facing where she had just come from and the wind was pushing her there fast.

On a sudden inspiration she turned herself around and started paddling. The stern became the bow. The wind kept the canoe aligned, and she pulled forward instead of pushing the canoe, paddling from the stern. It meant not wasting energy keeping the canoe straight. Pleased with herself, she kept paddling. She knew she had to go straight south. Kneeling in the canoe, she put her compass on the seat to correct her direction. "I'm going to make it," she yelled at the wind. The spray of a wave felt like sandpaper across her face.

Her muscles strained as each paddle stroke felt like her shoulders were tearing from her chest. Her ribs stung as her muscles tore at their attachments. But an hour later she recognized a break in the trees that she knew was the bay to the boat landing. The landing was yet hours away, and she had exhausted her strength. "Stay focused. Get there or die," she yelled at her faltering confidence.

She was startled by a voice. "Young lady, do you need some help?"

CHAPTER 6

> If you are really in difficult places ... and you come
> back, you feel that you got again a chance for life. You
> are reborn. And only in this moment, you understand
> deeply that life is the biggest gift we have.
> —Reinhold Messner, solo climber of Everest

Another wave splashed her face. She dared not take her focus off the channel ahead for even an instant. Then a canoe approached from behind on her left side. An older man with a gray beard peeking out from the hood of a green rain suit was in the stern of a canoe. She thought he must have been the one to first call out to her. In the bow was a young man, wrapped in a rain poncho. He had a full beard and straw-colored hair that stuck out in all directions from his stocking cap. As they approached her, the younger man grabbed her gunwale. The turbulent waves splashed up between the canoes.

"I'm Troy," the young man said. "Mr. Svenson back there is my boss. We're outfitters. What are you doing out in the middle of the lake all by yourself?"

"Trying to get to that landing," she said, pointing to the inlet. "What do you expect?" The wind muted her sarcasm.

"Looks like you could use some help. We'll tie a rope to your bow and keep you lined up. We're going to the same landing."

Lisa struggled with her thoughts. *I can make it on my own. I made it this far. Only a couple more hours and I could reach the landing.* Then she felt a cramp in her right gluteal muscle. It grabbed her so intensely she grabbed the gunwales to keep from jerking the canoe over. "Thanks, I could use some help," she said.

Troy held the canoes together and nodded to Mr. Svenson to tie a rope to Lisa's bow. "Now when you swing around, don't fight it, or you'll flip. Just let it swing you around. Turn and face the other direction while we're holding you. And get low in the canoe."

Lisa turned to face the opposite direction. She hadn't come as far as she thought. She could still see the portage.

Troy shoved Lisa's canoe to the side. It caught the wind and swung her violently to the side. It felt like a ride at the fair. The centripetal force threw her into the waves. When the rope became taut, her canoe jerked into alignment behind the other canoe. The two men dipped their paddles, and Lisa felt a surge forward. She added her paddling to the motion, and with each stroke, she could feel the thrust and strength of the other canoe. It felt great.

The wind howled, and the waves splashed, but within an hour they were in the wind shadow of the bay. The paddling was easier, and the lack of wind allowed Lisa to be heard. "Thanks, guys," she called out. Her pride would not allow her to add, "Couldn't have made it without you," but she knew it was true.

"Anytime," said Troy as they arrived at the landing dock. "How long have you been out?"

Lisa counted. "Ten days, I think. I may have lost a day or so."

Mr. Svenson went to get their vehicle. Troy took off his hat and faced Lisa. "By yourself?"

Despite the bleached and weathered hair that stuck out from underneath his hat, his hair was dark and straight underneath. It tossed about his face. Lisa pictured two eyes peering out from under a haystack.

"By myself." She wanted to add, "Do you see anyone with me?" but refrained from the sarcasm.

"Get your car, and I'll help you load your canoe."

Lisa felt rebellious. *I don't need help,* she thought, but she bit her tongue. *That is no way to treat these guys who have just saved me hours of paddling and maybe saved my life.* "All right, let me dig out my car keys." She found her keys in the bottom of her pack in a ziplock bag and went for the car, pack on her back. *He wasn't going to help her with that.*

Unlocking her car, she slid into the seat and started the engine. Instant pain seared her buttocks. It was so intense she jackknifed out of the seat. *I hadn't thought about having to sit to drive.* She settled on her left butt and drove to the landing. She set the emergency brake and left the car running.

Mr. Svenson and Troy had already loaded their canoe. The older man was sitting behind the wheel of his car. Troy grabbed the bow of her boat and Lisa the stern, and the two of them hoisted the canoe into position on top of the Jeep. Lisa grabbed the straps out of the back. Troy secured the canoe.

"What did you do to your bow?" he asked.

Lisa flushed with embarrassment. "I had a little trouble on the Wickstead portage."

"You took that portage?" He paused, wild eyed. "By yourself? It's been closed for years! Didn't you see the sign?"

"Yes, I took the portage by myself, and no, I didn't see any sign. The canoe slipped off my shoulders coming down that goat trail at the end."

"That cliff is a killer. We always had to line our canoes down that cliff. How did you ever make it without killing yourself? I'm impressed. You must be the only girl—I mean, woman." She felt his eyes scanning her figure. "Let me start over. You must be the only person to have ever done that. You are one awesome … woman." He yelled to his boss, "Hey, Mr. Svenson, she came across the Wickstead portage—alone."

"Invite her for lunch."

"You heard the man. You're having lunch with us."

Lisa hated being told what to do, but Troy was handsome, and if he was impressed with her, then maybe she should accept. She climbed behind the wheel of the Jeep. "All right, if you insist. I'll follow you."

Troy held her car door open. "Can I ride with you? I'll show you where the outfitter is. So you don't get lost."

"Sure, no problem on my end."

He waved to his boss and yelled, "I'll show her the way." With that, Mr. Svenson left the parking lot and drove down the road. Troy ran around the front of the Jeep and slid into the passenger's seat as Lisa took off her wet raincoat and soaked fleece, tossing them in the backseat. With the car doors closed, it was silent: no wind, no rain. It felt to Lisa like a sacred sanctuary. She felt secure. She turned on the heater full blast, enjoying the warm air blowing in her face. Her butt screamed, so she shifted slightly but refused to wince with Troy sitting next to her.

"Now, tell me this again," he said. "You've been on a ten-day canoe trip by yourself and went across the Wickstead portage?"

"Yes. What of it?" His admiration was annoying.

"Let's start with names. It was too windy out there to properly introduce myself. I'm Troy Vogel. Mr. Svenson and I have been out for a couple of days checking on campsites and portages. And you are?"

"Lisa Zuccerelli. I just graduated from high school and needed to get away for a while." The words stung. She was sure that she hadn't graduated. She turned to look at him. He was checking her out. She realized that her soaking wet T-shirt was probably quite revealing. Her nipples were as hard as rocks. *Maybe I should have worn a bra to come back to civilization*, she thought.

Lisa put the Jeep in gear and drove out of the parking lot.

Troy said, "You sure got great biceps, Lisa Zuccerelli. Mr. Svenson and I were impressed with the way you handled your canoe. Oh, turn right on that next gravel road. I hope you like chili. Mrs. Svenson always makes chili and cornbread when we come back. Imagine, a Swede who loves chili. This wilderness does strange things to people."

Lisa turned onto the gravel road and followed Troy's directions to the outfitter where canoes were stacked alongside the parking lot. Her butt was throbbing, but she had managed to sit straight in the seat despite her pain. But when she stopped the Jeep, it made her wince. She climbed out as quickly as she could get the door open.

"You're limping. Did you get hurt?" Troy asked.

"Just a little bruise on my butt. Nothing bad."

"Well, follow me." Troy led her into the log building. Packs hung upside down on the wall. Dehydrated food filled the shelves. The smell of new equipment mixed with the aroma of dehydrated fruit. The computerized cash register in the corner seemed out of place next to the rustic gear. He motioned for her to follow through the maze of equipment to a door marked Private.

Inside the door was a small kitchen. A pine dining table filled the open space. Eclectic spoons and bowls rested on red cloth napkins. Mr. Svenson stood as Lisa entered.

"Her name is Lisa Zuccerelli," said Troy.

Mr. Svenson nodded.

His wife turned from the chili to greet her. "I'm Helga. It's nice to meet you, Lisa. Don't mind Ernie; he's Swede. They're naturally shy. He doesn't say anything unless he's got something important to say, and then you need a crowbar to get it out of him.

"Now, I just put the cornbread in the oven, and the chili has to rest for a few minutes to improve its flavor, so you just go take a shower, and when you come back, everything will be ready. Troy, honey, show her where the shower is."

Troy blushed and said, "Follow me." Once outside he turned to her and said, "I still blush every time she calls me honey. I know it's silly, but I can't help it." It had started to rain, but in comparison to what she had been through, the few drops hitting her face seemed a gentle mist. They walked over to a log building with doors on each side and stood under the eaves. "Men's bunk is on the right; women's is on the left. But it doesn't much matter, as we won't have any groups coming till tomorrow."

"Thanks, Troy. Let me grab my clean clothes from the Jeep. A hot shower sounds great."

"See you back at the kitchen. 'Honey' is going back to smell the chili." He blushed again. "Helga is sweet, though." He turned and headed back to the house.

Lisa grabbed the clean clothes she had stored in a plastic bag in the back of her Jeep, and without anyone watching she limped in a less-painful gait toward the showers. She was tempted to use the men's just because she could but opened the left door and went into the women's bunk room. Six bunk beds lined the walls. In the back corner was a doorway that led to a spacious bathroom with three showers.

Now to check this wound. She stripped, untied her binder, and turned on the hot water. It felt glorious. Soap and shampoo were provided, and clean towels were stacked by the sink.

Never had hot water streaming down her body felt so good. The silky sensation intensified as she turned the water hotter. Her skin turned red in a rush of pleasure. "Oh, this is great." She turned so that the force of the water was on her wound. It didn't look infected, but the scab was cracked in places. Near the edge of the laceration some of the scab fell off in the pulse of the shower, and she found healed skin underneath. *Good, signs of healing, so no need to seek medical attention.*

Despite not wanting to ever leave, she turned off the shower and dried in a fluffy towel, careful to only pat her wound dry. She adjusted her posture to look at her wound in the mirror. It was ugly but did not seem too red or inflamed. She went to reapply her binder and realized how filthy it was. *It looked clean when I tore it from my towel.*

She noted some torn sheets sitting on a shelf to be used as rags. She took one and bound it around her hips, spreading the piece of sheet out to encompass her wound. It felt better as she slipped her underwear over the binder.

She smelled her clean clothes. The refreshing scent of laundry detergent pleased her as she put on her pants. She held up her bra. *I suppose I need it to go home, but Troy will probably be disappointed.* She slipped it on. It felt uncomfortable and restricting. She took it off. *Maybe later. Lucky Troy.* She put on a clean T-shirt and looked in the mirror. She tickled her nipples till they stood up. "I do look cute, and I do have nice biceps, but maybe that's too much of a good thing," she said to the image in the mirror. She put on her flannel shirt. *Comfort is more important today, Troy.*

Back in the kitchen the cornbread was coming out of the oven. All eyes stared at her as she came into the room.

"Aren't you a sweet-smelling sight," said Troy.

"Did I smell that bad before?"

"You just ignore him, honey, and sit down," Helga said. "You look famished. What did you eat out on the trail? Birch bark?"

"I had plenty of oatmeal and soup with beef jerky mostly and lots of fish, except for the one a turtle stole." Lisa sat on the hard wood chair and found that as long as she kept a straight posture and rolled her hips forward, she was comfortable.

"Done a lot of canoeing?" asked Ernie.

"I learned to canoe with my father. We've canoed hundreds of miles together, but he was too busy working this time to come with me."

"You've got a lot of guts to do what you did." He turned to Helga, "She was out there ten days."

Helga interjected, "He means gumption and tenacity, honey."

"I love the wilderness, and I enjoy being alone. I left June 10, ten days ago. Right?"

"Eleven," said Ernie.

Helga served large bowls of chili to each and cut the pan of cornbread into four chunks, serving one to Lisa. She set a pot of honey next to Lisa and cut off a chunk of butter and plopped it on top of Lisa's steaming cornbread. It melted and dribbled down the sides. "Now if you need more cornbread, honey, you let me know," said Helga. "I'm not going to finish mine. But you watch that Troy. He'll gulp his down and have his eyes on yours before you're half done."

Troy smiled and shook his head, apparently to negate the remark.

The only sound in the kitchen was hunger being quenched. Lisa ate like a wolf discovering fresh kill. She kept looking up to find Troy staring at her.

Ernie was half done with his chili when he asked, "Have much trouble with the Wickstead portage?"

Lisa looked up. Every spoon was in suspended motion. "It was a challenge. I thought it might kill me."

"Not many groups have crossed that one. You're the first person I know who's done it solo. There is supposed to be a closed sign. I've been outfitting trips for over twenty years, and I've never heard of such a thing. How did you deal with that cliff? Is that where you got your limp?"

No one was eating. Lisa took a deep breath. "That swamp in the middle must be where every mosquito in Canada has their relatives." Everyone smiled at her humor. "And yes, that cliff banged me up pretty badly. I tried to carry the canoe down on my shoulders."

"You drop it at the top or near the bottom?"

Lisa winced. "Sort of in the middle."

"Didn't knock any of the rivets loose, did you?"

"No, it didn't leak."

"You should line the canoe down the cliff next time." He returned his focus to his chili.

Troy explained, "If you're by yourself, tie a long rope to each end, loop one rope around a tree or something, then throw both ropes down the cliff. You can keep the canoe away from those rocks by pulling the lower rope and letting the canoe down by gently loosening the upper rope. When the canoe is down the cliff, you just yank down the rope from around the tree above. A lot easier."

"Sounds easy. I didn't think of it."

"That's all right," said Ernie. "I admire you. I'm pleased to make your acquaintance, you being a young woman and all."

It was quiet as each person finished his or her chili. Ernie popped the last of his cornbread into his mouth. "Now, Helga, are we sharing that apple pie with our brave guest, or are we keeping the whole thing for ourselves?"

Helga didn't answer but smiled and cleared the plates. Lisa was embarrassed that she had eaten all her cornbread. The honey bowl was almost empty, and much of it had ended up on her portion. She wasn't sure when that slab of butter had disappeared. Helga set dessert plates in front of everyone and went to the pantry. She served large wedges of apple pie and offered cheese to go with it. Lisa wasn't sure she nodded agreement, but a large wedge of Wisconsin sharp cheddar cheese appeared on her pie.

"Sorry, honey, we don't get much ice cream here very often," Helga said. "Troy brings the cheese from his home."

Everyone dug into the pie as if they hadn't eaten. As she devoured hers, Lisa became aware of Troy's gaze. She smiled.

"You're amazing," Troy said to her. "I have never met a woman like you. Where are you going to school? Which university?"

Lisa thought, *This guy who is more impressed with my biceps than my breasts is fascinating. At least that's what he said. He seems so gentle yet was no wimp by the way he and Ernie paddled. What should I say? I'm tired of school. I'm not planning on going to college. I have to finish that stupid English class this summer or maybe next fall. Then go to university? I doubt any university would accept me.* She replied, "There is a branch of the University of Minnesota in Duluth, my hometown."

"I'm from Eau Claire, Wisconsin, and am going to the University of Wisconsin in Madison. I'll be a freshman in business administration. My parents aren't too well off, so I need in-state tuition. That's why I'm working for Mr. Svenson. He pays me all right, and there isn't anywhere for forty miles in any direction to spend it. Besides, Mrs. Svenson makes good grub."

"She sure does. Well, I better get going. I have a long drive ahead of me."

"You can stay in the bunkhouse and leave in the morning if you want," Helga said. "It's important to be well rested."

"No, that's fine. I drive well at night." Lisa got up and gave a wave of thanks.

"All right, honey, you stay safe." Helga got up and gave her a smothering hug. Ernie clasped Lisa's right hand with both of his. He didn't say a word.

"I'll take her out to her car," said Troy. Lisa turned and walked out the door through the front, past all the camping equipment. Troy grabbed a pen and paper from the cash register, scribbled something, and followed her to the Jeep. He handed her the paper. "I would sure like to get to know you better. Would you write or call me?" He bowed his head slightly and lifted his eyes to meet hers. "Excuse me if you think I'm flattering you and coming on too strong, but seriously, I have never met anyone like you. Please keep in touch, would you? Please?"

Lisa took the paper and climbed in the Jeep. "I'll keep in touch. Nice to meet you, Troy." She put the key in the ignition, waved, and drove down the gravel road to the highway.

• • •

A half hour later, despite twisting in odd positions, the pain was so severe that she had to stop. Tears gushed from her eyes as she pulled to the side of the road. Her tears blinded her.

CHAPTER 7

S hit, that hurts," she screamed as she scrambled out of the Jeep and leaned over the hood for relief. She turned and vomited chunks of chili in the ditch. The soft seat pressed on her laceration in just the wrong way. *I can't concentrate to drive.* She thought about driving back to the Svensons' place and accepting their offer to stay the night. *But would it be any better in the morning? Besides, I would have to admit I was hurt. I can handle this myself; no one needs to know.* She spit the last vomit out of her mouth. *Especially my parents.*

She sobbed on the hood of the Jeep, thankful that no one was driving by. *How could those hard kitchen chairs be comfortable and my car seat hurt so much?* With a sigh she lifted her head, and her eye caught a child's orange life vest in the ditch. She picked it up. It had not been in the ditch for long, as it was still clean. She squeezed it and found it to be solid foam. *Someone must have left it in their boat after hitching up the trailer, and driving this gravel road flipped it out of the boat. This is a gift of the wind.*

She stuck it on the seat, straps underneath, then eased herself onto it, positioning her wound into the hole. She felt instant relief. She adjusted her seat belt and started her car. With a little wiggle to check position, she drove off. "Much better."

• • •

Driving up to the US border control, she was glad that there were no lines. It was well after midnight. She slowed to the border station and opened her window, turning off the ignition.

"Good evening, miss. May I see your driver's license? Where have you been?"

"Canoeing." She handed the officer her license. He did not give it back but added it to his clipboard.

"Do you have any fish or food products?"

"No. I ate them all."

He walked around the car with his clipboard and scribbled something down. "Can I please have you open the back?" He garbled something into the walkie-talkie attached to his shoulder.

Lisa got out and opened the back. He fished around inside, checking her backpack and plastic bag of dirty clothes. There was a squawk on his walkie-talkie.

"Can I have you come into the station, miss?" he said.

"Yes, sure." She became aware that he wanted her to lead. They walked into the fluorescent lights of the glassed station. Lisa tried not to limp.

"Please be seated." He offered her a plastic chair and stood in front of the door.

Another border control agent was on the telephone. "Yes, sir. Positive ID, sir. Yes, sir. She is walking with a limp, sir." He turned to her. "Elizabeth Zuccerelli?"

"Yes."

He handed her the telephone. "There is someone who would like to talk to you."

"Hello?" she said.

"Elizabeth."

"Yes, Dad."

"How was the canoe trip?"

"Excellent. I had a great time."

"We missed you." There was a long pause. He didn't say any more.

"I'm on my way home if I can get past the border guards. They stopped me and won't let me through."

"Let me talk to them."

"All right."

She started to hand the phone over, but then her dad said, "Elizabeth?"

"Yes, Dad."

"One more thing."

"Yes, what is it?"

"I have your diploma. You graduated."

She turned her head and covered her mouth. Removing her hand, she said into the phone, "I thought I flunked."

"The school board overruled Mrs. Burns. We didn't find out until the week after graduation what was so complicated. They decided to force Mrs. Burns to retire. It wasn't about you. And before you think I manipulated the system, I had nothing to do with it. But your pediatrician is on the school board."

"I graduated," she said. "I can hardly believe it." She looked at the officers staring at her and quelled her tone. "Seriously, I graduated? You're not just saying that to get me to come home?"

"Yes, seriously. And another thing."

"Yes?"

"We're sorry we've been too busy for you. After you left the auditorium, you were awarded Most Valuable Player of the year. Your mother and I were ashamed as we accepted your award that we hadn't even been to one of your basketball games. We talked to your coach after the graduation ceremony." He choked. "We're sorry. We love you very much. Do you know that?"

"I know that, Dad. I'll see you soon." She handed the receiver to the border patrol officer and danced around so he wouldn't see the tears in her eyes, tears of joy. Sharp pain made her stop.

The officer said a few words that Lisa didn't hear and hung up the telephone. "You're free to go, miss. I'll raise the gate," he said as he offered her a tissue.

"Thank you, Officer."

She positioned her buttocks into the hole in the child's life jacket, attached her seat belt with exaggerated flourish to make sure the officer saw her put it on, and drove off waving to the two border patrolmen as she left. *It will be good to be home. But will my parents really change?*

• • •

About seven thirty in the morning she turned into the driveway and pushed the buttons on the security panel. The gate opened, and she drove the winding drive to the "big house," as her grandfather called it. She turned off the ignition and stared at the massive structure. Grandfather had had good ideas and good friends who had helped him start his factory despite his lack of education. He had paid his help well and managed to become wealthy. He'd built the mansion that Lisa called home with local labor, except for the Italian sculptor he imported to carve the fireplace mantel. She remembered sitting on his lap when she was little. He would give her a hug and tell her, "We have a responsibility to spread our wealth, Lisa."

The house looked like a Gothic chateau with its faux-wood-and-masonry exterior and the large stained glass window facing the driveway. She had loved playing hide-and-seek with Linden when they were growing up. She had been able to hide in so many different rooms. Her favorite had been the solarium filled with plants. She'd imagined that she was hiding in a jungle. Linden had seldom found her there because he'd been afraid to get messy.

She loved the library with books to the ceiling that required a ladder on wheels that rode on its own track around the upper shelves. It wasn't the books so much as the ladder that she enjoyed. There was even one room that her grandfather had thought would be a private chapel, but it had become a recreation room. Grandfather later called it the ballroom. He would dance with Grandmother late at night when everyone was in bed. Lisa had caught them several times when she couldn't sleep. They had been so graceful.

When Grandmother had died, Grandfather had measured the ceiling height and had suggested putting up a basketball hoop, but Lisa's parents had thought it would "desecrate the ambiance."

But as much as Lisa loved the house, she felt self-conscious of it. Whenever her classmates had seen where she lived, they'd always treated her differently afterward. She'd learned not to invite friends over. It was better that way.

She felt stiff as she opened the Jeep door. She planted her left leg and stumbled out of the seat. It felt good to be standing and not putting any pressure on her wound. She pulled the canoe off and hung it on the rack on the side of the garage. The dent didn't look too bad. She hoped her father wouldn't notice. She turned to retrieve her pack.

Her father was standing in the driveway holding her pack. "I was so worried about you, Elizabeth."

He was the only one who ever called her Elizabeth. "I'm home safe and sound, Dad. You taught me excellent canoeing skills."

"We missed you at the party. It was for you."

She started her memorized script. "I didn't deserve a party—"

"Elizabeth," he interrupted. He dropped her pack and faced her, holding her shoulders with his strong hands. "I love you very much. I was seriously worried. I know work has gotten in the way, but a lot of people depend on me. You know that, don't you?"

The script didn't fit. Lisa didn't know what to say. She watched a tear stream down his cheek. "I love you too, Dad. I am sorry I made you worry. I just thought that I was such a major disappointment to you and Mom."

"You have great strengths, and I'll do whatever I can to make those gifts blossom." They hugged, their tears flowing on each other's shoulders. "Oh, it is so good to have you home. Come in the house, and tell me all about your trip."

"Don't you have to go to work?"

"I took the day off."

They walked inside, his right arm over her shoulders.

"Look what I found out on the driveway," he said to her mom.

Her mom jumped up from the kitchen chair. "Oh, Lisa, you're safe. Whatever possessed you to do that?"

Lisa froze.

Her father looked stern. "Helen, she went on a canoe trip, but she's back safe and sound. Let's go out for lunch. She can tell us all about it."

"I just had to work some things out in my head, Mother."

"Did you decide anything? You made me so upset. I could hardly focus at work."

Lisa glared at her. "Are you a prosecuting attorney or my mother?" Helen stepped back and said nothing. "I can't argue with you. I don't know how." Lisa took a step closer, unsure of her predator. Helen did not respond. "Since Dad told me that I graduated, I've decided to go to the university. Does that satisfy you?"

Her mother's eyes softened. "That's a wise decision, but I don't think it is worth thirteen days of worry."

Quit exaggerating; it was only twelve, Lisa thought.

Her mother choked and swallowed. "You're my only daughter, Lisa." She held out her arms. "You're limping. What's wrong?"

"I bruised my hip falling down on a portage trail. It's nothing." Lisa attempted to correct her gait and walk more normally. "Tell you what: I've been driving all night. Let me take a shower and a nap, and you can take me anywhere you want for lunch. I'm so tired of camp food. How's that?"

Her parents' eyes seemed to connect and communicate. She was sure that they were resolving two weeks of anguish and arguments. Not a word was said. Her dad grabbed her mom's hands as they faced each other.

"That's a great idea," he said. "You take a shower and get some rest, and I'll make reservations at the Brewery."

"Yes, get some rest. I'll come and wake you up about noon," her mom said.

"Sounds great." She shifted her weight to her left leg. "Mother?"

"Yes."

"Are we still friends?"

"I'm sorry, Lisa. I know I sounded harsh. I want to be your friend." She grabbed the pack from Paul and looked inside. "Looks like I have some laundry to do."

"I'll do it. It's just that I am so tired. I drove all night to get here."

Her mom gave her a kiss on the forehead. "I'm your mother. I'll do it for free and love it. An attorney would charge."

Lisa smiled and climbed the stairs to her room. She felt her parents watching her, so she tried not to limp, but it was very painful. With her back turned they couldn't see the grimace of pain on her face.

She enjoyed her room. Her mother had let her choose which room she wanted when she was five years old. When she was older, she got to decorate it. It was the only room in the house with cherry paneling. Her bed was a Tudor-style canopy, with massive corner posts like trees in a forest. Green fabric across the top was drawn together at the corners like leaves cascading down the trees. Her bedspread and comforter with a pattern of green and yellow leaves scattered across a beige background complemented the antique cherry bed. The stain was so dark it was almost black, but the walls were bright and cheery with a pastel-green ceiling. She closed her door and locked it.

Disrobing, she discarded her clothes in the bathroom hamper. By angling three mirrors she was able to scrutinize her wound. It frightened her. There were signs of healing on the edges, but green purulence exuded from beneath the scab, which was surrounded by red, inflamed tissue. She gritted her teeth, grabbed the scab, and ripped it off. She almost screamed, but no sound escaped. As pus poured out, the pressure decreased, but she almost fainted. She bit into a washcloth as she twisted at the waist and put one hand on each side of the reddened area and squeezed. Green, coagulated mass exuded to the surface. It was grotesque. Another intense squeeze and clotted pus squirted onto the sink and floor. She wiped up the splatter with a washcloth and rinsed it in the sink. *I just can't let my parents know about this, or they will not let me go to the wilderness again. They'll at least give me a really hard time about it.* Digging her fingers into the wound, she felt splinters of wood. Pinching the fibers, she yanked them out.

"I need a shower," she gasped. For the first time since her mother had remodeled all the bathrooms in the house she was glad for the handicapped rails in her shower. Warm water and her favorite shampoo and soap excited her. She turned the handle on the body sprayers and hung on to the handicap bar as she was sprayed from all sides. With just a slight twist she directed one of the sprays right into the infected wound. She lifted her leg to open it more. The washcloth was still stuffed into her mouth to prevent her from screaming.

She shampooed her hair and spread scented soap over her body. The intense pain subsided, and she took the washcloth out of her mouth. *I made it. No matter what happens. I went solo, and I made it back. No one can ever take that away from me. I survived fog, getting lost and blown off course, and … If my parents find out, they won't let me go again.* Her thoughts turned to Troy. *He seems so gentle, controlled strength. I loved the admiration in his eyes when I told him about the portage. And I even completed the Wickstead portage … alone.* She laughed. *And it looks like I'm going to the university.* She pictured her mother's expression when she'd told her.

She turned off the body sprayers and rinsed her hair once more. Only fatigue and necessity made her turn the water off. Large, fluffy towels greeted her skin as she wiped off. She dried her wound with a towel. It was still draining yellowish fluid, but at least it was mostly clear. She taped a feminine napkin over the wound to absorb the drainage.

Am I going to be able to sleep? As she popped two Tylenol, she noticed some Bactrim that she had been prescribed for a urinary tract infection. She had taken only two pills, and her symptoms had resolved, so she'd never taken the rest. She examined the prescription. "Take for fourteen days." *I think I'll finish these. The doctor said to take all the medicine. Better late than never.* She swallowed a pill and went to bed.

• • •

Lunch at the Brewery was better than expected. The corned beef sandwiches drenched in mustard were tasty. It was so good to eat something that wasn't fish or soup. The french fries were hot and crispy. Lisa ate as if she had never tasted a french fry before. Plus the restaurant had hard oak chairs, and by adjusting her pelvis and sitting very straight she was almost comfortable.

The adventures of the canoe trip charmed her parents. Her father was impressed with her survival skills. "I would never have thought of listening for the waterfall in the fog. That's amazing." He bit into his sandwich. "How did you get that fire going in the rain?" She explained to rapt audience.

Stirring his coffee, he said, "So you caught quite a few fish."

"Yes, walleye, and the bass fishing was great."

Her mother looked horrified and kept repeating, "At least you're safe," followed by, "I don't think you should do that again."

The waitress came to take their plates. "Can I interest anyone in dessert?"

Her mother said a polite, "No, thank you."

Lisa gave her father a longing smile. "I'm sure you can interest us in dessert," he said. "What do you have?"

After ordering one to share, Lisa told them about the last day's wind and Troy and Mr. Svenson's rescue. She didn't mention that she'd run out of food. She was sure that would have precipitated a lecture about proper planning.

Her mother seemed intrigued by Troy. "Imagine finding a University of Wisconsin student in Canada. Are you intending to keep in touch with him?" she asked.

"Yes, Mother. I really liked him," Lisa said as she rolled the velvety smooth chocolate cheesecake around in her mouth.

She and her father fought over the last bite like hockey players after a puck. He scooped it up. Lisa resolved to let him have it, so she was surprised when he put it into her mouth. "You are very precious, Elizabeth."

She rolled the flavor around in her mouth. "Is that why you called the cops?"

He smiled. "Yes."

CHAPTER 8

Two weeks later Lisa still had not registered for classes at the University of Minnesota, Duluth (UMD), even though her mother had completed her application months before. She was focused on healing. Her wound made her feel depressed because it was so painful to exercise. She tried throwing a few baskets in the driveway, but any demand on her right gluteal muscles sent a fiery sensation down her leg. At least she could sit without pain on hard chairs. She sat on the couch one afternoon, and the pain catapulted her up so fast it scared her. Her limp disappeared as long as she concentrated on a normal gait. The ten days of Bactrim cleaned up her infection.

After two weeks she was frantic to run no matter how much it hurt, so she put on her jogging shoes, shorts, sports bra, and a green T-shirt and drove to the university track. She had to park off campus without student identification on her vehicle. The walk to the track stretched her muscles, so once through the gate she was ready to run.

She went once around the track, and her right hamstring felt tight. She stretched and ran again. Muscle spasms stopped her. When the spasm released, she walked the track, stretching out her gait. She tried to run again, but more spasms immediately prevented her.

"I guess that's enough for today," she said as she walked off the track. Passing the basketball court, she noticed a ball sitting on the court. She walked through the chain-link fence and shot a few baskets. She didn't have the jump she wanted on her right leg, but the first four shots from three-point range swished in the basket. She dribbled in place, spun on her left leg, and shot. Swish.

"I like your form, but I haven't seen you before."

Lisa looked up to see a trim, fit woman in a maroon-and-yellow jogging suit. Lisa recognized UMD's colors. "I hope you don't mind. The ball was just sitting here. I'm trying to recover from an injury."

"If you run that well and shoot that well with an injury, I can't imagine what you'll be like when you heal."

"I'm sorry. Is this a restricted area?"

"Are you registered for fall semester?"

Lisa grabbed her towel, wiped her brow, and tried to look innocent. "No, not yet."

"I'm Amanda Hammond. I'm the basketball coach. I would really like you to try out for the team. Did you play basketball in high school?"

Lisa extended her hand. "I'm Lisa Zuccerelli. Yes, I was MVP my senior year. I ran track, played soccer, and was on the swim team. Could I do that here at UMD? I thought you had to be recruited or something."

They shook hands, and Amanda laughed. "I think I'm recruiting you. Is money an issue? There are scholarships available."

"Money's not an issue, but procrastination is. If you really want me, you'll have to entice me to register."

"What's your major?"

"Do you have a major in basketball?"

Amanda laughed again. "You're something else, Lisa Zuccerelli. I'll tell you what: if you major in exercise physiology or coaching, I'll be your adviser."

"That's great. Where do I sign up?"

"Come with me. I'll take you to the administration building."

• • •

At supper that night, Lisa's mother was delighted to hear that Lisa was registered for classes. "Are you sure you don't want to major in political science, business administration, or let's see …"

"You're just thinking of things that will get me into law school,

Mother. I don't want to be a lawyer. I want to be a coach or something athletic. I'm an action person, not a sit-at-a-desk person. Besides, Professor Hammond is really neat; I want her for my adviser."

"Then you have to be the best coach ever."

Lisa sensed resignation in her mother's voice and gave her a hug. "I promise. Now you got me into the university, so be happy. You got your wish. Who knows what might happen next."

"By the way, we had an employee quit today. Do you want to work at the factory loading pallets till classes start?"

"I'd love to, but Coach Hammond wants me to meet some of the other faculty tomorrow."

"Loading pallets is a great upper-extremity exercise. It would build your arms for basketball."

"And probably be as boring as lifting weights, right? I'll tell you what: Let me see how this goes tomorrow. If I have time, I'll load pallets."

"Lisa, I was just teasing you."

"The promise remains."

• • •

At Coach Hammond's suggestion, the soccer coach, Coach Larson, offered Lisa an invitation to try out for the team. After loading pallets and practicing her running, she was as fast as most of the others. On a sprint, the only one at tryouts to beat her was Cheryl, another freshman. Once Lisa recovered completely from the Wickstead portage she knew she could beat even her.

They started some soccer relays, working the ball down the field, passing to one another, and then trying to steal it from the other player. "Lisa, lower your arms to your sides. You're using too much energy; relax when you run," admonished the coach.

"Yes, Coach." Lisa lowered her arms and tried to feel more relaxed. *How can you be relaxed and sprint at the same time?* she thought, but she followed Coach's advice as they ran back and forth across the soccer field. Coach blew the whistle, and they slowed their pace.

Cheryl came along beside her as they rounded the track for their last required lap and asked, "How long have you been playing soccer?"

"Since sixth grade."

"You're fast; that's for sure. Now I know who my competition is."

"I'm not too much of a competitor in soccer. I just like to run. It keeps me calm. It's a stress reliever. Besides we're on the same team."

They sat on the grass and stretched before taking another cooldown lap. Cheryl said, "I've been playing soccer since junior high school. I'm here on a scholarship, so I have to look good. You want to go jogging sometime for fun?"

"I'd love to. Just let me know when and where. Then we can go out for a hamburger or something."

They slowed to recover their breath. "I'm vegetarian. Are you from here? I'm from Pennsylvania."

"Yes, grew up here like a weed."

"Then maybe you would know some good vegetarian restaurants. I haven't found any."

Speech came easier as their breathing slowed. "Let's go for a slow long-distance run this weekend, and I'll take you to a great vegetarian restaurant."

"Sounds fun; I'll treat."

Lisa was shocked. No one had ever offered to treat her. They finished their cooldown and slowed to a stop.

"A few stretches, ladies," Coach yelled.

"Are you living at the dorm?" asked Lisa.

"No, I found an apartment off campus."

"All right, I'll meet you here Saturday morning at ten o'clock, and we can drive to the restaurant when we're done. See that green Jeep?" Lisa pointed.

"Yeah, see you then."

Talking stopped as Coach lined them up to do stretches and then blew the whistle to head for the showers. Near the entrance, two young men caught Lisa's eye. Cheryl ran up to the shorter of the two, turned to make sure the coach was distracted and gave him a quick peck on the lips. "Hello, Kevin. Were you here to talk to me or just watch all the pretty girls head for the showers?"

"I have to admit the local fauna around this part of the university is sure worth seeing."

"You're bad," Cheryl said, arching her back and sucking in her midriff. "Your eyes are supposed to be on me."

"Oh, they are."

"By the way, this is Lisa. She just joined our team." She nodded at the taller fellow and then at Lisa. "Are you two interested in a date this weekend?"

Lisa shook hands with Kevin, who introduced his friend Craig.

"Nice to meet you," Craig said. He was about as tall as Lisa. He was muscular and wore a UMD T-shirt and jogging pants. His smile was beautiful.

Coach appeared at their side. "Let's get to the showers, girls; there's enough time for fraternizing with the guys later."

"See you," said Cheryl.

"See you this weekend, Craig," Lisa said with a wave.

She and Cheryl went into the building, with Coach right behind them. The girls stripped and headed for the showers.

"Where did you get the nice tan, girl?" one of the more-pale-complexioned girls asked. "How do you tan without getting tan lines?"

"And where did you get those abs?" asked one of the seniors, slapping her own belly.

"Naked, outdoors, doing a lot of work," Lisa answered. She soaped her belly and down her legs. As she leaned back to soap her buttocks, she found her scar still sensitive. She kept it toward the wall.

As they towel-dried, Lisa whispered, "Craig is sure a beautiful specimen."

"He is," said Cheryl, "and he's nice too, not arrogant like some of the other football players."

"How long have you been going with Kevin?"

"Ever since this summer. We met at the beach playing volleyball."

"This should be an interesting date." Lisa pictured Craig in her mind. Surely it would be different from the awful experience with Roger. She thought about kissing a handsome fellow like Craig. She felt a rush of heat in her groin. What it would be like to have sex with such a guy? Maybe this tall, handsome guy was just the one to give her that experience. But what about Troy? She'd written a letter to him. No response. She'd called and left a voice mail. No response.

"See you around, Lisa," Cheryl said, interrupting Lisa's thoughts. She was dressed and ready to stow her locker basket. Lisa was still wrapped in a towel daydreaming.

"Oh, yikes, I promised to work an extra shift at the factory tonight. See you later, Cheryl." She slipped on her clothes and put her locker basket away and headed for her Jeep.

She still had enough energy to stack pallets as she turned onto Industrial Road. She liked working in the factory. It was demanding, physical work. Most of the employees knew she was the owner's daughter, so she tried to set a good example by working hard and not taking advantage of her status. It wasn't just exercise; she was accomplishing something. She could look at her pallets at the end of the shift all shrink-wrapped like Christmas presents and know that she had stacked every item.

The other aspect of the factory she appreciated was the noise. Everyone was required to wear hearing protection, so if someone spoke to her, she could pretend she couldn't hear them. It gave her time to think without interruption.

She and her brother were supposed to take over the factory when they got older. It was all planned out. Her brother would be the CEO, and she would be the corporate lawyer. Linden was doing his part. He was at Harvard getting a degree in business administration. The day he'd left for Cambridge, she'd wandered into his room while he'd been packing.

"If I make it big playing concert piano, you have to take over the factory," he'd said.

"Not a chance. You take over the factory, and don't count on me being your lawyer either."

"But Mother says you're argumentative enough to be a good lawyer." That always made Lisa angry. She'd chased him into the hall.

He'd stopped at the top of the stairway and held up his hands. "All right, hit me, but spare the hands."

Lisa had socked him square in the stomach. He'd doubled over in pain. She'd said, "You deserved that."

He'd stood up, rubbing his stomach, "Guess so, but it doesn't change the facts."

Lisa had been preparing to hit him again, harder, when their mother had yelled from downstairs, "What are you two doing?"

"Nothing, Mother," he'd yelled. He'd turned to Lisa and said, "I think we better go play tennis before I get hurt."

Lisa loved Linden, but they always competed. Fortunately, they had enough different interests that they could respect each other as well. Lisa loved to hear him play the piano and had gone to his concerts during high school. He wasn't that excited about basketball, but he'd promised, "You come to my piano concerts; I'll be at your basketball games." He'd kept his promise. She would have rather had her father there, but her brother had done a great job of cheering for her.

Lisa took a deep breath. Her first pallet was stacked. She put shrink-wrap around it and called her supervisor. She was ready for the next pallet, but there were not enough cases to put the first layer down. Besides, she stacked faster than the line.

The line supervisor, Bob, put his hand on her shoulder and yelled, "Good work, Lisa. I'll call the forklift." He pulled out his factory walkie-talkie. "Pallet ready on line seven. Over." He turned to Lisa. "You want to go out for a couple of drinks after work?"

"No, thanks." Lisa pushed his hand off her shoulder. She considered Bob a penis with a position. She knew from talking to the other young women on the line that his goal was to get into every girl's pants that he could. She treated him with respect since he was the supervisor, but she hated him as a person.

She'd told her father not to trust him, but he hadn't seemed interested in the details and had brushed her off. "He gets more work out of his employees than every other line supervisor. I can't fire him for his social life."

She finished two more pallets before closing and started a third, which was not the responsibility of her shift, but she did it anyway. Finished, she pulled off her gloves and punched out at the clock: 23:34. *I wonder if mom will give me four minutes of overtime.* She laughed and headed for her Jeep. Her muscles felt warm and stimulated, and her back felt stretched and supple. She was satisfied with her workout. She thought about how the soccer coach encouraged upper-extremity exercise and squats. Certainly it was good for basketball. As she unlocked her car door, she felt a hand on her shoulder.

Bob spun her around and grabbed her breasts. "Doesn't the boss's daughter need a little fun in her life?" He grabbed her hair, jerking her head back. "And you won't tell anyone, will you?"

Lisa smelled the stench of tobacco on his hot breath. Disgusted, she kneed him in the groin, then spun around and punched him in the stomach. "I believe that constitutes assault." She shook her fist at him. "Mustn't touch the boss's daughter."

He doubled over, grabbing his scrotum.

She opened the door, climbed in her Jeep, and drove home.

The rest of the summer he treated her very formally, and he never put his hands on her again, so she never told her father about the incident. But she remained wary of him because he often gave her a look that was either anger or lust.

CHAPTER 9

Lisa plunked down on the hard wooden chair in Coach Hammond's office to have an adviser meeting. Classes had just started one week ago. Coach was organizing some papers on her desk. "I hated the beginning of classes in high school, Coach. In fact, I hated school."

Coach looked up as she placed the papers in the open file cabinet behind her desk. "You will do just fine, Lisa."

"This freshman English course is required for graduation," Lisa said, jamming her finger at the UMD bulletin. "Papers are required every week starting next Friday. And this geography course you said would be easy, the professor passed out the course requirements today, and they don't look easy to me. There are lots of handouts to do and chapters to read. The whole book has to be read by the end of the semester. I don't think I have ever read a whole book before in my life, much less a textbook. And then I have this physiology class …" She gasped for breath as the books fell off her lap. She stared at Coach as she finished her sentence, "Which is for my major, but it's in the science building. Science scares me. The only class I am not afraid of is my calculus class. I love math, and I'm good at it, easy A." Her eyes welled with tears. She looked up at the ceiling to prevent them from dripping down her cheeks. "I'll never pass English."

Coach handed her a tissue. "Lisa, this is like a race. If you try to win it all at once, it's overwhelming. Just take one lap at a time. I've reviewed your high school grades. You'll make it."

"You saw that I flunked English? I only graduated on a technicality. English killed me."

"I saw that. Do you want a tutor? It can be arranged." Coach clasped Lisa's trembling hands. "I've watched you work out. You have tenacity and determination. I've seldom seen an athlete that stays so focused. What I want you to do is use that focus to study. I'm not asking you to be a perfect student. You just have to meet academic qualifications. I've chosen you for my basketball team because you have what it takes to be a champion. Apply that, will you?"

Lisa snuffed her tears. "It's embarrassing to have a tutor. Whoever it is will laugh at me."

"No, they won't. Now calm down. You'll make it." Coach stood her up and hugged her. Lisa quivered. Coach tightened her hug till the convulsions quelled. "Now don't trip getting out of the gate."

"Thanks, Coach. I'm sorry to be such a problem. I'll try to focus. I promise." She turned and walked out of the office, wiping her cheeks. She didn't see anyone, so she headed for the bathroom to blow her nose and splash cold water on her face to remove the blotches. She looked in the mirror. *I'm not ugly. Why has Troy not written back? If he only knew how difficult it is for me to write letters to him. I'll just have to call him again.*

Cheryl appeared in her practice suit. "Ready for a good run around the track?"

"That's for sure. Just let me change into my running gear."

During scrimmage, Cheryl stole the ball from Lisa when she suddenly got a cramp in her right butt. She tried to get in Cheryl's path, but the searing cramp dropped her to the ground.

"What happened, Lisa?" the soccer coach asked, trotting over to where Lisa sat on the field.

Lisa was massaging her muscle. "I got a cramp. Did Cheryl score?"

"Yes. I was surprised that she got the ball away from you."

Lisa pressed on the spasm in her muscle till she could stretch her leg out.

"Lisa."

Her voice was so commanding. Lisa thought of all the ways she could apologize but decided she would just take the criticism. "Sorry, Coach, I guess I need to stretch more before the games."

"I didn't come to criticize you. I came to tell you that I was amazed how you managed. That was the fastest limping I've ever seen. Most girls would have quit. You have the tenacity that I'm looking for." She put her arm over Lisa's shoulder and hugged her. "Good job."

Coach searched her clipboard. "Cooldown, girls; then head for the showers. Game on Friday. Be early."

Lisa walked out her cramp. Each step came easier. At the other end of the field, she squatted to do a hamstring stretch.

Cheryl was beaming over her goal. "Did you do that on purpose? You had control of the ball; I saw the whole thing."

"I didn't do it on purpose. I got a spasm in my butt. Do you want to feel it? It's still there."

"I'd rather not, thanks anyway. It's just that—"

"Cheryl, there is no way I would have let you take the ball from me. I am too proud and arrogant. Does that make you feel better?" Lisa finished her stretch and stood. "Run with me. I think I'll be all right now." They ran around the track together.

They slowed to a stop, and Lisa felt her muscle. There was no further spasm.

Cheryl wiped her bangs away from her eyes. "Get your hand out of your pants, girl."

"I was massaging my spasm."

"Massage your spasm in the locker room. You're embarrassing me." Cheryl ran off to help collect balls from the field.

• • •

The tutor was fifteen minutes late. Lisa was trying to read a novel that she was supposed to summarize for her English class. She had a few notes scrawled in her notebook. She felt a sense of panic. Where was her tutor?

"Hard at work?" a dark-complexioned girl with long, black hair said as she sat down beside her. She had a muscular physique but was still feminine with plenty of curve, not fat but solid. Lisa wondered if she lifted weights. The girl asked, "Are you Lisa Zuccerelli?" Lisa nodded. "I'm your tutor, Heidi Barton."

Lisa was calmed by Heidi's demeanor. Heidi had dark-brown eyes, like Lisa's, but her face was so different. She had prominent, high cheekbones and thicker lips. Lisa said, "I tried to read this book this weekend. It took forever. Now I am supposed to write a summary. We have another book for this week and another summary to write, and I can't even get this one done."

Heidi scanned Lisa's notes. "I'm having trouble reading this. You have dyslexia, don't you?"

"Thanks, I needed that pointed out. Yes, and it's embarrassing."

"I'm not trying to embarrass you; I'm here to help you succeed, to heal your wounds. Did you finish the book? You can be honest with me. No one else needs to know."

Lisa glared at her. "I did read it. I'm a slow reader, and I can't spell, and what other deficits of mine shall we discuss?"

"People have really hurt you over this, haven't they?"

Lisa opened her mouth, but nothing came out. Heidi had a mystical calming effect on her. All the anger she intended on throwing at her tutor dissipated.

"I'm sorry you hurt so much," Heidi said. "Now tell me about this book."

Lisa started describing the book. Heidi interrupted her and said, "Wait a minute." She pulled a legal pad and pencil out of her backpack. Setting it comfortably in front of her, she said, "All right, start over." Heidi's pencil skated over the paper as Lisa described her impressions of the book.

Twenty minutes later Lisa gasped for breath. "So that's what I want to say, but how am I going to write it?"

"Pick up your stuff, and let's go to the computer room."

"That's another thing. I can't type either."

Heidi said nothing, and Lisa was forced to follow her out of the library and down the hall to the computer room. It was a long, rectangular room with rows of computers in packed configuration. Most were unoccupied. A few students were clustered about the room doing more talking than computing. Lisa observed that some were browsing the Internet. Cheryl sat down at a computer in the far back corner. Lisa cringed, expecting a typing lesson. To her surprise, Heidi pulled out the legal pad, set it in a holder beside the computer, and started to type.

"How fast do you type?" Lisa asked as a whirring sound flowed from the keyboard. Lisa could not even hear the individual keys being pressed.

"About a hundred and twenty words a minute," Heidi said without even a pause in the beat. "There, your paper's done. You might need to edit it. Do you have a floppy disk?"

"A what?" How could she explain that her life was sports and all this technology was just not for her? "I'm a jock, not a geek. What's a floppy disk thing?"

Heidi grabbed her backpack off the floor and took out a blue plastic device. "I'll give you this one. We get them free in the chemistry department." Heidi popped the disk into the computer and pressed save. The light in the computer drive lit for an instant. "Check the printer in the corner. It should be printing your paper."

Lisa obeyed and found the printer spewing out pages. She looked at them as she walked back to the corner. "I can't turn this in. It isn't right for you to do my homework for me."

"I didn't, silly. That is what you said. Read it. I just took dictation and typed it. It is all your work, not mine. I did not add one word to what you said."

"I said this?"

"Yes. And I personally think you have very good insight into the book. What you dictated was well organized and succinct. I read that book last year, and I didn't think of half that stuff." She put her arm around Lisa. "You just need a secretary that's all. You sure aren't very tech savvy, are you?"

"No." She scanned the paper that had spewed out of the printer.

Heidi grabbed her backpack. "Next week, same time?"

"Huh? Oh, yes, same time. Please don't be late; it scares me."

"If it needs editing, just download it from the disk, fix it, and reprint it. See you next week. Don't worry; I promise not to scare you next time. I'm Anishinaabe; we have trouble with time."

"What's that?"

"First Nation? Ojibwa Indian?" She smiled when Lisa finally recognized what she was talking about. "See you next week." Heidi flipped her pack over her shoulder and walked out of the computer room, leaving Lisa reading page four.

. . .

Lisa's team won their first soccer game. Although Lisa didn't get much playing time, she paid close attention to the seniors on the team and watched their ball handling. Some of their moves were like ballet. Coach Larson put her and Cheryl in for a few minutes to rest some of the other players. Lisa was playing defense and managed to steal the ball from an offensive player to the cheers of her teammates. After the game, Cheryl and Lisa decided they needed a few laps to unwind.

"So what is Kevin like?" Lisa asked.

"Oh, he's sweet. He's an economics major, pretty smart with money. His dad owns an investment company. He already has some investments that have done pretty well."

"Is he sensitive?"

"Very."

"Do you and Kevin have sex?" Cheryl didn't say anything as they finished a fast lap. "I'm sorry. That was too personal? I was just curious."

Cheryl caught her breath as they started a slower lap. "Yes, we have sex, silly. It's good too. He knows just where to touch me. It drives me nuts. I love it." Their feet beat the ground in rhythm until they stopped at the other end of the track. "My turn to be personal, since you started it. How about you?"

"Oh, I had a date with a guy in high school who was pretty crude. I didn't like him pawing me one bit. What do you think about Craig? I've enjoyed the dates we've been on so far. He treats me with respect; he's intelligent and can discuss a wide variety of topics. I like him."

"I think he is charming. You two are good together."

"Do you think we should ... you know?"

"Kevin says he likes you a lot and is anticipating a good time on our double date tonight. I'm sure he would be game for some hooking up. I'll make sure we have a good supply of condoms tonight at my apartment."

. . .

The Indian Continent restaurant had the best ethnic food in town, and the menu wasn't limited to vegetarian. Lisa loved the aroma of Indian food. She could taste the flavors in the air from the parking lot. *Pretty clever to vent the kitchen into the parking lot*, she mused.

Cheryl, Kevin, and Craig had already registered for a table as she walked into the small, bright-orange waiting area. It had a leather couch on one side and two overstuffed leather chairs on the other. Craig stood as Lisa entered. He was dressed in black slacks and sports coat with a crimson polo shirt.

"You're looking good, Craig." Lisa hugged him, and he gave her a kiss on the cheek. "I'm really hungry. How about you?"

"Our table should be ready in five minutes," said Kevin.

Just then the waitress appeared. "I'm Lakshmi. Welcome to the Indian Continent. I'll be your server. Your table is ready. Are you having the buffet, or do you need menus?"

They all looked at one another. "I want the buffet," said Lisa.

"I've never been here before. May I have a menu, please?" asked Cheryl. The men followed in Cheryl's wake and asked for menus as well.

"Certainly." The waitress smiled and handed menus to Kevin, Craig, and Cheryl as she seated the group. "I'll be right back for your order. What would you like to drink?"

"Oh, just water for me," said Cheryl. Kevin and Craig looked vacant.

"Try the mango lassi; it tastes great," said Lisa.

"Then I'll have one too," said Cheryl. The men nodded their heads. The waitress left to get the drinks. "Do you come here often, Lisa?"

"When I am feeling exotic."

Craig gave Kevin a look. To Lisa, Craig acted like a rabbit caught in an open field by a hawk. "I'm not sure I understand anything on this menu," Craig said.

Lisa thought an explanation might make him more comfortable. "The menu is divided into vegetarian and carnivore food, North Indian and South Indian food. The buffet has a little of everything." Her explanation didn't seem to help.

When the waitress returned with their drinks, all four ordered the buffet. The waitress was delighted and invited them to the center island. "Enjoy. I'll bring your bread sampler. It goes with the buffet."

"I've never seen such a variety of vegetarian food," said Cheryl as she sat down at the table. Her plate was overflowing with an array of colors from crimson to bright yellow, green to ivory.

"I haven't a clue what I'm eating," said Craig. "This yellow stuff is good, and so is this red chicken."

Lisa glanced at his plate and laughed at his description. Kevin had all vegetarian choices, picking only what Cheryl had chosen first. Lisa had a mound of saffron rice across her plate with individual puddles of various meats and other delicacies. A large Tandoori chicken thigh sat on top. She rolled the food around her mouth, relishing the flavor. "Isn't this great? There is always something new every time I come here. They haven't had this lamb before."

"Which one is lamb?" Craig eyed the samples on Lisa's plate.

"This green one. It's cooked in vegetable leaves and nutmeg."

"Oh."

"You want to try some? I'll give you a taste."

"I don't eat green things."

"You're missing a real taste treat." Lisa spooned some of the greens and lamb into her mouth. She lowered her voice. "The flavor is so sensuous." She laughed.

Cheryl convinced the guys to pay for the meals even though they had eaten very little. Lisa stuck a better tip under her plate when the others weren't looking. As they walked out of the restaurant, she stuffed a handful of licorice bits and caraway seeds into her mouth.

Craig plopped a spoonful in his palm, scrutinized the contents, and changed his mind, dumping his handful in the nearby trash. "What is that stuff?"

"It refreshes your palate," Lisa explained.

"I'll pass. Looks like what my mother puts in her bird feeder."

As they left the restaurant, Cheryl suggested they rent a movie and go to her place. The guys agreed to go get the movie, and Lisa and Cheryl went to get some Diet Coke and chips.

Cheryl's apartment was about the size of Lisa's closet. There was a couch across one wall with the television on the opposite wall. A coffee table intervened and prevented walking easily between. The kitchenette was small enough that Lisa could put one hand on the refrigerator door and the other hand on the counter that separated the kitchenette from the living room. To the left of the couch, a door left ajar led into Cheryl's bedroom. Lisa could see clothes scattered across her bed. Barbells sat in the corner opposite the television on top of an exercise pad. A length of pipe hanging from the ceiling on piano wire held most of Cheryl's dresses.

"Nice place," said Craig.

It reminded Lisa of a gerbil cage. She made a mental note not to invite these people to her house. The two guys sat on the couch as Cheryl put the movie into the DVD player. Lisa sat on the opposite side of the couch, next to Kevin, while Cheryl put the chips in a bowl and placed them on the coffee table. She wedged herself between Lisa and Kevin. As the movie started, everyone became silent.

Halfway through the movie, Cheryl got bored. She got up from the couch and pulled Kevin upright. "I think I've seen this one before. We're heading to the bedroom." She grabbed her purse and dug around inside. "Here are a couple of condoms for you two." She smiled as she set them on the coffee table next to the bowl of chips that only the guys had eaten. She grabbed Kevin to give him a kiss, and they disappeared through the door into the bedroom. Lisa heard the lock click.

Craig and Lisa finished watching the movie. He scooted closer and put his arm around her shoulders. During the final scene of the movie when the two protagonists fell in love with each other, he put his hand on her thigh and squeezed her quadriceps.

Now we're supposed to have sex, she thought. She quelled the butterflies in her stomach that she got when making a critical free throw. "Good movie. I enjoyed it. You want to make out now?"

"Sure." He sat up from his slouched position.

Lisa's heart was pounding, and her mouth went dry as she stood and surveyed the scene. *This is it. I want to try this sex thing, but ...*

Lisa stripped. Craig stared. Lisa couldn't understand the expression on his face. *Was he shocked? Embarrassed by her body? Was she missing something?* "What's wrong? We have to be naked to have sex, don't we?"

"Yes, I guess we should. It's just that ..." Craig seemed uncoordinated as he pulled off his shirt and tried to get his ataxic hands to unbuckle his belt. "Nice tan," he said as he untangled his underwear from his feet. His eyes twitched as he scanned her lanky form. It was as if he was a blind man who now could see. He reached out and touched her muscled belly. Her pectoral muscles boasted firm breasts, her rib muscles rippled with each inspiration, and her groin was tight. Her sartorius muscles caught his attention and led his gaze directly to her pubis.

He ran his hands down her sides. She sat next to him and kissed him. He responded by kissing her breasts, fondling them into his mouth. She hugged him until she noticed his response and opened a condom and handed it to him. Clumsy with excitement, he applied it. Lisa watched his evolving physiology with intense curiosity.

He became frantic with anticipation and started ejaculating. Lisa pushed him down on the couch and jumped on top of him. He thrust a couple of times, but his limp member barely entered her. The anticipation in her belly just turned to a cramp.

"Sorry, you took me by surprise," he said.

She kissed him on the forehead and dressed. "That was interesting," she said and put her clothes back on. All dressed, she turned to him and said, "You're riding home with Kevin, aren't you?"

"Yeah, I suppose."

"See you at the university." She turned to see the condom still dangling on his limp penis as she headed out of the apartment. *Can't say that that was much fun,* she thought as she shifted her Jeep into gear.

• • •

Cheryl asked the next day, "Did you enjoy Craig? He's a hunk, isn't he?"

"He's all right, I guess."

"Did you two have fun? I found the used condom in the garbage."

"If watching premature ejaculation is supposed to be fun?"

Cheryl covered her face to avoid laughing. "Not so good, then?"

"No orgasm if that's what you're asking."

"Maybe you need someone with more experience?"

CHAPTER 10

When basketball season finally arrived, Lisa was ecstatic. She practiced every free moment that she wasn't reading texts or writing—that is, dictating—papers for her classes. Lisa was standing outside the three-point line in the empty gymnasium one day when Coach Hammond said, "Lisa, I have to close the gym now."

Lisa turned to see Coach standing by the door and said, "Just three more shots and I'll have sunk a hundred three-pointers."

Coach watched with her finger on the light switch. When the third shot went in, she switched off the lights. The glow of the exit lights and the open door to the women's locker room directed Lisa. Coach walked beside her. "You're doing well. You will definitely make the team. Don't overpractice."

"I wasn't, Coach. I was getting rid of my stress over English class. I can't read all those novels without exhausting myself first."

"But you're doing well. I checked with your English professor."

"If it wasn't for my tutor, Heidi, I wouldn't be doing that great. I have to dictate all my papers to her. And every week we have another paper to turn in." Lisa pounded her fist into the wall.

"Hey, be careful of my locker room," Coach Hammond said.

"Sorry. I just get so frustrated."

"How are geography and physiology going? I know you enjoy calculus."

Lisa flexed her biceps. "I love the muscle physiology class. I've learned a lot about how to stay in shape. In geography we are studying the Canadian Shield. I've gone canoeing there. Now I know about all the rock formations I've seen up there."

Coach grabbed her shoulders. "You're going to make it. I know you're struggling, but it's like basketball: you practice, and when the game comes, you deliver. Are you willing to play guard?"

Lisa twirled out of Coach's grasp. "Oh yes, I'm so ready."

"Then you have the position when I need you."

Lisa wrinkled her brow. "When you need me?"

"You'll be my first backup for the starters."

Second string, still, Lisa thought.

• • •

One evening Lisa took a hot shower to settle down before starting to read her required English novel in her bedroom. She hated getting dressed after showering, so she sat naked on her towel, curled up in her chair like an oyster in its shell.

Her father knocked gently on her door and asked, "Are you busy?"

"Just reading for my English class."

Her father opened the door and stepped in. He glanced at her and quickly stepped back out of the room and closed the door. "I'm sorry. I didn't know that you weren't dressed," he said through the door.

"You're my dad. I didn't think it would embarrass you. You used to change my diapers, remember?"

"Elizabeth, you are no longer prepubescent. Put on a robe or something."

Lisa slipped on her silk bathrobe. "Clothed. Come in."

Her father entered with some hesitation. Lisa was sitting at her desk enveloped in silk. She was laughing so hard she had to wipe her eyes with a tissue.

"What's so funny?" he asked

"That word, *prepubescent*. I just spelled it six different ways on the computer, and according to spell-check they're all wrong. I guess I'm creative if not accurate." She turned to look at her father.

"Listen, your mother and I have been talking, and we're quite impressed with the way you've been studying. We've seen a real change in your attitude since you started at UMD, and I just wanted to tell you that we're proud of you."

"Thanks. I love you both. That canoe trip changed my focus. I hope to be a much better daughter now."

"We'll love you no matter what."

"Even if I don't work for the company?"

His Adam's apple bobbed as he swallowed hard. "Even if you never work for the company."

"Thanks, Dad." Lisa got up from the desk and gave her father a hug. She sensed that her silk robe was a bit too revealing, but it didn't matter.

"I love you, Elizabeth." He turned.

"Dad?" she said as she returned to her desk. "How do you spell *prepubescent*?" He spelled it for her, and she typed it into the computer. "Accepted, yeah! No wonder I couldn't find it in spell-check."

He walked out and closed the door.

"Dad?" she called.

"Yes?"

"Can I take off my robe now?"

"Yes, Elizabeth."

"Thanks, Dad."

"You're welcome."

• • •

The months whizzed by. Thanksgiving came, and she called Troy, but there was no answer. She concluded that he must be with his parents. She left a message on his answering machine to call back. It was almost Christmas, and he hadn't called yet. She worried that he wouldn't. Despite the guys she had dated, she saw in Troy the characteristics she valued most: endurance, stability, and tenacity. The way he picked up a canoe, the way his muscles tightened with each paddle stroke, charmed her. And that funny hair sticking out like a haystack was adorable. But he still hadn't written. *Maybe I'm just fantasizing about him?* she thought.

Classes were going better than expected. With Heidi's tutoring, she was not only passing everything but had a B average in English. When she was discouraged, Heidi sang to her. Lisa didn't understand the words, as it was in some Ojibwa language, but the songs calmed her.

After a lot of studying, she finished exam week and felt a sense of relief. Linden flew in from Logan Airport, and the two of them volunteered to decorate the tree. Their mother had a professional decorator for the part of the house where she entertained guests but allowed the "children" to do the tree.

"So you're becoming an intellectual?" Linden said as he held the stepladder so Lisa could put the angel on the top of the Christmas tree.

"I made it through the first semester. A in calculus and Bs in physiology, geography, and *English!* And of course an A in my physical education class." She added a candy cane to a branch as she climbed down. "Pretty good for your dumb sister, huh? I'm going for a coaching certificate." She picked up an ornament she had made in third grade and put it on a lower branch.

"Lisa, I never called you dumb. I just said that you weren't applying yourself; that's all. I'm very proud of you." He added a glass sphere with a carved castle inside that their parents had bought on a trip to Germany. It was heavy enough it needed to be on one of the more substantial branches. "I hear you've been dating."

Lisa flushed; her face felt hot. Did he know that she'd had sex with some of her dates? The first time had been a disaster, and subsequent experiences hadn't been that great either. Did he know that? She glanced around the room at all the Christmas decorations to stabilize herself before she answered. "I never let my dating interfere with my studies. Ask Mom. I only date on weekends," she said and then added, "if I don't have an exam the next week and all my homework is finished. See, I've become disciplined." She added tinsel to the back branches. "Are you positive you never called me dumb? I thought you did."

"Don't be so defensive. You deserve a date once in a while, and no, I never called you dumb; I would swear it in court." Linden unwrapped the tissue paper from the last glass ball and placed it on a solid branch. They both stood back to admire the tree. "Dating anyone I know?" he asked.

"I don't think so. They're mostly guys on the football and basketball teams on scholarship from out of town. No one from our high school."

"Any steady boyfriends?"

"Most have been pretty disappointing. One guy didn't even know what filet mignon was, so I ordered it to show him."

"Did you make him pay for it too?"

"No, we went Dutch, but he ended up eating half of my filet mignon. He didn't touch my green beans, though. Can you imagine that?"

"What did he order?"

"Some hamburger thing. Not very creative. Haven't dated him since. In fact, I haven't dated any of them more than twice—well, one guy, Craig, who was very nice, three times. But the rest were so socially inept."

"Maybe you're dating the wrong kind of guys?"

"Could be." She stepped back and handed him some tinsel. "Are you just going to watch me do this, or are you going to help? Besides, let's talk about your life in Boston for a while, shall we? Are you getting all As? Who have you dated?"

He hung some tinsel. "Lisa, I am so glad you haven't changed."

Their mother came to see their progress. "Very nice," she said, looking at the tree from several angles. As she turned, she held up a postcard and said, "Oh, Lisa, there is a postcard here for you from Troy somebody, address in Wisconsin. Someone you know?"

Lisa snatched it. "It's from the outfitter I met when I was up in Canada."

"Oh, I remember you mentioned him when you came back from your runaway canoe trip," her mother said without smiling and walked out of the room.

Lisa looked at the card. It was a picture of a wolf with snow on its face. The other side said, "Merry Christmas. Been busy, sorry I didn't return your calls. See you next summer? Troy."

Linden looked over her shoulder. "Another boyfriend?"

Lisa hugged the card to her chest. "No, just someone I met at the landing who invited me to have lunch at the outfitter."

"Oh, really," Linden said with a playful smile.

• • •

Spring semester Lisa registered for the second required English class. It would be no different from the first except that they would read different books. She was grateful that Heidi was still willing to be her stenographer.

She'd been disappointed with the final exam for fall semester because the essay questions had made her hand cramp. Her spelling had been atrocious, which had lowered her grade on the final to a C-, but all As on her weekly essays had kept her final grade at a B.

Her professor called her into her office before spring semester began. "Please sit down, Lisa. I need to ask if you wrote your own weekly papers last semester."

Lisa felt lightheaded. She clenched her fists to the chair. "I need to explain." She described how she struggled with spelling and that she dictated to her tutor. "Heidi is willing to confirm what I am telling you if you don't believe me," she said. "There is not one word in those papers that didn't come out of my mouth. And if that is a double negative, it is for emphasis."

"It isn't a double negative."

"Oh, good." Her legs cramped as she prepared for the professor's scorn.

"Talking to your tutor won't be necessary. I can see the same concepts in your final exam that you wrote in your weekly essays. You are quite creative and insightful."

"But I can't spell, and I read very slow. Is it supposed to be slowly?" Lisa said, anticipating the professor's correction.

"Lisa, I'm certain that you have a learning disability. You are clearly dyslexic. I could have you tested and then make accommodations for your exams. Wasn't this done in high school?"

"No, it wasn't. Since I was getting passing grades, the school refused to pay for any testing. My parents sent me to a special psychologist. He tested me and said I had some kind of dyslexia, but I didn't want anyone labeling me. I feel different enough as it is. I don't want to get special privileges just because I can't spell." Her professor looked at her as if what Lisa had just said was incomprehensible. Lisa continued, "As long as you understand and I can get a B, I'm content."

"You would have gotten an A for the class if we had accommodated your learning disability."

"That would have blown my mother right out of her chair." Lisa stood. She wanted this to be over. She said in her most polite way, "I am so pleased that you understand my problem. That means more to me than any grade."

They shook hands, and Lisa left, but she could tell that the professor wanted to pursue the problem. As she walked down the hall, she felt as if she had just jumped the biggest hurdle on the track, freshman English.

Since her fall classes had gone well, Lisa decided to examine the class bulletin and try one more class. Anthropology of Northern Native Americans seemed intriguing. The bulletin description promised to include Ojibwa culture, Heidi's tribe and the tribe of the canoe country. The bulletin abstract claimed that the professor had actually lived with the Ojibwa in Northern Ontario for three years.

When Lisa walked into the class, she was surprised at how many students there were. She was ten minutes early, and the large auditorium was already packed. She scanned the room. There were two empty seats in a row next to a girl with exceptionally long, black hair. Lisa walked down the aisle and sat two seats away from her. The other girl brushed aside her hair, and Lisa recognized her. "Heidi! We get to take a class together. Wow." She got up and sat next to her. "There sure are a lot of people in this class, aren't there?"

"It's always filled. Dr. Clossen is such an interesting lecturer. Many of these students aren't even signed up for the class. They just come to hear him speak, well, tell stories. Are you registered?"

"Yes. I've canoed in Canada and wanted to learn more about the people who have canoed there before me."

Heidi laughed. "Since I'm Ojibwa, I was hoping for an easy grade. Where have you gone canoeing? You never mentioned that when I was tutoring you."

"I guess I was too uptight about my papers." Lisa related some of the major lakes she had canoed—Lac la Croix, Crooked Lake, and Kashipiwi. Heidi seemed to know them like the back of her hand, describing the rocks, portages, and islands in each one. *It's like she's describing her living room*, Lisa thought.

Dr. Clossen entered dressed in a red-and-black flannel shirt and blue jeans. "He's not much for fashion," Heidi whispered in Lisa's ear. From the first sentence Lisa was fascinated. He spoke about rituals and relationships, filling the hour with examples. In a moment, the hour was over. The students got up to leave.

"Just a minute, class. There will be one term paper, a midterm, and a final exam. Each will represent thirty percent of your grade. You may work on the term paper with a partner, but you will each get the same grade, so pick your partner wisely. The midterm and final will include fifty percent questions from my lectures and fifty percent from the assigned reading. You are dismissed. See you Wednesday."

"That sure went fast," Lisa said to Heidi. "When he was telling about making an offering of a tobacco twist to avoid offending the beaver, I was on the edge of my chair."

Heidi laughed. "At least he's accurate. I'll give him that. His stories sound just like my uncle's." She closed her notebook. Lisa saw that she had taken no notes, whereas Lisa had pages of notes. Heidi asked, "Do you want to do the term paper together? I sure would like to do it with someone who is interested in canoeing."

"Really? I wouldn't drag down your grade?"

"We're going to get an outstanding A plus on our paper. How would that drag down my grade?" She laughed.

"I'm in favor of outstanding. What should we write about?"

"Let's write about plants that the Ojibwa use for food or medicine, if that's all right with you?"

Lisa was too excited to speak. Heidi probably knew all the plants in Ontario, and that could be valuable on her next canoe trip.

"Unless you have a better idea," Heidi said to Lisa's silence.

Lisa felt a tear come to her eye as she was overwhelmed with joy. She sniffed her nose to draw it up. She stuttered, "No, I think that's a great idea. Can we go out in the woods and get samples?"

"I don't think we need that for our paper, but I will be glad to show you some of the plants I know, if you are interested."

"I'm interested. I'm very interested."

CHAPTER 11

Lisa had just finished swimming a mile in the Olympic-length pool. She surfaced and took a deep breath. It had been invigorating. She felt so free in the water.

"It's awkward the way you bring your arms around," the swimming coach said.

"It feels weird to do it any other way," Lisa protested. *She knew she had improved her lap times. Why was he bothering her about her arm position?* She watched as everyone else headed for the locker room. She jumped out of the pool and stood dripping at the edge.

"Try it like this," the coach said, demonstrating the technique. "I know what I'm talking about."

"Yes, Coach, I will." She felt like a marine responding to her sergeant. She turned to head for the locker room.

"Well then, get in the pool, and do it."

"Yes, Coach." She jumped back into the water and swam as fast as she could, bringing her arms around as the coach had instructed. She finished the lap. "Is that how you want it done?"

"That's an improvement. I want you to practice that. Now hit the shower," he said.

She was fast enough to qualify for the team, but she wasn't really interested in competitive swimming. She just liked to swim. She had plenty of endurance, but the swim coach annoyed her.

As she climbed out of the pool, the men's team entered. Lisa liked their sculpted bodies. She had dated one of the swimmers. It hadn't gone well. He had been more interested in his athletic prowess than any conversation. Lisa had tried to discuss literature, politics, or even religion, but within minutes he would be talking about some trophy he had won. *Cute hunk but what a bore,* Lisa thought as she grabbed her towel. She notified the swim coach a week later that she had decided to just play basketball.

. . .

One Saturday morning Lisa was having breakfast with her father. She scooped her poached egg out of an egg cup. She had already eaten half her croissant smeared with cherry jelly. The other half she was dipping in her egg yolk.

Her father was reading the newspaper, interrupted by spoonfuls of broiled grapefruit. "It says here that the UMD women's basketball game was won because Coach Hammond had a strong bench. A certain Lisa Zuccerelli scored thirteen points."

"Coach sent me in because the other team didn't know me. The other girls set me up, and I made all my three-point attempts; plus I got two fast breaks. Our center got the rebound and threw me the ball. Then the other team started guarding me, and Coach took me out. I guess the damage was done. You should have been there."

"I thought about going, but I didn't think I would get to see you play. You're second string, right?"

"So far."

"You really want me to come, don't you?"

"Yes." Lisa wiped the tear forming in her eye with her French lace napkin.

"I will then."

"When?" she asked, but he didn't answer as he was lost in reading another article in the newspaper. Lisa answered for him in her mind: *Never.*

. . .

Toward the middle of spring semester Coach Hammond called Lisa into her office. Lisa never missed an appointment. "Sit down," Coach said, motioning to a chair and dropping her whistle on the desk. Lisa was still in her volleyball uniform for her physical education class. "So how is it going, Lisa? You're almost done with your first year at the university. Your parents must be proud."

"I appreciate your encouragement, Coach. I never expected to go to college after my disastrous experience in high school."

"I knew you could do it. How's the English class going?"

"I went to the professor and told her that my tutor was typing my essays, and she said that was fine. I don't do well on the exams because I can't write fast and I spell worse than my brother did in third grade, but the professor is very understanding. I've gotten As on every one of my weekly papers."

"And the other classes?"

"Psychology is fun. The tests are multiple-choice. I was the last one out of the midterm because I read so slowly. I didn't get to finish all the questions, but I got a B. I'm happy with that." Lisa shifted in her chair. Her sweaty uniform stuck to the seat. "Of course, Calculus II is a whiz, easy A."

"Not very many of my advisees even take advanced mathematics."

"I'm good at sports, but my brother is so smart he made me feel dumb. But I used to help him with his math homework. He was a grade ahead of me, but my math was boring; his was interesting. Of course, the next year I was bored again because I had already done all the problems in his books."

"You're a very gifted young woman. Just because you can't spell and write means nothing except that as a professional, you'll need a secretary."

Lisa pulled herself forward, pulling her jersey off the back of the chair. "I've never thought of myself as professional material. I want to be a coach, remember?"

Coach came around the desk and grabbed Lisa's hands to pull her out of her chair. The Velcro sound of Lisa's jersey peeling off the seat made them both chuckle.

"Lisa, start thinking differently. Don't sell yourself short." Coach gave her a hug.

"Don't you want to hear about my anthropology class?" Lisa bristled with enthusiasm.

Coach held her by the shoulders. "You're enjoying it, aren't you?"

"I love it."

"Some other time then. I have a faculty meeting. I'm proud of you."

"Thanks, Coach." Lisa turned to walk out of the office.

"One more thing, Lisa." Coach Hammond picked up a folder she apparently needed for her meeting and grabbed her coffee cup.

"Yes, Coach?"

"When we're having these adviser meetings, you may call me Amanda. But don't you dare on the basketball court."

"Thanks, Amanda." Lisa choked on the word and started to cough.

Coach patted her on the back as they walked out the doorway. "It takes some getting used to, doesn't it?" She shut the door behind them, making sure it was locked, and walked away. "You need a shower, Lisa."

"Yes, right away, Professor Coach Hammond." Lisa stripped off her uniform.

Coach turned, took one last look at her standing in her sports bra and panties, and shook her head. "You might want to do that closer to the showers."

· · ·

"I enjoy this anthropology class so much," Lisa said as she and Heidi closed the anthropology reference books they had been studying in the library.

"Is that why you're always fifteen minutes early?"

Lisa's face flushed. "No, I come early to talk to you." She adjusted the notes on the table in front of her. "It looks like we have enough material for our research paper, right?"

"I think you just like to hear me tell stories." Heidi tossed her long, black hair over her shoulder.

"Well, that too," said Lisa. "I did take notes on all the stories you told me."

"How did you do on the first test?" asked Heidi.

"I got an A minus. I lost a few points on the essay question. In brilliant red ink Professor Clossen wrote, 'Good insight, elaborate in your essay for full credit.' It was better than I expected. If I had elaborated, I would have just spelled more words wrong. I'm just no good at this stuff."

"Oh, Lisa," Heidi said, "your dyslexia has nothing to do with your value as a person. You had nothing to do with it. Forget that; let's review what I've found about medicinal plants and food preservation." She pulled some papers out of her folder and handed one copy to Lisa. They reviewed the notes and made a rough outline for their term paper.

"By the way, what are you doing for spring break?" asked Heidi.

"Not much," Lisa said. "I think we have a basketball clinic scheduled." *Actually I was thinking that it might be a good time to venture to Wisconsin to see the evasive Troy*, she thought. *Just a couple of postcards with animal stories is all I've heard from the rascal.*

"That's too bad. I was going to invite you to come home with me. We could talk to my uncle Marten and get some more information for our paper. He knows a lot more about medicinal herbs and plants than I know."

"Come to your home? I don't want to miss that. I'll ask Coach if I can miss. Some of the other girls are going to Mexico, and she's letting them go, so I am sure doing something required for my anthropology class would qualify." Lisa grinned so hard it made her cheeks sore. *Troy will just have to wait*, she thought. "Will your family accept me? I'm half Finnish and half Italian. I get my olive complexion from my Italian side, but my dishwater hair won't exactly blend in with First Nation black."

Heidi laughed. "Don't try to blend in; just be yourself."

"Let's do it then. When do we leave?"

"That's another thing," Heidi said. "I'm probably taking advantage of you, but would you mind driving? I don't have a vehicle. My uncle just dropped me off here at UMD."

"Not a problem. I have a four-wheel-drive Jeep; will that do?"

"Perfect. Pick me up Saturday morning at the dorm. I'm at Evan Hall, room A-8."

"I'll be there at eight o'clock."

"Thanks." Heidi got up and walked a few steps away. "Oh, Lisa?"

"Yes?"

"Dress casual."

"I always do."

The ride to Heidi's home felt as if Lisa was escaping from prison: no tests, no English papers, no lectures—freedom. The sun was shining, the birds were singing, and it was unseasonably warm. Lisa had finished her reading for English and had met with Heidi to draft her papers, which were now written and edited, ready to hand in on the Monday after break. Calculus was done, and the psychology professor had not assigned homework. Lisa felt euphoric. When she'd explained her plan to go to Heidi's to her father, he'd said, "This is a rare opportunity for you." Her mother, however, had only been pleased that she wasn't "heading to Mexico to shack up with a couple of guys."

Lisa and Heidi drove the freeway north and talked about school activities. Lisa felt a catharsis of frustration.

"So what is physical chemistry about?" Lisa asked.

"How different atoms bind to each other. We have to know the electron-cloud structure of all the elements in the periodic table and explain mathematically how they react and how the bonds hold together."

"The only word I understood was *mathematically*. I'm glad you're taking that class and not me."

"It's the hardest class I've ever taken. If I were to miss one lecture, I'd be lost for the rest of the semester. So don't feel bad about not understanding. How is your psychology class going?"

"It has been interesting. We discussed post-traumatic stress disorder last week. The treatment is quite controversial, but it seems that talking out feelings and experiences is therapeutic. Stuffing it inside can be lethal."

"In our tradition the person would talk to the Mide and be given a medicine, but more often, the Mide would sing to the person or advise them to take a sweat bath to get out the evil."

"I think having someone singing to me after a traumatic experience would be very therapeutic, like when you sang to me before that English test."

Heidi looked out the window. "I'm hoping to go to medical school." She paused. "Maybe I'll sing to my patients after I give them their prescriptions."

"I'll sign up to be your first patient."

As they drove off the highway and headed down a gravel road, Heidi shared some of her experiences living on the reservation. Lisa felt as if she had entered a parallel universe. Small houses, cars in the yards, men out working on the vehicles, and women sitting at tables in the yard just talking all seemed so strange. At the far end of the community, Heidi directed her to turn into a driveway.

"Mother must be at work," Heidi said as she got out of the car and ran through the door of the small house covered with tar paper and unpainted siding. Lisa was surprised that the door wasn't locked. The living room was sparse. An icon of Mary, mother of Jesus, had a prominent position over the fireplace opening. The fireplace had been replaced with a woodstove with the stovepipe stuck up through the chimney. It was chilly in the house. Lisa noted the few pictures on the wall. Some were sepia pictures of relatives, clearly quite old. The couch along the wall was threadbare, and the two chairs in the room were plastic lawn chairs. Despite the lack of furniture, the room was immaculate. Lisa wandered through the dining room and kitchen, which were just as clean but devoid of decoration.

"Mom's at work," Heidi said.

"Is this where you grew up?"

"Yep, come down the hall, and see my room."

Lisa followed into Heidi's room, which had a full-size mattress on the floor with no frame. The walls were covered with pictures of horses torn from magazines. In one corner was a pine bookshelf loaded with so many books that the bottom shelf was warped from the weight. There was a small dresser with a hand mirror facing down. The tiny closet had no door and had almost nothing in it.

Heidi seemed to have followed Lisa's eyes and explained, "Most of my clothes are at my dorm room." She pushed the empty hangers to the side. "You want a snack?"

"Sure."

Heidi led the way back into the kitchen and found some bread in the refrigerator and a jar of peanut butter. She took out two pieces and smeared them with the creamy substance and then asked, "You like jelly? It's from currants that my mother picked."

Lisa nodded, and Heidi pulled a jar out of the refrigerator and spread the jelly over the bread. She handed one piece to Lisa. The taste was tart.

"I hope it isn't too sour for you. Mother doesn't like to waste sugar. Plus, she's diabetic and can't eat a lot of sweets."

"Tastes fine." They smacked their lips as they finished.

"Do you want to hang around here, or should we go over to my uncle Marten's house? I'd like you to meet some of my family."

"Let's go to your uncle's. Should we leave our suitcases here?"

"Yeah, let's just put them in my bedroom."

They unloaded the car and then returned along the road they had driven through the community. Down a side road they arrived at a small, white house. There were five cars in the yard and one in the garage. The house would have been a ranch style if it were larger.

"Does your uncle have company?" Lisa asked.

"No, he fixes people's cars."

When they got out of the Jeep, they could hear a radio blaring. In the garage elaborate tools were displayed on several workbenches. The car in the garage was in a state of disassembly. The radio seemed to be coming from the backyard. Lisa followed Heidi around to the back of the house. She noticed the back screen door was closed but that the other door was wide open. They walked around the Skelgas tank and into a family gathering in the backyard.

"Uncle Marten, this is my friend Lisa." Uncle Marten set down his soda but remained seated. All conversation ceased. A slight woman stood, and several children assembled behind her. They all seemed shy.

"Very pleased to meet you, sir." Lisa extended her hand.

He was muscular and dressed in a torn flannel shirt, sleeves removed, with faded blue jeans. Grease was streaked down the front of his jeans. His black hair was silky and rolled down his back in a long ponytail. "Just call me Marten." His voice was coarse. He did not respond to her hand.

"This is my aunt Bidah; she's like a mother to me," Heidi said.

"My pleasure, madam." Lisa bowed her head and shoulders but wasn't sure why she did it or if it was appropriate.

"And these are my nieces, Shelly and Tanya, and my nephew, Hank."

"Hi, Lisa," they said in a chorus. Shelly was early high school age, Hank looked a few years younger, and Tanya was tall but seemed to be in grade school. The formalities out of the way, Lisa stood like a statue at a museum while the family ran to Heidi and gave her hugs.

"Mom wasn't home, so we came here," Heidi said.

"She is working late tonight and won't be home till after midnight. You're supposed to eat with us," Bidah said.

"How is that university treating you?" Marten asked.

"They're being very nice to me," Heidi said. "Classes are going well."

"You don't have to go to that government school to be a healer. You're already a Mide. You can doctor here without going through all that, you know."

"I know, my favorite Marten." She bent over and gave him a kiss. "But I want to learn as much as I can. It is part of my vision, remember?"

"Don't get too smart, or you'll end up in the city, and we'll never see you again."

"I promise. I won't get too smart."

He grabbed her and gave her a hug around the waist, and then he turned his attention to Lisa. "So you're Lisa. What are you going to school for?"

It sounded like a reprimand, but Lisa maintained her composure. "I hope to be a coach."

He pointed at Hank. "You think you could teach him anything?"

Lisa looked at Hank and smiled. "What are you interested in, Hank?"

"I like basketball," he whispered. His voice was so timid Lisa had to strain to hear him.

"Is there a place to play around here?"

His eyes brightened, but he did not say anything. He just ran to the garage and came back with a battered basketball.

"Well, let's go play." She turned to Marten. "May we?"

"You go right ahead. Teach him everything you can, Coach."

Hank and Shelly seemed excited to play. Tanya shied away to her mother. Hank threw the ball to his older sister. "Come on, Shelly; let's play."

Heidi led Lisa, her niece, and nephew down the dirt road to a cement court. A single rusted hoop hung to a warped plywood backboard at one end. There was no net. Lisa looked at Heidi. "Hank and I against you and Shelly—is that fair?"

"Sounds great," all three answered.

The game was rough. Hank and Shelly had no idea what was legal and what was foul, so they decided that if both Heidi and Lisa agreed, the person fouled could shoot a free throw. Heidi played defense well but had trouble shooting. Shelly was lithe as an antelope and could jump pretty high, so she made some nice inside shots. Lisa realized the best defense was not letting her have a lane to shoot. Hank was the most enthusiastic. What he lacked in skill he made up in determination. He was all over the court.

The game was frequently tied. With the score tied at fourteen, Heidi signaled time-out. Shelly ran to get something to drink. She returned with four plastic glasses and a jug of water. They quenched their thirst and then agreed to play to twenty-one.

Hydration and rest intensified the game. The score was soon tied at twenty. Heidi missed a shot. Hank grabbed it, dribbled to the other side of the court, and advanced. Lisa knew he was intent on shooting and would likely miss, so she made her move under the basket and waited. Impatient, he shot before he was set. Lisa could tell it was going to miss the backboard. She jumped at just the right time, grabbed it in midair, and dunked it into the bucket.

"Nice pass, Hank."

Everyone collapsed on the cement. "Good game," Heidi said, breathless.

"Did you play in school?" Shelly asked Lisa.

"Yes, when I was your age, I played on the school team. How about you?"

"No, they said I wasn't good enough," said Shelly.

"Well, I think you're plenty good. If I was the coach, which I hope to be someday, I would have you on my team."

"You play like a professional basketball star, just like on television," Hank said with a high five.

As they wandered back, they found Marten hunched over the pieces of the car in the garage. As they approached, he stood, wiped his hands, and said to Lisa, "You like that Jeep?"

"I do. It's been a good vehicle for me."

"Let me see the engine."

Lisa opened the hood, and Marten stood looking at one side then shifting to the other. He checked the belts and the spark plug wires. He tapped on the distributor. "Let me hear it once; start it up."

Lisa started the car and let it run till he told her to turn it off.

"I thought so. It didn't sound quite right when you drove up." He invited Lisa to come to his side. "See how this belt is a little frayed on the one side. It's not tracking right. It's going to wear out. I'll line it up for you." He ran and got a wrench, loosened a bolt, aligned the shaft pulleys, and tightened the bolts. Then he had her start the engine again. Even to Lisa it sounded smoother, but she would not have been able to tell there was a problem before.

"Thank you, Marten."

He wiped his hands on a rag that hung from his belt. "Time to eat." They all followed him in through the garage door. Lisa had not seen anyone use the front door yet.

Bidah had the table set with plain dishes, forks, spoons, and knives that didn't all match. Serving dishes were steaming with potatoes, squash, wild rice, and some kind of meat. She waited till everyone was quiet, and then Marten said a prayer. They all crossed themselves and then grabbed for the serving bowl nearest them.

The meat was in dark gravy. Marten took the platter and handed it to Lisa. "Elk."

"Looks good," she said.

There was little conversation until everyone finished eating. Then they sat back. Marten prompted the children with two-word questions, "School all right?" And then, "Learning anything?" The children broke into animated conversations. The whole room filled with laughter as stories and foibles were related. By the end of the evening, Lisa felt like part of the family.

At ten o'clock Lisa looked at Heidi. She was exhausted. Heidi took the hint and said, "We better get home and get some sleep."

"You can stay in my room," Shelly volunteered.

"Thanks, but Lisa and I are going back to my house. I want to be there when Mother comes home from work."

"If you get scared, you can come back," said Tanya.

Heidi smiled. "If we get scared, we will come back and crawl into your bed, all right?"

Tanya pursed her lips, hugged herself, and smiled. "That would be so good, Heidi."

After giving hugs to everyone, Lisa climbed in the Jeep with Heidi and drove back to her house. Everything was dark. There wasn't a streetlight in the whole community. Yard lights were scattered across the darkness. Heidi turned on the kitchen light as they walked in. "The shower is back here. You should sleep next to the wall because I am going to get up when I hear Mother."

Lisa headed for the shower. The showerhead and wire soap dish were held with drilled inserts into the concrete wall. There was no curtain, but the floor sloped so the water went to the drain in the middle of the room. Lisa stripped, setting her clothes on a plastic chair, and showered while Heidi gathered blankets and went to put a clean sheet on their mattress. Lisa was wrapped in a towel when Heidi returned.

"My turn," Heidi said as she took off her clothes.

Lisa went to the bedroom and put on an oversize T-shirt and underwear. She crawled next to the wall. Heidi returned from her shower in T-shirt and panties, wiping and combing her long, black hair. "It takes forever to dry," she said. "I've considered cutting it short, but that isn't culturally acceptable around here." She finished drying her hair and lay beside Lisa.

"My family likes you," Heidi said.

Lisa looked at Heidi. "How could you tell? I sure felt like an outsider at first."

"They talked to you. If they don't like someone, they don't talk. It's our way."

"I'm thankful they talked to me then. Your nieces and nephew seem nice. I wasn't sure about your uncle."

"He's testing you. He is deciding whether to share any information with you."

"Oh, did I pass?" Lisa stared at the blank wall.

"The test isn't over yet. Did you enjoy the basketball game?"

"I loved it. Was that part of the test?" Lisa twisted on the mattress and nestled up against the wall to face Heidi.

"Probably," said Heidi with a laugh. "Hank will probably exaggerate the basketball story to all his friends. He'll tell them that he was playing with a TV star and he passed the winning shot."

"That's all right. He's a great kid, lots of enthusiasm. By the way, the food Bidah prepared was great." Lisa glanced up to see the light from the full moon make odd shadows across the ceiling. Lost in thought about her evening, she said, "I didn't know what to say when Marten fixed my car."

"That was a compliment. That's his way of telling you that he accepts you."

"Does that mean he'll let me interview him for our paper?"

"He might, but it will take a couple of days to be sure, and we can't ask him."

"Why not?" Lisa asked, puzzled. "How will he know what we want?"

"I'll ask Mother to ask him. In a couple of days he will decide if you are worthy of the information."

Lisa scrunched closer to the wall and thought about what Heidi had said. Lisa lay motionless in the dark, scanning the shadows on the ceiling. "Why did he call you a Mide? And you said something about a vision."

Heidi sighed deeply. "I was afraid you heard that. My mother is a Mide healer. She has advanced through three stages of the Midewiwin Society. As her daughter, I was tested and deemed worthy to become a healer as well. That's part of what prompted me to try to get into medical school. When I was in high school, I was initiated into the Midewiwin Society at first level." There was a long pause. "So, you see, Lisa, you are sleeping next to a certified witch doctor."

"Did you have to go on a vision quest, like Dr. Clossen talked about?"

"Five days of fasting, ritual cleansing, and meeting with the whole Midewiwin Society. Yep, I went through the whole thing."

"You had a vision?"

"Yes."

Lisa waited for Heidi to elaborate, but she remained silent. Finally Lisa said, "I think you will be a fine physician, Witch Doctor."

A car drove into the driveway two hours later. Lisa noticed, but only as in a dream. Lisa felt Heidi get up, but then Lisa fell back asleep.

CHAPTER 12

By the time they rolled off the mattress in the morning, Heidi's mother had left for work. The house was silent. "What does your mother do at the casino?" Lisa asked.

"She's a floor boss."

"What does that mean? What does her job involve?"

"Several things. She makes sure no one is cheating. That's her main job, but she also gives out free passes to the shows for people who have lost a lot of money, and at the end of each shift she transports the money to the counting room."

"Sounds like a responsible job."

"Yes, but she works awfully hard and has to confront upset people, and it requires long hours."

Lisa opened her suitcase. "So what are we doing today? How should I dress?"

"The suckers are running, so I suspect we're going fishing. Don't wear anything you're not willing to throw away." Lisa wrinkled her brow, not understanding, but dressed in her grubbiest clothes and joined Heidi in the kitchen.

Heidi was flipping pancakes. "This maple syrup was harvested right here on the reservation. Yours is on the table." Lisa sat down and tasted her pancake. She savored each mouthful. As she rolled her last piece of

pancake in the little puddle of maple syrup on her plate to pop into her mouth, the door burst open. Lisa jumped, spilling syrup on her T-shirt.

Hank was frantic. "Come quickly! The suckers are running."

"We're ready," Heidi said.

"Dad said to meet him at the creek. I'm supposed to ride with you."

Heidi turned to Lisa, who was sponging syrup off her shirt. "Do you mind driving?"

"No problem, as long as you know where we're going."

"I'll show you," said Hank, "but hurry; let's go. I'm sorry I made you spill, Lisa, but don't worry, because it won't matter." Lisa grabbed her keys, and they ran out the door.

Hank squirmed in the front seat between the two girls. He popped up out of his seat at key moments to give directions. The final turn put them on two tire tracks through swamp grass. Lisa switched to four-wheel drive to navigate the muddy, rutted trail. When they reached the creek, several families were already there. They were netting the suckers and putting them in baskets. Uncle Marten called to Heidi, "Take these baskets to the pickup truck."

They were full of flopping fish. As strong as they were, Lisa and Heidi had to work together to carry the baskets to the truck and lift them into the back. Several fish jumped out, and Lisa grabbed them and put them back. Slime from the fish was slopped all over their shirts by the time they finished. Marten jumped in the driver's seat. "We need to get these cleaned, girls. Follow me in your Jeep."

Lisa tried to wipe her hands in the grass, but she still smelled like a combination of fish and mud. Lisa saw that Heidi was a mess of fish slime as well. They climbed in the Jeep trying not to touch anything. Lisa hesitated to grab the steering wheel, but it was necessary. They waved to Hank as he pranced around grabbing fish that flipped out of the nets and putting them in the baskets.

They followed Marten's truck, but there was no road that Lisa could see. They arrived at a clearing where women were waiting with sharp knives and pots on top of portable tables. They looked excited to see the truckload of baskets.

"Here's how you do this, Lisa." Marten picked up one of the knives and demonstrated gutting the fish, cutting off the heads, and flaying out

the meat. He passed the fish on to the women waiting in line. They put the heads in a pot of water and the flayed meat on a rack. Then they searched the guts for roe. "All right, get to work," Marten said, handing the knife, covered with fish slime, to Lisa. Heidi took a place at the table opposite to Lisa and picked up another knife. Marten hauled the rest of the fish-filled baskets to the end of the table.

"You're looking good there, Lisa," he said.

Lisa looked at herself. She was a mess of fish guts and slime all down her shirt. Fish eggs stuck to her forearms. She didn't even want to look at the mud encapsulating her shoes. *This is good*, she thought.

She was slower than Heidi, but after the first dozen fish she became more efficient. They worked as fast as they could, but there always seemed to be more fish. Other families brought more baskets of fish, but they didn't see Marten the rest of the day. By nightfall, without so much as a break for a drink, Lisa was hungry, thirsty, exhausted, and as slimy as the suckers they had cleaned. She saw Heidi cleaning her hands in the grass and joined her.

"Are we done?" Lisa asked.

Heidi laughed. "Unless you can work in the dark. The older ladies will be out here all night minding the fires to smoke the fillets, and those young men with the rifles will be here to see if the smell attracts bears. But we can leave that job for them. Let's get our pot."

"What do you mean 'our pot'?"

"We worked all day. We get some of the fish. It's our reward." Heidi smiled and grabbed one of the smaller buckets. An older woman with deep wrinkles in her face put her hand on Heidi's pot to stop her and scooped some roe into the bucket, a handful of fresh fillets, and a few fish heads for garnish. Without saying anything, she released the bucket to Heidi.

Heidi picked up the basket. "This is our pot, so let's go have supper. I'm hungry enough to eat these raw."

Lisa felt nauseated from the smell of fish guts and unsure if she wanted fish for supper, but she was hungry. They hadn't eaten since breakfast. *I think I should have eaten more pancakes.*

Lisa did not understand why the lady had thrown roe in or why the fish heads were on top, and Heidi didn't explain. As Lisa drove the

Jeep following Heidi's directions, she glanced at the bucket Heidi held carefully between her legs to avoid spilling.

"On to Marten's house," Heidi said.

As they turned into the driveway, the headlights caught Marten in the garage leaning over a car. He waved a wrench as they pulled to a stop.

"Looks like we're having fish for supper," he said. "Bring them to Bidah, and wash up." He turned back to the car.

Lisa and Heidi walked in through the garage door. Bidah met them with a broad smile as Heidi handed her the bucket.

"What an excellent catch. Nice pot for so little work." She poked a finger into the roe. "I see the ladies were impressed with you girls." She turned to the stove, dumped the fish heads in one pot, and pulled out the frying pan. She put the rest in the sink. "Get washed up, and supper will be ready soon."

"Where are the children?" Heidi asked.

"Oh, they're at their friend's house. It's just us for supper tonight."

"All right," said Heidi. "We'll get cleaned up." She turned to Lisa. "Follow me."

Lisa felt slimy from head to toe. She looked at her shirt, jeans, and shoes, all sticky and smeared with fish guts. She followed Heidi to a concrete laundry room. Heidi locked the door behind them. There was a washing machine and laundry tub in one corner and a shower in the other. There was no partition or curtain. Heidi undressed, putting her clothes in the laundry tub. Lisa stood in the middle of the room unsure what to do.

"Add your stuff to the pile," Heidi said. Lisa peeled off her T-shirt. The thick fish slime stuck to her skin right through her shirt. Her pants weren't much different. *I think I should have worn a bra. No, I would have ruined it.*

She joined Heidi at the laundry tub. The two of them in their underwear scrubbed their clothes by hand, removing globs of fish guts and slime. With the third rinse, they seemed clean enough to put into the washing machine. Heidi gave the clothes to Lisa, instructed her how the old washing machine worked, and rinsed the laundry tub with bleach while Lisa added soap to the washing machine. As the washing machine started churning, Heidi stripped off her underwear and added them to the load. Lisa did the same.

Lisa noticed a small seashell on a leather thong bouncing between Heidi's breasts. "Nice necklace," said Lisa.

"It's sacred. It was given to me when I became a Mide. I'm not supposed to take it off, but sometimes I do." She smiled. "Don't tell my uncle."

"Our secret."

"Now let's wash off these fish guts. I'm sorry, but my aunt and uncle do not have hot water, only cold." Lisa cringed. Heidi continued, "We'll rinse, then soap up and rinse off the soap." She paused and smiled. "If you still don't feel clean, we can take a hot shower tonight at Mom's house." Heidi turned on the shower, took a deep breath, and got wet all over. With a gasp, she stepped out of the spray and invited Lisa to get wet while she soaped up, including shampooing her hair. It was a brand of shampoo Lisa had never seen before.

Lisa gasped too. The water felt like icicles driving into her skin. She almost screamed but clenched her mouth, so nothing came out. Her hands still smelled like fish guts despite washing the clothes and rinsing with bleach. Within minutes she felt frozen and was sure her skin was blue. Her skin prickled, and her nipples were so hard they hurt. She turned off the water, then scrubbed her body with a large bar of yellowish brown soap, partly to get rid of the fish smell and partly because the friction made her feel warmer. When she was done, she really did not want to rinse, but she started getting soap in her eyes. Every blood vessel in her skin constricted when blasted again by the cold water.

Towels, stacked on a table beside the washing machine, smelled musty. When she was dry, Lisa asked bewildered, "What do we wear till our clothes are clean?"

Heidi laughed and handed Lisa sweatpants and a sweatshirt. "Bidah set these out for us."

"I am definitely awake now," said Lisa. "I thought I was too tired to be this awake."

"Did you like the soap?"

"What do you mean? It's like laundry soap."

"They make it here on the reservation. It's an old-fashioned recipe, bear fat and lye." She slid up the baggy sweats. "Ready to eat?"

Bidah was serving as they entered. Their places were set, and Marten joined them. He smelled of grease remover.

Lisa's plate was stacked with fried fillets and something she did not recognize beside a generous bed of wild rice. A bowl of soup consisted of vegetables with a fish head swimming in the middle.

Lisa ate some rice and a piece of fish, then cut off a piece of the unknown thing and tasted it. It was the strangest combination of sweet and salty. The flavor exploded in her mouth. "This is good. What is it?"

"Finish it and I'll tell you," said Heidi, putting a big piece in her own mouth.

"Don't worry about telling me. I really like it."

"It's fish eggs fried in oil." Heidi smirked. "Actually, rendered bear grease." She swallowed. "With maple syrup on top."

"Wow," said Lisa partly from shock and partly from the flavor in her mouth. "I have never eaten anything I can even compare it to, but it's good."

By the time they finished, Lisa was so tired she could hardly speak. "I need to go to bed," she whispered to Heidi when she got the chance. They gathered their clothes from the laundry room, only spun dry, put them in a plastic bag, and excused themselves. After hugs, they climbed in the Jeep and headed back to Heidi's house.

As they walked in the door, Lisa asked if she could take a hot shower. "Not a problem, but be quiet; Mother is already in bed. While you're showering, I'll hang up our clean clothes. Nobody has a drier around here. They'll be dry by morning."

Lisa grabbed a T-shirt and clean underwear from her suitcase and took a very hot shower. Warm again, she crawled alone onto the mattress, face to the wall, and fell asleep.

· · ·

Lisa awakened still facing the wall. It felt as if she hadn't moved all night. She focused on the paint that was peeling around the floorboards. Her hands were swollen and sore and still smelled like dead fish. She pushed them under the covers so she couldn't smell them and then rolled flat on her back.

Heidi was awake and asked, "Did you sleep well?"

"I don't remember."

There was a long pause as they stared at the ceiling. The sun was coming through the window making oblique streaks across the walls. Heidi sighed. "The sap is running."

"What does that mean?"

"It means that Uncle Marten will want us to help carry buckets." She stretched under the covers. Her toes hit Lisa's foot, and she pulled away. "Mother left for work, but she got some eggs for us yesterday, so we can have a nice breakfast before we head out."

They ate a hearty breakfast of fried eggs, hash browns, orange juice, and milk. Lisa did not hold back, remembering the lack of lunch the previous day. Stuffed, she went outside to wipe down the Jeep's interior with a soapy rag to remove as much fish smell as possible. "Remind me to buy one of those air fresheners at the gas station on the way home," she told Heidi as they climbed into the Jeep. "All right, where to today?"

Heidi directed her to the maple orchard. There was already a chaos of activity. As far into the forest as Lisa could see there were buckets hanging on the sides of maple trees. People were hauling sap, boiling it down, and gathering wood, and two women were bottling the maple syrup as it finished the concentrating process.

Uncle Marten appeared. "Good morning, girls. Slept in pretty late I see." Without waiting for an answer, he continued, "You're responsible for emptying the buckets from these trees." He brought them to the trees they had been assigned. After Lisa and Heidi started hauling sap, he disappeared.

"Slept in late?" Lisa asked.

Heidi laughed. "We were supposed to be here at sunrise; that's when the sap starts flowing."

The work was fast paced. The sap ran much faster than Lisa expected. It was already spilling over when she made it to her assigned trees. She saw Heidi only in passing as she ran with buckets from her trees. They worked without a break. Constantly running, Lisa felt hungry and exhausted, but she wasn't about to lose any sap from her assigned trees. She wasn't sure where her endurance came from; she had never run so fast for that long in her life. *Good training for long-distance track*, she thought.

As the sun fell below the horizon, the air cooled, and the sap stopped running. Oblique shadows enchanted the forest floor as Lisa raced to her buckets and found them only half full. The dripping had stopped. "Someone turned off the faucets," she yelled at Heidi and then collapsed on a stump.

"Good aerobic workout, right?" Heidi said.

"I think I was anaerobic after the first hour. It doesn't really matter that Coach let me off practice this week."

That night, after another meal of fish and a hot shower, Lisa lay in a cadaver position on the mattress. "My arms hurt, my hands are sore, my legs ache, and my feet are numb," she said to Heidi, who was beside her. She swallowed her saliva. "But I'm not bored. This is the most amazing spring break I've ever had. When will we get a chance to interview Marten?"

"We'll get a chance. Do you understand now that he is testing you to see if you are worthy of the knowledge?"

"Is that what's ..." The final s slurred into a snore.

• • •

The next day was the same: hauling buckets to the boiling pots. The sap ran fast, as it was an especially warm day despite the nighttime frost. By the end of the day she was delighted with bread and fresh-smoked fish for supper. In the middle of the third day, Marten came to the maple grove, and Lisa watched him pull Heidi aside. "Roast bear meat tonight," he said, "no fish."

"This is the day," Heidi whispered in Lisa's ear as they ran past each other.

"How do you know?"

Heidi gave no answer.

They left early, others willing to take their trees so no sap would be lost. Lisa had worked harder than ever before in her life, running constantly from sunrise to sunset. She'd dreamed about bear meat all afternoon. It had to taste better than fish.

At Lisa's request they took a long, hot shower at Heidi's house before going to Marten's for dinner. Lisa felt refreshed but was afraid that once her hunger was satiated she would fall asleep. They arrived to the smell of bear roast, baked onions, and vegetables. Shelly, Tanya, and Hank were seated at the table. As Lisa pulled out her chair to sit at the table, Marten asked, "Would you mind splitting some wood for the stove?"

Lisa looked at Heidi, then at the pile of wood stacked beside the stove. Remembering what Heidi had told her, she said, "I'd be glad to do that." She walked out in back of the house, grabbed the ax, and split an armload of wood. She gathered it up and brought it back, stacking it on top of the wood already beside the stove.

Food was on the table when she returned. Everything was tasty—wild rice, vegetables, and huge portions of roasted bear meat. Everyone ate with famished appetites. Bidah served wild rice candy for dessert. Lisa was stuffed and ready to fall asleep at the table.

Marten sent the children to bed and then said, "Lisa, when bear came up from inside the four layers of the earth, he gave gifts to men. Some were for healing. Bear has strong claws to find roots and taught us which roots were good for medicine and which were good for food."

Lisa was intrigued. She gave Heidi a desperate look and mouthed, "I don't have a notebook."

Heidi mouthed back, "Don't worry," and smiled.

Uncle Marten took out his parfleche and pulled out some small specimens. "I don't know what others know, but I know a little something about these. This one"—he pulled out a crumbled root with some dried, white flower petals—"is very good for a sore mouth."

Heidi explained to Lisa, "You put it in hot water and strain it. It is very soothing when you have sores in your mouth. That root is alum, and the flowers are a form of sumac."

Marten ignored the interruption. He pulled out what looked like yellow strings. "Wrap these around a sore tooth, and the ache goes away."

"That is the xylem, the inner bark of a birch tree. It has salicylate in it," Heidi whispered, "like aspirin."

He took out a black, blob-like mass. "I've used this when my cousin had an epilepsy attack. You set it on a clean, hot rock beside the child, and the seizures stop."

"That's balsam sap," said Heidi. Lisa recognized the pine smell.

Marten pulled out some gooey substance in a tiny wooden container. "This will cure bad wounds. I even used it on Uncle Loon Tail when he had gangrene from his diabetes. The ulcer healed within days. It's very potent."

There was a brief exchange between Heidi and Marten in Anishinaabe; then Heidi translated, "It's a combination of very young white pine stem and wild cherry with wild plum bark. It's boiled together and then pounded with a wooden mallet into a mash. He keeps it in that wooden container because it must never touch metal or it will no longer work."

The lesson continued late into the night. Each root or flower or concoction had a story about a patient Marten had treated and how the patient had responded. Sometimes there was a social lesson or a moral lesson to explain the efficacy. His stories were enchanting, and Lisa's only concern was that she could not remember everything.

Hours later, all three were exhausted. Lisa bowed and asked, "How do I thank you, Marten?"

"No need. You are part of our family. You don't need to thank family. You only need to treasure the stories and use your knowledge wisely. Never use what you know for selfish reasons." He got up from the table and went through the side door with no further comment.

Heidi walked out the door, pulling Lisa behind her. When they got outside, they paused under the mercury-vapor yard light, and Heidi asked, "Do think that's enough for our paper?"

"The question is can we get even half of it on paper? That was fascinating. And every medicine had a story."

"Some I knew, but I learned a whole lot too."

"But how can we remember it all?" Lisa said with concern in her voice.

Heidi put her arm around Lisa's shoulders. "Remembering is part of my culture. Oral tradition has been passed down for generations. Don't worry: I'm a Mide; I'm trained to remember." They climbed into the Jeep.

Lisa started the engine and turned to Heidi. "Marten is Mide too, isn't he?"

"Fourth level."

"What about plants used for food? He didn't mention any of them."

"I know some of that, but we'll talk to Bidah tomorrow. Now let's get home and go to bed. Mother will already be asleep. We don't need showers till morning, do we?"

"For the first time in my life, I am so tired I think I would drown if I took a shower."

Lisa was deep in thought as they drove back. Heidi instructed her to turn off the headlights as they drove into the driveway since her mother's bedroom faced the road. Quiet as mice, they slid into the house, dropped their clothes, slipped into their T-shirts, and crawled onto the mattress, covering up with clean sheets and blankets. Lisa's muscles and hands throbbed so that she could count her pulse in her fingers. As her heart rate slowed, she drifted off to sleep counting buckets of maple sap.

It was midmorning when they awoke. They stretched and did a few exercises in Heidi's room to loosen up. Out in the kitchen, Heidi's mother had left a note with instructions for breakfast. They ate cheese, homemade biscuits, and fried eggs and then showered and dressed for a woodland hike.

Bidah greeted them as they pulled into the driveway. The garage was closed, and there was no sign of Marten. Bidah took them into the grove behind the house. They walked through the sweet smell of the morning sun on the birch trees. After a brisk walk, the trees changed to jack pine until they came to a corridor of cedar. It was so dense Lisa stopped. Bidah brushed away a few cedar branches, exposing a path neither of the girls would have found. They followed Bidah into the swamp. The mosquitoes were ferocious until Bidah smeared some white sap on them.

She hiked up her skirt and knelt in the mud, pulling up an arrowhead plant root. "This is like our bread. Just cook it well. Otherwise, you'll be shitting all the way to the outhouse." She laughed and then became serious. She pointed to a cattail. "That root is just like potatoes. It has to be cooked well too. But if your bowels aren't moving well, just don't cook it so much." She showed them plants that would flower in midsummer, plants that could be used as spices, and plants that would have berries in the fall. She coddled a low bush cranberry. "My favorite. I love the tart flavor. Won't have berries till just before rice harvest."

Lisa realized that Bidah loved her swamp. This was a radical concept. Lisa had always avoided swamps. She recalled her experience on the Wickstead portage. She sneezed, just thinking about the sewage smell. Now she saw the swamp with new eyes. *I wonder what special plants I missed in that swamp. I should go back there and check it out.*

They spent hours learning rare plants and reviewing their use. It was getting dark as they headed back into the birch grove. Bidah quizzed Lisa on what she had taught her and showed her some new plants along the path that they hadn't noticed before.

"The swamp is like a breadbasket," Heidi whispered.

• • •

Lisa contemplated all the experiences of the week as they drove back to the university. "I was disappointed that I never got to meet your mother. I am thankful for her hospitality and talking her brother and sister-in-law into telling us about plants. Would you tell her how much it meant to me?"

"I will, and I am sure she knows. One thing about Anishinaabe, they talk to each other a lot. Mother probably knows every word you said the whole week. Remember we had an oral tradition before Europeans had a printing press. You'll probably be a legend by the end of the year." Heidi smiled and put her hand on Lisa's shoulder. "You handled yourself very well; you would make a good Anishinaabe. Most white people aren't subtle or patient enough to get along in our culture. I am proud to be your friend."

Lisa choked on her tears. She turned to Heidi to thank her but couldn't get the words out.

"Don't say anything; I know what you mean. It's the Anishinaabe way."

CHAPTER 13

Lisa was expecting an A on their anthropology term paper. She had never worked so hard and felt so confident about a paper in her life. But when Professor Clossen returned the graded papers to the class, Heidi and Lisa did not receive theirs. They looked at each other as Professor Clossen explained what was going to be covered on the final exam. Then he dismissed the class.

"Heidi Barton and Lisa Zuccerelli, would you accompany me to my office, please?" Professor Clossen said as he walked out.

Lisa looked at Heidi. "Are we in trouble?"

"I don't know. Let's go find out." Heidi's chipper response allayed Lisa's fear.

Dr. Clossen was looking at their term paper as they stepped into his office. "Be seated, ladies." He flipped over the last page. He looked at Lisa. "What did you do for this paper?"

Heidi started to answer, but he held up his hand to stop her. "Lisa?"

Lisa felt hot all over, ready to faint. She turned to Heidi for support. "Dr. Clossen, I don't type very well, so I had to dictate my part to Heidi. She types over a hundred words a minute. So I didn't type it." She looked at her shoes and rubbed them together like a schoolgirl.

"That is not what I meant. Where did you get this information?"

"I did some reading, and then ..."

"Yes?"

"Then Heidi and I went to the Nett Lake Indian Reservation where her family lives, and I interviewed her aunt and uncle. He's fourth level Midewiwin. The medicinal part comes from him." *And worked to exhaustion for four days to be worthy of the information,* she thought but didn't say. "His wife is quite the cook; the food part comes from her. We hiked all day back in the swamp to find out what plants she used. We got their permission. I'm sorry. I did not quite know how to reference that in the bibliography. Did I do it wrong? We wrote ... I did the best I could." She dropped her hands in her lap and looked at the professor like a sheep ready to be slaughtered.

"My interest in your paper is that much of this is unpublished information. I am aware that Heidi knew quite a bit about the subject, so I wanted to hear what your contribution was. And I wanted to know your references. Ladies, this is an extraordinary monograph. I would like to help you publish it in the *American Anthropologist.*" He stood to give them their paper. "Oh, by the way, neither of you will be required to take the final exam. You both have As for the class. I'm only sorry I can't give you a higher grade."

Tears burst into Lisa's eyes, and she tried to cover them with a tissue from her purse. Heidi took the paper from the professor. There was a large red A on the paper. Heidi gave it back to him. "Go ahead and publish it, but I will need to write an acknowledgment before it goes to print."

"Not a problem. Who should be first author?"

"Lisa Zuccerelli." Heidi smiled.

"Elizabeth," Lisa corrected as tears dripped down the back of her throat. Lisa and Heidi held hands as they walked out of the office.

"How does it feel to be such a lousy speller and a published author at the same time?"

"Great." Tears burst from her eyes again. Heidi gave her a tissue.

"My goodness, Lisa, control yourself." Heidi gave her a hug.

• • •

Lisa was ecstatic when the semester was over. She and Heidi went out for dinner and talked about their experience. "I'm leaving to go home for the summer break," Heidi said, "but I'll be back in the fall. You can imagine Uncle Marten will be quizzing me about you."

"After that experience I will never complain about working hard again." They parted with hugs and tears. Heidi left in some beat-up car that someone had driven down from the reservation for her. It looked terrible, but the engine hummed. *Marten's work*, Lisa thought.

Back at home, Lisa felt drawn back to the Canadian wilderness and another canoe trip. She dreamed about returning to her secret campsite and lay awake planning her menus and what equipment to bring. *Will Troy be there?* She felt so ambivalent about him. He never returned her telephone calls and sent only a couple of lousy postcards before Christmas. But she liked him in a way that was so different from the other guys she had dated. He was rugged and yet gentle; he was masculine, but he didn't act macho.

The Friday after summer vacation, Cheryl called to ask if Lisa wanted to go on a double date. Lisa was not too interested, but Cheryl had introduced her to some nice guys, so she hated to turn her down. "Sure. Where should we meet?"

"Oh, just meet at my house. This guy's name is Jake. I don't know him. Kevin doesn't know him very well either. He was on the bench of the football team, never played. He told Kevin that he had heard so much about you and just had to take you out."

"A blind date then? And he'd heard so much about me? From whom?"

"Sounds like a blind date, doesn't it? All he told Kevin was that he'd heard about you while 'just asking around.'"

The four of them met at Cheryl's house and had some sodas and chips. Jake was a mousy-looking guy, shorter than Lisa by half a foot. She was surprised he was on the football team, but as they talked, it turned out that he was the water boy. Lisa preferred guys who were more athletic, but that wasn't what made her apprehensive. The whole time at Cheryl's house he just sat on his chair looking at her, never once participating in the conversation. *Some date this is going to be,* she thought.

Finally, she got up to go.

Jake stood as well and said, "Oh, I want to take you for a ride and get something to eat."

Lisa was still hungry as chips and salsa were not her idea of a meal. She had anticipated supper at a restaurant. "Where should we go?"

He turned to Cheryl and Kevin. "See you around." He took Lisa's arm and said, "My favorite place."

Lisa took her arm out of his grasp. "Aren't Cheryl and Kevin coming with?"

"Oh, no, just the two of us. It'll be more romantic." They walked outside. He kept trying to take her hand, but she withdrew.

"I'm taking you in my car." He jangled the keys in her face. He was parked behind her Jeep. He got in the driver's side and leaned across to unlock the door.

"Where are we going?" Lisa asked. She didn't really want to spend much more time with Jake. Most of her blind dates with Kevin's friends had at least been fun, though Lisa usually found the guys short on conversation. Jake was a surprise. He didn't look right. He was dressed in glitzy clothes, but they were sloppy in the way he wore them. And he did not seem physically fit.

They went to a Mexican place to eat. The service was fast, and the food was greasy. Jake gobbled down his food as if he was in a hurry and still didn't say much. He didn't even brag about his prowess or achievements. Lisa lost interest. Jake was rude to the waitress. There was no way he was getting into her panties. No sex tonight. She had worn a skirt and a button-down blouse, expecting a nice evening at a fine restaurant. She wished she had worn jeans and a sweatshirt.

They got in Jake's car, and as he drove, he said, "We'll just go up to the Skyline Drive to watch the stars. Doesn't that sound romantic?"

"Not particularly. Why don't you just take me back to my car? We don't have much in common." *I'd rather be in Canada watching the stars from a campsite.*

He sped on up the hill and turned onto Skyline Drive. He raced to the first overlook and stopped the car. Lisa saw another car there and figured it would be safe. She doubted that short, pudgy Jake could outrun her. "We're here; let's look at the stars," he said as he opened the car door and stood by the guardrail in front of the other car.

Lisa expected him to be more of a gentleman, but no such luck. She looked at her shoes. At least they weren't high heels, but maybe she should have worn running shoes. Tired of waiting, she got out of the car to join him.

She stood beside him. "You know, Jake, this isn't working out very well. I think you should just take me back."

He looked at her and seemed fidgety. He swallowed hard, then said in an unconvincing voice, "Take off your clothes."

"What? I'm not going to take off my clothes. Take me back." She started backing up, contemplating where to run.

He stammered, "I asked you to take off your clothes. Craig said you would."

"This is ridiculous. I am not taking off my clothes. Craig and I were dating at the time. It was mutual. Did he tell you that I would just take off my clothes for anyone?" They were miles from her car and her home, but Lisa started calculating how long it would take her to run the distance. Down the hill would be fast and then to Chester Park.

"He said to take off your clothes," a man said behind her. Lisa felt the cold steel of a gun on her temple and recognized the voice of the plant supervisor. "So you're in on this, Bob?" She noticed the Zuc Industries logo on his shirt. He was still wearing his supervisor uniform.

Jake whined, "You said she would have sex with me, Uncle Bob. You didn't say anything about guns."

Lisa ducked her head and tried to run. Jake grabbed her arms as Bob put the gun to her forehead. "You're not being very cooperative, Lisa. Now my nephew Jake wants to fuck you. And this gun says you're going to let him. Then I'm going to fuck you too. You owe me that after the way you treated me in the parking lot." He grabbed his crotch.

"To tell you the truth, I'm feeling a little suicidal today. So why don't you just shoot me. Since this was so well arranged, that would be premeditated murder. My friends know who I left with. Jake, you're going to spend a long time in jail with your loser uncle."

She turned to Bob. "You will never work for my father again." She spit in his face.

"I'm the company's most productive foreman, and when we're done with you, you aren't going to tell your rich little daddy anything. I'll make sure of that. Now, enough of your mouth. Just because you are the plant owner's daughter, you think you can treat people like shit. Jake knows all the guys you've fucked. He's been doing his homework."

His homework, Lisa thought. *Sure, Cheryl's arranged lots of dates for me. I had sex with some of them, but it was mutual. This is different.* Fear rose up inside her gut, making her nauseated, but more than fear she was angry. Adrenaline surged through her veins. *The game is on the line. I need to keep my head. I need to escape*, she thought.

Bob pulled out duct tape from his left jacket pocket, tore off a piece with his teeth while keeping the gun in place, and slapped it over Lisa's mouth. He handed the roll to Jake. "Tape her hands behind her back, and do it right." He jabbed the revolver into her stomach. She involuntarily lunged forward as Jake torqued her hands behind her back.

"This isn't the way you said it would be. You said she would be willing," Jake said.

"Shut up. Tape her arms," Bob said.

Jake wrestled Lisa's arms behind her back. She was stronger than he was, but eventually he secured her hands together, which dampened her struggle.

"I got her," said Jake.

Not very well, thought Lisa as she wiggled her sweaty palms together.

Bob grabbed Lisa's jaw. "All right, Lisa, darling, let's begin." Out of his left pocket he produced a utility knife, the box cutter he used at the plant. With the precision of a surgeon, he cut off the buttons of her blouse. With each lost button he spread her blouse with the gun barrel. When her blouse was free and blowing in the wind at her shoulders, he smiled. "I've waited so long for this." He grimaced as he wiggled the box cutter under her bra and between her breasts. The metal was cold against her skin. Then with one wild pull he cut her bra in half. The two cups flopped at her sides, exposing her breasts. He smiled as he flipped her nipples with his pistol. "Nice, just like I expected."

Lisa felt Jake behind her still struggling with the tape. She kicked her left heel into his groin. He let go of her arms and screamed as he fell to the ground grabbing at his scrotum. Just then lights appeared on the road coming up the hill. Bob grabbed at her arm, tearing her blouse and wrenching her left elbow. He yelled at Jake, "Drive the car, you moron."

He pulled her back to Jake's car and stuffed her into the backseat, careful to maintain the position of the gun to her temple.

The car smelled like stale cigarette smoke. She sneezed. As the stranger's car drove by the overlook, Bob crouched, grabbed the back of Lisa's blouse, and pulled her down. She resisted, tearing the back of her blouse. Her bra now dangled at her wrists.

"Calm down," he ordered, shaking the gun in his right hand. Lisa continued twisting her hands in the tape. Bob opened the door a crack with his left hand. Jake was rolling around on the ground. "Jake, you good-for-nothing son of a bitch, get in the car and drive."

Lisa watched out her window as Jake crawled painfully to the car. He used the car handle to pull himself up. Still guarding his groin, he climbed into the front seat. "That hurt, Uncle Bob." He started the car and put it in reverse, squealing the tires as he turned the car around. "Where are we going?"

"To Chester Park. We can have some privacy there."

My neighborhood, thought Lisa. In her terror she started formulating a plan. Chester Park adjoined her parents' property. Either Bob doesn't know where I live, or in some diabolical way he wants to commit the crime in my backyard. If I escape, I'll be close to home.

"What about your car?" Jake asked.

"I'll get it later."

"This isn't the way you said it would be."

"Quit whining and drive."

Lisa's breasts felt cold; the torn ends of her bra and her shredded blouse were twisted behind her back. Poor Jake couldn't do anything right. The tape was now loose as she wiggled her wrists without moving her shoulders.

Jake drove in silence. Lisa could see that his jaw was clenched and he was grinding his teeth.

Bob kept his revolver pointed at her head but was salivating over her topless torso. "The scenery is sure pretty back here," he said to Jake.

"What scenery? It's pitch dark out," Jake said.

"Just drive, you idiot. I'll show you when we get there."

As Jake turned onto the street that led to Chester Park and her house, Lisa focused on what was around her. Jake's car was an old-model clunker, and the back door on the passenger's side where she was sitting wasn't locked. She stared at Bob but was really focused on the door mechanism beside him. Her side would be the mirror image. Slowly she maneuvered her sweaty hands so she could slip a fingernail through the edge of the duct tape. A rough place on her nail tore the fibers of the tape, and she pushed her hands apart, snorting through her nose in a show of frustration to disguise the sound of the tape tearing. She looked ahead. They would be driving past her driveway in a few minutes. She grunted again, tearing one side of the tape free.

This time Bob jabbed the gun into her breast. "Shut the fuck up, and quit wiggling." He put a cigarette in his mouth and lit it with his lighter, all the time with the gun on Lisa.

Lisa grimaced with pain as dramatically as possible. She kept her hands together so Bob wouldn't notice any change in her posture. It was going to hurt and maybe tear some of the skin on her wrists, but with one thrust she could free both hands. *What's the next step? I'll wait until we're right in front of my driveway and then jump out.*

Jake stopped at a stoplight at the bottom of the hill. Lisa sat still. He asked, "Can I have a cigarette too? I'm nervous."

"Later, Jake; just drive." Bob smiled, apparently fascinated by the flashing traffic lights dancing across her chest. Jake floored the gas pedal when the light turned green.

I should have made my escape there. We were stopped. But there was too much light. Bob would have seen where I was going and probably shoot me. I need darkness.

She planned a new strategy. Just past her driveway, there was a streetlight that was burned out. It would be dark there. Bob's gun would be worthless if she could get into the woods. She knew the trails well, and Jake and Bob were unlikely to find her in the dark. But how could she get Jake to stop or at least slow down? He was driving like a jehu.

As they passed her driveway Lisa tensed her muscles, ready for her break. She rehearsed her moves in her mind. *Open the door and roll. Cover myself since I'm not too well protected on top. Then get to my feet, run down the trail, and hide when I hear them coming.* She again focused on the door handle on Bob's door.

123

Suddenly Bob pointed the gun toward the windshield and screamed, "There's a deer, you idiot."

Jake slammed the brakes. The car swerved to the left. The brakes screeched as the car swung left and skidded into the oncoming lane. Lisa took it for an opportunity. She wrenched her hands apart, opened the car door, and rolled across the pavement into the ditch, covering her chest from the impact. As she rolled, she hit her head hard on the fallen deer-crossing sign. *How ironic*, she thought. She lifted her head to see what was happening to the car. She needed to get up to make her escape.

The deer turned in the middle of the street and ran back into the forest untouched. Jake overcompensated and swung the car to the right, then left in an erratic arc. An oncoming Dodge Ram pickup truck came around the corner and smashed into the driver's side. The impact crushed the car. Lisa saw the truck driver straighten his arms to hold his position as he screeched to a stop. The car spun in wild erratic arcs and crashed into an oak tree. The truck came to a stop and turned on his flashers. Lisa lost consciousness.

CHAPTER 14

Lisa sneezed at the smell of smoke. The taste was acrid in her mouth. But there was another smell. Her boggled mind trying to place the scent. Ah, it was a man's aftershave and leather. She opened her eyes. There was a leather coat draped over her. Goose bumps lined her arms as shivered. She felt bruised, sharp, stabbing pains in her chest. Everything hurt. Red and blue lights were flashing. Someone was speaking to her. She shook the dizziness out of her head.

"Are you all right, miss? Oh, God, make her all right," the man shouted. Lisa thought this must be the man from the pickup truck. She bent her head to see police cars, ambulances, and a fire truck.

Everything was lit up. The man bent over her, protecting her with his coat.

"What's happening?" she asked.

"The car is on fire. Oh no, the driver!" he screamed.

Lisa looked up at the canopy of trees overhead. Now she could smell the stench of burning tires and the faint whiff of burning flesh. Firemen were containing the blaze. Police were all over. She heard the soft voices of two attendants coming toward her. She looked to the side. A policeman was standing behind the man from the pickup. "So you saw this woman exit the car before you collided?"

"No, I found her here in the ditch after the collision. She must have flown out the door when they lost control."

"Why did they lose control?"

"Officer, when I came around the corner, they were in my lane sideways. I put on the brakes but hit the back driver's side. The car spun around and smashed into the tree. I called 911 right away and then searched the wreckage. The guy driving was still alive, but I couldn't get him out of the car. The doors were so smashed up I couldn't get them open. I searched around while I was waiting for help and found her here in this ditch. I turned around, and the car burst into flames. Poor girl, I found her shirt ripped, and her bra had been cut off, and she had duct tape on her hands and mouth. I put my coat over her. I'm sorry I removed the tape from her mouth, but I was worried about her breathing properly. The tape is on her forehead if you need it for prints."

"You did all the right things, Mr. Craft. But I still don't understand why they were in your lane." He took the tape from her forehead and placed it in a forensic bag. He leaned over to get out of the way of the EMTs who were focused on their assessment.

"Miss, what's your name?" one of the EMTs asked.

"Deer," Lisa mumbled.

"I'm sorry; I didn't get that. What is your name?"

Lisa gasped and took a deep breath. Sharp pain shot through her chest. "Elizabeth Zuccerelli."

The ambulance attendants inspecting her wounds said, "Vitals are stable, Officer, looks like just a few lacerations and bruises." With discreet care, one rolled back the leather coat to listen to her heart and lungs with a stethoscope while the other took her blood pressure and put her neck in a brace. They replaced the jacket with blankets and gave the jacket back to Mr. Craft. The police officer nodded.

"Deer," Lisa said louder.

The officer squatted closer to hear her. "What is that, miss?"

Lisa took a deep breath. Every rib screamed with pain. "A deer jumped out, and they tried to avoid it."

"Why was there tape on your mouth and wrists?"

"They were planning to rape me."

The officer stood and spoke into his shoulder-mounted police radio.

The police code meant nothing to her, but she understood, "St. Mary's Hospital. Name is Elizabeth Zuccerelli."

The attendants placed a neck brace on her and then rolled her onto a stretcher. She was glad to be out of the mud. *Jeans and a sweatshirt next time*, she thought. "We need to go, Officer," one of the EMTs said. "She's hypothermic and needs attention."

"That's fine. We can complete the investigation at the hospital. Did you find any identification?"

Mr. Craft responded, "I found no purse or wallet."

The ambulance was so bright inside and smelled of disinfectant. She closed her eyes but opened them when she felt a sudden sharp pain in her arm. The attendant was starting an IV as they sped away. She started shivering, and the attendant applied another blanket.

She was transferred to an emergency department stretcher, and a short-haired brunette nurse replaced her ambulance blankets with hospital blankets. They were nice and warm, but the hospital stretcher was hard.

An ER physician entered her exam room and pulled the curtain over the doorway. "I'm Dr. Harris." He slid the blankets down her chest, exposing only her left breast, and listened to her heart and lungs. "Grace, help me roll her onto her right side. I need to see if there are any lacerations."

The nurse held her neck brace as the physician grasped her back and shoulder to roll her on her side. Her ribs screamed, and she gasped. "These lacerations won't need sutures, but they do need some careful cleaning. Get an x-ray of her neck, a chest x-ray with bilateral rib detail, and draw the usual blood tests. Set her up for a pelvic; police said this is a potential rape case." The doctor left her on her side, propped against the side rail of the stretcher. Lisa couldn't see him, but she heard him leave.

"Ms. Zuccerelli, I'm Grace, your nurse. I'm going to clean these wounds. You've got a lot of gravel embedded in your back. If I clean them well, they shouldn't leave any scars." She removed Lisa's remaining shreds of clothing and put them in a paper bag. She labeled the bag with permanent marker, put sterile water in a basin, and started washing Lisa's wounds.

It burned like fire, but Lisa didn't wince. *This is nothing compared to having a stick poking into your buttocks and hanging upside down on a cliff,* she thought. *I escaped, and I wasn't raped, just bruised and beaten. But wait till I see Cheryl. All those guys I dated, Jake is history! No more blind dates for Lisa Zuccerelli. I'm done.*

She squeezed the side rail instead of screaming as the nurse poured hydrogen peroxide into her wounds. She could feel it foam.

"Sorry," the high-pitched voice behind her said. But she didn't sound a bit sorry. She had done this many times before. Lisa knew it was necessary.

The phlebotomist entered and looked at the nurse. "Can I draw blood while you are doing that?"

"No problem."

The phlebotomist turned to Lisa and introduced himself. "Your physician has ordered certain blood tests. I am going to draw a small sample of blood."

"Go ahead," said Lisa. She was feeling better, although having her backside exposed was chilling. She watched the blood jet into the tube. It was so red, so vital looking.

"Got it," the phlebotomist said and left the room with his tubes of blood.

The nurse scrutinized each laceration on Lisa's back and buttocks. Lisa felt her meticulous probing of each wound as she worked down her back.

"Why do you have this scar on your right buttock?"

"Canoe trip injury."

"Oh, what happened?" She continued scrubbing.

"I fell on a stick."

After what seemed forever, the nurse announced, "All done here. Now let's check your front side." She closed the sliding glass door beyond the pulled drapes. Returning to Lisa's bedside, she pulled Lisa's gown down to her waist, exposing her breasts and abdomen. There were a few abrasions Lisa could see looking down, but the neck brace inhibited her from seeing very much. Her breasts were sensitive and stung when the nurse cleansed the wounds. "There is a circular bruise on your left breast. How did you get that?"

"That's where he poked his pistol into my breast." Lisa searched the nurse's face, expecting sympathy. She was disappointed.

"Forensics will need pictures of that. Are any of these abrasions from the assault?"

"No. I think they're all from bailing out of the car."

The nurse covered her top and exposed her belly to her groin. "Any tenderness in your abdomen?"

Lisa was quick to say no; she never wanted to admit she was in pain. But when the nurse palpated her right upper abdomen, it was tender. Lisa jumped in spite of herself.

"We need to check that out," the nurse said. "Maybe you have a broken rib or something."

Through a crack in the sliding glass door someone said, "X-ray."

The nurse pulled Lisa's gown down and tucked it behind her shoulders. She opened the glass door, and the x-ray team entered.

"We are going to carefully remove your neck brace. Do you have any neck pain?"

"No."

Two female technicians removed the brace and slid an x-ray plate under her neck. The nurse left as the techs put on lead aprons. Click. "One more," one tech said, holding a plate alongside Lisa's neck while the other positioned the portable camera. Click. They grabbed their films and pulled out their machine.

Grace returned with a camera. "I'm so sorry, Lisa, but this is a forensic case, so I must take a picture of that bruise." She closed the glass door, put the curtain in place, and again pulled Lisa's gown to her waist and took a picture.

"You're not putting that on the Internet, are you?"

"No. I'm sorry this is embarrassing for you, but it's important. Now we have to do a pelvic exam."

"He didn't rape me. He threatened to but didn't get a chance. A car came by."

"I'm sorry, but it's still necessary. I'll be right here while the doctor does the exam." She went to the door and called, "Doctor, we're ready."

The physician returned, and Grace put Lisa's feet into stirrups. Lisa appreciated the soft touch of Grace's hand on her shoulder as she readied herself for the exam.

Flash.

"You have to take a picture of my vagina?" she asked.

"Yes, it's required," said the physician.

"But he didn't rape me. He was interrupted when a car came by."

"Sorry. Proper procedure requires it. I'm putting in the speculum now."

Lisa resisted the instinct to tighten her belly and pelvic muscles when she felt the speculum enter her vagina. She had never had a pelvic exam before. Grace let go of her shoulder and assisted the physician with swabs and bottles. The doctor removed the speculum and then put two gloved fingers inside her and pressed lightly on the outside of her pubic area. "Does this hurt?"

Lisa felt a cramp. "Yes."

"I'm done. You can relax now." He turned to Grace. "Don't forget to comb her pubic hair. Here is the forensic bag."

"Yes, Doctor. By the way, she has a bruise that she says is from the assailant sticking a gun into her breast." Grace pulled the left side of Lisa's gown down to expose her breast.

The doctor looked at the bruise intently, palpating the bruised area. It hurt. "I see. Did you get a picture?"

"Yes, Doctor."

"Good." He left, closing the glass door behind him.

Grace lifted the bottom of Lisa's gown and exposed her groin, gently covering her legs with a blanket. She combed Lisa's pubic hair several times with a small comb, then put the comb and the retrieved pubic hair into a plastic bag. She sealed the bag and signed her name over the seal.

"Grace, why do you have to do all this when I said I wasn't raped?"

"Proper procedure, Lisa. Many women deny they have been raped, so we have to do these things on anyone where there is even a suspicion of rape."

"I will never say that you haven't looked me over carefully." Lisa thought it was a cute joke. Grace did not respond.

"X-ray," one of the two x-ray technicians said as they both entered the room again. "Doc said the neck's okay, so we can do the chest. Can she sit up?"

"Yes, I can sit up," Lisa said. "You can talk to me. I'm not in a coma."

Grace chuckled and left the room.

"Sorry," one of the women said. She put a large x-ray plate behind

Lisa. The technicians already had on their lead aprons. Click. Another plate and a click. "Done, Ms. Zuccerelli. Sorry, I didn't mean to be disrespectful. We're busy with a lot of trauma tonight." One backed out the machine while the other ran off with the film case.

Grace and the physician returned. "Your tests look good," the doctor said. "There is nothing broken in your neck, but I am worried about this tenderness the nurse said you have in your abdomen." He lifted Lisa's gown, pulled up the blanket, and palpated her belly. Lisa grimaced when he palpated the right upper part. "Maybe a little rebound, no rigidity," he said to himself. "We need to keep you for observation. There are important things like your liver there, and sometimes you can have delayed bleed. We should know for sure by tomorrow. I've asked the academic medicine team to watch over you since you don't have a physician." He shook her hand. "You should do just fine."

"Thank you, Doctor."

They both left, and Grace dimmed the lights on their way out. Lisa mentally checked herself over. *I got all my limbs. Nothing was cut off. The lacerations will heal. Every orifice has been scrutinized. Looks like I just survived a close encounter. It sure is embarrassing to have your vagina photographed. I wonder where they keep those pictures. I hope I don't end up in some medical journal. I feel violated even though I wasn't raped. Is this what women go through?* She closed her eyes, but visions of the fire and the stench of burning kept her awake.

Outside the door in muffled tones Lisa heard, "She's in room five, Officer."

A female officer entered the room. "I'm Officer Riley, from the special victims unit. You're Elizabeth Zuccerelli? May I ask you a few questions about what happened tonight? Are you comfortable?"

No, I hurt all over, Lisa thought but said, "Surprisingly, I am very comfortable, Officer. Every inch of my body has been searched. Nothing was left uncovered."

The officer did not respond. "Did they give you pain medicine?" she asked.

"No, I don't need any. I've been hurt a lot worse than this."

"So what happened tonight?"

Lisa told the whole sordid story in as much detail as she could remember. Officer Riley wrote everything down but showed no emotion. "I woke up on the side of the road with that nice Mr. Craft putting his coat over me. I was freezing. I think there was water in the ditch, mud and gravel too based on what the nurse dug out of my back."

"That will be all for now. I understand you will be here overnight for observation. I will let you know if we need anything else."

"Officer, did Bob and Jake survive?"

"One of the occupants of the vehicle was dead at the scene; the other is hospitalized in critical condition. They have not been identified yet, madam." She stepped out.

With her wounds attended to, she just lay still. It didn't hurt too much if she didn't move. With the glass door closed, she could hear almost nothing of the chaos in the emergency department. Lisa loved the quiet. Her mind flashed with anger, resentment, and fear, a maelstrom swirling inside her. The quiet of the room was the refuge of a rocky island in the midst of a storm. *That was sure a narrow escape. God, you must want me around for something. I'm not just poor Lisa, the misfit in the rich family. What is my purpose, God? I guess you aren't ready to take me to heaven yet, if I'm going to heaven. Too many adventures like this and I might not make it. Thanks, God, for saving me.*

She fell asleep, awaking later to Grace saying, "Your parents are here. May I send them in?"

"You may. Her Highness is accepting guests."

"You're something else. How can you be so casual about this?"

"I survived, didn't I?"

"Yes, but most women … I'll send your parents right in."

"Oh, Elizabeth, what happened?" Her father shot in the room like a mustang escaped from a stall. Her mother followed.

"I'm fine," Lisa said. "They're taking good care of me."

"The police told us that you were assaulted."

"Don't worry; I'm fine. But, Dad, remember that line supervisor, Bob, that has such high productivity?"

"Yes?"

"He just quit his job." She twisted on the hard mattress. "He is either dead or in the burn unit."

"What do you mean?" her mother asked. "How did you get yourself in such a mess? This is going to be in the papers, you know."

"Calm down, Helen," her father said. "She's alive. That's what counts."

Amid hugs and her mother's interruptions, Lisa told the story to her parents. At least they were both here for her. "Some blind date, huh, Mom?"

"Lisa, I am glad you are safe. It's just that … Listen, if you need counseling, we'll pay for it. This has been a traumatic event. You're bound to feel depressed after this. I know a counselor who deals with post-traumatic stress disorder."

"Mother, I'll let you know if I need counseling. What I need right now is sleep."

Grace appeared. "We found you a room in the observation ward. We'll be bringing you up there shortly. Any questions, Mr. and Mrs. Zuccerelli?"

"Lisa answered our questions, thanks," her mother said.

"Elizabeth, we love you very much. We're here for you." Her father bent down and gave her a kiss on the forehead. The adhesive left from the tape pulled on his lip. "What's this?"

"The man who found me put the tape that was over my mouth on my forehead. The police took it for forensic purposes," she explained with a smile. He was not amused. Lisa decided that this was more than either of them could handle. "I love you both. Come get me in the morning. I need some rest now. Thanks for coming."

• • •

At 3:38 a.m., Lisa awoke with shaking chills. The nurse noted a fever. More blood was drawn, and the surgeon on call examined her. Her belly was much more tender than it had been in the emergency department. By four thirty antibiotics were pumping into her IV, and she was taken to the operating room. In her delirium she saw her parents' faces as she was whisked into surgery. It all seemed like a dream.

Later that morning her head started to clear from the anesthesia. She felt hungry yet nauseated. She shook her head to get rid of her confusion. She pushed the call button that someone had put in her hand. The floor nurse asked her what she needed. "I don't know. I'm groggy, but I'm hungry. Did I get breakfast?"

"No, because you were in surgery."

"Did they fix me?"

"You're going to get better fast."

"Good. Send me food," she said. She paused. "I'm sorry; please bring something to eat. I'm starving."

"You can't eat until the surgeon gives the order. Here, suck on these ice chips. The infectious disease resident, Dr. Rachel Johnson, is here to do a consult. I'll send her right in."

Dr. Johnson came in and introduced herself and told Lisa, "Ms. Zuccerelli, I already examined you just after surgery, but I need to ask you a few questions."

Dr. Johnson looked as if she could be Lisa's slightly older sister. She had wavy, brown hair that flitted over her shoulders as she moved her head. She was of medium height, thin, and adroit. Lisa thought she must look very pretty dressed up, but right now she looked tired and disheveled. Being on call all night had depleted her attractiveness. "Just call me Lisa. I'm feeling pretty clear now. I told the whole story to the police. What more do you want to know?"

"Lisa, we did an emergency surgery early this morning. The surgeons were worried that you might be bleeding from your liver with the trauma you've been through, but you weren't bleeding."

"What did they find? Did they fix it?"

"I'll explain that in a minute. First let me ask you about your lifestyle."

"I go to the university. I'm majoring in exercise physiology so I can coach basketball. I do not drink alcohol when I am training. Sometimes in the off-season I have wine with dinner. I don't smoke, never have. I eat my vegetables and meat, and I have never been accused of anorexia or bulimia. I had all my baby shots. How's that?"

"That's good. That's all the information I needed. Ever been in the hospital before?"

"No."

"Previous surgeries? You have a scar on your right buttock."

"Not a surgery. I was canoeing in Canada and fell down a cliff with a canoe on my shoulders. Got poked in the butt by a sharp stick. Hung there upside down for who knows how long."

"Who helped you?"

"No one. I was solo, up in the wilderness. I had to pull myself down and pull the stick out myself." Lisa watched the expression change on Dr. Johnson's face. Lisa continued, "When I finally I got to a lake, I reached in the wound, pulled out the leftover leaves and sticks and washed it out."

Dr. Johnson cringed. "I'm impressed." She made some notes. "Now, are you sexually active?"

"I wasn't raped."

"I know. But are you sexually active?"

"This is confidential, right? You're not going to tell my parents?"

"Confidential."

"Yes, I am sexually active."

"How many partners?"

Lisa paused. "Is that important? I tell them to wear condoms, but sometimes they tell me that I get them too excited and they forget." Tears welled in her eyes.

"So how many?"

"Six. I have to be honest, right? Maybe eight. Why does it matter? They're all neat guys from the university, basketball players and football players mostly, nobody dirty."

"Lisa, at surgery the surgeon found your liver covered with infection. It's called Fitz-Hugh-Curtis syndrome, which is caused by sexually transmitted diseases. Your cervical swab taken from the pelvic exam was positive for gonorrhea and chlamydia. Have you had an HIV test recently?"

"Gonorrhea and chlamydia? How did I get that? Oh, yikes, you're freaking me out."

"It must have been from one of those guys who got too excited to wear a condom. May we have your permission to check you for HIV?"

"Yes, I want to know what's wrong with me." The guys she'd had sex with flashed through her mind. *Which one? Who gave me these STDs?*

"I will personally let you know the result as soon as we find out. We have to notify the health department. This is a reportable disease, but they will be very discreet about your contacts."

Guilt hit Lisa like a rock. She felt dizzy, like when she was tumbling down the cliff on the Wickstead portage. "They have to know the names of all the guys I had sex with?" She gasped as Dr. Johnson nodded her head. "What are you going to tell my parents?"

"What do you want me to tell them?"

"Tell them something was wrong with my liver."

"I'll tell them that you have a liver infection. I don't have to discuss how you got it with them. The good news is that we caught it and are treating it with the proper antibiotics. You should feel well in a couple of days."

"Can I go canoeing?"

"Certainly."

"Thanks, Dr. Johnson. You're awfully young."

"Young enough to be a physician."

"Right. Thanks. Wait a minute, could you answer a medical question for me?"

"Sure, what is it?"

Lisa blushed. "It's just that with all the sex, since you brought it up, I've never had an orgasm. How do you get one of those? I've read about them."

"Well, you might need to be in a committed relationship to feel safe and secure. Those feelings of security are important for the hormones in the hypothalamus, the part of the brain that sends out hormone signals. Then it requires some fairly slow, gentle foreplay in your erotic zones. Every woman is a little different, but those are usually around your nipples, the inside of your thighs, inside your vagina, and the sensitive area of your clitoris. Then with penile insertion you are properly primed for an orgasm. Many women have difficulty reaching orgasm through vaginal insertion alone and need additional stimulation of their clitoris. Does that help you understand?"

"That explains a lot. I clearly haven't been doing this right. Are you married?"

"Yes."

"Do you enjoy sex and get orgasms?"

The doctor cleared her throat. "Yes."

"Thanks, Dr. Johnson, I needed to know that."

As the physician left, Lisa looked out her window. Biting her lower lip, she yelled at the window, "I'm never having sex again!"

Why did I ask about that? Guys just take advantage of you. Look at the mess I'm in.

Her anger momentarily depleted, she whispered, "Sorry, God, I haven't taken very good care of the nice body you gave me. Can you get me through this mess? Forget it. I know I don't deserve it." The window shapes and colors blurred in her tears. She picked up her remote control and turned off all the lights, then stared at the shadows on the wall. By divine mercy she fell asleep.

She awoke to a humming sound. Someone was holding something on her belly. The room was dark. She opened her eyes but could see nothing at first. As her eyes adjusted, she saw a young dark woman. It was Heidi. Tears were streaming down her cheeks like rivers. The seashell on her leather necklace swayed with her movement. She was chanting in a slow rhythm. Lisa listened, following the cadence of the song. She sensed what the words meant even though she could not understand them. *It must be Anishinaabe,* Lisa thought. It felt as if the song entered her soul, like a healing hand deep inside, stretching into her body, putting her back together.

That's when she noticed that her gown was pulled up. Something was resting on her belly. Lisa reached to touch it. It was just a stone, but it felt hot as Heidi continued to sing and rub it along Lisa's abdomen. There was also some kind of powder on Lisa's skin; she could feel the silky texture, but it was too dark to see it.

When Heidi finished the song, Lisa felt the strong grasp of Heidi's hand on her own. Heidi picked the stone off Lisa's belly, whisked the powder into the air, and sat in the chair beside the bed. Lisa heard her friend sobbing.

Lisa clasped Heidi's hand. "Thank you, Heidi. I needed your touch. I needed the healing song. How did you find out that I was in the hospital? And how did you get in here?"

"You will heal, Lisa. The healing song released you from this evil."

"You are much nicer than the emergency department physician who searched all my orifices or the surgeon who cut me open last night or the nurses taking care of me. I know they care and are giving me the best medicine, but no one came to heal me like you."

Heidi said nothing more but leaned over and kissed Lisa's forehead. Then like a phantom she was gone.

When Lisa awoke the next morning, she felt so much better. *Did I dream that episode with Heidi? Was that real or just my imagination?* She lifted up the sheet. On her belly and on the edge of the sheet were traces of ocher powder. *What will the nurses think of that?* she wondered.

. . .

In the afternoon her parents returned. Her father appeared weary and distraught. He paced in the room, stunned by the intravenous lines, cardiogram wires, and nasal oxygen, which Lisa had removed and tossed on her pillow. He maneuvered between the pieces of apparatus to hug her as tears dripped down his cheeks. "Oh, Elizabeth, I am so sorry. We heard that you have a liver infection and have to stay a few more days for antibiotics. The doctor said that it's treatable, though."

Lisa lifted her gown to expose her belly. She ripped off the gauze pad. "See. It's just a tiny little incision. No big deal. They do it with a scope."

Her mother pulled down her hospital gown and placed a newspaper on top. "Bob was killed at the scene. Jake died in the burn unit last night. You're lucky to be alive, young lady."

Lisa anticipated her mother's reasoning. "Yep, no more blind dates for this collegiate."

Her parents sat in the bedside chairs. Within five minutes they were chatting about Linden, how he had done on his exams at Harvard, and what flowers were blooming in the garden. Lisa turned on some classical music with her bedside remote and relished the inane pleasantries. The alternative topics of discussion were too painful.

"Did you pick up my Jeep? It was at Cheryl's house."

"It is safe and sound in the garage. Cheryl called and brought it over to the house. You left your car keys at her place. And the police found your purse in the wreckage."

Lisa cringed. *Cheryl's seen my house. Will she still be my friend? Will she change on me?* She repeated, "No more dates. I'm done with that scene."

Her mother looked stern. "I think—"

Her father grabbed her mother's arm. "Helen, not now." She didn't finish her sentence.

From a paper bag her father pulled out a scorched, mangled mess of leather. "I guess this is what is left of your purse. I've ordered duplicates of your credit cards, since they were melted. It doesn't look like you had much cash with you."

"It looks like it needs to be trashed, Dad."

"Yes, it is all replaceable." He had tears in his eyes. "I gave you this purse for your sixteenth birthday." He choked on his words and brushed his hand through her hair. "But you're not replaceable, my dearest Elizabeth."

Her mother stood and placed her hand on Lisa's arm. "We love you, you know."

It sounded like a legal pronouncement.

• • •

Two days later Lisa was lying in bed feeling weak but no pain, no tenderness, and no fever. *Now, to find out if I have HIV or another STD, that would be a game changer.* She was disconnected from the intravenous pump because she had already received her morning dose of antibiotics. She felt a new freedom not being attached to a pole, oxygen, or the cardiac monitor. With the nurse's permission earlier that morning she had walked the halls with the nursing assistant assigned to her care, turned around at the nurses' station, and did another loop. It felt good. *I've got to start training for track and basketball.*

Dr. Rachel Johnson burst into the room. "I have good news for you. You came back negative for HIV and for syphilis."

"No HIV, no syphilis!" Lisa screamed as she leaped out of the bed and pirouetted around the room. Her hospital gown flying through the air concealed nothing of her physique, but she didn't care. It was time to rejoice. Besides, she knew Dr. Johnson had probed and prodded every inch of her body inside and out.

The ecstasy of a second chance overwhelmed her. In fact, she struggled to pay attention as Dr. Johnson explained, "However, there is a thirty percent chance of infertility because of the damage done to you fallopian tubes."

"You mean I can't have children?"

"Thirty percent chance."

"I don't care about that right now. I feel great. I survived." She jumped for joy.

"You are clearly ready for discharge. You need to take the oral antibiotics I've prescribed till they are all gone. That will give you the best chance of healing properly. It will take the nurses a while to get all your paperwork in order, but you can get dressed. Is someone coming to pick you up?"

"Yes, I think my parents are coming. Thanks for everything, Dr. Johnson." The physician extended her hand. Lisa pushed it away and hugged her. It still seemed like Dr. Johnson should be one of her classmates at the university, not a doctor.

Dr. Johnson grabbed her by the shoulders. Her grip was firm, almost painful. It caught Lisa off guard. "The way you are having sexual relations is high-risk behavior. I would hate to be standing here telling you that your HIV test is positive and you are going to get AIDS. You need to think through the choices you are making."

Lisa's exuberance dissipated. "I've made a decision to change. I've had enough. This is like a second chance. I won't blow it. This sex stuff can kill a person. Thank you for helping me."

"You're a very gifted young woman. I pray that you make healthy choices from now on, especially about your sexual relationships."

"I will. I promise," Lisa said. Dr. Johnson released her grip and walked out.

Lisa shed her gown and tossed it to the ceiling. Then she dressed in the clothes her mother had put in the closet. They seemed a bit too fashionable for leaving the hospital, but she was thankful anyway. She sat in the chair and turned on the television while she waited for her parents. The program was a soap opera. There was some young man cooing over some lovely young women. The next scene, three minutes later, they were in bed together. It disgusted her, and she turned it off. She sat in silence looking at the unmade hospital bed she had been lying in for four days.

There was a tap at her door. It was so gentle that if she had not turned off the television, she would not have heard it. "Come in."

"I'm so sorry. This is all my fault." Cheryl stepped into her room like a fawn into a wolf den. Her face was flushed; tears were streaming down her cheeks. "I talked to your parents."

Lisa bolted across the room to hug her friend. "No, Cheryl, this was a premeditated assault. Even if I had been raped and murdered, it would not have been your fault. Bob would have found a way to get to me. He wanted to abuse me because I'm the plant owner's daughter. Please don't blame yourself."

Cheryl wept at the sound of murder and rape.

Lisa hugged her. "You're my friend, remember? Don't bail out on me."

"Thanks, Lisa. I thought you would be so mad at me. Kevin is out in the car. He's afraid to face you."

"I am just glad that car came up the road when it did. Bob was ready to rape me there at the overlook on Skyline Drive, but because some car came by, they decided to take me to the park. That gives *coitus interruptus* a whole new meaning, doesn't it?"

Cheryl laughed in spite of the tears dripping down her chin. "Lisa, you're ridiculous."

Lisa became serious. "Tell Kevin that I think I am out of the dating market. But if you invite me, I'll be glad to go out with you and Kevin. I promise not to take him from you."

Cheryl started to laugh and then sobbed. "It's a date."

"Poor choice of words."

"Sorry." She blew her nose with a tissue from Lisa's dresser table.

"Are you taking me home? I heard that you returned my Jeep." She hesitated. "You saw our house, didn't you?"

"Yes, it's beautiful."

"You don't think less of me because of where I live?"

"No, why should I?"

"I figured if you knew I was rich you wouldn't like me anymore."

"Lisa, I like you rich or poor. I'm your friend. I'm just amazed that you're still *my* friend after all this."

"All right, could you take me home?"

"Sure, I'm ready."

"Good, let's get out of here."

The nurse appeared at the door. "Wait a minute, young lady. I need to take out that heparin lock in your arm and go over your discharge instructions." She sat Lisa on the edge of the bed and with an alcohol wipe removed the lock from her arm. Lisa winced at the sudden stinging pain in spite of herself. The nurse gave her the prescriptions and reviewed how they were to be taken and potential side effects. Cheryl stood like a statue in the corner.

Just as the nurse rose to leave, Linden appeared. "Lisa, I'm taking you home." He stood as resolute as a military officer.

CHAPTER 15

Lisa froze. She dropped the instructions the nurse had given her. "Linden, what are you doing here? I didn't know you were home from Boston. When did you fly in?"

"Mom and Dad told me what happened. I got the first flight available."

"Are you missing classes?" Lisa rose to give Linden a hug. It was like hugging a statue. *Where's the brotherly love?* she thought. *What did I do now? What does he know?* She pretended not to notice his insensitivity. "I'm so glad you came." Lisa turned to introduce Cheryl. "I met her on the soccer team, and she's on the basketball team with me."

He nodded at Cheryl, then asked Lisa, "You ready to go?"

"Yes." Lisa turned to Cheryl. "Thanks for the offer to drive me home. I guess I already have a ride."

"All right, see you at UMD. Go Bulldogs." She disappeared out the door.

Linden picked the prescriptions and paperwork off the floor. "Do you have everything?"

Lisa nodded. Without saying another word, he left the room. Lisa followed in his wake, but the nursing assistant, an attractive African American young lady, stopped them and said, "I'm required to discharge you by wheelchair." Lisa wanted to argue. *Hadn't she accompanied me rounding the floor on foot?* But her fight was gone, and she complied.

She popped out of the wheelchair as soon as the nursing assistant set the brakes and bounded toward the parking lot. She jumped in the car and put on her seat belt. Linden climbed into the driver's seat but did not put the key into the ignition. They sat in silence. Lisa felt the sweat trickling down her lower back. She waited, staring straight ahead.

"Do the guys you have sex with wear condoms?" He was staring out the windshield.

Lisa's lower lip trembled. *How does he know? Does he know everything about me? His friends must have told him.* A tear felt hot on her cheek. She felt like opening the car door and running home, but he would just corner her later. No escape.

"Did they test you for sexually transmitted diseases?" he asked.

More silence. Lisa bit her lip to keep it from quivering. Linden intimidated her, just as he had when they were children and he would tattle on her. *What should I tell him? How much does he already know?*

He said, "I am not starting the car till you answer me. I have ways of finding out, so don't give me any crap. Tell me the truth." He turned to stare at her. His gaze burned her face.

Lisa spoke so slowly she had trouble remembering what words she'd already said. "I was checked ... I don't have HIV ... or syphilis." Her tongue traveled around her mouth, giving her time to form the next words. "They found gonorrhea." She choked on the word. She felt nauseated and wanted to vomit, but she swallowed and gripped her seat belt with her sweaty fists. "And chlamydia." Ashen, she focused on her seat belt buckle. She felt faint. He was silent. She turned to him. An understanding passed between them that she still had not answered his question. She took a deep breath. "So I guess that proves ... that some," she said, searching his eyes for compassion and finding none, "of my sexual partners ... were not wearing condoms."

Her eyes flooded with tears as all the unsheathed penises that had entered her vagina paraded through her mind. She turned and leaned her forehead on the passenger window. Tears dripped on her blouse, and her respiration fogged the window.

His hand touched her arm so gently she had to look to make sure it was really him. "Lisa, I love you. You will always be my favorite sister."

"The only one you have," she garbled through her tears. "It's a good thing I don't have any competition, isn't it?"

"I don't want to lose you. You're special. Are you willing to give this up? I want you to find some young man that loves you someday and appreciates how special you are. Are you willing to wait for someone like that, or are you going to keep screwing around? It would break my heart to get a telephone call to come to your funeral."

"You almost did," she said as she unbuckled her seat belt and hugged him, tears pouring onto his shoulder. Her body quivered in his grasp, shaking as an abscess of regret and guilt burst from her soul. In a squeaky voice only audible because her mouth was in his ear, she stammered, "I thought I was the black sheep of the family. I thought that you were so much better than me."

He tightened his grip on her shoulders. "Don't compare us. You have gifts I will never have. Don't be jealous of my gifts. God made us different. But screwing every available jerk isn't the reason for your existence."

She lifted her head off his shoulder and held his face in her hands. "I've learned my lesson. I don't want to be a well-sculpted cadaver. I'll change."

Linden hugged her as she wanted to be hugged. "I can't believe I almost lost you. Lisa, you were almost raped; you could have been killed. I need my little sister."

Lisa felt a rush of cleansing pour through her. A small curl to her lips was the beginning of healing. "Let's go get my prescriptions filled so I can be cured."

He put on his seat belt and started the car. "Put on your seat belt."

"Yes, brother, sir." She put on her seat belt and looked out the windshield. Before he pulled out of the hospital parking lot, she put her hand on his wrist. "I don't know how you figured everything out, but do I have to tell Mom and Dad everything?" She closed her eyes and took a deep breath, awaiting his answer.

"I have my sources, but the question is, are you willing to tell them everything?"

She hesitated. "Yes."

"Then you don't have to." It was an absolution blessing, a new beginning.

Lisa twisted around and looked straight out the window. *I sure would like to know who his spies are.*

. . .

Amid hugs and kisses, her parents welcomed her home. "Go up and change your clothes into something nice; dinner is almost ready," said her mother. "I've catered it, and I want everyone dressed up."

Her father danced and spun around. "We have a lot to celebrate. My daughter is alive."

Lisa went up to her room and took off the clothes she had worn home from the hospital. She looked at the dresses in her closet. *These dresses have one purpose, to attract guys. And look at the mess that got me into.*

She pulled out a long dress with a high bodice and ruffled shoulders and laid it across the bed. *This won't put pressure on my tender belly.* She looked at herself naked in the full-length mirror. She checked her breast. The bruise from Bob's pistol had faded to yellowish green. *I could have been a dead body, raped and left in Chester Park. I sure wish none of this had happened.* She thought about how slimy and disgusting Bob was. She imagined him putting his penis into her vagina and gagged. She ran into the bathroom but only dry heaved. The nausea passed, and she looked at her surgical incision. She touched it. It was only a centimeter long and almost healed, not even sensitive.

She put on bra and panties and slipped into the formal dress. *It's not fair. I wanted to have sex with those guys. But now, because of Bob, I don't want to ever have sex again. I need more of that healing powder. And Heidi needs to sing to me.*

She looked in the mirror and put on a subtle shade of lipstick and light-blue eyeliner and passed a comb through her hair. *Is this just a facade for Mother to pretend nothing happened? I just can't think about this right now, or I'll get sick during dinner.*

There were candles lit on the table, and the lights in the chandelier were set low. Lisa smiled when she saw three forks and three knives, including a fish knife, beside each plate. One tiny spoon was at the head of each plate as well as the two spoons beside the knives. All the leaves were taken out of the table, which was set for four cozy places. Her father and brother were standing, dressed in suits waiting for her. Her mother stuck her head out the door that led to the prep room when she heard Lisa enter. She gave a quick word to the caterers and motioned for her family to sit down. Her father pulled out her chair for her. He gave her a hug, and she sat.

There were six courses served in traditional style with dramatic presentation. Crème pâté with little crackers stimulated their appetites; then a lettuce salad with no two leaves from the same kind of lettuce preceded the baked fish in foamed celery seed sauce. Little spears of carrots set off the fish for color. The main course was filet mignon in a puddle of horseradish sauce, separated from a coin of twice-baked mashed potatoes with a strip of bacon. Her father had chosen the wine. He made her promise, as always, not to tell anyone of her underage drinking.

"After what you've been through," he said in a toast, not finishing his sentence. He took a sip. "Note the floral in this wine, Lisa. It's sensational."

She smiled to herself, remembering her first glass of wine. She and Linden had been in Paris for her parents' twentieth wedding anniversary. They'd expected to stay in their rented apartment, but then their parents had invited them to join in the celebration. The waiter had made such a fuss out of "two fine young couples" that he'd given them free champagne compliments of the chef. He'd refused to believe that such a young couple had been married for twenty years. Lisa had liked the champagne because it had fizzed but had liked the wine they'd had with dinner better because it had been so fragrant in her mouth.

"Great wine," she said as she took a sip. "I am done training till fall, so I can enjoy this. I've been invited to be a starter on the soccer team this coming season."

The beef was so tender it hardly needed chewing, but Lisa kept chewing it to extract the flavor. "This is sure better than hospital food. Thanks, Mom." Everyone was silent. *Now what did I say wrong?* she wondered. So she added, "How are your studies going, Linden? Have you gotten to play any concerts?"

Linden explained about his classes, all As of course, and then described his piano recital. "Not many students majoring in business administration at Harvard are trying to minor in music." He sipped his wine. "But I'm more excited about the gig I got to play at a local pub. I had them dancing between the tables. Boston is quite an artists' village."

Dessert was crème brûlée with fine slices of strawberries and kiwi on top. The juicy flavor, which she so enjoyed, made her think about not having this dinner if she had been killed. Fruit always made her emotional.

The final course of chocolate truffles with a thimble cup of cognac completed the meal. Her father gave her an inquiring look as he served her. Lisa nodded as she remembered going to Ireland for her father's birthday when she was sixteen. They had stayed in a castle south of Dublin. That night the host had served twenty-year-aged Jameson. She remembered her father's concern, but it had been so smooth. It had immunized her against the cheap stuff her friends would offer her at parties, sending her on a search for a plant that needed watering.

Conversation stopped. Her father focused on her. "I am so glad you're safe. We just wanted to show you how much we love you." Tears were in his eyes as he choked up.

Her mother continued, "Lisa, I am sure that was very frightening. I can't imagine what it must have been like for you. I haven't slept well since it happened."

Linden said nothing. He just looked to her for a response. She put her hands through her hair and then folded them in her lap. "I'm safe. I'll be healed when I finish my medicine, and I really appreciate the way you have shown your love. I am very thankful," she said, turning and looking at Linden, "for a thoughtful and caring family."

She looked at the ceiling and sighed. "I've also made a couple of decisions." Wind rustled through the shutters. "I'm out of the dating scene." She saw her mother exhale with relief that she would not have to give her speech. "And I don't think I can work at the factory this summer. I think I'll help the gardener haul rocks and put in flower beds instead."

"You don't have to do that," her mother said. "The gardener—"

"I want to, Mother. Consider it my rehabilitation."

Her mother pulled an envelope from under her plate and gave it to

Lisa. "The girls on the pallet line sent this to you. And here is another card from Troy in Wisconsin."

Lisa opened the letter and read it out loud: "We're glad you're safe and sound, thanks from all of us."

"What are they thanking you for?" her dad asked.

"For helping work on the line when they were short," Lisa lied. She knew the real reason: she had released them from nonconsensual sex.

Lisa read the card from Troy. He wanted to see her again and was going to be working with Ernie. "There is one more thing." She looked up from the postcard. "As soon as I feel stronger, I'm going on another canoe trip." She turned to her mother and thought about how she could get her mother to agree without an argument. "I need the trip to heal my post-traumatic stress." She looked at her father. "That is, if you don't have the border guards retain me."

"I'm sure they'll be friendlier this time." He pushed his chair back. "I almost forgot. There was a package delivered to you yesterday." He went into the living room and returned with a large box. "It's from a Mr. Craft. I think that is the man who first found you at the scene."

As her dad got the package, her mother said, "You know they cleared him of any charges because of your testimony about the deer. They eventually found deer tracks beside the road confirming your story, although at first the detective told me he thought you were hallucinating."

Lisa opened the box. It was the leather jacket he had covered her with at the scene. Inside there was a note: "I had it cleaned, but I couldn't wear it after seeing you lying in the ditch, exposed like that. I think you need it more than I do. A tall girl like you must be my size."

"I don't think that's appropriate," said her mother.

"Oh, Mother, this is so thoughtful." She slipped it on. "Doesn't go with this dress, though, does it?" She stared at her mother to see her reaction.

"I don't like it. Send it back to him, or throw it away."

"Don't you understand what this means? I was kidnapped and two f—" She covered her mouth at the word. "Two jerks tried to abuse me, and along comes this *man*," she emphasized the word, "who doesn't even know me, and he is kind enough to cover me up and not take advantage of me. I will treasure this coat. I'm glad there are still men in this world who are kind and respectful of a young woman. Besides"—she wiggled in the coat—"it fits and feels good."

Her father laughed at her tirade, and her mother gave her a hug. "I'm proud of the way you handled yourself in this horrible situation," her mother said, "but I still think this is inappropriate."

Her father stroked his chin. "Yes, I think you should keep the coat and remember that there are still gentlemen in this world."

"Like you, Dad?"

He smiled. "Exactly."

As the caterers cleared the dishes into the kitchen, Linden gave her a hug as well and whispered in her ear, "Act wisely, Sis."

They all went to the living room.

"Thanks for the fine welcome-home dinner," Lisa said. "I am very thankful for my family. Linden, are you going to play something nice for me?"

He got up and adjusted the bench at the piano. "This is a special Mozart nocturne for my resilient sister."

The music was so therapeutic. It calmed her frustration and quelled her anger. The smell of the room made her close her eyes and breathe in the deep richness. When he finished the piece, Lisa clapped. "Thanks. Now I think I need to go to bed. Good night, everyone." She curtsied and headed toward the stairs, her leather coat under her arm. *Now to plan a canoe trip*, she thought, *and see Troy. But no sex.* "Thanks for the special concert, Brother dear."

He started playing some razzle-dazzle jazz piece. She paused and smiled. He was so talented. When he finished, he smiled. "Glad to do it for my favorite sister."

"And your only sister. Don't forget it." Everyone smiled.

As she ascended the stairs to her bedroom, she thought, *I'll be glad when he returns to Harvard. Those friends of his are probably the ones who tattled on me.* She took another shower just to feel the massage of the water, dried off with a fluffy towel, and crawled naked between the sheets. *I hate pajamas.*

CHAPTER 16

Lisa's arms were sore, and her biceps felt warm as she pushed the wheelbarrow full of stones. She was pleased that the gardener was allowing her to help. Lisa viewed the labor as preparation for her upcoming canoe trip. She remembered Troy admiring her muscles. *This is great workout, and I know Troy likes my biceps.*

"Where do you want these stones?" she asked the gardener.

He pointed at a flower bed. "Place them around the flower beds. And make it look nice."

"Yes, sir." Lisa hauled the stones to the flower bed where she had spent all morning digging. She placed the stones in a border around the flowers the gardener had planted. She thought about the acres of dirt she had shoveled that week. Her arms were so sore and strong. Her mother had quite an imagination for flowers, especially when it involved other people's labor. Lisa closed her eyes for a minute to rest, but flowers danced in her vision. She almost screamed.

"Taking a break?" the gardener asked, standing over her.

"Just collecting my thoughts."

"I appreciate having such a great assistant," he said. "You're strong, not like the rich, frilly girls of my other clients."

"I've learned a lot from your expertise," Lisa said. "Besides, the physical exercise has tuned up my muscles."

"I've got another job this afternoon, so when you're done placing those rocks the way your mother wants them, that will be all for today."

"Thanks," said Lisa as she positioned another stone next to a group of marigolds. She sighed. The sun was so bright and warm that she decided to use the afternoon for some nude sunbathing on the tennis court. Her Italian complexion tanned quickly, thanks to her copious melanocytes, a genetic gift from her paternal grandmother. *A nice tan should prevent burning on the canoe trip*, she thought.

Canoeing was always on her mind. As she lay naked on her towel, she reviewed her menu. *I'll need a few groceries, candy bars, peanut butter, pancake mix, and condiments that will make my meals more fun.*

Later that evening she went over her menu with her father in his study. "What do you think?" she asked. He had taught her to love camping, and he had been so clever about preparing food over an open fire, back before he'd become CEO.

"Looks great to me, but you'd better get your mother's blessing as well. She will worry about you otherwise." He smiled.

"Yes, Father dear. I will show Mother dear my menu as well." He gave her a paternal swat as she left his office.

She wrapped each day's food in a separate bag and filled the pack. She weighed it to make sure it was not more than she could carry with a canoe on her back. "No double portages," she promised herself as she hoisted the canoe on her shoulders and walked down the driveway.

Finally, she had all her gear together. She packed her car, leaving her injured aluminum canoe behind. She'd decided to rent a canoe instead of dealing with the transport and the damages of her own. *Besides, it will give me an excuse to see Troy.*

The drive was uneventful. She squirmed in the seat remembering how painful this road had been the year before. She smiled as she went through the border. The guards seemed so disinterested compared to her previous experience. As she turned into the outfitter, she looked for Troy. She saw Ernie sorting through muddy packs left by a group that must have recently returned.

"He's been moping around like a kicked pup," Ernie Svenson told Lisa. "He's out delivering one group, and then he is going to wait for a pickup from the same landing. He won't be back till late this afternoon. But I'll take you to your landing."

Lisa laughed at Ernie in spite of her disappointment. *I guess I will just have to wait until I return to see him.* She jumped into the van, and Ernie took her down the road to the landing. Along the way he explained some of the lakes she would be going through and some of the portages.

Ernie dropped her off, and Lisa hurried to get out on the water. The wind was just a gentle breeze. The warm sun caused the cedar trees to lift their boughs and permeate the air with their scent. The rocks of the Canadian Shield welcomed her in a special way, now that she had taken that geology class. The loons sang to her as she poked the embers of her cooking fire that night. She wondered if Troy was still moping. She pictured Ernie and Helga prodding him to do his work.

Ernie had proposed a different route with grand waterfalls and fast-moving rivers. She felt at home. The falls were majestic but too dangerous to swim down the cascades. She had managed to enjoy swimming in the current swirling below the falls, and that was refreshing. Besides, she swam every morning before breakfast no matter where she was camped.

One night she awakened in a panic with Bob sticking a gun to her chest. She had fallen asleep curled near the campfire. Now the fire was out, and the breeze off the lake sent a cold chill down her back. She forced a laugh, realizing that it was just a dream. She got up and crawled into her sleeping bag under the canoe, and the nightmare didn't return.

The chain of lakes she canoed all one morning ended at Ramshead Lake. It was copper blue with a sheer rock face on the east side. She stopped at a rock that had fallen off the face of the cliff in the geologic past. It jutted into the bay and lay almost horizontal. It made a nice table for a picnic lunch. After eating, she noticed sufficient footholds in the cracked granite to climb the rock face. At the top, she was rewarded with a breathtaking view hundreds of feet above the surface of the water. Ramshead Lake appeared like a puddle in a dense pine forest with this phallus of granite rising into the sky on the eastern shore. Except for the hum of insects near the water, there was silence. Ernie had promised her solitude. "I have tried for years to send people that way, but they're scared off by all the portages," he'd told her, "but I know that won't have any effect on you."

He was right. She had not seen another group since the first day when she had taken a mile-long portage to the west. The group that she'd passed with all their gear on the previous portage had waved their paddles at her as if she were going the wrong way.

The solitary environment certainly improved her tan. She was already quite dark as she lay naked on top of the promontory. The sun felt so good. Even the smell of her sweat seemed to belong to nature. She rolled on her back, adjusting her baseball cap to shade her eyes. Her skin prickled as a faint breeze wafted across her torso. She tightened her abdominal muscles. It was so good to not feel pain inside her belly anymore. She felt cured and healthy. Without looking, she felt the one-centimeter scar where the surgeon had put his scope. The surgeon had said that she might be sensitive there for a while, and she was, but only slightly. She pressed on her right upper belly and smiled. There was no more liver tenderness. She put her hands on her hips and then followed her pelvic brims with both hands sliding across her inguinal ligaments. As her fingertips touched her pubis, she pressed her fingers deep into her vagina. Could she feel the tip of her cervix? She thought so, but there was no pain. "I declare myself healed," she informed the scraggly jack pines that struggled to survive among the moss on the top of her granite bed.

She stretched skyward, twisting in the breeze, thankful to be alive. She felt her right buttock. There was still a numb area where the scar was. She palpated the healed skin, remembering the big, green, slimy hole it had once been. *I'm so thankful for healing.*

She dressed and scampered down the rock face to where her canoe was wedged between the rocks. It was thirty-five pounds of Kevlar. She felt as if she could portage it all day. But she knew its light weight was also a liability. If a strong wind came up, she would be blown like a leaf across the water any direction the wind chose. At least her lightweight Grumman had a sharp keel and was more stable. But down the rivers and on these small lakes none of that mattered. She slid through shallows that would have been a struggle with her aluminum canoe.

Pushing off, she headed for the northern shore where she found the portage to Shag Lake. *What an odd name for a lake,* she thought. From what Heidi had taught her, it was probably an abbreviation for an

Anishinaabe name that white men couldn't pronounce. The portage trail angled between cracks in the large granite wall. Lisa wondered, *What geological force cracked this rock as big as a house in half, and how long did it take to fill in the crevice with debris to form this trail? Did an earthquake or ice split it?* One semester of geography was not enough to answer the question, but it was enough to ask it. *Maybe I should take a geology class next.*

Straight up through a poplar-and-birch forest she found a gradual landing. The map showed an L-shaped lake where she was on the short arm. She couldn't see much ahead of an upcoming bend in the water, but everything to her left was birch, and everything to her right was cedar and jack pine. Surprised by the difference, she kept comparing the two shores as she kept to the middle of the lake. *What enchantment made the two shores so different?* When she had paddled the entire length of the lake, she decided to find a campsite. There were two choices. There was supposed to be a site to her right, but she couldn't see it. Consulting the map, she searched for a rock jutting out between the cedar trees. She found it and spotted the small campsite back in a shaded cove. The site looked small and dark. The other site marked on the map she could plainly see. It was wide open, like a forest service campsite in a national park. She headed for the open camp, frowning at the other site. *Who would want to camp there?*

The campsite was idyllic. A collection of rocks formed a pleasant fireplace for cooking. The beach wasn't sandy, but the gradual rock shelf formed a perfect landing for the canoe and swimming. She unloaded her pack and turned the canoe over to make her shelter. Instead of the soup that had been her staple supper, she cooked up pasta and added the freeze-dried sauce when the noodles were soft. It tasted so good; each mouthful was a thrill. It had been her mother's suggestion.

"This is sure a lot better than soup, but it still doesn't taste like home-cooked spaghetti," she said to no one. She headed behind the camp into the birch grove to look for a good latrine. As she searched, she found some unripe blueberries. As she investigated the forest floor, she realized that there were blueberries as far as she could see up the ridge, but none were ripe. *I should come back in a couple of weeks.* She walked along a path that was well groomed and rolled her nose when

RICHARD R. ROACH, MD, FACP

she stepped in some poop. She scraped it off her shoe, and after digging a latrine for herself, she added it to her own feces. "Who could possibly be so careless?" She felt indignant.

There was a red streak on the horizon as she finished washing her dishes and closed up her pack, sliding it under the overturned canoe. She took off her clothes, folded them, and stuffed them into the head of her sleeping bag. Then she ran out into the water for an evening swim. The rock shelf ended at about knee depth and dropped off to twenty feet. She climbed back up on the shelf and dived into the deeper water. It was dark when she climbed the shelf for the last time and headed for her campfire. The coals were still hot as she dried first her backside and then her front in the heat. She listened to the loons and scanned the sky for shooting stars. The site had no large trees, so she packed up her food pack and put it under the canoe before crawling into her sleeping bag. Sleep comforted her like a mother.

. . .

She awoke with a start. The canoe was tipping upright, and out of the corner of her blurred vision she saw a face and smelled hot breath. Her pack disappeared. She peered into the darkness trying to understand what was happening. She unzipped her sleeping bag and jumped to attention. In the moonlight she saw the form of a bear with her pack in its mouth ambling along the path behind her camp. She screamed, grabbed a piece of firewood, and banged on the canoe and then threw it at the bear. The bear did not even change its gait, let alone let go of her pack.

In her fury she screamed and ran after the bear. The bear only quickened its pace, carrying its precious treasure farther into the woods. She yelled, "I need that pack!"

A few minutes later she was gasping for breath, and her bare feet hurt from stones and sticks along the path. There was no sign of the bear or her pack. Everything was silent and black as the trees closed in around her. She picked her way back to her campsite through the woods. Her pupils dilated as she searched in the moonlight for the trail. She stopped. *This is stupid. I'm stark naked in the middle of the woods. I need to stop and think. I should have put the pack up a tree, but there are no large trees on this site, just a lot of blueberry bushes.* She stood perfectly still. Silence. *How could a bear be so big yet so quiet?*

She folded her arms across her breasts and shivered. Her skin cringed with goose bumps. The moon lit up the trail, and she walked carefully back to camp. *How did I run this barefoot?*

She stepped on something squishy and soft. "Oh, shit." Immediately she understood what she had buried that evening. "Bear scat and I just stepped in more." She recognized some of the trees along the trail and found her way back to camp. She ran to the water's edge and washed the feces off her foot, then headed for her sleeping bag. She put on the clothes she had bundled up for her pillow. With shorts and a T-shirt she felt warmer and less vulnerable. Her boots were at the foot of the sleeping bag, and the canoe was unharmed despite the way the bear had tipped it over.

I have only the clothes I'm wearing, my boots, the canoe and paddle, and a sleeping bag. No food, no pots, no raincoat, no supplies such as insect repellent, bandages, or flashlight. She felt in the pockets of her shorts. At least she had matches, and they were dry. She had a small plastic bag in her pocket too for litter, and her camp knife was buckled to the belt of her shorts.

She added wood to the fire, and the embers burst into flames. The warmth was comforting. *What should I do? What if the bear comes back?* She sat still listening to the night. No loon songs, no frogs croaking; it was that time of the night when everything was silent. Or was nature mourning her loss? *The bear won't come back,* she thought and then yelled, "There is no food here anymore." That made her hungry, and she knew the sensation was going to get more intense before it got better. *I'm two or three days' paddle from the landing. That's a long paddle without food.*

She packed her few things into the canoe and paddled in the moonlight to the other campsite across the lake. It was small. *Why am I doing this? The bear won't come back. I have no more food. But I'll just feel more secure.*

There was a tiny clearing for a tent between the cedar trees. She overturned her canoe on the spot, took her sleeping bag out of its sack, and undressed, putting the clothes into the top of her sleeping bag for a pillow. They had become very valuable, like a treasure to be hoarded.

She crawled into her sleeping bag, and her stomach grumbled. She pushed her belly with her hands. "Settle down, stomach; there is nothing to eat. It hasn't been that long since supper. You're just overreacting." She rolled on her back and took a deep breath. Mosquitoes attacked with a vengeance. She crawled deeper in her sleeping bag and closed the opening. Resignation and exhaustion put her to sleep.

. . .

The warmth of the sunshine awakened her, and she wanted to swim. The air was warm and sultry. A brisk wind had blown away the mosquitoes. With her sleeping bag zipped up, she had broken into a sweat. The shore was full of fallen trees and rocks covered with green-black slime. The foliage was so dense that the rocky place where she had landed her canoe was completely shaded. She squatted on a rock and eased into the water, feeling the slime squeeze up between her toes. *I can wash that off, but how am I going to get back up? I guess I'll save that decision. I can only handle one decision at a time this morning.* She swam out to where the sun warmed the surface, floated on her back, and thought. *Don't panic. You aren't hurt or anything. Woman does not live on food alone.* She spun over and did a breast stroke, looking at the campsite in the birch grove across the lake. She felt betrayed.

Suddenly she understood the events of the night. *I get it. That side of the lake was burned in a forest fire. The birch and poplar are the first trees to grow after a fire. But blueberries come up first, sometimes even the first season after a burn. Bears like blueberries. I should have recognized the poop as bear scat. Never again. How stupid. All the signs were there: the blueberries, the young birch trees, and the too-perfect campsite. I know to check for bear scat before ever camping at a site. What's wrong with me? I guess I needed to learn a lesson.*

She swam back to her site. "Oh, God, why didn't I think of that yesterday? You are a harsh teacher. Don't get me wrong, God. I am thankful that you sent the deer to keep me from getting raped and killed, but did you have to send the bear to steal my food? Couldn't I have learned that lesson in an easier way?"

As she swam near her camp, she searched for a way up the slimy rocks. "One other thing, God, I'm hungry. How do you plan to feed me?"

She stepped on the slimy rocks, balancing on her toes before shifting her weight from one foot to the other. With one surge she jumped up onto a dry rock. "Did you think I was too fat and needed to go on a diet?" She stretched and pinched the skin on her belly and yelled, "I don't think so, God; there's not much fat here." Her voice reverberated through the cedar trees.

She stood near her canoe dripping. *Right, the bear took my towel.* For a moment she thought about making a fire but decided it would be a waste since she had nothing to cook. It was chilly in the shade, so she squatted to conserve heat.

Choices. I could fish and try to get something to eat, or I could paddle as fast as possible. She grabbed at her slim thighs. *Not a lot of reserve there. Should I try to make it back before I get too hungry?* She stood, almost dry, but was covered in goose bumps. *I have one easy decision. I am not staying here.*

She dressed and bolted into action. She hauled the canoe down to the landing, stuffed her sleeping bag, and put her few belongings into the bow of the canoe. With each stroke of the paddle she felt warmer. She thought about the route she should take and realized the map was in the pack. She headed back to her fateful camp.

I've got to get what's left of my pack. Her thoughts were braver than her feelings. *That darn bear won't eat my map or my aluminum pot. If he didn't go too far after I quit chasing him, I should be able to salvage something.*

She landed on the gradual granite rock that she had enjoyed so much the night before. She followed the trail and found the scat she had stepped in. She laughed as she paused to urinate in her latrine. She slowed her pace to watch for broken branches or paw prints in the moss. Careful observation allowed her to follow the trail. An hour later, she came to a clearing in the birch trees. There sat her pack. She froze. No sign of a bear. Approaching the pack, she saw the moss packed down where the bear had sat enjoying her food. Vigilant, expecting the bear to jump into the clearing, she snatched the pack.

Plastic bags were scattered around, especially the ones that had held peanut butter or grease. White powder, her pancake mix, was flung over the moss, but the bag with the sugar for her syrup was licked clean. She searched the perimeter but didn't find anything to salvage. The pack had huge rips down the back, but the leather straps closing the top flap were still buckled. She held the two ripped sides, took one more look around, and decided to continue her investigation back at camp. She walked backward across the clearing, sure she would see the bear, but when she came to the edge of the clearing, she turned and bolted back to camp.

She dumped the contents out. The oatmeal packets had been ripped apart, and the candy bars, fruit bars, and jerky were gone. The bear must not have cared for the breading for fish, as that remained. Her pots were dented, but she bent them back into usable shape. Her raincoat was ripped, but her towel was still usable. The large plastic bags that protected her clothes were in shreds, but her fleece and flannel shirt were intact except for a ripped sleeve. She found bear-claw rips through the seat of her jeans. *Maybe I can start a new fashion trend, bear-claw jeans. I'll have to copyright that as soon as I get home.* Her flashlight and first-aid kit were still in the flap pocket undisturbed, and there was the map. She shouted for joy.

Pasta was scattered in the bottom of the pack. There was as much dirt as pasta, but two sauce-mix packets had no claw marks. She found a plastic bag with only a small puncture in it, so she tied off the hole with a twist tie. Then she blew the dirt off each noodle and placed them one at a time in the rescued plastic bag. *I'll boil it well. It can be one meal.* Nothing else was salvageable. "So much for creative meals, Mom."

What do I do with this pack? She slumped, head in her hands. Then she remembered the baskets Bidah had in her house and how they were put together. *I wish I could find some cedar roots to sew it together.* She lifted the torn pack into the bow of the canoe, careful not to lose anything out the rip. She scanned the sky to anticipate the weather and shoved off. Once in the water she consulted her map and headed for the portage. "I rename this Bear Lake," she yelled in exasperation.

The portage was a problem. She hated crossing twice, but it was necessary with a torn pack. Besides, it was only twenty rods. She portaged the canoe first and then put the pack on backward, across her front, so she could use her hands to hold the torn part together and try not to drop anything. She was glad to leave Bear Lake. Over her shoulder she snarled, "Just stay there, Bear. I'm leaving it to you."

Finding a small stream on the other side of the portage, she sat on a rotten log and scanned the map. *First I portage into this stream, which meanders through a swamp according to the map. There are a couple of short portages. It'll take me all morning to get through this.* The next portage was into a large lake and was two hundred rods or two-thirds of a mile. She noted a campsite marked on an island in the middle of the lake. *That's my goal. One hard day of paddling, and then I'll be a within a day of the landing. I can make my pickup on time and see Troy.* The goal made her feel better. *If the weather holds, I can make it, food or no food.*

As she paddled through the narrow stream, the red-winged blackbirds bolted from cattail to cattail along her route. It reminded her of what Bidah had taught her about edible roots. As she paddled up to a beaver dam, she noticed some arrowhead plants off in a small cove beside the dam. *Just have to cook them well,* Bidah's voice echoed through her brain. With the canoe docked on the beaver dam, she took off her precious clothes and put them in the canoe. Then she swam to where the arrowhead plants and cattails grew in abundance. It was deep.

She followed an arrowhead plant down its stalk with her feet until her face was in the water. She dove in the muck and pulled with both hands. No bulb, nothing to eat. She tried again, following her hand to the bulb, but the water was so deep it meant her face was under mucky, foul water. *This isn't going to work.*

Then she remembered what Bidah had said: "Dig them out with your toes." She burrowed her foot into the muck to find the tubers. *I can't do this without the canoe.* She pulled the canoe into the water and swam it to the cove. By holding the canoe she had the leverage to dig with her toes. "How do I find them once I dig them out?" she asked. Her toes finally popped one free. Plop, it floated to the surface. "Oh, that's how. Now I remember."

With a vivid imagination it looked like a potato. She worked some more out. Plop, plop. It was fun, and the more she dug, the more appetizing they appeared. Next, she focused on some cattails. She pulled them up. It required more force, but they were bigger for the effort. They didn't pop up, but by holding the canoe she could use both feet to lift them to the surface. In no time she had enough for a reasonable meal. She threw the roots into the canoe and pulled the canoe back to the dam. She felt like a beaver as she washed the roots off in the cleaner effluent going over the dam. She placed her harvest in the canoe and then focused on cleaning the muck off her body.

The water was murky, rust colored, and muddy, disturbed from her scrounging, and she felt slimy, covered with mud, as she climbed onto the beaver dam. Squatting in the sunshine, she waited till her skin was dry and then brushed herself clean before she dressed. She was covered in a scaly crust as she climbed into the canoe, but her harvest was worth the trouble. "At least I won't starve. I hope these roots taste good with pasta sauce," she laughed. "I don't think that's how Bidah serves them." She felt lighthearted as she paddled toward the long portage. About noon she landed the canoe. She recognized some of the plants Bidah used for spices and picked them, wrapping them in some ripped plastic bags she had salvaged.

Her stomach growled. No breakfast and now it was lunchtime. She had never craved a candy bar so much in her life. She felt hostile toward the bear that had scarped down all her candy bars. She'd drank as much water as she could that morning in the lake, but the brackish water of this stream was too dangerous to drink. "A bear probably pooped in it," she said, shaking her fist, "and the beaver did for sure." She remembered reading that giardia was a contaminant from beaver feces. *Glad it's not a problem in the big lakes.*

To get her mind off food, she decided to fix her pack. With her camp knife, for which she was so thankful, she dug around a cedar tree, following the roots till she pulled up a long, thin one. She dug it out, getting as long of a tendril as possible. Then she sat down with her torn pack, stripped the bark, and made tiny slits along the shredded rip. She tied off the root, not sure what kind of knot to use. Her knot came undone.

She contemplated the problem and tried to visualize Bidah's baskets. *Don't try to tie a knot, silly; weave it back on itself,* she could almost hear Bidah reprimand her. She wove it back into the slits and then pulled it tight. It held. She wove some more through the slits, and when she finished, it looked horrible, but it was secure. She put her stuff back in the pack, reserving the sleeping bag till last. As she stuffed in the sleeping bag, she heard a tearing sound and stopped pushing. The sleeping bag had to come out. It was too much stress on the ripped canvas.

She strapped the sleeping bag to the outside. Motion at her feet startled her. She noticed a group of frogs that had gathered while she was sewing. She smiled. "The congregational meeting is over. You'd better hop away before I eat you." She remembered a fancy restaurant her parents had brought her to once. She had ordered frog legs and decided they were pretty tasty. She looked longingly at the beautiful thighs of the largest frog as it scampered away. *It would have used too much energy to catch them,* she rationalized.

With her pack on her back, she flipped the canoe on her shoulders. The sleeping bag was soon dangling from the straps and knocking into her legs. *I'll just have to walk with a smoother rhythm,* she thought. Within a few yards she had a gait that kept the sleeping bag from swinging into the back of her legs. She had to slow her pace because when she tried to speed up, the bag's motion became too chaotic. Two hundred rods later she was looking out over a beautiful lake.

As she loaded the canoe, she pulled out her fishing pole strapped inside the canoe and cast into the bay, then trolled the line behind as she paddled. It was a large lake filled with small islands. The wind whipped up while she paddled, but since it blew from behind her, it improved her progress.

By late afternoon she saw the island that was her proposed camp. "Today's goal is attained," she declared, spinning her paddle in the air. She pulled up her lure. She'd gotten nothing, not so much as a snag on her fishing line. She contemplated eating her roots.

Setting up camp was simple: flip the canoe, and roll out the sleeping bag. Her stomach gnawed at her as she rested on a log. She got a pot of water and set it on the fire, thankful for matches. She counted her matches. Four left. She would bank her coals tonight so she would not need another match in the morning.

The roots were easy to scrape clean. She cut them in small chunks and added them to her pot of water. *I wonder what constitutes well-cooked arrow plant and cattail root? Should I cook them together or separately?*

Squatting by the pot, she watched the cooking process. Never had a novice cook paid more attention to her work. As they boiled, she poked them periodically to assess their texture. When they were mushy, maybe overcooked, she didn't know, she drained them. "Now the taste test." She spooned some of the white, pasty stuff into her mouth. It had no flavor, reminding her of riced potatoes. She got one of her sauce mixes the bear had left her and sprinkled it onto the mush. "More flavor, but not exactly a culinary delight." She kept spooning it into her mouth, thinking about the roast she had eaten at Bidah's house and how the gravy would taste on her concoction. *This might even be a delicacy with some meat. But I shouldn't even think about meat.*

When she was done, she felt her belly. At least it wasn't growling, but something was clearly missing. She undressed, found her soap, and went for a swim, hearing her mother's words in her mind: *Don't swim right after eating; you might get a cramp and drown.* She decided that her mother's words applied to hot dogs and hamburgers on picnics, not to a belly full of cattail roots. Besides, she needed to wash off the dried muck crackling on her skin from the beaver swamp. "I should have washed up before dinner," she said laughing, knowing that she was far too hungry to have waited. "I'm such a pig."

She stepped into the crystal-clear water and dipped her soap. The foamy lather rolled across her ribs. She imagined racks of pork ribs roasting on the grill dripping with barbecue sauce. *Oh, that was a mistake. I can't let my mind wander like that.* She scrubbed her thighs. She reprimanded herself, "Next thing I'll be thinking what a nice ham I'd make. Get your mind off food, girl."

All soaped up, she dove deep, rinsing off the muck and soap. It felt wonderful, a normal thing to do, and normal was distracting. She swam around her island. It wasn't that big, and if she got a cramp, she would be close to shore. As she returned to where she'd started, she spun over onto her back and scanned the sky. Huge cumulus clouds were forming in the western horizon. *A storm is coming.*

She climbed out of the water and dried off, thankful that the bear had had no interest in her towel. She looked through her gear. Her jeans were wearable, immodest for a shopping mall but good protection for her legs in a thicket. Her flannel shirt with only a rip along one sleeve was wearable. Her concern was the raincoat. It had suffered the most as it had interfered with the bear's access to the food. The back of the raincoat was torn in several places. When she held it up, huge triangles of fabric waved like spinnakers in the breeze. *How can I repair that?* She made a mental note to bring wax and sewing kit on the next trip. *If there is a next trip. With trips like these, my mother is never going to let me leave the house again.*

She laid the raincoat on a rock. Digging into her pack, she recovered a spoon. She remembered the sticky sap on the pine trees and searched the trees on her island. She managed to get a heaping tablespoon of sap and returned to her campfire to heat it up. She wasn't sure how long to cook it, but when it turned black and bubbling, she poured it on the ripped parts of her raincoat and waited for it to cool. Most of the triangles seemed to hold. There were still rips that were open, but the coat would give her some protection now. The spoon was ruined. She kept it anyway in case she needed to cook more pine sap.

She sat on a large rock on the peak of her island to watch the sky. The sunset was magnificent as the brilliant crimsons turned into indigos. *It would be more beautiful if I didn't know what it meant, Lisa thought. It would make an excellent photograph or painting. I guess it would have to be a photo, a painting like that would be considered psychedelic. No one would believe it was real.*

The beauty of the sunset put her in a prayerful mood. "God, am I going to make it? On my last canoe trip you gave me self-esteem; you talked me into going to college. That hasn't been too bad. But the guys I've been dating you probably wouldn't approve of, would you? But I'm quitting the sex thing, God, really. It's too bad I go to a Presbyterian church. I could become a nun if I was Catholic."

She squirmed on her rock to get more comfortable and leaned back on the ledge behind her and continued her prayer. "But this university experience has been good. I never thought I could do it. I packed much better for this trip, and I had my parents' approval. I have a much better relationship with them. I love Dad. All right, I love Mom too, but she still treats me like a client. I've made new friends. Some of the guys aren't exactly friends, are they? I wonder who gave me gonorrhea and chlamydia. I hope the health department has fun finding out. You're right, God; I can't blame them for my problems. I'm the one who chose to have sex with them. It isn't their fault I got them so excited." She fondled her breasts, remembering her coital experiences. Then she giggled. *Thinking about sex takes my mind off food.*

The horizon exploded with light as the sun set. "Heidi's a good friend. You approve of her, don't you, God? And I am going to be a published author. That's me, who can't spell. You probably don't care if I'm a published author, do you? Cheryl's my friend. She sort of led me astray. No, I shouldn't blame Cheryl. I made my own stupid decisions. Hey, God, I'm confessing here. I'm not blaming anyone. That's good, right?"

In her mind she charted the next day's course. "And I'll see Troy. He is such a neat guy. If he likes me … okay, if he loves me … could I renegotiate that no-sex thing with you, God? Oh, he would probably never want a girl with my past. Probably not an option. Maybe I should convert to Catholicism, so I can be a nun. Don't Orthodox churches have nuns?

"Are you going to feed me? I'm still hungry. Cattail roots, even well cooked, are not real filling." She got up off the rock, went back down to the beach, and cast her line. "A nice walleye would be so good. I could bake it carefully over the coals. I wouldn't even need grease, which probably isn't good for me." She cast till her arm was sore. Nothing. "Oh, I suppose I should close with 'amen.' Thanks for talking with me, God."

She banked the coals to conserve her matches and piled the rocks close to the coals. She put a large flat rock on top to protect the coals from the coming rain. She put on her flannel shirt, putting her arm down the sleeve slowly so as not to lengthen the tear. She put on her torn jeans, laughing at how her bare buttocks stuck out. She put on her raincoat, avoiding any stress on the cooked sap. She wrapped the remainder of her clothes in the shredded plastic bag and stuffed them into her pack, careful to avoid any stress on the stitching. Ready for bed, she turned over her canoe and rolled out her sleeping bag. A few dry split logs found a protected place under the canoe beside her. The few stars on the horizon disappeared into blackness.

The loons sang in frantic a cappella as the storm approached. She crawled into her sleeping bag, fully clothed, and listened. The loon music, which refreshed her most evenings, seemed like an alarm. But even alarms could be calming if one was warm and tucked dry under a canoe.

This is the first time I have gone to bed with clothes on since I was a little girl—well, except at Heidi's house, but that was different, she thought as exhaustion and peace with God comforted her to sleep.

CHAPTER 17

She wasn't surprised by the violence that awakened her. Lightning shot out of all corners of the sky. The wind blew in sheer force under her canoe, lifting her tarp. She adjusted her raincoat to protect her sleeping bag from getting too wet. She also made sure that she was positioned under the overturned canoe so she was protected from the onslaught of the storm. Thankful to be dry, she curled on her side, but that exposed part of her sleeping bag to the rain, so she resumed a straight cadaver position, afraid to move. Lightning lit up the sky like daylight. As the deluge descended, she repositioned to avoid getting wet. She wondered how birds kept their nests dry and fell back to sleep listening to nature's version of Tchaikovsky's 1812 Overture all around her. *Gives surround sound a whole new meaning,* she thought.

Morning was a constant drizzle. At least it wasn't pounding rain like during the night. She crawled out from under the canoe and stood looking at the water. The wind was whipping the lake into whitecaps. *What should I do? I don't think that I can fight this wind. If I paddle from the bow, it will be exhausting, and this is a big lake. No place to hide.*

She was on the last island between a large expanse of open water and the next portage. *If I swamp the canoe, I'll die. If I stay a day, it will be a huge struggle to get to the landing on schedule, and that assumes that the wind will die down.* She had read stories of early pioneers to this area being stranded for days by fierce winds. *Not a good thing to think about.*

The other problem was what to eat. *Maybe I should have saved some cattail roots from last night's supper. Maybe I should have picked more. Why am I always thinking about food?* She shouted, "Because I'm hungry." Her voice echoed around the bay.

Anyway, I can't paddle safely against this wind. Discouraged, she walked to the other end of the island and sat in the wind shadow of a large boulder. It was peaceful and quiet yet odd to watch the whitecaps crashing on the shore. A log bleached white from the sun became her couch. By noon the drizzle had almost stopped, and it felt warmer, but her hunger was intense.

"Time to go fishing," she said to her pole. She threw her fishing lure into the wind, and it plopped far from the island. She reeled in, impressed with her cast. "Any fish will do. I'm not fussy here, God," she prayed as she cast several more times. An hour of persistent casting in every direction caught no fish. She set the pole aside and decided to swim instead. It would use more energy, but she knew swimming would focus her mind.

Her clothes were only damp, as her body heat had kept up with the drizzle. She undressed and folded her clothes, stuffing them under a rock shelf to keep them dry. The leeward side of the island was rocky, so she jumped from rock to rock until she was in thigh-deep water and then dove. The water was so placid in the wind shadow of the island. She swam several yards and then floated to contemplate. It was soothing, but as she crawled onto the rocks, she was even hungrier. *Should I try fishing again?*

She absentmindedly kicked a small rock and saw a crayfish scurry away. She picked her way closer to the shore and stumbled on another crayfish. *I think I could eat crayfish. Why didn't I think of this before? They should taste good with my salvaged pasta.* She jumped rock to rock to get to the shore and then sprinted back to her campsite.

She pulled out her cooking pot and said a quick prayer, "Thank you, God, for this food I am about to eat. Give me quick hands and sure feet so I don't stumble and crack my head open. Amen."

The fierce wind on her bare skin felt like sandblasting. She turned her back to the wind and ran back to the leeward side of the island. Without wind she warmed in the sun that peeked through the intermittent drizzle. Squatting in the water, she flicked rocks with her left hand and tried to grab a crayfish with her right. After a few missed attempts she got the motion correct. She also understood which rocks were likely to hide crayfish. One had two. She grabbed the biggest with her right hand and somehow managed to grab the smaller one with her left.

Within an hour her pot was full. She turned over a few more rocks to make sure there were plenty she hadn't captured, confirming that her resource was renewable in case she was stranded here another day. She dressed and headed for the other side of the island to cook her prize.

She filled the pot with enough water to cover the creatures. She felt bad about boiling them alive but knew no humanitarian way to kill them first. So she thanked them for sacrificing their lives to appease her hunger and added fuel to her banked coals. By the time the pot was boiling they had magically changed from blue-green squirming crayfish to brilliant, appetizing, crimson delicacies. She poured in her picked-over pasta. When it was all boiled together, she was unsure if she should save the water. *Would it have any nutritional value? Not enough,* she decided and dumped it onto the wet moss that surrounded the fire. She sprinkled the sauce packet over the whole thing and stirred it.

She took her culinary masterpiece to a place out of the wind and set the pot on a rock. Squatting beside the water, she carefully washed her hands. "I don't need to get sick over this." Returning to her rock, she straddled it like a horse and started to eat. The tails were great. *Just like shrimp cocktail.* She wasn't sure what else she could eat, but she was so hungry she tried to eat everything, crunching the carapaces between her teeth and sucking out the juices. The green livers were particularly tasty, adding flavor to the tails. When she'd eaten every morsel of crayfish, sucked every carapace dry, and inhaled every bit of pasta, she paused. Using her finger to scrape the starchy spices left around the kettle, she stuck the last morsels in her mouth. The flavor was satisfying. She rubbed her stomach. The sensation of being full and satisfied was so pleasant. A pile of remnants that looked like a raccoon's feast surrounded her rock table.

On the windy side of the island, she washed her pot and returned it to her pack. The wind was even stronger, gusting spray as the waves hit the rocks. But at least it had stopped raining.

Time for a postprandial nap, she decided. She crawled into her sleeping bag, adjusted her raincoat in case it started raining, and fell asleep.

Magic stillness awoke her. She remembered that in the Canadian wilderness, no matter how strong the wind is during the day, in the evening there is a magical time when the air and land are the same temperature. She recalled Heidi describing the phenomenon. "Twice a day this phenomenon makes the water tranquil, often smooth as a mirror with no wind." Lisa jumped out of the sleeping bag and looked at her map and then at the lake. The water was still as a mirror. The sky was gray. The sun would set in an hour. Dare she paddle at night?

I'll go. I'm well rested. I've slept most of the day, and I have a full, happy belly. She noted her position on the map and set a compass direction. She looked to the heavens. "I should be able to do what I couldn't during the day. If this is a bad decision, God, help me."

She dumped a bucket of water on the coals to smother them and put everything into the bow of her canoe. The water was silky. "To the landing to see Troy," she shouted in triumph. Her canoe slid like a greased knife through the glass-smooth water. She made it to the portage and looked across the lake. There was hardly a ripple on the surface of the water.

As she portaged her canoe and pack, the sun sank below the horizon, leaving her in total darkness, no moon and no stars. She tripped several times but didn't fall. She strung the flashlight around her neck. It bounced around when she needed both hands to keep the canoe stable but she was able to keep from stumbling on rocks and roots. Her progress slowed as she had to check each footstep. She was surprised that she could stay on the trail, but the thick brush on each side kept her on track. The dip in the horizon where the gray of the trees intercepted the black of the sky kept her heading in the right direction. When she saw the ripple of water at the end of the portage, she was thrilled. "Congratulations, girl, you've just crossed a portage at night. You've never done that before."

She loaded the canoe and started out again into the ink of the lake. *I'm amazed how much I can see in the dark; my pupils must be maximally dilated.* The water was so distinct from the shore, and by compass and flashlight she crossed the next lake.

Encouraged, she took the next portage in the same way, monitoring each foot step for stability, but she left her flashlight off this time. She discovered that it left her blind to the nuances of the darkness. The hardest part was going downhill because she had no idea where her feet would land. One wrong turn and a sprained ankle would paralyze her evacuation.

The next lake was trickier. Magic hour, as the Anishinaabe called it, was over, and a breeze started prancing across the water. The greater problem was that she could not just set a compass course. There were islands and peninsulas in the way, and she had to keep consulting her map, which required turning on the flashlight. *I better keep going. The wind might be too strong by morning.*

She stopped to reconnoiter. Her finger on the map followed the flashlight trail across the lake. Where could she get lost? Could she end up in the wrong bay? She noted the spots on the map where going on the wrong side of a spit of land could send her down a wrong channel.

She felt like a turtle with everything she needed with her. But she so wanted to do it right. She didn't have energy to waste getting lost. She charted a compass course to a spit of land, then paddled around it, and set another course. As she set each compass course, she tried to match it with a distinctive notch in the skyline so she could save her flashlight batteries. Step by step, she found herself at the next portage just as the sun was breaking the horizon. She was still a bit behind schedule and exhausted from paddling all night.

The early-morning light made the portage easier, but as she cleared through the brush at the end of the trail, she despaired. The wind had returned with a vengeance. Morning magic was over. She stalled. "Why is the wind always against me?" she yelled. She searched for likely hiding places for crayfish, succulent cattails, or arrow roots, anything she could eat, but found nothing. "Back to fishing," she said.

The wind was so strong by the time she had her gear ready that she could not cast her lure. She tried, and the lure almost snagged her ear as the wind blew it right past her head. "I'm not doing that again." She piled everything in her canoe, hidden in the brush a good ten feet from shore, out of the wind.

Now what? She curled up in a mossy place behind her canoe to think. Exhaustion narcotized her to sleep, and she dreamed of her nocturnal paddling.

The moon smiled at her as it directed her path. The lake was silky. Glittering sparkles in the water showed her which way to go. She hardly had to paddle as fish swimming beside the canoe glided it along. Everything was smooth and still. Her canoe was an ice skate coursing along silently. "How beautiful," she said. She looked at the fish carrying her canoe. "Could I eat one of you?"

She awoke from her dream with a gnawing pain in her stomach and sat up with a start. The wind whistled as it blew past her ears. "Still going nowhere," she said as she lay back down. But the gnawing prevented her from returning to her dream. *I shouldn't have thought about eating the fish, and I wouldn't have busted my dream. Now I'm wide awake and hungry. It must be about noon.* She grabbed her fishing pole and headed back across the portage.

A sudden cramp sent her into the forest to defecate. "Diarrhea, that's just what I needed." The cramps quelled as her intestines discharged their watery load. She felt lightheaded and grabbed a sapling as her bowels finished moving. She knelt in the moss and used handfuls of it to clean herself. "Am I going to make it, God?" She pulled up her pants with renewed determination. "I guess I didn't cook those cattail roots long enough. Thanks for the warning, Bidah. No constipation on this trip."

She picked up her pole and cast into the bay. She started systematically casting into the left side of the bay, moving about ten degrees with each subsequent cast. By the time she was casting along the right-hand shore, she got a bite. The line whizzed back and forth. Hunger-induced desperation required that she land this fish. It was lively, but when she finally plopped it on the rock beside her, she was disappointed. It was a perch. Although fairly large for a perch, it was too small to quell her hunger much. She hoped it would stop her diarrhea. She thought about how much fish she had left on her plate at Marten's house. *I'd love to have that back,* she thought, but it did remind her that she could boil the fish, head and all. She made a dozen more casts into the bay but did not even get a snag.

She ran back to where her canoe lay like a lame duck in the moss. The wind was so strong that the whitecaps were splashing her ten feet back from the shore. She moved the canoe farther into the brush. She found a sheltered place and used another match to start a small fire. Two left. She scaled and gutted her perch. It was a female full of roe. She cradled it into her pot and inspected the liver. It had no spots, so put it in her pot as well. She skinned the fillets and added them, covered everything with water, and set it on the fire to boil. The smell was overwhelming. She started salivating uncontrollably. On a hump of moss a few yards up the portage and out of the wind, she sat with her pot between her legs and ate everything but the bones she had missed when flaying the fish. She even sucked the vertebrae dry. When there was nothing left, she looked at the water she had boiled the fish in and drank it. She poured more water in the pot to wash it, and after scrubbing the scum along the inside of the pot with her fingers, she drank that too.

Now there was nothing to do but wait. She sat with her empty pot between her legs and watched the sun, wind, and waves. As the sun dipped into the horizon, the wind quelled. "It's magic. Time to go. This is what I have been waiting for all day." Canoe loaded, she was on the water within minutes.

A check of her compass and she was paddling with a quick, consistent stroke. She made it to the next portage before it was completely dark. She was euphoric with her progress and planned another night of paddling to arrive at the boat landing by noon the next day when Troy was supposed to meet her. Another compass setting and she was off. This was a large lake with a multitude of bays and islands to confuse her. But when she got to the next portage, it would be only a couple of hours to the landing. For the first time since the bear attack she felt confident that she would finish the trip. She smiled. *And see Troy.*

It was after midnight when she heard a strange roaring sound. At first she was uncertain as to what it was. Twenty minutes later she knew. She secured her life jacket, tightening the straps. The drizzle that she had tolerated all day had become a torrent. A wall of rain advanced toward her. She flattened onto the bottom of the canoe, crawling forward to her pack. She was a long ways from shore, so tipping would be fatal. Grabbing her pack, she pulled out her raincoat. *Now to test that boiled pitch.* She just managed the sleeves and popped over the hood when the rain hit. It roared like a typhoon. At least there was no wind, but the drops were so big and hitting so hard that they stung when they hit her hands. She wondered if it was hail, but it was too dark to tell. Besides, she saw nothing but water accumulating in the canoe. The water surface piqued like spiked hair. Lightning lit up the sky in every direction.

Maybe I shouldn't be on the water during a lightning storm, but should I hide under a tree? She kept paddling, thankful to be able to periodically see where she was going. All night she paddled in the rain. Twice, when she neared an island, she stopped, turned the canoe over, and emptied out the water. She tried to bail while she paddled, but it was too difficult and wasted her energy.

Theoretically, the pine pitch was effective. It kept the torn flaps of her raincoat in place, but within an hour she was soaking wet. She worried about her sleeping bag but convinced herself not to worry. "If I paddle all the way, I won't need it." It was about four in the morning when the intensity of the rain diminished. The lightning was farther away and the thunder more distant, so she took a deep breath of relief. It was still raining, and she was soaked, but at least the canoe was not filling up with water. Vigorous paddling kept her warm, but it used up a lot of energy. She felt famished.

As sunrise changed the sky from black to scarlet, she saw the portage trail at the end of the lake. "I'm almost there. I can make it."

Her arm muscles screamed as she paddled toward the portage. But her emotional adrenaline dissipated as the calories from her perch soup ran out. A hundred yards from the landing, the wind returned. In a last furious fight with the wind, she landed the canoe at the portage. She knew it would be a maelstrom on the other side. Her pickup was in six hours.

She got out of the canoe, loaded her pack, and flipped the canoe on her shoulders. "Might as well cross the portage. I can't conquer this wind worrying about it," she said, but her voice was lost in the roar of the wind. The portage was 180 rods, but she relished stretching her legs. All along the way she noticed summer flowers blooming among the trees.

The scent of humus, things rotting and flora growing, was intoxicating. Branches hung over the trail, scratching the canoe like an orchestra maestro tuning his violin section. She paused to hoist up her pants. They'd gotten pretty loose. But this was the last stage. "Onward to the landing," she whispered, "I can make it."

"I can't make it," she yelled as she set down her canoe. Immense whitecaps beat the shore and destroyed her hopes of getting to the landing. The defiant spray splashed her face. On the far horizon she saw the channel that led to the boat landing. "So close."

She put her packs in the stern, knowing she would have to paddle from the bow. The wind was too strong to maintain control, even from the middle of the canoe. Too wet and tired to care, she walked the canoe into the water and climbed in. The wind immediately shoved the canoe back, and the stern hit a rock, but with a few deft strokes she was away from the shore. It took constant vigilance to make progress and keep from tipping over as the waves slammed the canoe with incessant regularity. After about an hour she looked behind her. She was making minimal progress. A gust swung her to the side, and she quickly corrected. She almost flipped. "No time to look back. Keep going."

The rain came in curtains blowing across the water. She flinched as each rain front pelted her. Every time the canoe was lifted up by a large wave that crested the gunnels, she checked behind her. The canoe was filling with water. There was no island or peninsula in sight where she could bail out. She was in a race with a canoe that was filling fast.

A sudden jarring and scrapping sound told her she was grounded. "In the middle of the lake?" she yelled. The waves splashed, but the canoe didn't budge. She searched over the side. "God, how can I hit a rock in the middle of the lake?" she cursed, but too exhausted to continue the harangue, she hunched over. Her arms collapsed, sore and depleted. She felt like a rag doll abandoned in the corner of a closet. Her head too heavy to lift up, she buried her face in the cleft of the raincoat. She took slow, deep breaths. Her gut gnawed with hunger or diarrhea; she wasn't sure. The rock held firm.

A streak of sunshine escaped through the clouds, striking her back. She straightened her back in the solar warmth. As she contemplated her situation, she realized that the excess weight of the water in the canoe was the reason she hadn't skimmed over the rock that she hadn't seen below the turbulent surface. "What is this big rock doing here anyway?" Under normal circumstances she would have been enraged. She imagined a motorboat shearing its prop. But she closed her eyes. "Oh, God, I'm thankful for this rock."

She breathed several deep sighs as a new curtain of rain pelted her back. The wet sap was weakening its hold on the ripped part of her raincoat. Everything was wet. She was wet, cold, and tired. Her shoulder muscles screamed. She focused on relaxing, muscle by muscle, till an infinitesimal portion of her strength returned.

She looked ahead and behind. She had made such little progress. The opening to the bay seemed as far away as when she'd started. But she was gratified that the portage was at least blurred in the distance. She was at best halfway, and Troy was scheduled to pick her up soon. She looked at her watch. "About now."

"Time to push on." She secured her paddle in the bottom of the canoe and stepped out of the canoe onto the rock. It was slippery, but she found a crag and secured her right foot. The wind tried to knock her off. She knew it was risky, but hand over hand she pulled the canoe to the stern and slipped on her backpack, always keeping a secure hand on the canoe. She flipped the canoe side to side in a rocking motion until it was almost empty. She laughed in spite of her fatigue to think how ridiculous it must look to be standing in the middle of the lake with a pack on her back beside her canoe. She paused. For a moment the rain had let up, and the wind wasn't gusting. But she had to be very careful to align the canoe into the wind so it wouldn't blow off course.

"Enough of this," she said as she flipped her soaking pack in the stern and cautiously climbed back in the bow to resume paddling. She was free and at the mercy of the tyrannical wind. She lost fifty yards of progress. "But I'll get it back," she yelled, frantic to regain the lost distance and then settle down to a pace she could maintain.

Several grueling hours later, she turned into the protected bay of the landing. At last, out of the wind. She paddled another forty minutes, but without wind it seemed easy. There was no one to pick her up at the landing. She expected as much. She was hours late. She couldn't expect Troy to wait that long for her to show up. But her disappointment wasn't logical, and she burst into tears. She shivered and shook from the beginning stages of hypothermia. With her last molecules of energy she limped to shore. Solid ground felt good, but she felt dizzy, the wave motion still stimulating her brain. She dragged the canoe out of the water and turned it over and looked around the parking lot. No one was there. A few locked cars gave no sanctuary. She walked back to her canoe, pulled her wet sleeping bag out of her pack and rolled it out under the overturned canoe. She took off her boots and crawled inside. It was still raining. She stopped shaking with chills, and the incessant rhythm of the rain lulled her into tranquility.

"I made it," she whispered.

. . .

"But, Mommy, I'm hungry."

"Lisa, you did not eat your salad, so you can't have dessert."

"But I ate my hamburger. I ate it all up."

"Quit whining, I hate it when you whine. You are not getting dessert no matter how much you beg. Now go to your room."

"But I'm hungry." Tears dribbled down her soft, chubby cheeks.

"You weren't hungry enough to eat your salad, so you must not be all that hungry. Now you will just have to wait till morning. Go to your room now before I give you a swat. Then you will have a good reason for those tears."

CHAPTER 18

Light danced across Lisa's eyelids, awakening her. She felt so warm and cozy that she didn't want to open her eyes. But she did. Canoe pictures were on the wall in front of her. She scanned the room and closed her eyes. *It must be a dream. I'm in heaven.* She reviewed the pictures in her mind. No recognition. She opened her eyes again and saw a fly-fishing rod with a collection of flies in a display case mounted below it. One corner of the room held a bookcase with a jumble of hardback books wedged on the shelf with a few paperbacks. The other wall held a bearskin that appeared soft and silky. There were two doors, one directly in front of the bed and another off to her left that was open. Rising up on her elbow, she could see that it was a bathroom.

Where am I? Did I die? If this is heaven, you should know, God, that I never went fly-fishing. She spotted a pair of men's coveralls hanging on a hook. "Not mine, I must be alive," she said to hear her voice. "But where am I?"

The strange environment heightened her awareness. She was too warm. Two heavy blankets were on top of her. She threw the top one off to the side, then ran her hands under the remaining blanket. "You're topless, girl," she told herself. She ran her hands down her sides and to her groin. "And there is nothing on your bottom either." She held up the blanket and looked. "Bare as the day you were born, but you still have all your parts and pieces, thank God. A little dirty, though, it appears."

I know I've never been here before, but this is definitely a man's room, and I am naked in his bed. Visions of Bob's face, the gun against her breast, and the car engulfed in flames raced through her mind. *Oh, God, I can't remember anything. What happened?*

She scanned the room again. For the first time in her life she felt self-conscious being naked. *What happened? Why don't I have clothes on? Where are my clothes?* Nothing in the room gave her the slightest clue. She scanned the pictures on the wall, the pine dresser in the corner, the light fixtures. Nothing was familiar.

A sharp tap on the door startled her.

"Yes, who is it?" She hid under the blanket, keeping only her eyes over the covers.

"Lisa, here are your clean clothes." The door opened a crack, and a hand appeared, placing clean clothes on the chair beside the door. "There's a shower in the bathroom to your left. Breakfast will be ready as soon as you come downstairs."

"Is that you, Troy?"

"Yes." There was silence. The door stayed open just a crack.

"How did I get here? What happened?"

"I will explain it all at breakfast."

She picked up the blanket and scanned her naked torso. "Did you take me clothes off?"

"Yes, I did, but—"

Clutching the blankets tighter around her naked body, she asked, "Troy, did you fuck me?"

She could hear him bang his head gently on the door. "No," he said, "I work as an orderly at the emergency department at the hospital in the winter. I know how to undress people without exposing them. Your clothes were all wet, and you were hypothermic. I had to take your clothes off to warm you up. I assure you: your modesty was preserved. Besides, I slept in the other bedroom."

She looked at the pillow next to her to see if it had been used. It hadn't. She looked under the blanket. The sheets beside her were crisp. It didn't look as if anyone else had been in the bed with her.

179

"I apologize for being vulgar, but it's just shocking to wake up in someone's bed with no clothes on and not even remember how I got here. And I was sober." She paused and then blurted, "Why didn't you take me to the doctor?"

"The nearest one is a hundred and fifty kilometers away. Besides, I took your temperature, and you were not in severe danger."

"Rectally? I know you orderlies do that."

Troy laughed. "No, orally. Now take a hot shower, get dressed so you don't feel self-conscious, and come down for breakfast. There is plenty of soap in the bathroom. I'm sorry if it is not your preferred shampoo, but it works. See you soon. I'm going down to get breakfast ready. How long will it take you?"

"I'm pretty dirty, probably twenty minutes."

"All right. See you in twenty minutes."

"Troy?"

"Yes?"

"Make a big breakfast. I'm very hungry."

"As you wish, miss."

"Cut the formal stuff, Troy."

Lisa climbed out of bed. Every muscle and joint hurt. No longer conscious of her nakedness, she looked out the picture window to reorient where she was. There was an unobstructed view across a small lake. No cabins, just wilderness. The water was still, not a ripple of a wave. *Maybe I should've waited a day.*

She turned and looked at her legs and feet. Dried mud streaked down her thighs, and her feet were black between the toes. Crusted dirt creased her belly and under her breasts. She headed for the shower. The bathroom smelled of men's musk aftershave. The scent caused her to picture Troy stepping out of the shower. She could see his towel slipping off his waist as he shaved and then splashed the lotion on his face. *Ridiculous,* she thought. *Why am I thinking like this? I'm tired and dirty. My emotions are whipped. How stupid.*

She climbed into the shower. Seldom had hot water been more appreciated. She giggled as the scouring torrent coursed across her flesh, dilating her capillaries. Euphoria swelled her brain. Safety, peace, warmth, and contentment rose from deep within her spirit. She felt as if she would explode and scream for joy. Soap was such a neat invention. She laughed as bubbles foamed across her breasts, and she blew them onto her belly. Her matted pubic hair curled and frizzed as she rinsed off the soap. The effluent streaming down her legs was black with the mud of portages and swamps. She rinsed, then soaped all over again until she was warm and clean. She ducked under the showerhead and closed her eyes, imagining a waterfall cascading over her body. She wanted to stay forever. She shampooed twice just for the thrill of the smell and the sensation of hot water on her scalp. Hunger brought her back to reality.

Stepping out of the shower, she found the mirror too fogged to see how she looked. The towels were on a heater rack and felt glorious as she enveloped her clean torso. She opened the bathroom door and steam poured out into the bedroom. She unwrapped her towel and laid it on the bed. She flopped, spread eagle, on top of the quilt to air-dry. She felt alive.

The ceiling was beamed with cedar. Her eyes followed the intricate grain across the wood. As the warm bedroom air-dried her skin, her mind wandered. She had canoed against whitecaps and survived. Now, she was very hungry. She jumped up as a faint smell of something frying wafted under the door.

Her eye caught the clean folded clothes on the chair. Unsure at first that they were hers, she unfolded each item and placed it on the bed. *Yep, these are mine. I wonder if I should be embarrassed that a guy washed my panties. I guess if he is the same guy who strips you naked and then claims he didn't take advantage of you, it's all right. Too bad I didn't bring a bra for him to wash.* She giggled as she slipped into her clothes. It felt good to be dressed. She went back in the bathroom to see if the mirror had cleared. The steam had dissipated. A crystalline reflection looked back at her. She thought her breasts were a little too prominent. She cupped her hands over her nipples to soften them and then tucked her shirt into her jeans. "I don't think I should let this happen too often. He might lose his orderly professionalism," she said to her reflection.

When she opened the door to the rest of the house, it seemed as if she'd entered a house in the Parade of Homes. Pictures of birds, moose, and bears graced the gallery along the hall. She paused on the balcony overlooking the living room. The sun sparkled through the two-story picture windows, highlighting the rustic furniture below. Out the window she scanned the majesty of the lake she had seen from the bedroom. Now it was drenched in wisps of fog exuding through the trees. She walked as quietly as a thief, relishing the treasures of the owner. Her bare toes touched the smoothness of the oak stairs. There was not so much as a creak as she edged down the steps. At the bottom, she followed her nose to the kitchen.

"I didn't know you could cook," she said.

Troy lurched with a large frying pan, spattering some grease on his hand. "I didn't hear you come down. You startled me. Welcome to my home away from home."

"I didn't know canoe outfitters lived in such luxury."

Troy smiled. "This is Roger Leland's house. He is a friend of Ernie's. Roger asked Ernie to watch the house for him. Poor guy broke his hip and ended up in the hospital, then was sent to a skilled nursing facility for rehabilitation. So I got the assignment to house-sit." He took a spatula and flipped his creation, added grated cheese, and folded it onto a plate. "Have a seat; your breakfast is ready."

Lisa sat down at the maple kitchen table. It had two hard wooden chairs, one on each corner. The table was set with forks, cloth napkins, and orange juice in crystal glasses. A small plate had three triangular-cut pieces of toast. She sat down feeling the comfort and support of the chair against her back. She wiggled, massaging her sore paraspinal muscles against the rungs of the chair. He served her omelet, turned slightly on the edges so that it was like a large, yellow smile. Two sausage rounds served as eyes, and a sprig of parsley set across the omelet for a nose.

"Go ahead," he said. "Eat. Don't wait for me. I know you're hungry."

"Yes, captain, at your command, sir." She dug into the egg and cheese with her fork. She snitched his fork, stabbed her sausage, and ate bites between mouthfuls of omelet. "You'll need another fork for yourself. I'm using yours," she managed between gulps of food. "Is there any coffee coming?"

Troy smiled at her two-fisted approach to her food as he served her steaming coffee. "Cream? Sugar?"

"Yes."

He placed a large pitcher of cream and a bowl of sugar with a tablespoon at her disposal. Returning to the stove, he made himself an omelet and sat down beside her. His upturned lips suggested that he was hiding something. Was he laughing at her unladylike approach to her food? His breakfast was barely half eaten by the time she took a piece of toast and wiped her plate clean of the melted cheese that had escaped her fork.

"Quite a trip, eh?" he said.

"Ernie sent me into the waterfall country. It was just majestic. I loved it." She relived her excitement as she related her experiences on the trip.

When she paused to take a deep breath, he asked, "So when did the bear take your food?"

"You're amazing, Troy. For someone who strips a girl naked, washes her panties, and then claims he didn't take advantage of her, you ask real personal questions." She glared at him till he lowered his eyes, and then she started to giggle. "I was two or three days' paddle from the landing—where there was no one to pick me up—Mr. Bear ate all my jerky, sugar, and candy bars and scattered everything else across a clearing the size of a basketball court."

"And ripped your pack and raincoat," he added and took a bite of toast. He laughed. "I assume you did not have the raincoat on at the time?"

"Did you see any slashes across my back when you weren't taking advantage of me?" She gulped down her orange juice and sipped her coffee that was half cream and sugar. His mouth was full of omelet. He didn't answer. She said, "No, I was quietly sleeping in my sleeping bag when the marauder struck. There were no big trees to hang my pack in as it was an old burned area with only scrubby birch and poplar new growth, so I put my food pack under the canoe. The bear grabbed my pack, tipping over the canoe. I jumped out of my bag and chased it down the trail yelling and screaming, but it wouldn't drop my pack. I guess I wasn't scary enough."

"So in the middle of the night you were running in your pajamas or whatever chasing a bear?"

"If you must know, I usually sleep in the nude."

"So you were running naked through the woods chasing a bear who stole your food pack. Do I have that right?"

"Yes." Lisa thought, *Should this young, virile male be hearing this? I wasn't going to even tell my parents. She sensed his mind was spinning the image of her words.*

He placed his index finger over his lips, securing them till he swallowed and thought through what he should say. She watched his gaze leave the ceiling and rivet on her feminine physique and then her eyes. She could tell that there were more questions he wanted to ask. *What will he allow himself to ask? Does he regret being so modest in his care?*

"What did you eat the last three days?"

She recounted the muddy details of collecting cattail and arrow plant roots. She described how she'd scraped and cooked them. She told him about finding the crayfish and serving them with the sauce mix that had not interested the bear. When she told about the perch, she exaggerated its size to prevent him from being too impressed with how starved she had been when he'd found her. She did enjoy how he gagged when she described how she'd cleaned every morsel of meat off the head and ate the roe and liver.

"All this talk about food is making me hungry," she said. "Are there any more omelets where that first one came from?"

He stood. "I'll make you another omelet if …"

Lisa fantasized. *What could possibly be his condition? I don't even know where the nearest road is if I need to escape. Talk about having a woman at a disadvantage.*

He continued, "If you tell me how you paddled against that wind. By the way, Ernie was there to pick you up. He waited an hour but decided you must have bunkered down in that terrible wind and left. Don't expect an apology from him. He hasn't apologized in thirty years to anyone, even his wife."

He went to the stove and cracked three eggs into a bowl and lit the gas under the skillet.

Lisa got up and stood by his side. "How many eggs were in that first one?"

"Four. Should I add another?"

"No. You mean I just ate a four-egg omelet, and now I'm having another?"

"That perch must have been pretty small, eh?"

For some reason she put her arm around his waist, hugged him, and laid her head on his shoulder. She felt her breast nudge his arm. "Barely a fingerling," she said. "Could a hungry young woman like me have another couple of sausages too?"

He tossed two sausages into the pan. She watched them closely as they cooked, hugging him close to her without obstructing his activity. When the sausages were flipped and cooked on both sides, he set them to the side and added the egg mixture. It bubbled in the grease all around the edges like the scallop of a lace doily. She hid behind him as the grease spattered.

He added grated cheese. "Sit down now. It's done."

She sat back in her chair as he served her another happy-faced omelet. He sat in his chair and sipped his coffee. She slid the second fork near his plate and ate with much improved table manners. She smiled at him as she chewed her food slowly, speaking only when her mouth was empty and setting down her fork between mouthfuls. She even used the napkin to wipe her lips.

"You have a promise to keep," he said.

"Oh, yes." She swallowed. "How I paddled against the wind. Those waves were pretty crazy. I paddled from the bow. It was like a roller coaster. Those Kevlar canoes have no keels, so you have to pull them into the wind. I was getting so exhausted, and there was no shoreline to cling to. You know that lake. Worst thing was the canoe was filling with water because it was raining so hard. Then I suddenly hung up on a rock." She grabbed another forkful of egg and half a sausage and chewed carefully, enjoying the anticipation she was building. He appeared anxious for her to continue.

"In the middle of that bay?" he asked.

"Right in the middle."

"What did you do?"

"Actually it was a lifesaver. It was raining so hard I had almost a foot of water in the canoe. My pack was floating inside. Anyway, I hit that rock so hard I was stuck. But I was stuck so well the wind didn't push me off, and it gave me a chance to rest. I have never been thankful for hitting a rock with my canoe before, but I was sure thankful for that one. I rested my muscles, caught my breath."

"How did you get off it?"

She grabbed another forkful, chewing slowly. She was becoming satiated. "When I was ready to go again, I climbed out onto the rock, flipped the pack on my back, and emptied the canoe by sloshing it out. You know the technique?" He nodded. "Without water in it I was free. I loaded back up and paddled to the landing."

"I'm sure there was more to it than 'paddling to the landing.' I am very impressed. You are one amazing woman." He stood. "But you must have looked pretty comical standing in the middle of the lake with a pack on your shoulders beside a canoe."

"Just laugh," she said as she swallowed the last of her eggs and stood as well. She grabbed him and hugged him. "Thank you for saving me."

He hugged her and then held her away with her shoulders in his strong hands. "Never have I met a woman that I respected so much." He glanced at his watch. "I got a pickup this morning. There's a group coming that didn't arrive yesterday because of the weather. Do you want to come to the outfitter office with me, or do you want to rest here for a while longer?"

"I could freshen up, and when you return, we could ..." She gave him a slow, writhing smile. *Why am I acting this way? What is wrong with me?*

He smiled and shook his head. "I think you'd better come with me. You didn't want me taking advantage of you, remember? I have the rest of your stuff already in the truck."

He turned and headed for the door. Without even looking back, he called, "Come on; I can't be late. This group is likely to be pretty exhausted. I don't want to make them wait."

They drove to the outfitter office and walked in the back room. Ernie was drinking his morning coffee. He was about to say something to Troy when he saw Lisa. "So then, the Lisa Zuccerelli pickup is completed."

Helga rushed to her side. "My dear, are you hungry? I can fix something for you. We are so glad to see you. We were worried when Ernie didn't find you at the landing. Of course, he'll never tell you that."

"Thanks, Helga, but I'm fine. I just had an omelet and toast before we came."

Troy looked at her. "She ate seven eggs with cheese and four sausages, Helga. Don't let her fool you."

"And toast and orange juice. Oh, and coffee, as long as we're being completely honest," Lisa said.

Helga held her sides. "My land, doesn't canoeing make a girl hungry?"

"You've got that ten o'clock pickup at Sandstone landing, right, Troy?" Ernie returned to business.

"I've got it, Mr. Svenson. I'm leaving right now."

"I'm leaving with him, if that's all right with you?" Lisa added.

"It's always good to have someone riding shotgun," Ernie said.

They rushed out the door together. Lisa jumped in the passenger's seat. As Troy started the van, she said, "Did you know I'm going to be a published author?"

"Really?"

"Yes, I spent a week on the Anishinaabe reservation interviewing a fourth-level Midewiwin healer. My friend Heidi and I wrote up our research for our anthropology class paper, and our professor submitted it for publication to the American Anthropological Society. It's going to be in the November issue. How about that?"

"What did you put in the article? It sounds intriguing."

She related the story of her week with Bidah and Marten, including a detailed description of the fish guts all over her clothes. Troy seemed enchanted by the story. He screeched the brakes to bring the van to a stop and watched the empty trailer in his side mirror to make sure it didn't jackknife. "You're a great storyteller," he said. "But I almost missed my turn. Fortunately, no one's behind me." He backed up a trailer length and made an acute turn onto the dirt road leading to the landing.

They were both silent as he maneuvered the corner and started down the dirt road, tempering his speed so the trailer wouldn't bounce. He seemed focused on the road. It had several large potholes that he eased the trailer through, as the road was so narrow he couldn't avoid them.

"Do you really work as an orderly in the emergency department during the school year?"

He squeezed the brakes to slow the trailer through a muddy spot. "Yes, St. Mary's Hospital in Madison. We see almost thirty thousand patients a year." Out of the mud, he sped up and looked at her. "Why?"

"I thought you just made that part up as an excuse to take off my clothes."

"Lisa." He sounded disgusted.

"I'm sorry; just checking."

He related how emotional he felt about some of the patients. "One young couple had just married. They were driving to their honeymoon, a lodge on a lake near Madison, when a drunk driver plowed into them. She was still alive, but he was dead on arrival. We worked so hard on her, trying to keep her alive, but there was just too much trauma. She died in my arms. I felt so helpless."

"I'm sorry." Lisa became silent, sorry that her coquettish question had provoked such sad memories.

They drove into the landing parking lot, and the group was standing there waiting. Lisa jumped out of the van as Troy came to a stop near the group. He shook their hands and welcomed them back to civilization. "Did you wait long?" he asked.

"No, we just finished hauling our packs up the hill. Boy, everything is soaking wet."

Troy discussed the group's adventures with them while Lisa grabbed the canoes and loaded them on the trailer. She then threw their packs into the back of the van and collected and loaded the paddles before she turned to look at the group. They were a grubby, smoky-smelling group of college students, four guys and two girls. They seemed quite relieved as they climbed into the back of the van. Lisa returned to her privileged spot.

"The waves were so high we just could not paddle against them," the leader said. "Besides," he whispered, "we had the girls."

Lisa said, "I'm a girl; I made it."

"Yes," Troy responded to the leader, "I understand it was really rough out there yesterday." He gave Lisa a quick poke in the ribs.

"I'm glad we had that arrangement that if we weren't here on time we would come in the next day at the same time. It worked out well. We had plenty of extra food."

The van engine roared as Troy lowered the gear to make it up a muddy incline. Lisa glared. "Extra food? What's that?" she muttered. No one but Troy heard her.

Once out on the highway, Troy sped up, watching to see that the trailer was tracking well and that the canoes were secure. She remained silent, periodically grinning at Troy over the conversation in the back of the van.

"My raincoat barely kept me dry; it was raining so hard. It came down in buckets. We even had hail," one of the guys said.

"We ate all our extra candy bars," explained one of the girls. Lisa smiled at the comment.

"Those whitecaps were sort of fun," said the other girl, "but we went backward as fast as I paddled. The wind was so strong."

"Well, you paddle like a woman," said one of the guys.

The girl kicked the speaker. "At least I don't zigzag all over the lake. And who caught the biggest fish, huh?"

"Caught a dozen nice walleyes at the narrows," the leader said to Troy. "Good fishing there, but we had to be patient. Pink jigs seemed to be their favorite."

"Carrie caught a nice walleye on a daredevil," said the other girl.

"That waterfall at Church Creek was beautiful," said the leader.

"But too cold for swimming," said Carrie.

"All you had on was that tiny bikini," the leader said.

"I didn't see you swimming, macho man. Besides, I thought you liked my tiny bikini."

When they arrived back at the outfitter, Lisa offered to put the canoes away while Troy settled the account. As he and the leader headed to the office, she overheard, "Cute assistant you got working for you. I haven't seen her before."

"Oh, she's a veteran, tough as bear, rugged as any man. She came in yesterday, alone," Troy said. "And she swam every day."

Canoes stacked, Lisa emptied the trash from the packs and stacked them neatly on the floor in the front office area. As the group turned to leave, the leader shook hands with Troy. "Good trip. See you next year."

One of the college guys looked at Lisa. "You want to guide us next year?" His girlfriend kicked him in the shin.

Troy laughed, waving them good-bye. He pulled out a drawer and picked out a set of keys, handing them to Lisa.

"Your Jeep is in the back."

She took the keys, then looked back with satisfaction to see him following her all the way to her vehicle.

He grabbed her arm gently and turned her around. "Do you understand now why I am so impressed with you? I have never met anyone so resilient and tenacious." They stood at her open Jeep door. He stared at her. No one moved. Then he asked, "Were you trying to seduce me this morning?"

Lisa hung her head, her tan face flushed. "That was inappropriate. I'm sorry. It's just that I was so hungry, and the food was so good, and, well, I woke up in a strange bed, and ..."

Troy spoke in hushed tones as if someone could overhear him. "I'll admit I was flattered."

She stammered, "I have never met a guy quite like you either. I want to ..." She gazed at the ground, not knowing how to finish her sentence.

He touched her cheeks with his hands. His hands were rough from exposure but so was her face. To her the caress felt as soft as baby skin. He held her face, forcing her to look him in the eyes. "Let's just take things one step at a time. We need to enjoy getting to know each other more first." He paused. Her face was trembling slightly. "You are so special, Lisa. I'll commit to you. I know that's hard when we are in two different states and universities, but I'll be faithful to you until you decide you don't want me. Does that take the pressure off?"

"Thanks. I promise not to try that again. Does your promise mean we're engaged?"

"Lisa."

"I'm sorry. I knew better. This is all so new. I—"

He kissed her, interrupting her sentence. Then he said, "Sort of, I guess. But I don't have a ring on me."

She laughed and hugged him, feeling his masculinity firm against her. She felt faint.

"I'll see you soon," he said, pushing her away, "maybe at Christmastime. I got some rough classes this next year. I'm not good at ... Well, you'd better get going."

She reached into the Jeep and pulled out one of her father's business cards. With a few brisk strokes she wrote her address and telephone number on the back and handed it to him. "This is an unlisted private number on the back. Don't give it out to anyone." She jumped behind the wheel. She couldn't say any more. Her throat was too choked up.

He gave her one last peck on the lips. "I really like you, Lisa Zuccerelli," he said, reading her last name from the Zuc Industries business card. He closed her car door. "Maybe I will stop and see you before classes start, unless Ernie keeps me busy." He handed Ernie's card to her from his shirt pocket. "We do have mail service up here. It's slow, but it works. My apartment address and telephone number in Madison are on the back. Write or call me."

"Why didn't you write me before? Besides those postcards?"

"I'm sorry. I'm focused when I am at the university. The classes are demanding and ..."

"Excuses?" she said.

"Yeah, sorry."

Her palms were sweating. She put the card in her shirt pocket and started the engine. As she backed up the Jeep, she waved to him. "I'll write or call," she said. As she drove toward the rural road, she added, "But I can't spell." She knew that he couldn't hear her.

She drove out the driveway and turned onto the tarmac. She managed to drive ten miles south before her eyes welled with tears. She couldn't see the road through the blur, so she pulled over onto the shoulder and stopped the Jeep. She bawled until the tears dried up and her vision cleared. Finished, she noticed tears and drool dripping down the front of her blouse. It made her laugh. "You slob, Lisa." She started the Jeep again and drove home.

CHAPTER 19

Lisa was sitting in Coach Hammond's office for her adviser meeting. Her muscles felt strong, and she was ready for basketball and soccer practice. She did not feel too ready for academic classes.

"I've outlined what classes I think you should take this semester and next," said Coach Hammond. She pushed a legal pad across the desk to Lisa. The courses were written in neat rows with the two semesters outlined.

"Do I have to take this biology class? Yuck, it will kill me. When do I have to do that? I will never be able to take all these classes." Lisa slapped the legal pad on her knee. "I hate school."

"You did well last year. I thought you enjoyed it."

"I did; you're right. But look." She held up the legal pad. "These classes are even harder."

Coach laughed. "The biology class is a prerequisite for the physiology class you need in your senior year for a coaching certificate, but I suppose you could wait until next year."

"I'll be more mature next year; let's wait."

"Don't put it off too long. Someone who hates school should plan to graduate in four years, not five. Reconsider. Take it this semester?"

"I need more success first. Couldn't I substitute a math class?"

"This isn't a restaurant. You have to take what's required."

Lisa squealed in frustration. "I know. I just did so poorly in biology in high school. You have to memorize bones and nerves, stuff like that. I dread it. Next to spelling, memorizing is my worst."

She saw Coach's expression and changed her tone. "Thanks for setting this up. I'll register for these courses as you've outlined them, but may I save that biology class until next semester? I can't handle it right now." She stood to leave. "I don't want too heavy of a schedule so that it interferes with basketball. I'm still on the team, aren't I?"

"Yes," Coach Hammond said, shaking her head. "I've watched you practice. I plan to use you as our three-point specialist this year. That's an honor for a sophomore, you know."

"So I won't even make second string? I'm a good guard on defense. Is this a downgrade?"

"You know I have lots of juniors and even two seniors who are good guards. You'll get your chance; be patient. Did you hear what I said?"

"You're honoring me with the three-point-specialist position. I heard it."

Coach Hammond walked around her desk and put her arm around Lisa. "Hang in there, kid; you'll get your chance. This is an important position for our team, not a downgrade."

Lisa looked behind her to make sure the office door was shut. "You've done so much for me, Amanda. I really am appreciative. I'm sorry for being immature and impatient. I'll practice hard and be ready when you need me. But what if I never make it to my junior year? This has been rough. I still hate school."

"I'm counting on you." She released Lisa's shoulder and returned to her desk chair. "Now go. Your sophomore year is starting. You'll make it. Soon you will be a junior. You'll surprise yourself. I prefer you take that biology class this semester."

"Yes, Coach."

"Shut the door gently. Don't take out your feelings on my door."

"Yes, my favorite coach, Amanda, professor, madam." Coach gave her a look of mock disdain.

She shut the door with feigned care and then screamed, "No more English classes!" She paused. *Now to conquer biology. Heidi is a science major, so maybe she can tutor me through the class.*

Psychology was a prerequisite for coaching. Lisa found it concrete and enjoyed it. The tests were easy. Besides, it explained a lot of her mother's weird behavior. Just knowing how her mother was trying to manipulate her made her willing to respond in a positive manner. During one of their spats, Lisa thought, *She is using the sandwich technique on me. Say something nice and then criticize me and follow it with something else real nice,* and responded without animosity. It quelled the situation. *That was sort of neat,* she thought as she walked away.

Lisa avoided dating. The experience with Bob and Jake was still fresh in her mind. Several young men did ask her out, which made her feel that she was still desirable, but she turned them down.

Dr. Johnson had made it very clear that Lisa had to have Pap smears every three months for a year. It had something to do with some abnormal cells scraped off her cervix. The first pelvic exam three months after her hospitalization had not been very pleasant, but at least Dr. Johnson had been gentle. Lisa knew the routine for the fall checkup and wasn't so anxious, but she still anticipated the humiliation of that plastic thing, that speculum, shoved up her vagina. *It's the punishment for all the guys you had sex with,* she told herself. *Now that isn't logical. Mother has Pap smears too.* But Lisa couldn't get the connection out of her head.

The night before her fall checkup, Lisa had a nightmare about Bob cutting her chest open with his box cutter. She awoke gasping, drenched in sweat. The next day she met Heidi in the hall. She pulled her aside to one of the study rooms in student commons.

"Two things, Heidi. Would you be willing to tutor me through biology? I have to take the class for my major. I'll be glad to pay you. Please?"

Heidi laughed. "No problem, I would love to. My needs are met; I don't need your money. And the second thing?"

Lisa looked around to make sure no one could hear them. "I need more healing. I had a horrible nightmare last night, and I have to have another pelvic exam this afternoon," she whispered.

Heidi put her arms around Lisa and sang a song in her ear. It was all in Anishinaabe. Then she said, "Now the nightmares will stop."

"How do you do that?" Lisa felt released. She remembered how Heidi had accompanied her to the first pelvic exam. She'd felt so threatened.

After she had undressed and put on her exam gown, Heidi had sung to her while they'd waited for the physician to return. Even introducing the dreaded plastic speculum and all the culture probes hadn't upset her at all as Heidi had held her hand.

"I'll come with you if you want, but I do have physical chemistry this afternoon."

"No, I'm all right now. I know what to expect. But what about tutoring?"

Heidi said, "Bring your biology book to my dorm room tomorrow. We'll go through it. Bring your syllabus so we can set up a schedule."

. . .

That afternoon in the physicians' waiting room, Lisa sat prim and proper, mentally avoiding the image of an execution. She was dressed in a loose, short jean skirt, cotton underwear, and a dark-green T-shirt with a quick-to-remove bra in anticipation of the examination of her breasts, heart, and lungs and the poking and prodding of her stomach to check her liver and spleen.

"Elizabeth Zuccerelli," the receptionist called.

Lisa dropped the waiting room copy of *Cosmopolitan* and went to the desk.

"I'm sorry, but Dr. Johnson is a bit behind. The patient before you had to be hospitalized. Would you like to wait or reschedule?"

"I'll wait. How long will it be?" *I'm all primed for this. I don't really want to come back,* she thought.

"About thirty minutes."

"Thanks for telling me. No problem. I'll wait. Oh, and just call me Lisa, please."

"I will. Thank you for your understanding."

When Lisa returned to her seat, she found another young woman was sitting in her place, so Lisa sat in the next seat and picked up her *Cosmo.* "Good afternoon," Lisa said in a mechanical way. The woman stood to shake her hand.

"I am quite fine. Thank you for asking so nicely." She had a strong Caribbean accent and was a hefty woman dressed in a colorful blouse and a black skirt with orange flowers. Dark complexioned, her bright-purple lipstick drew attention to her rounded face. Her black, curly hair was adorned with ribbons.

"Are you here to see Dr. Johnson?" Lisa asked.

"I am being Portia Bustamante. It is a pleasure for me to be meeting you. Dr. Johnson is not the name of my doctor. But I am not remembering his name."

Lisa stood to shake hands, and then they both sat down.

"I'm an artist," Portia said. "In my village in Jamaica I did a lot of painting, but my mother, she wants me to get a university degree. So I am here. I like it. I just wish this Minnesota place was not so cold all the time. And it is so far from the ocean, but I like the big Lake Superior. It is not warm like my ocean. The food at the cafeteria is being bad all the time."

"I agree with you about the food. Try Little Angie's. The owner sent his cooks to the Caribbean to learn some recipes. I think you might like it."

"I am very grateful to hear the name of that restaurant. I've been losing a lot of weight with cafeteria food."

Lisa thumbed through her *Cosmopolitan*. An article caught her eye, "Enjoy Being Naked."

Portia glanced over at what Lisa was reading. "And that's another thing," she said. "My professor Dr. Henderson is a great artist. She teaches us many good things, but she is having so many troubles finding models." She pointed at the page. "Maybe more people should read that article so we could have models for our class. In Jamaica we like our bodies. They are a gift from God. Don't people around here believe in God?"

Lisa laughed. "Do you think I would be a good model?"

"Oh, yes. You have a beautiful body. I would like to draw you."

"Tell me where to sign up."

"Lisa Zuccerelli," a nurse called, "Dr. Johnson is caught up, so she can see you now."

"My doctor is ready," Lisa said. "Nice to meet you, Portia."

Portia stood. "I am very happy meeting you, Lisa Zuccerelli. Just talk to Professor Henderson. I'll be drawing a great picture of you. I am making you a promise."

• • •

The idea of being a nude model sounded intriguing. *Look but don't touch*, Lisa thought of the male students who would be in the class. A week later, Lisa had an appointment with Dr. Henderson. Her office was in the art building, one of the oldest parts of the university. The neo-Gothic architecture on the outside was reflected by high ceilings, tall arched windows, and ornate moldings on the inside. Lisa walked into the art department secretary's office. "I have an appointment with Dr. Henderson. My name is Lisa Zuccerelli. She should be expecting me."

The secretary led her to an ornate office that would have been orderly if it hadn't been for paintings stacked along each available wall. Lisa had been expecting a bent, gnarled woman with oil paint in multiple colors on a smock. Dr. Henderson was the opposite. She was a tall, stately, elderly woman, immaculately dressed, who stood to greet Lisa. Her white hair added to her dignity.

She requested identification and then sat at her clean, organized desk. She motioned for Lisa to sit as well. She spoke with an Eastern European accent. "I am looking for a model for the human-figure drawing class that I can depend on for a group of classes. I have used an agency in the past, but I have to explain each time what I want them to do. If I had a model I could use consistently, I could focus on the needs of the students and not my model."

"I talked to Portia Bustamante."

"She is a fabulous artist. I am very privileged to be her instructor." Dr. Henderson's eyes were piercing. "From your CV I understand that you are a student here at the university, majoring in ..."

"Exercise physiology."

"Yes, I've reviewed your work history. And you're interested in canoeing?" She leafed through Lisa's form. "You have not done any exotic dancing or nude modeling in the past?"

"No."

"Fine. I have had some problems with models the agency sent who have been exotic dancers. They have the wrong idea." Dr. Henderson dropped Lisa's CV onto her desk. "You understand that this means *nude*." She emphasized the last word, peering over her glasses.

"I understand."

"Good. I'm glad to see you have an athletic background because you have to maintain a pose for the students for almost an hour. That requires a significant level of stamina and determination. You can't move."

She filed Lisa's application in her desk drawer. "Do you have a boyfriend?"

Lisa paused. "Sort of. He is a student at the University of Wisconsin."

"I apologize for asking, but we have had some boyfriend problems, even with the models from the agency." She seemed to be waiting for a response. Lisa said nothing. "So have you discussed this with him?"

"No. We aren't that close."

"So you don't think he would object?"

"No."

"And your parents?"

Lisa had no intention of letting her parents know about the modeling, and besides, she was almost twenty-one. What could they do? Kick her out of the house? Not likely. This was a university project, not a pornography thing. "No problem."

"You'll be comfortable nude in front of your classmates for two hours at a time? What if one of the students in the class is an acquaintance or a friend?"

Lisa thought about all the people she knew at the university. The girls on the basketball team had all seen her in the shower, and the boys she had dated had seen her body parts as well, unfortunately. She couldn't think of anyone she would feel shy about.

Dr. Henderson added, "I do recommend that you avoid dating anyone in the class. Now I am not able to enforce that recommendation, but you may find it a useful policy to avoid unwanted attention outside of class."

"I've quit the dating scene here at the university. I had a bad experience. And to answer your questions, I am comfortable in the nude, and no, there are no fellow students that would make me feel uncomfortable."

"I think you would be a good choice for my class. I will have you start next week then with some of my senior art students. It is a small class, and these students have all painted nudes in the past. If you are comfortable with them, we can advance to the larger, less-experienced classes." She stood and extended her hand.

Lisa stood and shook her hand. "Thank you for this opportunity."

"Oh, you are doing me a great service. I anticipate that you will be comfortable with this. I will have the contract drawn up, and you can come by tomorrow and sign it. That also gives you a day to think about it. Don't worry. I won't be disappointed if you choose not to do this. Not everyone feels comfortable being nude and having a class full of people scrutinizing their bodies."

They walked out of her office, Lisa leading the way. Dr. Henderson said, "Janice, run off a contract. Lisa Zuccerelli will come by tomorrow if she is still interested and sign it." She turned to Lisa. "I will have Janice write up a schedule so you know when the classes are. Sign up for as many as your schedule allows. Remember, I can still use the agency."

"Thank you for being so accommodating. I look forward to working with you."

Dr. Henderson turned to go back into her office and then stopped. "Oh, by the way, Portia is in that senior class. Will that be a problem?"

Lisa could feel the professor watching her face for a response. "I assumed she was after meeting her. It will not be a problem."

• • •

Lisa talked to Cheryl the next morning.

Cheryl asked, "How could you do that after what you have been through? Every guy in the class is going to be gawking at you."

"Dr. Henderson does not allow models to date anyone in the class, and I'm out of the dating scene, remember?"

"You can be cute if you want, but I know Kevin would never allow me to model for the art class. Naked. That's disgusting, especially now that he has promised to marry me."

"You're engaged?"

"Well, no ring yet. He's saving up, but yes."

"Then I can understand that he wouldn't want his soon-to-be wife posing nude. Besides, you've been sexual partners for a couple of years. I'm sure that would affect him. But that isn't true of me."

"Well, I think you are just asking for trouble."

"It's art, Cheryl, not pornography." *I need this to get over my fear,* Lisa thought. *Besides, I enjoy being naked, and Mother will never find out. I'll make sure of that.*

"But other people will see you."

"That's the idea. They're supposed to draw pictures of me. You've seen me in the shower. Don't you think I have a nice body for drawing? I'm in good physical shape, sort of classic, like a Greek statue."

"Maybe it's right for you, but I wouldn't be caught dead posing nude for an art class."

Lisa put her arm over Cheryl's shoulder. "Don't worry; I'll be careful. I don't want to be caught dead either."

Cheryl pushed her away. "Lisa, be serious."

• • •

Heidi went over Lisa's syllabus for biology. She went through the chapters pointing out what to focus on and what was likely to be on tests. "You are an auditory learner, so describe the anatomic parts out loud to yourself, and then during the laboratory test the words will pop into your mind." She pointed to a graphic of a dissected frog in her book. "Say it out loud, so I can hear you."

Lisa yelled out the terms to Heidi's amusement. Suddenly stern, Heidi closed the book and drew a frog. "What's this?" she asked, going through each anatomic item. Lisa answered them all correctly. "See, I told you. You just have to study the way you learn."

Lisa put her book and notes away in her backpack. "There's something else I want to ask you."

"Fire away."

Lisa described her opportunity to be a nude model for the art class. Heidi was logical and unemotional. "I think that's wonderful that you feel comfortable posing nude. It's a service to the art community, and you're physically fit and will make an excellent model. I'm sort of stocky and don't have curves in the right places. But I think you'll do great. Are you nervous?"

"I don't think so, not being naked. When I'm canoeing …" She wrung her hands. "But do you think I'm being narcissistic? I learned that word in psychology. Just don't ask me to spell it."

"We're all narcissistic to some extent. We enjoy people giving positive feedback about what we say, how we look, and what we accomplish. You know I was raised in a tradition where it's improper to put yourself above others, but my culture also requires me to be thankful. So just enjoy the experience, but don't let it rule your life; don't let it become who you are." Heidi held Lisa firmly and gave her a hug. "You're so much more than an attractive nude body, Lisa. But if this experience is a celebration of the way God made you, then enjoy it."

CHAPTER 20

> As long as you grab for what makes you feel
> good or makes you look important, are you really
> much different from a babe at the breast, content
> only when everything's going your way?
> —The Message

L isa arrived a half hour before the first class as instructed. She thought through everything Cheryl and Heidi had said. But now she had no qualms. *I need this for healing.*

Dr. Henderson was picking up clutter. Lisa wandered around the room, checking everything out as her pulse slowed. The room was stark with wide drawers along the wall for the students to keep their work. Above the drawers were windows that stretched to the ceiling. The room smelled of linseed oil and expensive paper. In the corners were various still-life arrangements, some covered in dust. The still-life fruits were papier-mâché. Canvases were stacked along the back wall, but there were no mounted pictures. To the right were two doors, one quite simple with no window, the other with etched glass in the window that led to Dr. Henderson's office. In the corner near the window was a small stage with a wooden stool.

Dr. Henderson said, "You are right on time, Ms. Zuccerelli."

"Please call me Lisa."

Dr. Henderson arranged the easels so the students could focus on the stage. "This is a senior class, only fifteen students. You already know Portia. This is where I will have you model." She directed Lisa to a stool.

"Try sitting there." She looked at Lisa from several angles. "Try standing beside it." Dr. Henderson put Lisa's hands and legs in various formations. When she was satisfied, she asked, "I know you're athletic, so can you stand that way for an hour?"

"I'm pretty sure I can." It was a casual pose with her left hand braced against the wooden chair back and her right hand on her hip. Her legs were positioned so that they were slightly flexed, leaning onto the chair.

"Good. Can you get into the same position after the break and maintain it for another hour?"

"Yes, I'm sure I can." Lisa felt her body position, where her arms and legs were, angles, and head position. "Am I supposed to smile?"

Dr. Henderson grimaced. "No, it's too hard to hold that facial position. It uses too many muscles. Just have a relaxed expression. This isn't photography. You have to be comfortable. Any change can make it difficult for the students to complete their drawings." She paused and looked at Lisa's position again. "Yes, that looks good. All right, the door on the left is for you to change. There's a cotton robe in there. Undress, put that on, come out, and make yourself comfortable. I'll be giving a few instructions before we start. The class will be here soon. These senior art majors always come early." She left for her office.

Lisa went through the door. *Are you ready for this, Lisa?* There was a moment of hesitancy as she started unbuttoning her blouse. The fresh cotton robe, still in a bag from the dry cleaners, hung on the door. There was a circular fluorescent light in the middle of the ceiling. *Now or never,* she thought as she took off her clothes. She bent and touched her toes and then stretched. *Oh, this feels good. Just think, I get to be naked in school, how neat.* Her mind transported her to the Great North Woods and reminded her of sun, wind, and loon calls. She put on the cotton robe, went out the door, and sat on the stool in the middle of the platform.

Portia was the first student in the door. "Hello, Lisa. You are being our model today. That is good. I have been anticipating this day with good expectations. I will remember to give you one of my paintings."

"Yes, I'm here. Look what you got me into."

Portia laughed, covering her face with both hands. She sat at one of the easels and gave Lisa an exaggerated smile. "I'll be watching you closely. Don't you be moving now. It will mess with my picture."

"I'll remain still as a statue."

Other students arrived but didn't pay much attention to Lisa. They kept busy organizing their papers and drawing supplies. Lisa winced when the first man came into the class. He was particularly handsome. For a fleeting moment she thought about him seeing her naked, and her mind flashed to some of her sexual partners. *Will these guys be thinking about having sex with me?* she wondered. Bob cutting off her bra, exposing her breasts, blazed into her memory. *This is different,* she reminded herself. *This is art class.*

Dr. Henderson came out of her office as a girl with three bags over her shoulders rushed in and scrambled to take her place. Dr. Henderson walked behind the students and shut the classroom door. "You almost didn't make it, Ms. Drake. Please plan to be on time so you can prepare properly."

"I'm sorry, Dr. Henderson," the girl replied.

"That's what you said last time." Dr. Henderson walked across the room and stood beside Lisa. "Today I want you to focus on form and shape. Our model is athletic, so I want to see that power in your pictures. And since she is fit, she should be able to maintain her position for the entire first hour. Put her form to paper during that time. In the second hour she will take the same posture, and I will have you work on shading to develop your three-dimensional image. Any questions?"

She turned to Lisa. "All right, take the position we talked about." As Lisa did so, she removed her robe. The air-conditioning fan came on, wafting cool air across her torso. Her skin prickled, and her nipples tensed. Dr. Henderson adjusted her arms. "Can you hold that?"

"It's comfortable."

"Good." She turned. "All right, class, begin."

As expected, Lisa didn't feel self-conscious, partly because her head position meant she couldn't see herself and partly because the students that she could see were intent on their drawings. Even the young man who had made her wince when he'd come into the room was busy drawing. *What did I expect? This was a drawing class,* she thought. She resisted the urge to shake her head.

The hardest part was not moving. She tensed and relaxed her muscles at times but was careful to maintain her position. On recommendation, she kept her face as relaxed and neutral as possible. *I might as well think about something while I'm standing here.* She remembered her secret campsite and the waterfall. She mentally climbed in the whirlpool at the top of the falls, feeling the water circulating around her.

She could not see the clock on the wall in the back of the room, so she was lost in thought when Dr. Henderson announced the break. Glad to be able to move, she looked at herself. Her nipples had relaxed, her areolae soft and round. *I wonder when that happened*, she wondered.

The students left the room, talking among themselves. Dr. Henderson picked up the cotton robe and handed it to her. "There is a break room down the hall with coffee and juice machines. They don't mind if you're in just your robe; they're used to art models. There's a bathroom near the break room if you need it."

Lisa put on the robe and found Portia waiting for her. Portia asked, "May I buy you a coffee?"

"Thanks, but I better have juice, so I don't have to go to the bathroom in the middle of the next hour."

"You are right," Portia laughed, "but the offer I am making to buy it for you still stands."

Lisa cinched her robe, and they walked to the small cafeteria together. It was a room that must have been an office at one time. Now it was set aside for the art students with a coffeepot and several juice machines. There was a jar on the counter full of coins. "Honor system," said Portia. "We use the money to buy the coffee and juice, and any profit goes to the art department for supplies." Portia directed Lisa to the juice machine where orange, cranberry, and apple juice were swirling in a cooler. While Lisa got a glass of cranberry juice, Portia fumbled with her purse, eventually depositing coins in the jar. "Let's sit over by the window," she said.

Lisa was surprised that the other students paid her no attention. They were engrossed in their own conversations. She actually felt more self-conscious than during the modeling session. The students were all completely dressed while she was covered only in a robe. It was odd.

"You did a very good job of holding still," Portia said. "You're a good model. Some of the models from the agency move just when I am following the line of their arm or torso. It is very aggravating. It is also good that you have good muscle definition. I studied the muscles in preparation for the class, but for most of our models, I can't see their muscles because they are fleshy like me." She laughed. "I have to imagine them inside their body."

Lisa found the conversation embarrassing, so she changed the subject. "Do you miss the Caribbean?"

"Oh, yes. I miss my home, the constant changing of the ocean, the green of the trees. There are so many greens. I miss the smell of the smoke drifting up from the cooking fires between the trees and the flowers. I so miss the flowers."

They talked about her memories as Lisa sipped her cranberry juice and Portia drank her coffee. They were deep in conversation when one of the male students stood and announced, "We got five minutes to be back." He walked out of the break room, and the others followed.

Lisa asked Portia where the women's restroom was and followed her directions. It seemed odd to be able to just slip off her robe and be naked in a public restroom to urinate. She put her robe back on and washed her hands.

She returned to the classroom just as Dr. Henderson was closing the door. She acknowledged Lisa with a nod and followed her to the platform. Lisa removed her robe and took her position as well as she could remember. The professor slightly adjusted her arms and legs and asked the class, "Is that close to the position she was in?"

One of the men raised his hand. "Her leg was extended just a bit more."

Lisa moved her leg, and he affirmed her position.

"I have looked at your drawings. They're coming along nicely. I want shading during this session. Look, she has good muscular definition here," Dr. Henderson said as she drew her finger across Lisa's chest, without quite touching her. "Note how her breasts are formed on top of firm pectoral muscles, different textures. So I want to see that in your drawings." She held her palm over Lisa's abdominal muscles. "This is not a flat plane. Since she is standing, there is a dynamic to her muscular tone; her power is evident. She is not a lump of clay. She is a young woman who can jump and run."

And canoe and swim, Lisa thought.

Dr. Henderson continued, "I want to see that tension. I want your drawings to reflect that she could jump off the paper. Proceed."

The second session was more difficult. Lisa wanted to jump and move. Standing perfectly still was difficult. But she was determined. She got a slight cramp in her leg and moved her leg slightly, then returned to her previous position. "Sorry, I had a cramp," she said. There was a mumbling through the class.

"Do you need a moment to move?" Dr. Henderson asked.

"If I could?"

Everyone put down their pencils and relaxed and started talking to one another. Lisa did some stretches, and they stopped talking. *How odd to be stretching naked while fifteen people watch,* she thought. The students were observing her motion. She had an urge to turn her back to them, but logic intervened. *They have been looking at me for over an hour; what's there to hide?* She glanced at her pubic hair and resisted the urge to cover her groin. Her nipples tightened and then relaxed as she finished her stretches. *Can't control that,* she thought. *It usually happens under my clothes.* Her heart settled into a comfortable tempo. Her muscles felt better. The cramps dissipated, and she returned to her former position. Being motionless felt less revealing.

Dr. Henderson made some minor adjustments, looking to her class for verification. Everyone picked up their pencils. Dr. Henderson whispered, "I should have anticipated your need. If you need to stretch again, just let me know. Most models stretch a couple of times during the hour. You've done very well."

When the class session was over, Lisa relaxed and did some more stretches. She noticed that several of the students were watching her. Dr. Henderson walked up to her and handed her the robe. "Don't be embarrassed. The students study motion, but mostly on film. This is very important for them to see how muscles and frame move in unison."

"I'm not embarrassed. Actually, it would be a lot easier to be able to move. Holding still is very difficult."

"For the freshman and sophomore class, I do have the model move every ten minutes during the first hour. That class is focused on drawing form quickly. Would you be interested in modeling for that class as well?

Understand that there are students in that class who have never drawn nudes before, so they are not as sophisticated as this class."

Lisa cinched the belt on her robe. "Sure, I'd be glad to."

"Great. I will have Janice go over the schedule with you. You did a great job. I hope we can continue working together. Thank you, Lisa."

Portia was putting her pencils and supplies away. Lisa went to Portia's easel to see her drawing. Lisa said, "Very nice. You are an artist." Lisa recognized herself in the drawing. She focused on the detail, noting how intricate the drawing was. Every line and curve of her torso was drawn. It was interesting to see herself through Portia's eyes.

"I don't usually do realism. I prefer flamboyant and surrealistic drawing, but this is training for me."

"Clean up, class," Dr. Henderson said. "The next session will be here soon."

"I better get dressed," Lisa told Portia.

"Yes, the next class is a freshman class, and they are drawing those papier-mâché fruit." She pointed at the still life in the corner. "They would not be ready to draw you." She smiled and shook Lisa's hand. "You did good."

Lisa went to the changing room and dressed. She felt an odd sense of disappointment that she had to put on her clothes. When she walked out, the freshman students were filtering into the room. A different professor was greeting them. It appeared that several of the young men had a good idea why she was walking through their classroom. She noted them whispering to one another. She quickened her pace.

As she walked down the hall to the more familiar part of the university, she thought about Troy. *What would he think about my modeling? Should I tell him? He really doesn't need to know everything about me, does he?*

The more she thought about Troy, the less interested she was in other guys. Yet as the weeks progressed, she still hadn't heard from him. She sent several postcards but received no response.

Then one day, a few weeks after she had started modeling, she came home late to find a letter for her on the table. Inside the envelope was a postcard of a loon nesting her young. *Why didn't he just send the postcard?* she asked herself as she turned over the card and read:

Dear Lisa,

Sorry I couldn't come and visit you before classes started. We had some late scheduled trips and I just barely made it back to school before classes started. I am really loaded this semester. I don't know when I have had to study so hard. And yes, I am still working as an orderly in the emergency department, honing my skills in case we meet under similar circumstances.

Thinking of you always, except when I am studying,
Troy

Lisa was angry. *Why couldn't he call? At least they could have talked for a while. Why was he so insensitive? He said he loved her. Did he really? On the other hand, what kind of catch was she for someone like Troy? He was probably a virgin from the way he talked and acted.* "So virtuous," she said in disgust. She decided to forget him and focus on her classes. *Finish this year and then you're halfway to being a university graduate. Then no more school ever again.*

CHAPTER 21

L isa had plenty to distract her by the time basketball practice started. She felt camaraderie with the other girls on the team, and exams were near. Practices were very demanding. Coach Hammond was passionate about the game, and that left little room for lack of focus. Lisa would never forget the speech Coach Hammond gave at the end of their first practice that fall.

"You are veteran players, especially you juniors and seniors. I expect you to be role models and teachers to the younger players. Basketball is learned by experience. Some of you have been playing longer than I've been coaching. I expect teamwork. Part of teamwork is improving the skills of your teammates. No matter how good you think you are, there is not a single person here who can win a game by herself. We work together. I don't want any heroes; I want a team. Do I make myself clear?"

"Yes, Coach Hammond," they yelled in unison.

"I hear only individuals. Where is the team?"

"Yes, Coach Hammond," they yelled louder, synchronizing their voices.

"Are you sure?"

"Yes, Coach Hammond, we are sure." The roar echoed through the empty gymnasium.

"Go Wild Broncos, go," Coach provoked them.

"Go Wild," they yelled back, slapping their hands together.

"Hit the showers, team."

Cheryl joined her in the shower. "You sure didn't put on any extra weight, did you? What were you doing? Working out all summer?"

"Hauling rocks." She flexed her biceps.

"I saw some of your three-point shots. Were you throwing the rocks through a hoop?"

Lisa laughed. "I wish. How was your summer?"

"Keith made our engagement official. Look at the rock he gave me." She held up her left hand.

"Congratulations." Lisa grabbed her hand, twisting the ring so it reflected the lights in the shower. "Mighty impressive. It looks good on you."

"Think it goes with my outfit?" Cheryl twisted her naked torso and slapped her left hand between her breasts.

"The diamond matches perfectly. But you'd better get out of the shower before you puff up too much."

Just before exams Lisa received a long letter from Troy. It was mostly about bears, wolves, and moose. It did not improve her ambivalence. She was thrilled to receive the letter and read it over several times. It told a good story with a charming ending, and he'd signed at the bottom, "Still faithful, love you." *But he didn't say anything about us or when we can get together. And it says nothing about the upcoming holidays. Will he just call me during break?*

She suddenly felt jealous of Cheryl's diamond. She went home and called the number Troy had given her. The answering machine picked up: "This is Troy. I'm probably busy studying. Leave a message."

"I left a message last time, Troy. This is Lisa." She slammed the phone down. How could he say that he loved her if he never communicated? Yet she cherished the letter.

She typed a response that night on the computer. She used spell-check, but there were some words that just weren't right, and she couldn't tell the difference among the words spell-check offered. Out of desperation she called Heidi.

After spelling the words for her, Heidi said, "You must really like this guy."

"Well, I do, but he exasperates me. And don't ask me how to spell *exasperate*."

"You are one special person. Don't let your dyslexia define who you are."

"Thanks for talking to me. You will make a great physician." Calmed, Lisa hung up the telephone, printed out the letter, and mailed it at the university the next day.

Lisa knew that her mother had not only a mother's suspicion but also a lawyer's scrutiny. Her mother would probably be suspicious of any reply from Troy, so Lisa checked the letters in the mailbox every day before her mother got home from the office, leaving them in the box. But there were no more letters from Troy, and Christmas vacation was fast approaching.

Lisa thought about driving to Madison, Wisconsin, to see Troy. She pulled out the map and mentally calculated the driving time. But then Coach Hammond announced the team roster and insisted on having one last practice the first Monday of vacation for those who were in town. Christmas was on Wednesday, so there was no reason not to practice. That left no time to make a six-hour drive.

Lisa never mentioned Troy to Cheryl. She only told Cheryl that she was still traumatized and out of the dating scene. Lisa was still unsure who had told Linden about her dating behavior, and she hoped whoever it was had told him about her celibacy as quickly as her promiscuity. "I wonder what he'll say when he comes home for Christmas about his sister the nun," she said, driving home from practice.

Coach had devised some new practice routines that used muscles Lisa hadn't stretched. She felt sore and tired after practice. Besides, she had thrown one hundred three-point shots after practice. She stretched her arms on the steering wheel as she came up to her driveway. A car parked in front of the security gate blocked her way. It was an older car, pockmarked with rust around the wheel wells.

Her heart raced. *Now what? Who's that?* She slammed her fists on the steering wheel. She locked her car doors and waited. No response. She flashed her headlights. No response. *Should I lay on the horn?*

She shifted into park and put on the emergency break. She unlocked the doors and slid out, leaving the Jeep running and unlocked. She edged toward the car. No movement. As she got closer, she could tell from the angle of the driver's neck that he was either asleep or dead. Ready to dial 911 for the police or an ambulance, she decided to tap on the car's rear window first.

Troy jumped with a start and rolled down his window. "Hello, Lisa. It's really hard to visit when you've locked me out of your life. What time is it?" He looked at his watch. "I must have been sleeping here almost an hour. Good to see you. It's chilly here in Duluth, Minnesota, in December."

She reached in and tousled his hair, long and straight just like in the summer but without the sun-bleached strands. It still reminded her of a haystack. "If certain people would announce their arrival, they wouldn't have to struggle so and get all cold and bothered. Your letter had great animal stories but nothing about your arrival."

"Oh, I thought I put that in at the end."

"No, you did not." She stood with her arms crossed, waiting to see what he would say next. *I like him; he's adorable but so frustrating. Why didn't he call? He just shows up instead?* Anger and resentment boiled inside her. *Maybe I should just smack him or ram him with my Jeep.*

He smiled, straightened his hair with his fingers, and sighed. "As you may have noticed, I'm in a bit of a jam here. I can't go through this gate. It's locked. And someone has parked in back of me, so I can't leave. Any suggestions?" He held up his hands in defense, like a mouse cornered by a voracious cat. He squeaked, "I love you."

Lisa laughed so hard she had to hold her stomach. "In that case I'll let you in. You sure know how to weasel your way into a girl's house."

"I'm trying to get into her heart, not her house"

"In that case I'll leave you out here." She shifted her hands to her hips. "Maybe you should get into her house first. Aren't you the one who said one step at a time?" *When he sees where I live, what is he going to think of me? Do I trust him enough?*

He folded his hands on his lap. "Miss Zuccerelli, may I please ask that you kindly open the security gate and allow me the pleasure of your company?"

"Yes, Mr. Vogel, you may." There was silence as they stared at each other. Neither moved. "You have permission to ask; now ask."

"Oh," he stammered. "Please open the security gate?" He unfolded his hands. "How was that?"

"Quite nice, Mr. Vogel." She turned to the keyboard and punched in the security code. The gate swung open. "Go in, and then let me pass you. I will escort you to proper parking."

After they parked and go out of their cars, he ran up and hugged her. "I've missed you so much." He kissed her on the cheek, hugged her, and kissed her again.

"That will get you somewhere," she cooed.

He stood in the driveway and looked around, his mouth gaping open. "Is this where you live?"

She pointed to the canoe hanging on the wall of the garage. "Don't you recognize the dent in the front of that canoe?"

"It looks vaguely familiar," he said.

"Then this must be where I live."

"If I had known you were a princess living in a castle, I would ..." He walked toward the front of the house examining the structure. He seemed to be in a trance.

Her anger surfaced. "You would what? Treat me differently? Maybe I should have called the police."

"Wait a minute." He walked around to the trunk of his car. "I brought presents." He turned to look at her. "I could use a little help since the big one is for you."

He filled her open arms with bulky presents wrapped in a chaotic manner and with an exuberance of bows. He followed her into the house carrying a large box. She led him through the back door and mudroom straight into the living room, which was decorated with ivy and pine in tasteful displays. The piano took command of the living room, and a large Christmas tree stood opposite. They set the presents under the tree.

"Back to the kitchen," she said.

"Wow, this living room is bigger than the whole downstairs of my dorm."

This is not going well. Now how will I be able to trust him? "My grandfather built the house and invited my parents to move in when my grandmother died. I was three years old, so it's the only place I've ever called home. Let's get something to drink, and I'll give you a tour."

"What a museum this is with the paintings, the furniture, and the artistic decorations. It is like a palace in Europe."

"Have you been to Europe, or are you just talking?"

"Yes, I went to France with my high school French class. We visited some of the castles in the Loire Valley. It was way too short of a trip." They walked into the kitchen. "Just milk, please," he said.

She poured him a glass of milk. They sat in the breakfast nook where there was a plate of decorated Christmas cookies. "Why didn't you tell me? You never mentioned any of this," he said.

She pulled up a wooden chair in front of him, dug her heels into the chair rungs, and stared at him. "Two reasons. First, you would never have believed me. Second, I make very sure people like me first before I let them know where I live. It's caused problems in the past."

He looked at the cookies. "May I?" She nodded. "I suppose that could cause problems." He ate two cookies and drank down his milk. "A guy gets thirsty sitting in his car by a gate. Could I have a little more milk? And could you stop staring at me? I feel like a lioness's prey."

She filled his glass. "All right, I suppose I can forgive you for showing up unannounced. And besides, I did want to see you. I've called several times and left messages on your machine. I even considered driving to Madison, but I would have told you *first*," she snarled, "that I was coming."

"I humbly accept your forgiveness, Your Highness."

She kicked his leg. "Cut it out." Another two Christmas cookies, a long drink of milk, and he smiled. His milk mustache curled at the edges. "I might as well give you a tour?" she said.

"Full belly, forgiven, and ready for the tour." He stood and reached for her hand. She turned away. "I am sorry. I thought I wrote that I was coming. It's been a rough semester. I should have called."

"Quit your blubbering, and follow me." She took him into the dining room. Troy asked questions about everything from the pattern on the china to the cut of the crystal. They toured the living room where he asked about the various ornaments, especially one gilded pinecone that seemed out of place.

"I made that for my parents in third grade. They keep all that stuff. My father is a bit of a romantic. My mother would have thrown it away years ago."

Then they went down the hall to see her parents' offices, the study room, and the library. Lisa climbed the ladder and wheeled it along the wall. "I always loved to do this as a kid."

The tour ended at the solarium on the far end of the house.

"This is like a jungle," Troy said. "You have everything from trees to geraniums in here."

"My mother loves plants. Although with her legal practice she has the gardener do most of the work. The orchids are her favorites."

In the center, a French café table and two chairs were set out. "I love this part of the house," Lisa said. "The sun shines through the glass ceiling all day and keeps it warm even in the winter. It always feels like an early June morning, even in December. The smell of sphagnum moss and potting soil gives the impression of an Elizabethan garden. Only the lack of frogs croaking reminds me that I'm indoors."

"This is enchanting."

"When I was little, I used to run around in here naked. I thought it was the Garden of Eden." She laughed at the memory. Troy stared at her. She was pretty sure she knew what he was thinking and changed the subject. "So, Mr. Vogel, tell me about your classes that have kept you so busy you couldn't answer my phone calls."

"I deserved that," he said as he described his classes, complete with comical stories of each faux pas he had made with teachers and classmates. She relaxed, enamored by his stories. Time slipped away.

"Lisa, are you home?" her mother yelled. "Whose car is that in the driveway? Are you in your room?"

"Mother," Lisa answered as she and Troy trotted down the hall to meet her in the living room. "This is Troy. He is the outfitter that I told you about."

"Troy, I'm pleased to meet you." She extended her gloved hand. "Lisa is quite impressed with you."

"He brought presents, Mother. They're under the tree."

Her father came through the door. "Ah, do we have a dinner guest? I didn't know anyone was coming." Lisa introduced Troy to her father. "We ate out while we were Christmas shopping," her father said, looking at Troy. "But do you mind leftovers? I can whip up something fairly spectacular in a few minutes. Did you have supper?"

Troy smiled. "I didn't even have lunch. I drove straight through from Madison, Wisconsin."

"Oh, my poor boy," said her mother, giving him a guest hug.

"Never fear; one feast coming up." Her father shook Troy's hand vigorously, then looked at his daughter. "I suppose you had basketball practice and haven't eaten either."

"True." She rubbed her stomach, glancing at Troy for a reaction.

"Now you two sit in the dining room, and the chef will get something ready."

Lisa and Troy sat at the dining room table. The table was already set for four, as it always was for her mother's sense of symmetry, complete with two knives, three forks, and three spoons at each place setting.

Her mother seated herself opposite Troy and started grilling him, asking about his parents and what they did, where he grew up, and his schooling. Troy answered in rapid succession. Lisa felt like telling her mother to stop being the grand inquisitor, but Troy didn't seem to mind. He appeared entertained by her questions. Lisa folded her hands in her lap.

In less than fifteen minutes, Paul appeared in his chef apron with hors d'oeuvres. "I'm reheating some leftover beef and mashed potatoes. Would you like an aperitif?" He set tiny, thimble-size glasses at their settings and proceeded to the liquor cabinet.

"None for me, Dad; I'm in training."

"No thanks, sir," said Troy. "I'm fine. I am afraid I drank most of your milk before you came home."

Her father seemed disappointed but took one of the glasses for himself and set the other in front of her mother as he headed for the kitchen. "All right, main course coming up."

They dipped their shrimp into the spicy sauce and munched the little rounds of garlic toast. As Troy licked his fingers, her father arrived with filet mignon and twice-baked potatoes, apologizing that they were reheated.

"This is fabulous, Mr. Zuccerelli. A peanut-butter-and-jelly sandwich would have been fine. I already had—"

Lisa knew he was going to mention the cookies, and she jabbed him in the leg. "Wait till you see what he brings for dessert," she interrupted.

In between bites, her mother's interrogation continued. Lisa quietly ate her food. Basketball practice always made her hungry. She kept one ear listening to her mother's questions, but Troy didn't seem to need any intervention.

Her father burst through the door, presenting his key lime pie. "One of my managers brought the limes back from the Keys in Florida." He gave Lisa her piece and put a double portion with mounds of whipped cream in front of Troy.

"I am pretty full, Mr. Zuccerelli, but I will give it my best. I did have a few Christmas cookies Lisa gave me when we first got here, before the tour." Lisa kicked him again. He didn't react.

"Oh, the tour is only half done," Lisa said. "I haven't even taken you upstairs." Lisa stared straight into her mother's eyes.

"We started in the living room and made it to the garden," Troy said. He turned to her mother. "I love your orchids. I tried to grow one in my dorm room, but it died."

Pie served, Paul joined them, still in his apron, with a piece for Lisa's mother and himself. Her mother explained the nuances of managing orchids, and then the conversation switched to other topics. Everyone was so animated that Lisa did not interrupt.

Her mother glanced at her watch. "It's getting late. Let me show you to the guest room, Troy."

"But I left my suitcase out in the car." He got up. "Let me run and get it." He ran out the back door.

"Did you invite him?" Her mother asked her, looking stern.

"No, I didn't even know he was coming. He was sitting, asleep in his car, outside the gate when I got home from basketball practice. I almost called the police."

"He seems like a very nice young man, but I expect the best behavior out of you, young lady. And he is not allowed in your bedroom. Do you understand?"

"Yes, Mother. I promise that I will be very well behaved," Lisa said politely, but she felt angry. *If Mother only knew that he took off all my clothes when I was in a hypothermic coma, then who would she be warning?*

"Linden will be arriving tomorrow from Boston," her father reminded her. "Troy seems like someone Linden might enjoy."

"May I be excused to show our guest his room, or ..." She meant to finish with sarcasm, but Troy entered with his suitcase.

Her mother stood. "Lisa will show you to the guest room. Are you staying through Christmas?"

"At least till we open presents, if I may, Mrs. Zuccerelli. I thought I wrote Lisa about my coming, but I guess I got carried away and didn't mention it. I apologize. I hope I am not causing any inconvenience."

"No problem at all. The guest room is always ready. The maid just cleaned it yesterday. Oh, and our son, Linden, is arriving tomorrow, and I am sure you will enjoy meeting him."

"Thanks. I am very tired from my drive. I would like to just get some rest, if I may." Lisa took his suitcase from him, and he followed her up the steps.

"Good night, Troy," her parents said in unison.

"Good night, Mr. and Mrs. Zuccerelli. Thanks so much for your hospitality."

Lisa headed up the stairs. His suitcase seemed light. Troy followed close enough to whisper, "I hope I didn't cause any trouble."

Lisa didn't respond as she opened the door to the guest room and pointed to the door opposite. "Shower and toiletries are in there." The room was paneled in oak with Tudor-style canopy bed and writing desk. A heavy matching oak chair with a padded seat and back reminiscent of medieval tapestry was in the corner. "This is beautiful. Very nice," he said loud enough so anyone out in the hall could hear. He hugged her and gave her a soundless kiss on the lips. "I love you, Lisa."

"You'll be comfortable here then?" she said loudly. Then she whispered, "You did get me in trouble, a lot of trouble."

"Yes, quite comfortable. Thanks." He pushed her out the door with his strong hands wrapped around her waist, tickling her belly with his thumbs. Like the whisper of the breeze drifting through the trees, he said, "I'm sorry. I'll make it up to you. See you in the morning." Once she was out in the hall, he closed the door.

Lisa stood outside his door and heard the latch click. She looked up to see her mother coming down the hall. "He's all locked in, safe and sound," she said as she walked past her mother, down the hall to her own room. "I'm exhausted from practice," she said as she turned in and locked her own door.

• • •

In the morning, after her shower, Lisa dressed in her robe and pajamas and scouted the hallway. There was no one. She went down the hall to the guest room. The door was wide open, the bed was made, and Troy's suitcase was standing at the foot of the bed. No Troy.

She went downstairs and found her father and Troy sitting at the kitchen table laughing. Her mother was pouring herself a cup of coffee. Everyone was dressed.

"Good morning, sleepy head." Troy got up and gave her a hug and a tiny kiss that was supposed to go unnoticed.

"So what's so funny?" she asked as her mother gave her a cup of coffee. She sat at the table, opposite her father, Troy next to her.

"Your father was just telling me stories about when you were growing up," Troy said.

"And which funny stories might those be?"

"Do you want eggs?" her mother asked her.

"Yes, thanks, Mother."

The sound of the eggs cracking and then sizzling in the pan broke the silence of the smiling men. Lisa poked Troy in the ribs under the table. He folded his hands in front of him. "Let's see," he said. "The story about you taking off all your clothes and running out in the rain, yelling 'I need a shower; this will save on water.' That's one of my favorites so far."

Lisa glared at her father. "Did he tell you that I was only seven years old at the time?"

Troy giggled. "I'm not sure that was mentioned."

"Dad."

Troy gave Lisa a hug. "Yes, that was mentioned; don't worry. But I especially liked the part about you taking soap and a bathtub boat with you and floating your boat in the puddle while you soaped up."

"Well, I wasn't well supervised as a child."

Troy laughed. Her father smiled.

"It wasn't very easy to supervise someone with such a wild

imagination," her mother said as she slid the plate with sausages and eggs in front of Lisa and handed her a fork. "So far we haven't told him the skunk story."

"Mother," Lisa said as she set down her fork.

Troy looked inquisitive. "What skunk story?"

"It's just a story about when I got into lots of trouble. Go ahead, Mother. I know you are going to tell it anyway. I'll just sit here like a chastened daughter and eat my breakfast while you humiliate me."

Her mother topped off her cup of coffee and sat next to Paul. Troy's eyes were intent on her as she began. "Our gardener was trying to get rid of some rats from the creek on our property, and he had been fairly successful using small beaver traps."

Troy reached under the table and caressed Lisa's knee. She wanted to stab him with her fork but continued eating.

"One day, instead of a rat, he trapped a skunk. It was killed instantly with its head in the trap. It didn't even smell. The gardener threw it in the trash. When Lisa came home from school, she changed her clothes and went 'exploring' as she used to say. She hated to be indoors even when she was young. Of course she found the skunk in the trash."

Lisa swallowed the last of her eggs. "It had very soft fur and a beautiful coat."

Her mother continued, "I have no idea how long she played with the dead skunk."

"Not all that long."

"But she decided to tie it with fishing line to the back of her bicycle."

"I wanted to give it a ride."

"When I came home from work, she was down at the gate. As the gate opened, she took off down the driveway, yelling, 'The skunk is after me, Mom.' I had no way of seeing the fishing line. All I saw was the skunk in pursuit of my daughter, so I tried to run over the skunk with the car and not kill my daughter in the process."

Troy was holding his stomach, his face red, as he struggled to breathe and laugh at the same time.

"When she got to the garage, she had no place to go, and that is when I discovered the ruse. I was in a panic, but when I saw the fishing line ..."

"She tried to kill me."

"I wasn't trying to kill you."

"No? You chased me around the house three times, yelling my name."

"I never could catch her, Troy."

"I kept my distance while we negotiated a truce."

"She never did get the corporal punishment she deserved."

"See, she was trying to kill me," Lisa said.

Troy gasped for breath, put his arm around Lisa's shoulder, and gave it a squeeze. "You are more charming than I even imagined." He turned to her parents. "I can see that she must have been a real challenge to rear."

"Oh, you haven't heard the half of it," her mother said.

"I think that is enough embarrass-Lisa stories for one morning," Lisa said. "Mother, as your dutiful daughter, may I have a glass of orange juice?" Her mother obliged.

Her father looked at his watch. "Linden should be here soon. He was going to rent a car so he could visit some of his friends this week, so we don't have to pick him up at the airport."

"When do you open presents?" Troy asked.

Her mother replied, "I saw the presents you put under the tree. We'll celebrate tomorrow morning."

"Great. I'd like to stay till then if I may. Then I was planning on leaving to spend some time with my parents."

"You're welcome to stay as long as you want," her father said.

Lisa took the last drink of her orange juice. "I'm going to get dressed." She excused herself from the table and bounded up the stairs. Closing her door, she discarded her robe and pajamas and plopped on her bed, hiding her face in her pillow.

She thought, *He certainly knows how to charm my parents. Now what am I going to do if I decide I don't like him? He does have a great laugh and a wonderful sense of humor even if it was mostly at my expense. Do I love him? I like him. He's fun, and we have been through a lot together. Does he have integrity? I'm not sure I believe that stuff about "I've been faithful to you." How do I know he's not going with some girl in Wisconsin? Darn it all, I think I love him.*

She turned and looked at herself in the mirror opposite her bed and thought about how the art students drew her form. "I suppose I need to put on clothes," she said.

She got dressed in sweats and bounded down the stairs. "Where's Troy?"

Her mother was sitting at the kitchen table with the newspaper, sale advertisements strewn in front of her. "He went with your father to pick up some groceries for dinner tomorrow."

"So Dad can tell him more stories about me?"

She looked up from the paper and smiled. "I suppose. He is certainly a charming young man. Your father really likes him."

"Now I'm trapped," Lisa mumbled to herself. Then to her mother she said, "I'm going for a walk."

"All right, honey, see you later. Don't be gone too long. Your brother should be here soon."

Lisa grabbed her coat and stormed out the back door. *She never calls me "honey." I wonder where that came from.*

The air was brisk; only a pittance of snow had fallen during the night. She walked back to the tennis court and then down the trail she maintained. There was a hole in the fence, but it didn't look like a hole. Lisa moved the links to the side and crawled through, replacing the fencing so it looked attached. Once through, her trail hooked up with a hiking trail through Chester Park. In the summer the trails were maintained by the city, but in the winter months they were abandoned since the park was officially closed. She saw no one on the trail and saw no evidence of human tracks. The chickadees were chirping, rejoicing in the bright sunlight. A rabbit stood in the middle of the path, and she paused, squatting on the trail to observe the creature without frightening it.

When the rabbit hopped off, Lisa had the urge to run. She knew the trails in Chester Park so well that she had a loop already mapped out in her mind that was about five miles. She ran as fast as her eyes could evaluate the sticks and rocks in the path. When she returned to the hole in the fence, she was breathless. Back at the tennis court, she lay down on the cement and did a hundred sit-ups and forty push-ups and then collapsed with her face on the cold concrete. *I think I can join that family of mine now. I am sufficiently exhausted that I won't lose my temper.*

She jumped up and dusted the dirt and snow off her cheek and coat.

As she came to the driveway, Linden drove in and parked. She also noticed her father's car. He and Troy had returned.

Linden climbed out of the rental car and smiled at Lisa. "How's my favorite sister?"

"Your only sister."

"That too." He gave her a big hug. "You're looking healthy. How's UMD treating you?"

"As and Bs. Much better than anyone around this household expected."

He hugged her again. "I am very proud of you, Lisa. You're special."

"You already got the report from your friends that I've been behaving myself?"

His Cheshire grin didn't deny it. "Whose car is that?"

"My boyfriend's."

"Interesting. I hadn't heard that you had a boyfriend. I need to meet him to see if I approve."

"Don't worry; Mom and Dad have already told him all the embarrassing stories about me."

"Even the skunk story?"

"Even the skunk story."

"They must really like him." He held one arm around her shoulder as they went in through back door. Lisa felt his warmth.

The house erupted with greetings and introductions as they walked into the living room. Her father had a tray with a teapot and cups. Little decorated sugar cookies were on a small porcelain plate. One was in Troy's mouth. Linden sat next to Troy on the couch even though Lisa was headed in that direction. After Troy accepted a cup of tea from her father, the family's questions began again. Her parents were sitting in the stuffed chairs adjoining the couch. Lisa served herself some tea, took one of the cookies, and stood in the doorway.

During a pause in the conversation she said, "I'm going to take a shower. I just ran five miles."

"All right, Elizabeth, join us when you're done," her father said. He added, "With clothes on, please." Everyone burst into laughter. Troy looked puzzled. Lisa bounded up the stairs, not waiting for the explanation.

When she returned, dressed in cotton slacks and a UMD sweatshirt, she slipped into a comfortable chair beside her mother. The tone of the conversation had changed. Linden was describing his experiences at Boston College, classes he was taking, and girls he had met and dated. He was especially animated telling about his piano-playing gigs.

Lisa was glad to have the focus on Linden. She edged in a few questions; he was enthusiastic to answer. *Anything*, she thought, *to keep the conversation off me.* Troy seemed to be enjoying himself. When Troy asked Linden to play something, Linden quickly obliged. His skill was the reason the piano was Lisa's favorite instrument even though she had never learned to play well. Her mother had tried to teach her, but Lisa had always been distracted with what was going on outside.

Linden played something from Beethoven. The music was enchanting. Lisa took a deep breath. *Maybe I will make it through the holiday*, she thought.

That evening her father made their traditional Christmas Eve turkey with dressing and various condiments. He spent most of the day cooking. Linden went to visit some friends, and Troy helped in the kitchen. He seemed to enjoy being with her father. They were constantly talking as her father gave him various culinary duties. Her mother decorated and set the table, and when she finished, she sat by the fireplace reading a book. Lisa helped with dinner in order to monitor what her father said about her, but by late afternoon she felt fidgety and needed a walk.

"Dad, can you release your sous-chef long enough to go for a walk with me?"

"Certainly," her father said. "We have everything under control. There is really nothing more to do till the bird is done. Go for a walk."

"You want to go, Troy?" she asked.

"Sure, let's go."

CHAPTER 22

Lisa led the way as they headed out the door. A brisk chill made them cinch their coats tight as the sun headed toward the horizon. "Look at the color of the sky," Lisa said, pointing to the west. "More snow tonight."

"I am really impressed with your family. Everyone is so warm and welcoming. I feel like part of the family."

You're not part of the family yet, she thought, gritting her teeth, but didn't respond out loud. She led the way behind the garage along the trail that lead to the tennis court. She contemplated what to say, but everything she wanted to say seemed wrong.

"You've got quite a spread here," Troy said as they came upon the tennis court.

"Yes, we have almost a hundred acres. And the property over there"—she pointed across the tennis court—"is a city park, so we are pretty isolated and private. The neighboring lot the other way has never been built on. I understand the guy who owns it lives in Florida and can't seem to sell it for the price he wants."

They walked through the tennis court and back along the forest path. Wanting to keep the hole in the fence and the access to Chester Park a secret, she led him along another trail to the granite escarpment that ended in the unsold property. The birds chirped, and occasionally a squirrel would voice his hostility toward the human invaders.

"This is beautiful," Troy said. "And your house is a castle. I never dreamed that the girl I found hypothermic under a canoe lived like this. What a paradise."

They came upon the place where Lisa had set a fallen tree on top of a couple of stumps years ago. It was a natural bench where she often came to think. *Now's the time to have it out with him. Then we'll see if he wants to be part of this family.*

She shoved him down on the bench and glared at him. "What are you doing? You come here unannounced. You charm my mother. You help my father in the kitchen. My brother plays a concert for you. What am I supposed to do? What if I don't want to be your girlfriend? What if I don't want to be friends with you at all? What will my family say? You're trapping me."

He reached for her, but she backed up. "I just came to see you and wish you a Merry Christmas. I didn't mean to cause trouble. You are one unusual woman, Lisa. You enjoy canoeing and camping, the things that mean so much to me, more than any woman I've ever met. And there are plenty of women in Wisconsin. There is just no one like you."

"Oh, stop it. You're a pleasant, handsome guy. I realize we have a lot in common; we like the same things. I even like your stupid humor, even though today it's mostly been at my expense. I just don't know if I like you enough to continue this relationship. I need time to figure that out." She took a breath. "And that doesn't mean I've dated anyone else. I have witnesses."

"Were you trying to seduce me, at Roger Leland's house?"

"Nice defense; make me the offender." She turned away as her eyes welled with tears. "I was grateful that you saved my life and was suddenly attracted to you. I was testing you."

He pulled her down to sit beside him. "Did I pass?" She turned away, so he continued, "I didn't mean to come on so strong. I enjoy your family. I'm not faking. They're fun. And I believe the record shows that I expressed my affection for you long before I knew you lived with the rich and famous." She jabbed him in the ribs with her elbow. "Ouch."

The sun was below the horizon, and the shadows were purple with silence. She took a deep breath and sighed. He hugged her. She didn't resist. "I guess I like you, Troy. But you make me feel like a cat trapped in a corner. I'd like to hiss and scratch your eyes out." She took another deep breath and turned to him. "No, I wouldn't. You're really sweet. You're the first boyfriend of whom my family has ever approved. If I promise not to seduce you …" She paused and searched his expression. "Would you promise not to ask them to tell you any more embarrassing stories about me? Please?"

He held her close. "I love it when you speak English so properly." He kissed her cheek. She felt warm, accepted, and supported. She ran her fingers over his face, "Thanks for letting me spout off without getting mad and running away. I expected you to get in your car and leave. I wouldn't mind another kiss …"

He kissed her again, with hesitation at first but then with commitment.

"Wow," she whispered when he let her breathe.

They got up and started walking back hand in hand. He said, "I couldn't have run away. I am totally lost out here. Which way back to the house?"

"This way, you rascal."

. . .

At dinner, Lisa relaxed. The conversation switched subjects from ecology and business administration to the music that Linden chose for his concerts. Troy was interested in corporate law, and her mother provided insightful examples. Lisa's foibles as a child weren't mentioned.

After dinner they moved to the living room where Linden played several piano pieces. Some were festive, Christmas classics, while others varied from Bach to Debussy. The lights on the tree, the festive decorations, and the smell of pine, cinnamon, and cooked turkey set the atmosphere.

Lisa felt emotionally and physically exhausted. It was only ten o'clock when she asked to be excused to go to bed. She kissed everyone good night, including Troy, which caused her family to hold their breath. Then she rubbed her eyes and waved as she headed up the stairs. When she reached the top of the stairs, she paused to hear if her name was mentioned. It wasn't, so she went to her room and closed and locked the door.

• • •

Christmas morning she awoke at five o'clock, put on her sweats, and tiptoed down the stairs. The house was quiet, so she went to the mudroom, put on her running shoes, snuck out the back door, and ran six miles on the road. It had snowed during the night, but the pavement was still warm and clear. The air was brisk, and the exercise was satisfying. Not a car in sight throughout her route. When she returned, she found her father in the kitchen making coffee. "Merry Christmas, Father."

He stopped what he was doing and gave her a hug. "Merry Christmas, Elizabeth. You're still my favorite daughter." Then he held her at arm's distance. "You're all sweaty."

"I just came back from a six-mile run; I should be."

"Well, no one is up yet, so there's time for you to take a shower." He handed her a cup and pulled the pot out. He filled her cup with the brew, then replaced the pot. "Fresh as can be."

"Thanks." She took a sip of coffee. "You like him, don't you?"

"He is a delightful young man." She watched him putter around the kitchen preparing for Christmas breakfast.

"So you approve?"

He filled his cup with fresh coffee. "If he makes you happy."

"Thanks, Dad," she said and walked up the stairs. No one was in the hall, so she went to Troy's door and listened. Not a sound, so she returned to her own room, stripped, and climbed into the shower.

She used her lavender soap that she saved for special occasions. It smelled so good and reminded her of the family outings in France. She shaved her legs and under her arms and shampooed her hair. The sensation of the water streaming down her skin as she rinsed thrilled her. She closed her eyes and stretched backward. The full force of the shower was on her face. She turned one cheek into the spray and then the other. As she stretched farther, the jets of water piqued the sensitive areas of her breasts. It tickled as she twisted so that the jets of water hit her areolas. She turned so the stream pulsated down her belly and coursed to her groin. It felt so good.

Drying off, she put on a minimum of makeup. She hated the stuff but presumed that it was necessary for Christmas. She splashed on a large dose of perfume that had been last year's Christmas present from her father. She laughed as she spritzed the perfume on one of her wrists. She pressed her wrists together and then dabbed her wrists against her neck. *See if Troy can resist me now.* She looked at herself in the mirror and asked her image, "Why are you doing this? This is a control problem, isn't it? How insightful of you, Elizabeth."

A red T-shirt with snow-covered pine trees over her lacy, green bra, silk green slacks, and an embroidered green vest she'd bought in Switzerland made her feel fresh and comfortable. She picked up her laundry, made her bed, and then flopped on top of the bedspread. "He doesn't return my calls; he charms my family and provokes them to tell embarrassing stories about me. But he is pretty nice," she said out loud. "I think I could … well, love him. But he's so aggravating."

Contemplating her dilemma, she went downstairs. There were voices in the kitchen. Everyone was drinking coffee and eating coffee cake. "There you are," her father said. "The pecan coffee cake just came out of the oven." In a mock whisper he added, "I didn't bake anything. It was frozen."

She sliced off a large chunk, filled her coffee cup again, and sat at the kitchen table next to her mother. Troy and Linden were deep in conversation. "Did you sleep well?" Lisa asked her mother.

"I did. It is so nice not to go to work."

"Merry Christmas," Lisa said.

"Merry Christmas, Sis," Linden said.

Troy smiled, and his teeth glistened. "Merry Christmas, Lisa."

Her father said, "I have the hors d'oeuvres ready, so I don't have to cook today. Can I have a little help bringing them out to the dining room table? Then we can open presents. How does that sound?"

"Great. I really should leave by early afternoon, I have a long drive ahead of me," Troy said.

"I wish you could stay longer," said Linden.

"Your hospitality has been sensational, but I really need to go. I have certainly accomplished my goal of learning more about Lisa." Everyone smiled except Lisa. She sipped her coffee as she glared at him.

They all helped carry trays of food into the dining room. Lisa moved the candle and pine centerpiece to the side to make room. Her mother pulled out dessert plates, spoons, forks, and some festive napkins. When everything from the refrigerator and pantry was set on the table, her father gave a Christmas prayer and then told everyone, "Fill your plates, and let's adjourn to the living room, shall we? We'll plug in the lights on the tree, light the candles, and celebrate."

Tempting their palates were olives and pickled herring, dill and sweet pickles, various kinds of crackers, and a cheese plate with samples from France, Italy, and Germany as well as cheeses Troy had brought from Wisconsin. Sausages and lacy ham slices completed the selections. Desserts consisted of apple pie, blueberry pie, and key lime pie, each with one piece missing. "I had to sample each of the pies to make sure they were good," her father defended.

They settled in the living room. Linden sat at the piano and played short pieces between bites. Troy sat next to Lisa, relishing his cheese and herring. Her parents sat in opposite overstuffed chairs looking more relaxed than hungry. The soft sounds of people savoring tidbits of cheese and meat spiced the air. No one had taken dessert yet.

"You're the youngest, Elizabeth; you pass out the presents," her father said, interrupting his chewing.

"I'm always the youngest, and I've always passed out the presents," Lisa protested as she set aside her plate and started reading the labels on the gifts.

Her mother broke a cracker in half and tried a piece of Troy's Wisconsin cheese. "This is good, Troy."

"It's from a cheese factory just north of Madison. My mother loves their cheese, and I didn't have a clue what else I could bring for Christmas."

Linden opened his first gift, a small package from Troy. He said, "I love chocolate. And this is from France. Thanks, Troy."

"My roommate did his study abroad in France. I asked him to bring some back."

The conversation continued as each opened his or her gifts and said thank you. Linden played a short composition to thank each giver. Hugs and kisses abounded as everyone seemed delighted with his or her presents.

When Lisa was done, she plunked down on the sofa to open her own gifts. Clothes from Helen, expected. Jewelry from Linden, expected. Perfume from her father, expected. Conversation hushed as she picked up the big box from Troy.

Linden played, in his words, "A little tune for opening presents." The gift was a large, bulky package but not that heavy. Lisa opened the envelope taped to the top first, expecting a frilly Christmas card. "What is it?" asked Linden.

"A year's subscription to *Walleye* magazine." She read out loud, "Next time you go canoeing you'll know everything about the habits of the fish and won't have to eat perch."

"Thanks, Troy." She gave him a quick kiss on the cheek, then proceeded to open her large package. As she tore off the paper, there still was nothing to suggest what it was. It was just a cardboard box. She looked at him quizzically and with some hesitation opened the box. She pulled out a dark-green Duluth pack with wide leather straps. As Lisa examined it, she found that it even had a trump line.

"Top of the line," Troy said. "I wanted to replace the one the bear ruined."

The piano music stopped. Three gasping mouths said, "What bear?"

Troy looked around the room. "Oops. You didn't know about the bear that attacked Lisa last summer?"

Lisa looked at her family. "He wasn't after me. He was after the food pack."

"Was it on your back?" asked her mother.

"No, of course not."

"How close did the bear get to you?" Linden asked.

She glared at her brother. "Close enough so I could smell its breath. I was sleeping under the canoe and had the food pack under the canoe with me. There were no good trees to hang it. The bear grabbed my pack and ran. I chased it but couldn't catch it."

"Were you sleeping like you usually sleep?" asked her father.

"Yes, Dad."

Linden covered his eyes. "I can just see my sister running naked through the forest chasing a bear. Oh my gosh."

"There was no one to see me."

"And that makes it better? The bear could have killed you," said her mother.

Lisa felt defiant. "And clothes would have helped that."

Troy looked from one speaker to the next in rapid succession. "I'm sorry; I thought you knew."

Lisa stood and put the pack over her shoulders. "This is really a very nice pack. I like it, Troy. I'll have to use it this spring when the ice thaws and the bears are roaming around looking for naked college girls." At everyone's insistence she told the story. A stern look to Troy told him not to elaborate on the parts she left out. "Everyone satisfied?"

"That's a great story," Linden said. "I can't wait to tell my friends in Boston."

Lisa sat on the piano bench next to Linden. "To make fun of me?"

Linden hugged her and said tenderly, "No, Sis. I am sure that none of my friends have a sister like you. I'm proud of you." He gave her a kiss on each cheek.

"I am just glad you are safe and sound," said her mother. "Oh, I can't imagine."

"I expect you to take good care of my daughter when she is up there canoeing, Troy," her father added.

"I'll do my best." Troy looked at his watch. "Hey, I better get going."

The whole family got up and hugged him good-bye. Her father packed some samples of his Christmas specialties for Troy to nibble on while he drove. Her mother asked a few more questions about his parents and family while filling a thermos with coffee for him.

"I'm sorry, but I've got to go," he said, protesting the delay. He grabbed the treats, and Lisa followed him to the mudroom. His suitcase was sitting by the door. He gave her a kiss on the lips, enfolding her in his arms. "I love you very much, Lisa. I am sorry that I keep embarrassing you."

"Wait a minute," she said. "I haven't given you my gift." She took a tiny box from her pocket.

He opened it to find a tie tack of a Bowie knife. "The little knife comes out of the sheath." She pulled it out to show him. "So be careful with it. It's solid silver from an artisan in Boston."

"I don't know what to say. I thought you would never talk to me again after …"

"It's certainly been challenging having you here. But you are," she said, pausing to take a deep breath, "very special, and I admire you. Maybe I even …"

"How did you get this when you didn't know I was coming?" Troy asked.

"I planned to mail it to you. It's fairly light."

"I love it, and I love you so much, Lisa." Tears sprouted from his dark-blue eyes as he kissed her again. "I've got to go. I promise …"

"I know," she said as he ran out the door. She followed and waved as he backed his car out of the drive. She ran in the back door to the remote control for the gate and opened it. *He would never think of that, and he would just sit there till someone came down the driveway.* She closed it behind him as she saw him leave in the security camera. Turning, she was startled to see her brother.

"He's a good choice for you. He is fun, athletic, and enthusiastic. He likes the things you like. He fits right into our family."

"Thanks. I suppose you didn't expect me to make a good decision about a boyfriend?"

"Come on, Sis, I'm complimenting you." He put his arm over her shoulders.

She hung her head. "I'm sorry. I'm a little sensitive after being the brunt of holiday conversation."

"He thinks the world of you. And I was glad to hear that you two are not having sex yet."

Lisa backed away. Her face flushed crimson. "You asked him about that?"

His sardonic smile gave her no relief. "Everything. We talked about everything."

"I guess I need a ticket to Boston to interrogate your girlfriend to return the favor."

He gently held her resistant shoulders. "Lucky for you, I don't have one yet. Too busy studying. Come on. Let's enjoy the rest of the holiday. Dad's making that eggnog you like."

CHAPTER 23

One afternoon, exhausted from basketball practice, Lisa needed to walk, so she walked the halls of the university. January had resulted in record snowfall, and now February had been so cold that she had been coming to UMD to do her morning run and exercises on the indoor track. This afternoon, as her heart rate slowed from basketball drills, she just wasn't ready to go home. *I need to think.* She ventured down the halls in the science building.

The glass cases along the hall caught her eye. She paused to look at the displays of physics experiments, chemistry research, and awards of various science professors, but most of it she did not understand. Her interest piqued when she arrived in the biology department. The comparative anatomy of skulls, variations on insects, and collections of fossils were more to her interests. At the end of the hall she came to the emergency exit, so she turned to walk back.

"You still feel foreign to this part of UMD?"

Lisa turned to the voice she recognized. "Oh, Heidi. Not so much anymore. I got a B on my final in biology, thanks to your tutoring. Did you have a nice Christmas break? I haven't seen you since the new semester. How have you been doing?"

"Too much studying, that's for sure. I need a break. President's Day gives us a long weekend; you want to do something?"

"We don't have any basketball games or practices, so sure. What did you have in mind?"

"Let's go for a winter camping trip. Uncle Marten has a trapping shack in the forest at the back limits of the reservation. We could snowshoe out there and relax. No people, no cars, and no place to study."

"And plenty of good exercise, right?"

"Do you have snowshoes or skis?"

"Both. My father used to take me snowshoeing when I was younger when he wasn't so busy, and I got cross-country skis for Christmas a couple of years ago."

"I have snowshoes," Heidi said, then paused.

"You know you can rent skis from the athletic department. They aren't top of the line, but they're inexpensive, ten dollars for the weekend."

As they walked down the hall together, they talked about what to wear, how they were going to transport their gear, and when they should leave. "What about food?" Lisa asked.

Heidi's eyes sparkled. "You bring frozen vegetables, and I'll be responsible for the meat?"

"Sounds like a plan."

"And let's bring some oranges. If they stay frozen, they're good. You just cannot let them thaw. I'll bring a half dozen."

"Great. I'll drive. We can leave Friday afternoon and drive ..."

Heidi finished, "Up to the reservation and stay at my house that night and leave in the morning." Heidi hugged her. "What a plan. See you on Friday. Meet me here after my last class."

"Where? By the fossils?"

Heidi smiled. "No, my last class is near the skulls."

· · ·

Lisa met Heidi by the skulls, and they went to Heidi's dorm room to pick up her gear. Lisa had her skis and the rental skis from the athletic department in the cartop carrier. *This isn't much stuff. The rest of her gear must be at her home,* Lisa thought as she threw Heidi's backpack in the trunk.

The conversation was animated on the way north. Lisa relaxed, knowing that she didn't have to think about courses or assignments for three days. She said, "I heard the temperature was going to be pretty cold this weekend, maybe ten below zero."

Heidi shifted in her seat, put her head back, and stretched out her legs. "That's a perfect temperature for snowshoeing. We won't get overheated, and when we ski, the snow should be slippery. But you won't get to hear the snow sing unless it gets a lot colder."

"What do you mean, 'hear the snow sing'?"

"At about thirty below zero the snow changes its crystal lattice structure and produces a high-pitched tinkling sound when you walk on it. Anishinaabe say that it's the snow singing."

"I'd like to hear that, but I'd like a warm shelter nearby."

"Don't worry; one time I heated up my uncle's trapping shack so much that I had to go outside and leave the doorway open to cool it off. Freezing on one side, too hot on the other."

"Sounds comical. I can almost see you spinning around at the entrance."

"Believe me; it is only comical in the telling."

. . .

When they arrived at Heidi's now-familiar house, no one was home. Lisa was disappointed to still not meet Heidi's mother. It was late, and there were only yard lights on. Even Marten's house was dark as they passed. There was a note on the kitchen table. Heidi picked it up. "My mother is visiting her sister. She took some time off and went to Wisconsin."

They looked in the refrigerator. There were eggs and sausages for their breakfast and a bag of oranges, but Lisa saw no other meat. "There are the oranges," said Heidi.

Lisa felt timid. "And our meat?"

"Oh, I'll take care of that. We'll have plenty of fresh meat." She rubbed her belly. "I promise."

Lisa followed as Heidi went back behind the house. A toboggan was stacked against the house along with a pair of well-worn snowshoes. "It looks like we are all set for morning," Heidi said. "You want a hot shower before we go to bed? This is the last chance till we return."

It was cold. Lisa realized that the weather report she'd read was for Duluth, and they had driven almost a hundred miles north of Duluth.

The house was not all that warm, so after their hot showers, they put on their long underwear for sleeping. Heidi started a fire in the woodstove, and in no time it was cozy in the living room. Lisa was tired, so she gave Heidi a hug and drifted off into the bedroom. She curled up in the corner next to the wall, her prescribed spot. She heard Heidi puttering with something in the kitchen. The smells of the woodstove and Heidi's familiar home put Lisa to sleep.

. . .

Lisa awoke to the sound of noise in the kitchen. It was still dark out the window. Lisa could tell by the smell that coffee was brewing, so she ventured into the kitchen.

"Good morning," Heidi said. "Ready for a good breakfast?" Lisa nodded. "Did you sleep well?" Heidi poured her a cup of coffee.

Lisa gave another nod as she sipped her coffee. It warmed her as it trickled down her throat.

Sizzling sausages and the splatter of the eggs in the frypan stimulated her appetite. Heidi served two plates and sat down. They ate in silence except for the sounds of cutting sausage and chewing eggs. Lisa, caffeinated enough to speak, said, "I feel totally disoriented this morning. I must have slept hard. I guess I am just recovering from studying. This is a great breakfast. Can I help wash the dishes? What time is it?"

Heidi looked at her watch. "Four thirty. We should be ready to go pretty soon. It's at least four to six hours by snowshoe to my uncle's shack if the snow is packed down."

Lisa realized why she was disoriented. She had never eaten breakfast as early as four thirty. They washed the dishes together and dressed. Within thirty minutes they were outside in the cold packing the Jeep. The toboggan went on top next to the ski carrier. They added a few items including the oranges, but Lisa still saw no meat.

"All packed," Heidi said. "Last chance to use a real toilet. You can go first."

Lisa obliged, and Heidi followed.

Climbing into the Jeep, Lisa asked, "Are we forgetting anything? Like meat?"

"Nope. We'll get it there."

"Oh." Lisa drove out the driveway and down the road, following Heidi's directions. For almost an hour they drove on a snow-packed, one-lane road, surrounded by forest and an occasional frozen lake. Then the road just ended. No parking lot, no sign, just a snowbank in front of dense forest. "Where do I park?"

Heidi looked at her. "You are parked. Turn off the engine."

They took the toboggan off the car and packed it. Lisa had dressed in layers, but it was so cold that just climbing out of the Jeep sent a chill down her back. She shivered. Heidi ventured into the woods but came right back. "My uncle has been here within the last week, so we can ski his trail. Just put the snowshoes on the toboggan for safety."

"Safety?"

"If we get a lot of snow, it will be difficult to ski out. Then we'll need the snowshoes."

An undisturbed canopy of snow covered everything around them as they followed the narrow trail through the dense forest. The silence was as intense as the cold. Periodic cracking sounds as tree limbs burdened with snow snapped and broke were the only interruption. It was easy to ski on Uncle Marten's packed snowshoe trail, as about an inch of new snow made it smooth. Lisa discovered how important this was when she skied off the trail. Suddenly up to her waist in deep snow, she looked up at Heidi. "I am so thankful for Uncle Marten. Tell him that when you see him, will you? And get me out of this snowbank."

Heidi laughed as she helped Lisa up. "I will. He'll be pleased to hear it."

Despite the cold, the exercise of pulling the toboggan kept them warm. As the sun rose, they came to a large lake. "Put on your scarf," Heidi said. "The wind will whip your face."

Away from the cover of dense forest the wind swirled around them, stinging exposed flesh. Despite the layers of warm clothes, Lisa's chest and belly were cold from facing the wind, but her back was warm. In the middle of the lake, they rested, turning their backs to the wind. "I feel like my whole front is frozen," Lisa said as she curled her arms across her chest. "My breasts have turned into Dreamsicles."

Heidi laughed. "My excess fat does have a purpose. See?"

"You're not fat. You just have a different structure."

"Right, my structure is warmer than yours." She rubbed her gloves together and moved her legs. "Do you remember that tall white pine we were skiing toward?"

Lisa had been following Heidi and didn't realize that they were heading toward anything in particular. "No." She turned her face into the wind to find the sentinel pine. "All right, I see it now."

"That's where we head back into the woods. We'll be much warmer then. Have you warmed up enough?"

"I'd really like to take a sauna or a hot shower for the rest of the day, but in the present circumstances, yes, I'm ready."

"All right, you lead."

They turned again into the wind, covering their faces with their hands when the gusts swirled spikes of snow at their faces. Heidi grabbed Lisa from behind and pointed at a miniature tornado of snow coming toward them. "Those are called snow devils."

Lisa did not have time to respond as both girls covered their faces and eyes as the snow devil hit them. Then it passed, swirling across the lake behind them. The discomfort drove them faster toward the forest. At times ice formed on Lisa's eyelashes so that all she could see was the dim outline of the tall white pine. She skied with her eyes covered with her gloves until the crystals melted and she could open her eyes again. Despite the whip of the wind, the work involved of pulling the toboggan kept their feet cool but comfortable. Unable to speak above the whistle of the wind, they soon developed a signal, a tap on the other's shoulder, when they wanted to change positions. Lisa preferred pulling the toboggan as it kept her warmer, and she skied so close to Heidi that she was in her wind shadow. It was the person in front who needed the switch.

When they reached the pine, they slumped into a snowbank. The snow was so deep that only face, hands, and skis were exposed. Getting out of her snow coffin was more difficult than Lisa had expected. "I'll take my skis off next time before I do this," she said as she struggled to right herself.

"I feel like a beetle trapped on its back," Heidi agreed. She rummaged through the pack. "Are you ready for a snack?" She pulled the oranges out. They were frozen solid but were surprisingly easy to peel if the girls rolled them first in their hands. The frozen sections exploded with flavor as they melted in their mouths. "Pretty good, aren't they?"

"They are. But I would never eat an orange this way at home."

"The amazing thing is they stay fresh as long as they don't thaw. I was out with Marten on his trapline for a week once, and the oranges were tasty the whole week. I brought one home with me and thawed it out, and it was terribly bitter."

"It really isn't too cold out of the wind, is it?"

"We're just getting used to it." Heidi spit out an orange pit. "We better keep moving. We still have a few hours before we get to the shack."

"I'll take the toboggan, since I don't really see the trail ahead."

"Follow me." Heidi started skiing between the white pines and a scrambled mass of jack pines. This was virgin forest. The pines towered above them with very little undergrowth. The snow was undisturbed. By careful observation, Lisa soon learned to detect the subtleties in the snow that marked Marten's trail, so she tapped Heidi on the shoulder, and they traded positions.

After a long uphill rise, they found themselves at the peak of a hill. "Take off your skis," Heidi yelled above the wind, tapping Lisa on the shoulder. They turned their backs into the wind. "We'll toboggan down. It's a long, straight stretch. But remember to fall off before we hit the trees at the bottom. I'll hold the rope. Fall off when I do, and then I'll spin the toboggan."

"Have you done this before?"

She gave a rakish grin. "Yes."

"And I'm supposed to trust you?"

"Yes."

The ride down the hill beat any roller coaster at an amusement park for excitement. The thrill was intensified for Lisa because she knew that they were three hours from the nearest help if anything happened. There was no safe exit along the trail, only bone-shattering forest to stop them if they got off the path. Lisa took her cues from Heidi, shifting her weight to steer the toboggan around the curves, avoiding trees by inches. Stretched out behind her, Lisa could not see where they were going. When she tried to look over Heidi's shoulder, she only got a face full of snow, so she was surprised when Heidi suddenly tumbled off the toboggan. The delay in Lisa's response flung her momentum forward instead of to the side. She spun face-first into a snowbank formed by the wind swirling between two large trees. She opened her mouth to yell, but that was a mistake. Her mouth filled with packed snow.

She rolled onto her back and with her tongue forced the snowball out of her mouth. Looking up at the bright-blue sky between the trees, she took a deep breath and laughed. "Am I in heaven yet?" she yelled.

Heidi ran through the deep snow to check on her. When she realized that Lisa was safe, she started laughing. She fell to her knees and held her stomach. "You were supposed to roll to the side." She gasped for another breath. "I rolled off and held the rope. You stayed on the back of the toboggan and shot like a slingshot stone into the woods." She got up and knelt at Lisa's face. "You're all right, aren't you? I shouldn't be laughing if you're hurt, but it sure was funny to watch."

Lisa was laughing so hard she had trouble breathing but was able to respond, "I'm all right, but I don't think we will be able to franchise this ride for Disney World." She twisted in the snow. "I may need some help getting out of this snowbank."

Heidi obliged, and the two followed her tumbled path through waist-deep snow back to the trail. They found the toboggan facing the wrong direction but unharmed.

Heidi said, "Marten is really going to get a laugh when he sees this track. He'll figure out exactly what happened. I can see an embarrassing evening ahead."

"Hopefully I won't be there," Lisa said as she surveyed her trajectory through the woods. "By the way, I'm warm now."

"Then let's get going." They put their skis back on. The trail for the next couple of hours went through dense forest, so although it was cold, they were protected from the wind. The trail was mostly level with only a few hills that they traversed at an easy angle.

By early afternoon, Lisa was starting to wonder where they were headed but kept quiet as long as she could. When they stopped to eat another orange, she popped the question: "Is it much farther?"

"I was wondering how long it would be before you asked that question. You did pretty well for a Caucasian. I'm impressed." Heidi gave her a hug but did not answer her question. She ate another section of orange, staring at Lisa. She put the last bite in her mouth. "Ready to go?"

"Do I have a choice?" Lisa asked, a bit unnerved.

Lisa grabbed the toboggan as Heidi led the way. Lisa took a sneak look at her wristwatch behind Heidi's back. It was three o'clock. They had been skiing since before sunrise. Despite the vigor of basketball practices, her thighs burned with fatigue. They skied through a low area that was forested with cedar. Lisa guessed it was a swamp in the summer. Heidi paused and squatted several times along the trail but said nothing. By the third time, Lisa figured out that she was looking at animal tracks in the snow.

They skied up a gentle incline and found themselves in a mature forest. The trees were so big that four people could not have held hands around most of them. They paused in a clear area formed by six towering hardwoods. A curious formation, like a beaver house, was in the center of the clearing. It was barely eye level and was buried in the snow. It could have been confused for a pile of brush. An indented path, drifted in with snow, led to it.

"The trapping shack," Heidi announced. She took off her skis. "Wasn't what you expected, was it?"

Lisa was dumbstruck. It did not meet any definition of *shack* that she knew. She stood stunned, disappointed, exhausted, and confused. She felt like running home and climbing into her canopy bed under a warm blanket.

Heidi grabbed one of the snowshoes off the toboggan and started shoveling away the snow at the entrance. She pulled away a large piece of elm bark covering a hole just large enough to crawl through. Heidi disappeared inside as Lisa stood gawking. There was a puff of snow on top as a snowshoe tip poked through.

Heidi's face appeared in the hole in the hovel. "Welcome to our weekend accommodations."

Lisa was still as a statue, holding the toboggan rope.

"Well, don't just stand there; come on in."

Lisa dropped the rope and unlatched her skis. She crawled on her hands and knees inside. Thick bark formed the outside of the dome. There were tools and traps on each side, with a second dome inside.

She crawled through a narrower hole and found herself inside a sapling-supported structure. It was just big enough for the two of them to crawl around. It smelled of tanned hides, cedar, and meat with a hint of stale smoke. There was a fire pit in the middle that corresponded to the small opening that Heidi had opened with her snowshoe. At one end was a pot, turned upside down, with utensils beside it.

"Cozy, isn't it?" Heidi said. "With a little fire, it will be nice and warm in here."

Lisa found herself sitting on a fur hide as her eyes adjusted to the darkness.

Heidi smiled. "Cramped quarters." She put on a pair of moccasins that were at the doorway. "I'll get your boots for you. Could you bring our supplies inside while I get us some meat for supper?"

Lisa paused on her hands and knees in the doorway as Heidi fetched their boots. "I'm off to get supper. Lean the toboggan upright on the shack after you unload it. I shouldn't be gone long."

With a quick twist of each foot Heidi put her snowshoes on her feet and disappeared into the forest.

Lisa listened. There was no sound to suggest where Heidi had gone. She felt alone. *What if Heidi dies out there?* She looked up at the sky. Twilight elongated the purple and crimson shadows that deepened with each minute. It would be dark very soon. "I better do my job," she said to herself. She untied the packs from the toboggan and carried them into the shack. When everything was inside, she noticed a rolled-up deer hide over the inner door and undid the rawhide ties, dropping it over the doorway. She backed out and lifted the empty toboggan out of the snow. She dusted it off and propped it against the shelter.

Her bladder was full, and she wondered where she should urinate. She followed the packed trail away from the camp that Heidi had left and squatted in the snow. Body temperature vapor rose from between her legs. The ammonia smell made her sneeze. She almost lost her balance. *Oh, that would be disgusting.* She grabbed a nearby tree branch to steady herself. She took a tissue from her zippered coat pocket, wiped her nose and then wiped her bottom. She turned to look at the yellow stain in the snow, unsure what to do with the tissue.

"It's easier to walk if you pull up your pants." Heidi was suddenly standing in front of her. Startled, Lisa dropped the tissue and pulled up her pants. Heidi was still on snowshoes, and a white hide, stained with blood, hung from her belt. A meaty carcass hung by a string over her shoulder. "Where have you been?" Lisa asked.

"To the grocery store."

Lisa buckled her belt.

"I wish I had a camera for the look on your face," Heidi said.

"I would hope you would wait to take the picture till I was decent."

"You model nude. What difference would it make?"

"The difference would be …"

Heidi laughed. "Lisa, you don't have to answer that. I was just making fun of you. Now, I got supper." She held up the rabbit. "So let's eat."

Lisa followed.

"Oh, I usually stamp down an area for the latrine with snowshoes. It makes it easier to squat. We can then cover everything up with snow before we leave. By spring it will all have disappeared."

"How did you get the rabbit?"

"I snared it. Remember the tracks we saw in the swamp when we came through? I followed the tracks and found a rabbit run. Set up a snare, waited patiently, and there's supper. You like rabbit stew, don't you?"

"I'm hungry enough to eat anything. The calories from our oranges disappeared a long time ago."

They returned to their shelter. "All right, supper," Heidi said. "First we need a fire and a pot of boiling water; then you add the frozen vegetables you brought, and I will cut up the rabbit and cook it all up."

"Inside the shack?"

"No, it's nice enough outside; let's cook here." Heidi kicked away some snow and uncovered black-tinged ground from a previous fire. "If we cook inside, the shack will get too hot. Remember the story I told you?" She kicked a lump of snow between two trees. "Here's the firewood; let's make supper."

Lisa retrieved the pot and filled it with snow. Heidi lit some tinder and added the dry, split wood Marten had left. Within minutes they had a nice roaring fire. As the snow melted, Lisa added some frozen vegetables. Heidi found skewers in the shack and deboned the rabbit and roasted the succulent meat over the fire. When the water and vegetables were boiling, she threw some of the roasted rabbit portions into the water. After the pot returned to a hearty boil, they were ready to eat their rabbit stew with rabbit shish kebabs. The well-cooked meat was juicy and tender. The vegetables, cooked in the broth, were tasty and filling. Lisa spooned the last of her stew into her mouth as darkness enveloped them.

A chill rolled over the clearing like a frosted blanket. Without the sun the temperature plummeted. Unseen clouds obscured the stars. There was no moon, just blackness. They huddled closer to the fire. "Are you ready for bed?" asked Heidi.

"Not much entertainment around camp, is there?"

They cleaned up their utensils, one holding the flashlight while the other cleaned the cooking pot and their bowls. After a trip to the latrine, they were both ready for bed. Heidi replaced the bark on the top of the shack. "We won't need a fire inside tonight," she said as they crawled inside, covering the outside doorway with the elm bark and the inside doorway with the doeskin. Undressing to their long underwear, they crawled into their sleeping bags, wiggling and squirming to generate heat. Finally warm they lay still.

"It sure is quiet," said Lisa.

"Just wait; the chorus will begin soon," Heidi said.

Within minutes of being settled the music started. First one lone wolf howled and then another. Soon they were in the midst of a concert. Lisa thought she could distinguish at least six or seven different voices. It was almost an hour before it was quiet.

"That was beautiful," Lisa said. "It was worth coming out here just to hear that. Thanks for inviting me to come to your uncle's shack, as you call it. Isn't it a wigwam or something like that?"

"It's a *weegiwahm*." Heidi spelled the Anishinaabe word for Lisa. "Or as you say, wigwam. But Marten calls it a shack. It is just a winter hunting lodge to him, a safe place to stay when he is trapping."

"I'm really getting cozy warm now; I can't believe it."

"Because one dome is inside another, there is good insulation. And he goes to a lot of work to lay grass and reeds underneath these hides on the floor. Then he places the rocks so he can have a small fire in here if it really gets cold."

"In my sleeping bag, it's nice; you're right we don't need the fire to stay warm."

"Yes, and it gets smoky in here with a fire, even with the little vent on top."

The wind was blowing outside making soft whistling sounds as it whipped through the trees. Periodically there would be a loud snap of a tree limb breaking under its load of snow. Now Lisa recognized the sound for what it was, not a gunshot as she'd thought the first time. In between such jarring sounds, there was intense quiet.

"Have you been dating anyone recently?" Lisa asked.

"Nope. It doesn't fit into my schedule. Besides, the Anishinaabe guys think I am conceited because I aspire to go to medical school, and I guess the blond, blue-eyed set don't care for my tree-trunk figure."

"They aren't attracted to your beautiful tan skin and long, silky, black hair? I'd love to have your hair."

"I could cut it off and make a wig out of it for you. I'm probably going to cut it if I get into medical school anyway. It's too much work."

"No. You should probably donate it to someone who is going through chemotherapy and has lost all their hair. Mine isn't that great, but I'm not much for wigs."

A lone wolf howled.

"How about you?" Heidi asked. "Have you been dating?"

"Well, sort of, but not like I was … before what happened. I will never forget you singing me back to health. That was such a wonderful gift."

"So what do you mean? Are you dating or not?"

"Not really. It's hard to explain."

"I'm not asleep yet; start explaining."

Lisa's eyes were fully dilated, but it was so intensely dark she could see nothing. It didn't matter whether her eyes were open or closed; it was exactly the same. She had never been in an environment so dark. After blinking a few times she said, "I met this guy when I was canoeing in Canada. He works at an outfitting place. He goes to the University of Wisconsin, majoring in economics or business; I'm not sure. He just works as an outfitter in the summer."

"Yes, I'm wide awake now."

"We've sort of done things together a couple of times when I've come back from canoe trips but not exactly going out. We drove together in the van to pick up campers returning from trips. He really likes me and claims he won't date any other girl until I tell him I don't want him. He's sort of ridiculous that way."

"Sounds like he is very interested in you."

"Yes. He even said he loves me, and he is great at kissing."

"So far so good."

"But I don't know. He doesn't call me back or write. He says he is overwhelmed with his classes, but then he suddenly showed up at Christmas. He was asleep in his car in front of our security gate. He could have frozen to death."

"Definitely dedicated."

"I suppose. But then he met my family."

"Did they like him?"

"That's the problem. He charmed them. They think he is wonderful. My mother wants me to marry him right away, my dad thinks he is great, and my brother, Linden, thinks he is the best thing that ever happened to me. But I just don't know."

"So what's the problem? He sounds smart, your family likes him, and he's dedicated. What's not to like? Is he ugly?"

"No. He has this straight, blond hair that falls over his face and a scraggly beard when he lets it grow in the summer. First time I saw him I thought of a smile creeping out from under a haystack. It's just that … Well, you know my past. I was, you know, fucking every guy I could, and then I was almost raped and quit all that, and now I want a guy I can be honest with."

"And you don't know how he will respond if you tell him what happened?"

"Right. Ambivalent." Lisa swallowed and took a deep breath. The air chilled her throat. "Every time I see him I plan to tell him. Then he comes across so darn sweet, and I don't tell him, and I just hate him for being so nice to me. Every nice thing he says to me makes me think, *If you only knew.* He just won't give me a chance to explain. I'm sure he'll drop me when he finds out. I could probably tell him over the telephone if he would just call, and then he would hang up and we would never see each other again." Lisa started crying.

Heidi said, "When you're done tear-dropping, you'd better turn your pillow over; it could be frozen in the morning."

Lisa sat up, bumped her head on something dangling from the ceiling, turned over her pillow, and wiped her eyes.

Heidi said, "I think you have a wrong mental image of yourself. You are so fixated on your past. If this fellow—what's his name?"

"Troy."

"If Troy loves you, he'll forgive all that past garbage. Remember: you are what you give; the rest is rubbish we carry along for a season and then discard. You can't give of yourself until you're honest. You have so much to give. You're sensitive, tenacious, and resilient. You have so many good qualities. Here, use this as a test. Tell him everything. If he walks away, he isn't as good as you think. If you tell him everything and he accepts you, then you will have a loving, giving, honest relationship that will last a lifetime."

There was a long silence, no wolves, no breaking branches, not even any wind. All of nature seemed to be waiting for Lisa's response. She wiped her eyes. "Sing to me, would you? You know, one of your healing songs."

Heidi said, "I'll sing you a very old Midewiwin song that has healed many distressed maidens over hundreds of years." Heidi's song caused Lisa to fall into a deep sleep.

• • •

The morning was cold; the bright sun glinted off the snow crystals in the air. The girls crawled out of the wigwam and visited their designated latrine, stretching and blinking in the sunlight. "Hungry?" Heidi asked.

"Sure am. But that rabbit quelled my hunger last night. I slept well, and I am sure it was warmer in the shelter this morning than it was last night. It is amazing how that dome conserves heat."

"It was pleasant, wasn't it?" Heidi got a fire going while Lisa filled the cooking pot with snow and placed it over the fire. In minutes the snow was melted, and they searched in their food pack for the oatmeal and Tang. Once the water boiled, they made their oatmeal and still had enough boiling water for hot Tang.

"I don't think I will ever drink Tang cold again. Wow, this is so good hot," Lisa said as she sipped the steaming liquid, "especially in this cold. It must be twenty below zero." She spooned a large amount of oatmeal into her mouth and chased it with another drink of hot Tang.

"You're good," said Heidi as she checked the thermometer dangling on the outside of her pack. "It reads eighteen below zero."

"Really? I was just making a joke."

"So what adventures do you want to have today, weather girl?"

"This is your neck of the woods. What are the big attractions here?"

"There is a waterfall not far from here. Would you like to see that?"

"Yes, and I would like you to explain the tracks in the snow to me. I saw you pause and look at the tracks yesterday, and I didn't understand what you learned from them."

"Those rabbit tracks showed me where to go to get supper."

"Are we having rabbit stew again tonight?"

"I thought you told me you brought spaghetti for tonight."

"Yes. The tomato sauce with spices is in a boil-in-a-bag container, and I figured it would be easy to boil the pasta."

"Then we can have rabbit cacciatore for supper." Heidi smiled. "Doesn't *cacciare* mean 'to hunt' in Italian?"

"How do you know all this stuff?"

"Oh, I just know a little something."

"I've heard that before." Lisa remembered Uncle Marten using the phrase. She knelt to rub snow in her bowl and cup to clean them. She handed them to Heidi. "Dishes are all done, Miss Knows-a-Little-Something."

They packed everything they were not taking inside their shelter, then put on their snowshoes and headed out of camp. The direction they traveled had not been traversed before, so they needed snowshoes.

"Now I really realize what an advantage it was to follow Marten's trail," Lisa said. She was breathless. "Still, it's fun to walk on top of the snow."

"We wouldn't make it very far without snowshoes, maybe fifty feet from camp." Heidi laughed.

"These must have been invented by a woman. What great thigh exercise! What every woman wants, great thighs."

"I don't know if it was a woman, but there is good archaeological evidence that it was an Athabascan."

They climbed up a hill and followed the ridge. A midmorning wind erupted, and Lisa was hoping to be able to get back into the woods. Heidi followed some kind of creature trail down the hill until they came to a river. It was frozen solid. Walking on the river was so easy they took off their snowshoes. The surface was blown clean in some areas, and in others the snow was so compacted that they could walk on top with their boots. Lisa could tell that they were hiking upstream by the gradual rise. They turned a corner and walked up frozen rapids. In some places she could feel the vibration of the water underneath.

Heidi suddenly turned, and Lisa ran into her outstretched arm. "The ice isn't safe here," Heidi said.

"How can you tell?"

"See the lace pattern?"

Lisa squatted and looked more carefully. She noted swirl patterns on the underside of the ice. The wind had blown away the snow so that the ice looked like window panes where frost had danced across. "Yes, now I see. They're beautiful patterns, like a fern."

"But deadly," said Heidi. "Those patterns are caused by swirling water currents underneath the ice. They eat away and thin out the ice. Hold my hand, and I will show you."

Lisa braced herself, counterbalancing Heidi's weight as Heidi stepped forward. The ice broke, and the swirling water boiled through. Heidi used Lisa's stability to jump back.

"The problem is if that's snow covered, you can't see it," Heidi said, leading Lisa to the other side of the stream where they continued walking. Eventually the stream narrowed as it cut through a rocky canyon.

The sun was at zenith when they turned a corner in the canyon and came face to face with a twenty-foot waterfall, frozen in motion. "Wow," Lisa exclaimed, "it's like a pipe organ." The spires of ice rose to the top of the falls. A dusting of snow intensified the contrasts. In several places the spires were so clear Lisa could see the water falling behind the ice. Deep azure blue, the color was the same as the sea in the Caribbean. She felt like a child as she took off her gloves and felt the stalactites of ice in spite of the cold. The vibration of the falls underneath was like music she couldn't hear. Moving from pipe to pipe, she inspected each along the way. She backed into the falls to feel the vibration against her back. "It's a natural massage. This is spectacular."

Heidi took the pack off her back and sat on a rock that protruded from the icy surface. She pulled out the oranges and frozen granola bars and tossed one of each to Lisa, who was still caressing the falls.

"This is so amazing," Lisa said. "I never dreamed of something like this. How did you find this?" She looked a Heidi and smiled. "Don't answer. You just 'knew a little something' that a falls might be here, right?"

"Well, I didn't know for sure." Heidi had her orange peeled and arranged the peelings on the rock as she ate. "These will be gone by morning. All the small four-legged creatures will devour these as soon as we leave." Lisa sat beside Heidi and added her own peelings. The citrine smell made her hungry. They ate, contemplating the beauty of the frozen falls in silence.

Lisa took a deep breath. "Did you see any rabbit tracks on the way?"

Heidi gave her a hug. "Are you getting hungry already?"

"No, just planning ahead."

"I think it is more likely that you don't trust me."

"A rabbit in the hand is worth two in the bush. I just want to see supper in your hand. Then I will trust you."

Heidi laughed as she packed up their gear. Lisa heard what she thought was a rifle shot. "Who's shooting at us?" she screamed.

Heidi laughed. "No one, silly; that's a tree branch breaking in the cold. You heard that last night."

"Well, it scared me. It was so loud this time, louder than anything I heard last night."

"It gets louder the colder it is. Some of my people could tell how cold it was just by the sounds in the forest." Heidi dusted the snow off her pants. "Now that you've heard it, you won't be so frightened next time, will you?"

"No, but I'll probably still jump."

Heidi put her arm around her. "You are such a great friend."

"Because I'm entertaining?"

"Partly."

Lisa's hunger pushed her to walk faster than they should have to return to camp. The result of not pacing themselves meant that they sweat under their layers of clothes. When they reached camp, Heidi took off her coat. "We came back too fast. You're like a horse returning to the barn. Now my long underwear is all wet."

Lisa peeled off her coat and found the same thing. "It's all right; we're back at camp."

"Not exactly all right," said Heidi. "I have to go snare a rabbit for supper, and remember that we slept in our long johns last night. They need to dry out before the hike back in the morning."

"Oh, can we put a fire in the shack and hang them from the saplings to dry?"

"Yes, let's try that. Otherwise it could be cold hiking tomorrow."

They went into the wigwam, took off their boots between the two domes, and crawled into the inner dome to strip. They hung their long underwear from small branches in the sapling supports.

"I feel ridiculous with no clothes on when it is twenty below zero outside," Lisa said as they put on dry panties. They covered up in flannel shirts, jeans, and sweaters and then went back outside to put on their coats.

"Twenty-eight below zero," said Heidi, checking the thermometer. "Now for some supper. I shouldn't be long if you want to start the fire and melt some snow. If you have the pasta cooking by the time I get back, I will cut the meat in strips; it will cook faster that way."

Heidi disappeared like a phantom into the woods. It was getting dark as Lisa filled the pot with snow and started the campfire. In no time she had a pot of water boiling. She added vegetables and fed the fire till it boiled again. Then she added the pasta and plopped in the sauce bag, stirring till the pasta was cooked. She emptied out most of the water, tore open the sauce bag, and squeezed in the now-warm tomato sauce, stirring it all together. She searched for Heidi, afraid to call out, fearing that she might scare away supper. She was so hungry that she thought about eating without Heidi. She let the fire die down and set the pot to the side to keep it warm without overcooking the pasta.

It was inky dark before Lisa noticed movement in the forest. Heidi returned with a large rabbit and another pelt tied to her belt. "This one was skittish. He didn't want to be our supper. I had to be very patient."

"The vegetables and pasta are a little overcooked, but they'll be all right," Lisa said as she watched Heidi cut the meat off the carcass into thin strips and put them on the skewers. In no time they were well cooked. Heidi slid the cooked meat into the simmering pasta.

They grabbed their bowls and ladled out large portions. Never had rabbit cacciatore tasted so good. As they huddled around the fire eating, their backs got cold, but their stomachs were full of hot, spicy food. Cleanup was a chore in the cold, but they needed a clean pot for oatmeal in the morning, so they had to face the cold and clean it.

"I am ready for bed," Lisa said as the first wolf howled.

"Me too. Let's take some of these coals inside the shack and heat it up so our long underwear dries." Heidi grabbed a large, gleaming coal with two sticks as Lisa opened the doorway. Dropping to her knees, Heidi lowered the coal into the small fire pit. "Now a few sticks, and we can heat this place up." With a pole she slipped the cap off the hole in the roof. A gentle breeze pulled the smoke straight up. "Just add a couple of sticks to that, and let's go to the latrine."

They relieved themselves and then crawled into the shelter, leaving their boots at the door. It was noticeably warmer. Lisa added another stick to the fire as they undressed to their panties and she crawled into her sleeping bag. They settled down, wiggling inside their bags to produce some heat, and then lay still, listening to the wolves howl.

"Thanks so much for bringing me on this trip," Lisa said. "I have learned so much."

"You're welcome. I am just glad to come with someone. I have done this alone for the solitude, but it is safer with two."

"Tell me a story."

"All right," Heidi said. "One cold January, the hunters could find no game. The women caught a few rabbits, but it wasn't enough to quell the people's hunger. The children were crying themselves to sleep. The hunters went out day after day to look for deer, but all they found were carcasses chewed and abandoned by the wolves. They were so hungry they would have eaten a wolf if they could have caught one. In desperation they huddled around the campfire at night, trying to decide where they should look for game.

"One old woman, who had seen many sweet summers, danced

around many warm campfires, and experienced just as many deadly cold winters, decided she was eating food the children should have. She waited until everyone was asleep and crept out into the cold. She didn't know where she was going, as it was too dark and her aged eyes were almost blind, but she just kept trudging through the snow. At daybreak the sun glinting on the snow was bright enough for her to see a buck and two does eating cedar in the distance by the edge of the ice-covered lake.

"'Now what should I do?' she said. She said to the deer, 'I know you have had a difficult winter too, or you would not be feeding on those cedar bows. But my people are hungry, and the children might die. Are you willing to give up your lives for them?' She wanted to tell the hunters where the deer were so they could bring meat to their families and especially the children. She ran in the direction she thought was back to camp but tripped on a root and fell in the snow, hitting her head on a rock. Blood gushed forth, but it was so cold that it froze to her face. She felt the gash. It was all across her forehead. She howled in her grief, a deep, prolonged, shattering howl.

"The hunters had decided that morning that there was no point in watching their women and children die, so they went out hunting, though they were disheartened and thought it unlikely they would find any food. Standing in a clearing searching for tracks, they heard the howl. One of them exclaimed, 'It must be a Windigo. I have never heard such a horrible cry from a two-legged or four-legged creature.'

"The hunters readied their weapons and strung their bows. 'We must protect ourselves from the Windigo, even if we starve,' they told one another and headed off in the direction of the howl.

"As they crept through the forest, they saw a horrible sight. A blood-streaked beast headed toward them. It sped off in one direction, hit a tree, got up, and ran in another direction. The beast howled again, and the archers shot at it. The other hunters raised their clubs in anticipation of the terrible creature's attack.

"Then they drew their knives, afraid that even as the Windigo fell it would rise again and attack them. They knew the Windigo had a heart made of ice and ate human flesh. They crept toward the monster. The snow around it was covered in blood. Taking great caution, they crept closer, but all they found buried in the blood was the old woman.

Deeply distressed, they searched the surrounding area. 'Look at these tracks. Let's follow them and see what evil made the old woman become a Windigo.'

"They followed her tracks expecting the worst, afraid that spirit creatures might suddenly appear, but as they crept to the edge of the lake, they saw the deer. Hunger replaced their fear of the Windigo as they shot the buck and one doe. The other doe got away. They thanked the deer for giving their lives and then cheered and chanted the victory song as they carried the meat back to camp. There was plenty for everyone.

"The hunters looked at one another trying to understand what had happened. 'The old woman must have died. That wasn't a Windigo. That was her spirit calling us to find the game.' They returned to the blood-stained corpse in the forest and gave her a respectful burial, hoisting her body onto a platform. Then they returned to the camp. Everyone feasted, thankful to the spirit of the old woman who showed them the path to the deer."

"That is a terrible tragedy, but the old woman did save everyone," Lisa said.

Minutes later Lisa could hear gentle, rhythmic breathing and knew Heidi was asleep. The wolves' howls were more distant now. Lisa watched the shadows cast from the flickering embers on the roof of the dome. She could just see out the vent and was fascinated as the smoke and occasional sparks flew upward. She shivered.

I better keep this fire going. There was a pile of kindling opposite the deer hide. She added a couple of sticks to the fire and rolled over in her sleeping bag.

• • •

"*Lisa, put your clothes on.*"

"*No. I don't want to, Mommy.*"

"*You can't play outside without clothes on. Now put your clothes back on.*"

"*No. It is too hot and sweaty out.*"

"*Lisa, don't tell your mother no.*" *Her mother grabbed her arm, but she got away and ran across the yard.* "*Come back here!*"

Her mother ran after her, but Lisa was so fast. Lisa saw ahead the shimmering light on the Tarmac and ran for driveway.

"No, don't!" her mother screamed.

Lisa stopped. Her feet were burning with pain. The shimmering heat rose all around her.

"Lisa," her mother screamed, "you're going to get burned."

. . .

"Lisa, wake up. Lisa, wake up! It is too hot in here." Heidi was shaking her. "Come outside."

Lisa shook her head. "It's cold outside; leave me alone."

Heidi grabbed her, put her boots on her feet, and pulled her outside. They stood in their underwear at the opening of the wigwam. The heat pouring out of the opening was so fierce that they only had to turn to avoid the subzero cold. "Did you put more wood on the fire?" Heidi asked.

"Yes, after you went to sleep. I just added a few so it wouldn't go out."

"Unfortunately you turned it into a sweat lodge. It is only necessary to build a small fire and then let it go out. Now we will just have to wait. We can't put the fire out, or the place will fill with smoke, and then we won't have a shelter at all."

"I'm sorry."

"Don't feel bad. I've done the same thing, as I told you. Besides, how often do you get to stand outdoors nearly naked at thirty below zero?" Heidi smiled and handed her a bottle of water. "Drink or you'll get dehydrated, and then you might get a urine infection. Drink."

Lisa drank the tepid water. Neither hot nor cold, the water tasted of campfire smoke. As she drank, she thought, *How odd. Here I am standing outside dressed in my underwear and boots because the shack is too hot.* Her back chilled, so she turned to face the weather. The heat pouring out from the opening warmed her backside, but her breasts and belly prickled with exposure to the cold. The breeze through the trees was gentle, but it deposited snowflakes on her skin.

They wrapped their coats over their shoulders and turned to face the heat. After about a half hour they huddled in the equipment area between the two domes, and by the end of an hour they were able to get back inside. It was still too warm to get inside their sleeping bags, so they lay on top.

"This is certainly an adventure of extremes, isn't it?" Lisa said. "I have never been so hungry and so full, so awed and so fatigued, so cold and so hot all in the same weekend."

"That's nature for you," Heidi said. "She teaches by extremes." Both were soon fast asleep.

By morning, both entrances were again shut and sealed. It was pleasant, warm, and comfortable outside her sleeping bag. Lisa rolled over to see that Heidi was still asleep, her back facing the white embers that had been the fire that forced them out of the shelter during the night. The smell of smoke permeated the air, but it wasn't acrid but pleasant as a wood-burning stove in a rustic kitchen.

The smell and its association made her hungry. She rustled around on top of her sleeping bag, changing positions. The light filtering through the vent on top lit up the scattered gear around the hut. She reached up and pulled on the leg of her long underwear hanging from the sapling overhead. It fell on her face. It smelled of body odor, her body odor, but it was dry.

Heidi whispered, "I suppose you're hungry, or did your bladder wake you up?"

Lisa put her hands on her belly, pressed her stomach, and then held her fingers over her groin. She leaped to her hands and knees. "Oh, that's my bladder. I got to go, bad." She crawled out the doeskin door. Painfully squatting and grunting in agony, she put on her boots, grabbed her coat, and ran off toward the latrine. Heidi joined her laughing.

"I almost peed myself," Lisa said. "Now I know where not to push. Why are you laughing?"

"You were certainly provoked into action. I couldn't contain myself seeing your antics. You are so funny, Lisa. I am glad I brought you on this trip."

"I hope I am more than just comic relief."

"Oh, you are. It's just that … Well, you should have seen yourself."

"Speaking of seeing ourselves …" Lisa finished urinating, pulled up her panties, and rolled her hips. Her coat flipped side to side across her bare torso. Heidi imitated. "Aren't we the sexiest advertisements for winter camping?"

"Coat over panties. I like it. Good enough for Victoria's Secret." Heidi howled like a wolf.

Breakfast was good and hot. They packed the toboggan quickly and dressed in their long underwear and multiple layers. Following their blazed trail, they arrived at the base of the steep hill in less than an hour. Climbing the hill was a challenge, not because they were out of shape but because they needed to climb the slope without getting too warm. By the middle of the afternoon they made it back to the Jeep, loaded it up, and headed back to town. Lisa invited Heidi to stay at her house overnight, so they spent the evening showering and sitting by the fireplace.

"It sure would be fun to have a sauna after a trip like that. Wouldn't it?" Lisa said.

"That would be great. Do you know where there is a sauna near a place to go winter camping?" asked Heidi.

"Yes, my uncle Toivo, my mother's brother, has a cabin with a sauna north of town. It is on a lake, but he is the only person on the lake as the rest is a state forest. It's totally undeveloped."

"Sounds like next season's winter camp to me. But we won't have Marten's shack as protection."

"I am sure we can come up with something. How about a tent inside of a tent?"

"That should work. Can't build a fire inside, though."

Lisa blushed. "That probably won't be necessary."

CHAPTER 24

If you have a positive attitude and constantly strive to give
your best effort, eventually you will overcome your immediate
problems and find you are ready for greater challenge.
—Pat Riley, LA Lakers' coach

Coach gathered everyone in a circle to start the game. "Forget
our streak of wins so far," she said. "This game will be the most
difficult of the season, despite being a home game. I promise."
She stared at each player. "I want teamwork. Without it we will lose. The
Comets' coach is a friend of mine and trains her team well. They are a
strong team. But I want this win." She smiled. "Do you want to win?"

"Yes," the team said in unison.

"I can't hear you," Coach said.

The team yelled in unison, "Yes."

"That's a little better, girls."

"Yes," they yelled louder.

"Now, ladies, let me see you play, so I can believe you."

Lisa sat on the bench as the seniors went out on the floor. She
remembered Coach Hammond's promise: "I will give you plenty of playing
time." She loved playing guard. Her three-point shots had become more
reliable. Every practice she shot a hundred three-pointers. The drills with
the team honed her skills and caused her to gain confidence in herself
as well as respect for the other players.

Lisa stopped daydreaming when Coach Hammond called a time-out.
Megan, the first-string guard, looked tired. "Lisa, go in until Megan gets

her wind back." Lisa headed for the court, and Coach grabbed her jersey. "No three-point shots. You shoot a three-pointer before I tell you, and I will pull you out for the rest of the game. Do we understand each other?"

"Yes." Lisa didn't understand, but she wasn't about to challenge Coach's threat. She played her position and passed the ball to the senior forwards, and they scored. Lisa wanted to shoot and had several opportunities, but she knew Coach had a plan. She passed the ball to the center, Allison, who scored.

Allison was a junior, six-foot-four African American with a vertical leap like a panther. Lisa had never seen her smile but was impressed with how focused she was on basketball. It was hard to get to know her. She seemed to have no friends, not even on the team. Over time Lisa discovered that she had grown up in inner-city Detroit and considered basketball her ticket out. Tutored through her classes, she just barely met academic requirements each semester. At the beginning of the season when everyone had introduced themselves, she had said, "My name is 'Allison,' and I do not appreciate nicknames. I was teased in high school, called 'Allie Cat.' I will not tolerate nicknames. Got it?" Coach Hammond had agreed.

Lisa respected Allison, and they had become almost friends. On the way home from practice one day Cheryl had told her, "She's like a grenade; if you pull her pin, she'll explode."

"We haven't walked in her footsteps," Lisa had said. "Give her some slack. I don't date anymore because of what I've been through. You don't hold that against me, do you?"

"You're right," Cheryl said. "I just don't like her."

"We're a team. Don't worry about being her friend. Just pass her the ball when she's in position, so the team wins. That means more to her than being her friend."

Lisa could see that the two teams were searching for each other's weaknesses. As Lisa observed the opposing bench, the Comets' coach seemed to be restraining them. The teams matched each other point for point. The spectators seemed bored, but Lisa felt the tension. It seemed as if each defense was testing the other team: a moment of sloppy passing or inattention to fundamentals, and they scored. Lisa returned to the bench and watched the seniors put on an aggressive show of strength.

The senior guard stole the ball and made a layup. The Bulldogs had a four-point lead as the buzzer sounded the end of the period. The team seemed euphoric as they headed for the locker room.

They met an angry coach. "This lead is nothing," Coach reprimanded. "I told you to stay calm, save your energy. They're just checking you out. Now they will take advantage of us. I want discipline." She slammed her fist on the whiteboard.

The Comets exploded in the second half. Within five minutes they had a ten-point lead. The girls on the Comets' bench were snickering. Coach Hammond called time-out. "We can do this, team, but we have to play much smarter. I want a strong defense, but slow down the game. On offense, make sure of your shots. If we play too aggressively, it will awaken their spirit. We want to sneak up on them. Just try to tie the game. Got it?"

The team calmed down. When Coach put Lisa in, Lisa passed the ball carefully to Allison and Megan, and the other forward had a couple of open shots. Cheryl stole the ball, but instead of a flamboyant layup, she passed it to Allison for a sure shot.

"Now," Coach said to Lisa. Lisa looked at her, unsure of what she meant. "Three-pointers, and don't miss." Lisa had three opportunities for three-point shots. She made the first two, but the player guarding her anticipated her third shot and tipped it, resulting in a turnover. The Bulldogs' defense prevented the turnover from scoring. Coach put the first string back in. Halfway through the second half of the game, the Bulldogs were under control, and the game was tied. Everyone seemed relieved.

Coach called time-out. "Now this game is going to heat up," Coach warned the team in the huddle. "I'll put in second string after the first few minutes, and I want you to match them. First string will be put in little by little when you're rested." She nodded at the key players. "The end of this game is going to be frantic. I promise you. But you can do it if you play like a team. Keep playing smart. No heroes." She turned to Lisa. "No three-point shots till I tell you, got it? They're onto you. Their coach knows you are the three-point specialist. I can see it in her eyes. Remember: I know her. She's my best friend."

"Got it, Coach," Lisa said.

Coach turned back to the team. "Get the ball to Allison as much as you can. It will work for a while, and then they will start to double-team her. Do you understand, Allison?"

"Yes, Coach."

"When that happens, I want Megan and Cheryl to come on strong. Pay attention to their defense. And rebounds, ladies. We need defensive rebounds. Don't give them second chances."

"Go Bulldogs!" the team shouted.

The crowd cheered, "Go Bulldogs! Go Bulldogs!" But the look Coach gave the team indicated that they should ignore the home crowd and control their strength.

Good defense gave the Bulldogs a two-point lead. They tried to maintain it, but after a bad pass by Tricia, the senior guard, the Comets tied it up. Coach put in a second string to replace Tricia. A minute later she pulled Lisa out as well. As Coach walked by Tricia and Lisa, sitting side by side on the bench, she pointed at them and said, "Chill."

The guards and forwards passed to Allison as much as they could, but the Comets recognized the weakness of the less skillful guards and took advantage. As the Comets were shooting two free throws for an unnecessary foul by the Bulldogs' exhausted guard, Coach sent Lisa in and said, "If thirty-six makes both of these, we'll be six points behind. Set carefully, and take some three-point shots. I want you warmed up for the end of the game. I'm pulling Allison so she can rest and putting in Katy. Feed Cheryl and Megan, and do some of those plays we practiced to pull the defense. Give Katy a chance if she gets open."

Lisa ran in and took her place, passing the messages on to the forwards. Comets 36 made only one of the two free throws, and the Bulldogs had the ball. Lisa set for a three-pointer, but it didn't feel right, and she passed it to Megan, who made a nice shot. When they had the ball again, Cheryl was way ahead of her defense. Lisa passed her the ball down half the court, and Cheryl made a layup undefended.

A moment later, Lisa had the ball. The Comets were defending better, sensitized by the last two baskets, but in a sudden defensive mismatch, Lisa had an open opportunity. Her three-point shot glided into the basket like a paper airplane.

The next couple of possessions Tricia, now well rested, shot well-directed passes to the forwards. The forwards missed their shots, but Katy got a rebound and made a beautiful shot.

Lisa thought, *I'm going to make first string next year.* While she was daydreaming, she got a bullet pass from the other guard right in her gut. Trained reflexes kicked in, and she caught it. Without thinking she swished a three-pointer. *All that practicing paid off,* she thought. The other girls slapped her on the back as Coach called time out.

"We're down by only one point. We're going to win this game, team, *if,*" she said, pausing to emphasize, "you keep your wits about you. Remember: control. Lisa, those two three-pointers are going to open the defense. I don't want you doing that again until they stop guarding you. Look like you are going to shoot, and then"—her eyes riveted on the other players—"do that alternate play we practiced. You know what I'm talking about?" Everyone nodded. "It will pull the defense to Lisa's side. Watch the clock. When their guard is down, pass it to the other side, and that should leave the forward open. Got it?"

"Got it," they cheered.

The play worked perfectly; the Comets fell for the "we're trapped" play, as Lisa called it. A few minutes later Coach called Lisa out and then Allison.

"Listen carefully, Lisa. I want to have you shoot some three-pointers toward the end. Hopefully they'll forget that you have that shot, when we need it. So when you go back in, pretend to go for three points and then pass to Allison, just like we practiced. They will think that you are too tired to shoot a three-pointer. I am counting on you two. Let's do it."

"Go Bulldogs," Lisa said and patted Allison on the back. She did not reciprocate.

The Comets watched the forwards carefully while trying to keep their eyes on Allison. Despite their attention, Lisa faked three-pointers twice, opening passes to Allison, who was then free to make two beautiful baskets, undefended. They were ahead by one point.

The Comets' coach called a time-out. The Comets' players stood at attention like soldiers. Lisa saw their coach giving strong, focused instructions.

The Bulldogs collapsed on the bench. Coach Hammond looked indignant. "The game isn't over, ladies." They knew they were in trouble when Coach called them "ladies" with that harsh tone of voice she reserved for chastisement. "Now suck it up. I want strong defense. I know this team. They come on very strong the last few minutes. That's how they win. If we defend well, we can burst their bubble, and then we'll get our chance. If you're sloppy, they'll have a ten-point lead and be out of range. Do you hear me?"

"Yes, Coach," the team said.

"Ladies, I can't hear you."

"Yes, Coach Hammond," they yelled.

"Now do it."

"Go Bulldogs!"

Despite the warning, the Comets swarmed around the Bulldogs. Stolen balls, intercepted passes, and sloppy shots resulted in a six-point lead for the Comets. Coach called time-out.

"You didn't believe me, did you?" she said. The girls hung their heads. "Now what are we going to do about this, ladies?" She waited for an answer, but no one said a word. "Slow the pace; we are not a team that does well on a frantic drive. I want careful passes. Feed the ball to Allison. Forwards, shoot carefully. We can win this, but you have to play with skill, not enthusiasm." She turned to Lisa. "I need a couple of three-pointers to catch up."

They returned to the court. Allison had the ball and was fouled by an aggressive Comet. She made both free throws, shooting with practiced skill. Megan grabbed the rebound, tossed the ball down to half-court, and Lisa made an undefended three-point basket. Then Allison caught one of the Comets' misplaced passes in midair and threw it to Lisa, who was standing at midcourt. She ran a few feet and swished another three-pointer. The Comets responded with their own shots, but all the Bulldogs worked together to slice the lead. Within a few minutes, the score was tied. The Comets took a time-out.

Lisa looked across the court. She was certain that the Comets were being reprimanded for blowing a six-point lead.

"Lisa, you aren't paying attention," Coach said.

"Sorry, Coach." Lisa turned to face a stern look.

"They're going to be watching you now. They're not going to let you do that again. They're going to keep one of their defenders at midcourt, so that play is dead." She scanned the team. "Let's use that to our advantage. There will be one less offensive player under the basket if Lisa hesitates around midcourt. Now for some rebounds." She looked at Tricia, who was their best rebounder. "This is your golden opportunity. Bring that ball down. Are you well rested, Allison?"

"I am, Coach." She nodded her whole massive frame. "Well rested."

"I want them guarding Lisa so the rest of the team has more opportunity. Do you understand the plan?"

"Yes, Coach. Go Bulldogs."

The plan worked well for a while. The Comets double-teamed Lisa, who thought she should get an award for her acting. Tricia got the rebounds, and Allison and Megan poured on the offense. But the Comet offense was keen as well. With only three minutes left the score was tied. Comets called a time-out.

"Their coach knows my style. She is expecting me to change our strategy. I'm only changing one thing. Lisa, I want you to move in on defense. That will give them a different look but keep the same strategy. Steal the ball, Lisa, then pass it, but don't run down the court. I want them to think you're tired, and then I'll take you out." She pointed at Allison, Megan, and Cheryl. "I'm counting on you three to get down the court as fast as you can. We need a few points' lead. This team is a terror in the last minute."

"Go Bulldogs!"

The next minutes were hectic. Both teams missed some key shots, but neither team could take advantage of it. The time flitted by with both teams missing opportunities. When the Comets' coach called time-out, the score was Bulldogs, 86; Comets, 87. The Bulldogs had the ball. They huddled with eight seconds to go. Coach Hammond pointed at Lisa. "You'll get the ball; they won't be expecting you to shoot. They haven't been defending you for the last minute. Set yourself properly, and make a three-point shot. Then if they get the ball back, they will need a three-pointer to win. The rest of you, scream for the ball. I don't want the Comets to know that Lisa's going to shoot. Got it?"

"Got it. Go Bulldogs."

Lisa drove the ball down the court. The crowd was screaming the seconds. The team was swarming as if they were anticipating a pass. The

Comets seemed confused by their strategy. Lisa set. Suddenly, Comets 12 ran and jumped to block her shot. The girl had long arms and just tipped the shot.

Lisa screamed, "Allieeee!"

Allison spun in position. She looked furious. Her anger focused on Lisa, but then she saw that the trajectory of the ball was wrong and recognized that the ball had been tipped. The ball was going to hit the rim and bounce to the side. Allison jumped with a gasp of rage and tipped the ball with both hands into the basket.

"Two, one," the crowd yelled as the Comets' center grabbed the ball and threw it across the court. Buzz. Game over.

Allison ran over to Lisa. "Don't call me that." Her face was burning red. "You know I hate that."

"I promise. I won't do it again unless we need you to win a close game. You did it." Lisa hugged her teammate. The rest of the team swarmed around her. Lisa shouted, "Allison, you're great." The team danced around Allison, and each team member hugged her. "Allison, go Allison, way to go, Allison!" they chanted. They tried to lift her onto their shoulders, but she was too heavy.

"Forget it," Allison said, laughing at their attempt. She smiled. "I love you all." Then she looked at Lisa, and her smile turned to a frown.

Lisa smiled when Allison approached her. "It's just too bad we hadn't practiced that shot, Allison. Maybe next year."

Coach Hammond grabbed Lisa's arm. "I don't know whether to commend you or chastise you. You didn't do what I told you. We only won by one point. What if the Comets had gotten the ball back? Which they did. What if their center had made that last-second shot? Which she might have." She gasped for breath. "On the other hand, you made Allison look good."

"Thanks, Coach, for the kind words. But I did what you said. The ball was tipped."

"Oh, I didn't see that. It must have been the angle I had from the bench."

Lisa smiled and joined her teammates to shake hands with the Comets. When they said, "Good game," they meant it. There were even several hugs between the teams. The Comets' coach gave Coach

Hammond a hug. "You deserve that one, very well played." As they parted, Lisa overheard, "I won't let that happen again, Amanda."

"Try not to," said Coach Hammond.

Lisa stared into the crowd as she always did, hoping to see her parents. But she knew from past experience that she would be disappointed.

Then she saw her father. He was jumping down the steps of the bleachers, and her mother was right behind him. He grabbed her. "Lisa, that was tremendous. I am sorry that I have not attended more of your games. You're an excellent player. And that last pass. That was the ultimate in humility. You really made that other girl look great."

"My shot was tipped; it wasn't a pass." She saw a total lack of understanding in her father's eyes. "Allison is great, Dad."

Her father looked over at Allison, who was still swarmed by her teammates. "Where are her parents?"

"Her mother's dead, and her father's in prison."

"Oh, I'm so sorry." He grabbed Lisa and hugged her till she was breathless. "This game was so exciting. I should've been coming to more of your games."

Her mother added to the hug. Lisa saw a tear dribbling down her mother's cheek. She said, "Yes, we should have been coming more often."

As Lisa headed for the locker, she was caught from behind. "Well done, *Sebiskukoque*." It was Heidi.

"What does that mean?"

"Woman with tough legs." Heidi disappeared into the crowd as Lisa's teammates pulled Lisa toward the locker room.

CHAPTER 25

Since basketball season was over, Cheryl suggested that the girls on the basketball team take Lisa out to celebrate her twenty-first birthday. Lisa was unsure that she wanted to celebrate with a beer bash, which was what Cheryl implied. "I don't know," Lisa said. "It's just another birthday."

Drinking alcohol was no big deal to Lisa. She had been sipping wine with dinner at home since she was twelve years old. Alcohol held no fascination for her. The wine her father selected for dinner and the aperitifs her mother selected for special celebrations were better than anything they had in the local bars.

"Come on; it's important. We'll just invite the other twenty-one-year-old girls on the team. You can legally drink now."

"I don't really want to go out. Do you want to come to my house? I can see if my parents will invite everyone. I am sure they have something special planned."

"We're not high school kids planning a slumber party, Lisa. Get real, girl. Let's hit the town." Lisa showed no sign of acceptance, so Cheryl said, "All right. You find out what your family is going to do, and then we can do something later. Your birthday is on Friday, isn't it? We could all go out on Saturday."

At home that night, her father met her at the door. "I'm making your favorite meal, Caribbean ribs with black beans and rice, for your birthday." There was nothing she loved better, and her father made it only for very special occasions because it took most of two days to marinate the meat and then slow-cook it. Her mother ordered a whipped-cream cake from the Swiss bakery for dessert, Lisa's favorite. It wasn't so much the flavor of the cake she loved as the sensuous texture of rolling the chocolate whipped cream around in her mouth. She definitely needed to be home for her birthday.

The next day Cheryl met her after class and prodded her about the party. "You're twenty-one years alive. It's the least I can do." So Lisa agreed.

That evening she found her father sitting at his heavy oak desk in his office working on the books for a financial meeting. Since she had been a little girl, this room and her mother's office had never seemed like part of their home. She had always felt that she needed to be invited to enter.

He looked up from his work as she slipped in the door. Before she could say anything, he said, "Are you excited about your birthday?"

"I am. You sure know the way to a girl's heart."

He smiled and put down his pencil, leaning back in his chair. It creaked.

Lisa sat down on the leather chair facing the desk. She folded her hands in her lap. "I have a dilemma."

"What's that?"

"Cheryl and some of the girls on the basketball team want to take me out." She wiggled her bare toes in the thick Persian carpet. "Should I go out after the party you and Mom have planned or Saturday night?"

"Why don't you invite your friends here? I always make too much." He laughed.

"Could I invite Heidi for dinner? She is actually a much better friend than anyone on the basketball team. I would not have made it through freshman English or biology without her."

He got out of his chair and came around the desk and hugged her. "I am so proud of you. It just took me awhile to appreciate how special you are. Juggling friends is a problem. Talk it over with Cheryl, and we will accommodate your plans. I'll make your birthday dinner either Friday or Saturday. I'm sort of selfish about my time with you. Big change, huh?"

"A change I like, Dad. But don't smother me."

He let go of her and held her at arm's length. "I can't make up for the past, but I'm trying to do a better job in the present."

"You're doing fine, Dad, thanks."

She turned and walked out of his office. She called Heidi and invited her over for Friday night.

"I would love to come over. Can I bring something?" she asked.

"Yourself, Heidi. You saw my house when we came back from the snowshoeing trip. Can you think of anything I could possibly need? But I need you at my party."

"I'll bring a wild rice casserole. What time?"

"Six o'clock or earlier if you want to go for a walk in the woods before supper. And I'll tell Dad that you are bringing the rice dish."

"I'll be ready. Besides, I need a break from studying all this chemistry. You'll pick me up Friday night? I don't have a vehicle."

Lisa said she would and hung up. She thought about Heidi. *She only had a mattress on the floor in her own room, yet she didn't seem overwhelmed when I brought her home. On the other hand, Cheryl is impressed by stuff.*

Lisa dialed Cheryl's number. "Hello, Cheryl. It's Lisa. My parents are pretty insistent about Friday night. How about Saturday night? We could go out then?"

"Sure, you will be twenty-one and a day, even better." They set the time for Lisa to meet at Cheryl's house.

Lisa returned to her father's office. "Heidi is coming for my birthday party on Friday. She is bringing a wild rice casserole." Her father looked quizzical. "I know you were making black beans and rice, but it is important to her, and she insisted. Besides, it is very exotic. We can have both." She knew *exotic* always caught her father's culinary curiosity. "My basketball friends are taking me out on Saturday night."

"All right, then we don't have to change our plans. Now Heidi, she's the one from …"

"She's the one that helped me with my anthropology project. Our paper is being published in next month's journal, remember?"

"Oh, that Heidi, the one you went winter camping with?"

"The only Heidi I know, Father."

"Right." He resumed studying his number graphs. Lisa knew the conversation was over.

• • •

Friday afternoon Lisa searched the chemistry department for Heidi. The chemistry department had its own library because most of the texts were used only by the chemistry faculty and students. Not another soul at UMD was interested in them. Heidi had told her that she would be there studying. Heidi was the only one in the room.

Lisa stepped in unnoticed and whispered, "Are you ready to go?"

Heidi shifted in her chair, surrounded by a pile of notebook papers. "You don't have to whisper in this library; it's a rule. Chemists are sort of a rebellious, antiestablishment lot. We have our own library, so we get to make our own rules." She looked up from the paper she was working on.

Lisa did not recognize a single symbol that made any sense to her and asked, "What is that, alchemy?"

"Inorganic chemistry, and actually it had its foundation in trying to make gold from base elements, so you're pretty close." She laughed, made a few more incomprehensible notes on the page, and put her papers away.

"I'm glad you're taking that class and not me. I have trouble spelling English, much less that stuff."

"It's just abbreviations for functions and elements."

"Like I know what that means."

"You make me feel so smart, Lisa." She closed her books and stuffed them in her cloth bag. "If I develop any doubts about myself, all I have to do is have you look at my assignments, and you'll make me feel better." She got up and gave Lisa a hug. "I need a friend like you. Come on; I'm ready to go. Let's party."

As they climbed in the Jeep, Heidi took a copy of the *American Anthropologist* out of her bag. "Look what came for your birthday. Dr. Clossen gave me his proof copy. Ours should come in the mail tomorrow." She thumbed through to their article on page 18.

Lisa was so excited she did not start the engine. She sat with the article on her lap, focusing on her name in print. "Did they spell our names right? I'm too excited to tell."

"They spelled our names right. See, you're first author, and Dr. Clossen is taking care of reprint requests."

Lisa started reading through the article as if she had never read it before. "Did we really write this? It is so … erudite." She looked at Heidi as she enunciated the word and gave her a hug. "We're good, girl."

"Yes, it is quite an honor. As undergraduates too! That doesn't happen very often. Maybe you should major in anthropology?"

Lisa turned the key and started the Jeep. "Nope, too many papers to write. I used all my words on this one."

Heidi laughed. "You don't give yourself enough credit, but it's your birthday, so I won't lecture you."

Lisa parked in front of the dorm so Heidi could get her casserole. She mulled over Heidi's response to her bedroom after their snowshoeing trip: "You were accepting of my house; why shouldn't I be accepting of yours? None of us got to choose who we were born to, did we?"

Heidi appeared with a casserole dish between hot pads. She had a gift bag looped on one finger.

Lisa felt the bow. It wasn't cloth but stiff like wood. "What is this?"

"Just a little birthday present. I wish I had made it for you, but Bidah did all the work. I shouldn't give you something I didn't make, but Bidah insisted."

"You made the casserole, didn't you?" She inhaled the earthy flavors coming out of the vented dish as she started driving.

"It just came out of the oven. Hope you like it. Should we tell your parents it is made with venison or keep that a secret? I don't know how sensitive they are about killing Bambi."

"My father will think it exotic, and I don't think my mother will care. But she is an animal rights advocate. Of course she is anybody's advocate. Lawyers are like that."

Lisa parked in the driveway, and they rushed through the back door into the kitchen. Lisa carried the journal and the gift. Heidi brought in the casserole dish with hot pads. As soon as they got in the kitchen, Heidi set it on the stove and said, "Thought I was going to drop it." She blew on her hands as she set the pads on the counter.

The dining room was set with Lismore crystal. The sideboard displayed a two-layer cake decorated with several different colors of green leaves interspersed with tiny blue flowers. "Happy Birthday, Elizabeth" was written in the middle.

"Very beautiful," said Heidi.

Lisa took a sample of the frosting, desecrating the foliage, and popped it into Heidi's mouth. "Does it taste good?"

Heidi licked her lips. "I suppose if anyone complains about the missing sample it will be my fault."

"And," Lisa said, putting her hands on her hips, "I wanted to make sure my parents weren't trying to poison me. I haven't exactly been easy to rear, you know."

Lisa's mom greeted Heidi and then noticed the smudged frosting.

"Heidi couldn't wait, so she tasted it," Lisa said.

"Right," said her mother but nothing more.

"I put my casserole in the kitchen, Mrs. Zuccerelli. I hope that's all right."

"That's most gracious, Heidi. We do not expect our guests to bring food."

"My pleasure. Oh, Mrs. Zuccerelli, take a look at our article?" She pulled the journal out of Lisa's hand and gave it to Lisa's mother. "Your daughter is a published author as of today."

Lisa's mother adjusted her glasses and scanned the title. "You wrote this, Lisa?"

"I dictated it. You know I can't type."

Her mother dropped into her place at the table scrutinizing each detail. "This is impressive. I thought you were just doing a little term paper and it was being published in the UMD bulletin. This is a national peer-reviewed journal."

"Yep, it sure is," Lisa said.

Her father came around the corner. "Happy Birthday, Elizabeth. We are pleased to have you join us, Heidi."

"Thank you, Mr. Zuccerelli, the pleasure is truly mine."

"Paul, look at this article," her mother said. "Lisa is the first author." Heidi winked at Lisa.

"My goodness, this is detailed," her mother said with a sigh, "and comprehensive." She puzzled over her daughter. "And you wrote this?"

Lisa turned to Heidi and smiled. "Heidi helped with the spelling."

Her mother didn't even hear her. She was engrossed. Her father was reading over her shoulder. "This was a lot of work," he said.

"A lot of work. We must have edited it a dozen times. And then all the references had to fit the journal's format. Heidi and I spent hours working on it, and then we had to meet with Dr. Clossen, and he edited a few things. But we got it done. And here it is on my birthday." She spun around. "Oh, and here is my present from Heidi."

Her mother put the journal down. "I'll have to read this more carefully later."

"Happy Birthday, *Sebiskukoque*," Lisa read as she opened the bag.

"What does that mean?" her mother asked.

"Nothing; it's just my Anishinaabe name." Lisa smiled at Heidi as she carefully preserved the bow and pulled out a basket that looked like a giant strawberry. With a little twist the green-dyed top opened off the red-dyed basket.

"It's made from strips of ash. It has to be treated, stained, and then woven in that shape. In the old days they used natural dyes, but they aren't as brilliant as commercial. Besides, Bidah"—Heidi turned to Lisa's parents—"she's my aunt, likes bright colors."

Lisa's father held the basket as if it were a bird nest that would fall apart. "Magnificent."

Her mother took the cover. "Oh, Heidi, this is a work of art. And I know art. I worked part-time as a docent at a museum while I was going to law school."

They put it back together and presented it to Lisa. "What a treasure," her mother said.

"I'm going to run it up to my room and put it on my dresser. Is dinner ready?"

Her father cocked his chef's hat. "It will be in about ten minutes. You brought a casserole, Heidi?"

"It's in the kitchen," Heidi said.

Her father left for the kitchen. "My very special Caribbean ribs are almost ready." Then her mother picked up the article and started reading, so the girls ran up the stairs with the basket.

Lisa closed the door. "Aren't they funny?"

"They love you. They're just being parents."

Dinner was not only delicious, but the conversation was animated. Heidi was conversant in economics of business and interested in food processing. Everyone enjoyed the wild rice, and Lisa's mother said nothing when Heidi explained that the casserole was made with venison. The whipped-cream cake was light and fluffy. True to anticipation, Lisa rolled it around in her mouth and found the subtle flavors and texture enthralling.

Her father offered everyone dessert wine.

Heidi put her hand over her glass. "None for me, thank you."

"Aren't you twenty-one? Lisa told me you were older than she is."

"Oh, I'm almost twenty-two. But my father was an alcoholic, and I don't want to tempt fate."

Her father looked embarrassed. "I'm sorry. Maybe we shouldn't ..."

"Oh, no, it's Lisa's birthday. Go ahead. Don't worry about my family problems."

Her father poured drinks for the three of them and then ran to get some grape juice for Heidi. "Now, a toast to Lisa, our most amazing daughter."

Lisa whispered to Heidi, "I'm his worst daughter too."

They sang "Happy Birthday," and then Heidi sang an Anishinaabe song. "It's a song of blessing," she explained.

Late that evening, Lisa brought Heidi home. "My parents enjoyed you. And it took the pressure off me. They had to behave with you around."

"Your father is a great chef; the food was excellent. Both your parents are interesting people. I enjoyed their company, but I can see why you had trouble growing up in their household." Heidi climbed out of the car and came around to the driver's side. Lisa rolled down the window. "Elizabeth, you are a special young woman, and I am proud to be your friend." She reached in and kissed Lisa's forehead, then turned and walked up her steps.

Lisa sat in the car. At first to make sure the light went on in Heidi's apartment but then to think. *Heidi doesn't care whether I'm rich or poor. She just likes me. Me.*

• • •

The next evening Lisa went to Cheryl's house. Seven fine-looking young ladies, dressed to party, stood at the curb.

"Divide up, girls," Cheryl commanded. "Some with me, the rest with the birthday girl. We're going to let this town know who's twenty-one."

The team shouted "Happy Birthday" in unison and danced around Lisa.

Cheryl whispered in Lisa's ear, "We're getting you drunk tonight, a birthday you will never forget, so I hope you have cab fare on you." She laughed.

Lisa followed Cheryl's car to the Loft, a college bar with loud music and tables scattered on the perimeter of the main floor. An overlook balcony with café tables gave the bar its name. Psychedelic lights floated about the room. The center was open for dancing. At the back a long bar stretched the width of the building. It was backlit with blue lights so the bartenders could see what they were doing. The lighting gave a mystical look to the bottles on the glass shelves.

The main bartender, Sylvia, owned the place. Once when she was a little girl, Lisa had barged into her mother's office unannounced, interrupting a client meeting with Sylvia. Her mother had introduced Sylvia. Lisa had been surprised that Sylvia was gracious about the interruption. After that encounter, as a teenager, Lisa had frequented Sylvia's bar for ginger ale with cranberry juice when she needed to hide away. Now Sylvia was in her sixties, but her respectful reputation still endeared her to college students. "They keep me young," she would say.

In the history of the establishment, no one had ever seen Sylvia drink an alcoholic beverage. She was as sober at three o'clock in the morning when the bar closed as she was at six o'clock in the evening when it opened. Despite her command of the place, she was playful, and the students loved her.

The group of seven girls entered, and an employee led them to a table off to the side. Chips were already laid out, and a birthday cake Cheryl had bought was set in the middle with "Reserved" signs on each side. After they were ushered to their table, everyone scattered. Some went to the restroom; others saw people they knew and went to greet them. Lisa went to the bar to talk to Sylvia.

"These are my friends," Lisa told Sylvia. "They want to celebrate my twenty-first birthday."

"Congratulations, Lisa. You're a big girl now."

"You mean besides being six foot tall?"

Sylvia laughed. "Have a good time tonight. You're only twenty-one once."

"I want you to promise me something."

"What is it, child?"

"I don't want any alcohol. No matter what my friends order for me, give me O'Doul's or 7 Up, but no alcohol. I'll give our waitress a big tip if you do that. Promise?"

"Whatever you want. But I won't tell your mother, if that is what you are worried about."

"No offense, Sylvia, but I've drunk some of the finest wine France and Germany have to offer, and I've had twenty-year-old Jameson in Dublin and Courvoisier in the Loir Valley that was smooth as silk. I don't need to drink tonight. Just keep your promise."

Sylvia laughed. "I pride myself on serving pretty good stuff here, but if that's what you want, that's what you get. I promise. Katy will be your waitress; I'll tell her. Besides, her husband left her, and she could use a nice tip."

The music became louder, most likely by someone's request. "You're the best, Sylvia."

Sylvia said something, but Lisa couldn't hear her and returned to her table.

Drinks were served, and everyone reassembled to give Lisa a hug. They sang to her and ordered another round of drinks. Cheryl asked Katy for a knife to cut the cake and little dishes to put their slices on. Lisa started to cut the cake, but as she did, Cheryl grabbed Lisa's hand. "Two drinks and already you can't cut straight," she yelled to everyone's laughter.

Hardly anyone ate the cake. Several of the girls mouthed, "Good," as they took a bite, but their plates remained untouched the rest of the evening. Lisa thought it tasted stale, but she took a large forkful and stuffed it in Cheryl's mouth, and everyone cheered. By the fourth round of drinks, several started dancing. Two of the girls that Lisa did not know very well sat in the corner and talked to each other, not interacting with any of the other guests.

Cheryl was the life of the party. She managed to find a couple of guys to dance with and brought them over to the table. She whispered at the top of her lungs, "Kevin said I could dance with anyone I want tonight as long as I get in bed with him when I come home." She flashed her engagement ring and roared as she grabbed one guy's hand and headed to the dance floor.

The other guy Cheryl left standing at the table looked at Lisa. She couldn't hear him, but he seemed to be asking, "Care to dance?"

"Are you good?" she yelled over the din. He nodded, and they danced. Lisa was as good at dancing as she was at playing basketball. Smooth and rhythmical, her every move was a flamboyant celebration of the beat. By the third song the other couples were making way for them and cheering when the number finished. Her partner was breathless.

There was a relative moment of solitude between pieces. "Can we rest for a minute?" he gasped.

"Sure."

Cheryl came up and walloped Lisa on the back. "Girl, you are good. Where did you learn to dance like that?"

"Playing soccer." The loud music started again, but her escort led her back to her party table. He said something and left.

Cheryl called for another round of drinks. Katy winked at Lisa as she served her.

"You're just drinking beer?" Cheryl said. "Have some good stuff. Bring her a martini, Katy. I'm paying."

Lisa caught Katy's eye and said, "Hold the olive."

When her order came in a large martini glass, Lisa was hesitant, but the look in Katy's eyes encouraged her. Lisa gave her a half smile as she took a small sip.

"Now isn't that better?" Cheryl asked.

"Tastes great," Lisa replied and then whispered to Katy, "I've always liked 7 Up, but the olive would have ruined it."

Long before closing, her friends were drifting off. Cheryl was still dancing but in an uncontrolled, ataxic way. The two friends in the corner weren't even talking to each other anymore, and the others were holding their drinks but had to rest their elbows on the table to hold themselves upright.

"I'm tired and ready to go home," Lisa told Cheryl.

She belted out, "Did everyone have a good time?" She sat down holding the table with both hands.

Lisa went to the bar. "Sylvia, here is the tip for Katy." She passed her two one-hundred-dollar bills. "Call a cab for boisterous one. Here's the address." She pointed at Cheryl as she gave Sylvia the slip of paper with Cheryl's address. "She should be asleep in a few minutes. I'll take the others home. They live on the east end, but Cheryl lives in West Duluth. Put the tab on Mother's bill."

"One cab coming up. Don't worry about the tab. Cheryl paid in advance for your cab fare." They both laughed.

"Thanks, Sylvia, for a nice birthday party."

Lisa walked over to the table and spoke sweetly in Cheryl's ear, "Thanks for the nice party; give me your car keys."

Cheryl grabbed her purse and flung it over to Lisa. Lisa caught it just before it hit the floor. She took out the keys and set the purse in Cheryl's lap. "Your cab is on its way."

"Great." Cheryl closed her eyes and laid her head on the table.

Lisa gave the keys to Sylvia. Katy, who was all smiles with her tip, offered to help Lisa haul the crew to the Jeep. Lisa had to put one girl in the back storage compartment, but the girl seemed comfortable. Lisa buckled everyone's seat belt, except for the one sleeping in the back, and headed down the road. She knew where most of them lived, and the ones she didn't were conscious enough to give an address. She stopped at the first house and pulled out the girl in the trunk. Lisa helped her walk to the door and pushed the doorbell, as the light in the room was on.

The girl's roommate came to the door.

"So why aren't you out partying tonight?" Lisa asked as she passed the girl into her roommate's arms.

"I got a physics exam Monday. Thanks. It looks like she will be quiet while I study."

"She might snore." Lisa walked back to the Jeep. She looked at her charges and calculated the next closest house.

She turned down the street, and one of the girls yelled, "I got to puke."

Lisa stopped the car alongside the road and opened the door just in time for the vomit to flow onto the pavement. The poor girl was hanging from her seat belt.

"Feel better now?" Lisa asked. She heard a faint groan of agreement.

Red and blue flashing lights reflected in her rearview mirror. A patrol car pulled up behind the Jeep. "Hands on the vehicle; spread those legs," the policeman said through the amplifier cone.

Lisa obliged, and a policeman came and frisked her while his partner got out of the car and stood in front of the police car's headlights.

"Who's the driver of this vehicle?"

"I am." Her passengers were too somnolent to respond.

"May I see your license and registration of this vehicle?" the officer said.

"They are in the Jeep. May I retrieve them for you, Officer?"

The officer was standing behind her with a large flashlight. He pointed the flashlight first at her and then scanned her passengers.

"They all have their seat belts buckled, Officer," Lisa said.

"Proceed. Keep your hands where I can see them." Lisa walked slowly to the other side of the car and leaned over and opened the compartment between the seats. She pulled out her papers, took her driver's license from her purse, and held them in front of her face as the officer shined the light directly in her eyes. He examined the papers and the license, maintaining the position of his flashlight.

"Name?"

"Lisa," she said. "I'm sorry. Elizabeth Tamara Zuccerelli."

"Spell it."

Lisa stammered, "Z-u-c ..." She paused, uncertain of the next letter.

The officer interrupted, "Have you been drinking tonight, Ms. Zuccerelli?"

"No, Officer."

He directed her out of the car. "Hold your arms up where I can see them." He had her walk a straight line. She was flawless. "Are you willing to take a Breathalyzer test?"

"Yes, Officer, I am willing. My arms are getting tired."

The other policeman was speaking on the radio. The police officer with Lisa told her to relax and motioned for his partner to bring the Breathalyzer. He instructed Lisa on how to use it, and Lisa blew into the device. As she finished, another police car appeared, blocking her car from the front. Two more officers approached.

"Name's Elizabeth Tamara Zuccerelli," said the officer with the flashlight in her face.

"Oh, I remember her," said an approaching woman officer. "We picked her out of a ditch about a year ago. Kidnapping and attempted rape."

"Same person," Lisa said. "You see, I just go out with girls now." The policewoman smiled. The humor seemed to be lost on the other officers as they focused their flashlights on the occupants in the vehicle. "They all have their seat belts on," Lisa said.

The first officer was looking at the Breathalyzer. "She's clean. First one this month."

"I'm the designated driver, sir. I'm just taking the girls home. They are all over twenty-one. Can I put my arms down now, sir?"

"Yes, relax."

"Thank you, sir."

The officer that recognized her said, "Did they get all that gravel out of your back? You were in awful shape."

"Yes, I healed quite well; thank you for asking."

"Sorry we were a little harsh," the first officer said. "Just doing our duty."

"I understand, sir."

"Drive carefully now. It's pretty late." He handed her license and registration back to her and directed her to the driver's seat as the other officer assisted the nauseated passenger back into her seat and closed the back door, careful not to put his foot in the emesis. He said, "This might constitute littering."

"I'll have her clean it up when she is sober, sir." He laughed. "Am I free to go, sir?"

The policemen stepped out of the way as Lisa started the car and turned the corner. They waited at the corner and watched as she took two girls who were roommates up the walk to their house. The remaining two she managed to deliver without further incident.

It was three o'clock in the morning when she arrived home. Her mother came down the steps to meet her in the kitchen. Lisa got a glass of milk out of the refrigerator.

"It was quite a night, Mother. I took all the girls home. None of them were fit to drive."

"You're sober."

"What did you expect?"

Lisa zipped up her jeans and threw on her sweatshirt in the changing room outside the figure drawing class. Modeling for the beginning class was easier. She had been apprehensive, as Dr. Henderson had said that most of the students had never drawn nudes. But after Dr. Henderson completed her orientation speech, Lisa did not feel the least self-conscious. Besides, she was able to move every ten minutes so her muscles didn't cramp. The time slipped by, and she spent the quiet moments thinking about basketball strategy and canoeing possibilities.

She remembered how she had dreamed as a little girl of being a model and had given up on the idea. Here she was modeling. But in her dreams she had worn fancy clothes. She smiled as she picked up her belongings scattered around the changing room and opened the door. Dr. Henderson was sitting at the desk in the back of a now-empty classroom grading assignments.

Settling on the stool on which she had posed, Lisa watched Dr. Henderson scrutinize the papers. With a blue pencil she wrote in the margins or circled part of a drawing. Her hair was pulled back, and Lisa could see the pulsations in her temples as she studied each student's assignment. After grading several papers she looked up. "This is the last class I will need you for this semester. If you are interested and available, I have some summer session classes."

"I would be very interested as long as I am in town."

"Good." She resumed her grading. Lisa sat still, observing her. Dr. Henderson evaluated each student's assignment as a scientist scrutinizing an experiment. *Why did she care so much? This was only an introductory class. Most of these students would never become artists.* Still her critical assessment flowed through her blue pencil.

When she finished the last drawing, she took a deep sigh and looked up. "Was there something else, Ms. Zuccerelli?"

"Dr. Henderson, how did you become so interested in art?"

Dr. Henderson's face became intense. Lisa felt scrutinized; Dr. Henderson was like an eagle eyeing its prey. The professor leaned back in her chair. "Is this important to you?" Her response was tainted with an Eastern European accent that she covered well when teaching.

"I'm intrigued by your intensity. I'm an athlete, and I focus to prepare for an event. You have the same focus toward art."

"All right, then, we've known each other long enough. I will tell you. My maiden name is Hochstrasse. Even though we were German, my family moved to Poland in the 1930s. When I was just a teenager, I was interested only in finding a cute boyfriend. I had no idea what was happening in the world. I studied French in school because there were cute guys in the class. I spent hours fixing my hair and scrubbing my face. My father was a businessman, so I had jewelry and nice clothes. Father gave me almost anything I wanted.

"Then the Nazis invaded our town. There was a shortage of everything. My parents sent my brother and me out to buy bread. We had no money, but Mother had given me some of her jewelry to exchange. The baker was reluctant because all his bread was supposed to go to the Nazi army, but he snuck us a loaf in exchange for my mother's diamond bracelet. When we returned, our apartment had been bombed. Our parents' bodies were somewhere in the rubble. My brother and I stood there not knowing what to do. A squad of soldiers came down the road. They grabbed my brother. I managed to get away and hide in the rubble, under part of the roof that had collapsed. They were yelling at him. We both spoke German because our parents spoke German at home even though we spoke Polish at school and to our friends.

"They were asking him why he wasn't in the army. He said he didn't want to fight, so they shot him in the head. He fell onto a pile of gravel, his blood and brains spraying onto the bricks of the collapsed building. The bread we had worked so hard to get fell from his hands, and one of the soldiers kicked it into the mud. Someone asked the squad leader, 'Where is that girl?' But no one remembered which way I had run. They searched for a while but soon gave up and marched away.

"I was so frightened, but after the soldiers left, I crawled out. I looked at my brother. He was lying in such an awkward way on top of the rubble. I straightened his neck and put his arms and legs beside him. I grabbed the bread out of the mud. With tears streaming down my face, I said good-bye to him and ran, clutching my muddy bread to my chest. I lived off it for a week.

"From that point on I only traveled at night. I pillaged garbage to find things to eat in the city, and when I got into the rural area, I slept in abandoned farmhouses. Several still had chickens running around. Some I killed and ate; others I couldn't catch, because I was too weak, but I found their eggs and ate them raw. I don't remember much about those days. They are all blurred. Somehow I stayed alive, but twice soldiers found me where I was sleeping and raped me. Somehow I managed to run away. I am ashamed that I stole clothing from people's homes and food from their kitchens, but I was desperate. Eventually I found myself in Paris."

"You walked from Poland all the way to Paris?"

"I did. I was so thankful that I had studied French, even if it was for the wrong reason. It helped me stay alive wandering through France. If I had spoken German, the French farmers would have killed me. When I arrived in Paris, I discovered two things that kept me alive. First, if I followed the German officers in the evening to where they were having dinner, there would be plenty of food to eat in the garbage. And the second thing that I discovered was that the Louvre, the art museum, was heated to protect the paintings. So I spent all day in the Louvre to stay warm. At first I slept in corners where the museum security people wouldn't find me, but when I was well rested, I would meander through the museum and study the paintings. They were a wonderful distraction from the horror outside. I could put myself into the paintings and find peace. By the time the war was over, I think I had read the inscription below every painting. I knew every artist and had scrutinized every brushstroke in the entire museum. So you see, art gave me back my life."

"But you have a doctorate in art. How did you get that?"

"When the war was over, the Americans came to Paris. I registered as a DP, a displaced person. All my known family died in the war. The Americans provided a way for me to come to the United States and helped me get a job. They also provided opportunities to get an education, so of course I majored in art. I went to Boston College.

"I guess I was pretty cute after I started eating on a regular basis, so Mr. Henderson, another student at Boston College, chose to marry me. He died of pneumonia five years after we were married. I was never able to get pregnant, probably because those soldiers gave me some disease when they raped me. Before he died, he insisted that I get my PhD, so I continued at Boston College. I cried like a baby when I got my doctorate because my husband died before he got to see me get my degree.

"Eventually, I adopted a daughter. Unfortunately we do not always get along very well, but I have a granddaughter of whom I am very proud. That is my story."

"So art saved your life?" Lisa said and thought, *And canoeing saved mine.*

CHAPTER 27

> We want to be perfect, well-rounded individuals.
> All of us have our quirks. We've got these
> embarrassing moments in our lives.
> —Rita Dove

Lisa had just finished her last exam the day before and was sitting with her mother having a pleasant Saturday-morning breakfast. "I can't believe that I'll be a junior. Pretty good for someone who can't spell," she told her mother. "But I'm tired of assignments and tests. I need a vacation. I'm going canoeing." *I want to see Troy,* she thought. *I'm done with him, and I'm going to tell him so to his face.*

"Much to my astonishment, you've always returned, in spite of chasing a bear through the woods naked. I still have nightmares about that."

"I promise not to do that again." She had in mind to do the Wickstead portage the right way, but she had never told her mother that story.

"I'll make a deal with you. You help the gardener put up a stone wall around my tulip bed and help with some of the landscaping, and you have my blessing."

Hauling rocks again, Lisa thought. Three weeks of intensive physical work prepared her for canoeing. She felt stronger and had more stamina. Now with the landscaping done to her mother's satisfaction, Lisa set off for Canada. As she got closer to the outfitter, she became more anxious about seeing Troy.

"Troy's picking up another group," Helga said when Lisa arrived. Lisa looked over the canoes and spotted a dark-green Kevlar canoe, not the usual yellow color. She threw it onto her shoulders and walked around the parking lot. It was heavier than the others, but in the shape Lisa was in, the difference was insignificant. She set the canoe in front of the building anticipating Troy's arrival.

Helga returned with a cup of coffee and a plate of gingersnaps. She invited Lisa to sit down at the picnic table with her. Helga said, "We are so glad to have you back again this summer. This is the third year in a row."

"The first year I didn't rent from you. Troy and Ernie just rescued me. It was pretty embarrassing."

"Don't be embarrassed, honey. You met a pretty neat boy that way."

"I suppose you're right, but he aggravates me." Lisa took a big bite of a gingersnap, stirred the cream and sugar Helga had already added to her coffee, and took a sip. "You heard that he showed up unannounced at my parents' house last Christmas, right? They didn't even know I was going with anyone. I had a lot of explaining to do."

Helga smiled. "That boy is quite spontaneous. But he is a good worker, and I have never once heard him complain. He will be a good man."

"I wished he would write or call like I asked him. After that disaster at Christmas I called him to thank him for my present. We had a squabble about how he arrived for Christmas unannounced and how focused he was on his studies. I thought maybe we had broken up and I didn't know it."

"All I can tell you, honey, is that he pranced around like a little boy who needed to go to the john the day you called to rent the canoe. He was so distracted he had to come back and ask Ernie what he was supposed to be doing." Helga took a drink from her cup and laughed. "He is definitely infected with a soft spot where you're concerned."

"I figured he was dating someone else. I called him in March and asked him why he hadn't called me. He said that he was busy studying, and then he said, 'I have a test tomorrow' and hung up on me. I called back that weekend, and he was all blubbery and 'I'm sorry' and whining, so I guess we made up. Then I called again and no answer. Then I get this adorable card in the mail telling me how much he loves me and that he is not dating anyone and only loves me. It was so …" Lisa threw her hands up in exasperation.

Helga finished her coffee. Lisa cradled her cup in both hands and took another sip.

Helga said, "Honey, why don't you go on a trip with Troy? You go on these trips alone, and I worry about you the whole time you're gone. What if the bear takes your food again this year? You were scrawny as a pencil last time. I'm glad to see that you've filled out some. Wouldn't canoeing with a nice young man like Troy be better for sorting stuff out?"

"I've filled out with muscle," Lisa said as she took Helga's hands in hers. "I'm sorry I made you worry. A lot of stuff at school and at home frustrates me. These solo trips help me sort things out."

Troy drove up with a van full of campers. Five young men and four young ladies climbed out the doors. Lisa immediately noted that they all spoke with an accent. All four young women were blonde, tall, and athletic. None were wearing bras despite having quite blessed figures. She sat at the table listening as Troy instructed them where to return their packs and cook kits. They were all smiles.

"Where is the bunkhouse and showers? I cannot go on like this," the tallest girl asked Troy. He directed them to the showers, and all four girls grabbed their personal gear and headed to the bunkhouse. Lisa recognized German words as they walked by but could not understand anything they said. The five men followed Troy with the empty packs and utensils to settle the finances.

"Sounds like they had fun," Lisa said to Helga, sipping the last of her coffee.

"Need a refill?"

Lisa smiled. "I'm fine. Thank you so much."

Helga picked up the cups and the empty cookie plate. "I'll make my special chicken and dumplings for you when you come back. I am sure you will be very hungry." She headed back to her private quarters and left Lisa gazing at the door of the outfitter, waiting for Troy's return. *He must have seen me*, she thought. *He is so focused. That's his problem.*

The German men came out first and headed for the bunkhouse, but Troy was in their wake. He came as far as the picnic table and sat down. "I see you have already picked out a canoe. The green ones are heavier you know."

"Who do you think carried it from the back lot?"

"I guess that was a stupid thing to say. You're mad at me, aren't you?"

"Yes. You jump into my life at Christmas, and then you are out. You're so hot one minute and then cold for months. Don't you think that is a little harsh to a girl's emotions?"

He reached out to clasp her hand, but she pulled it away. He said, "I'm sorry. I had a great time at Christmas. That was the most fun Christmas since I got a fire truck when I was six." He smiled.

She didn't respond.

"I had a hard semester, and I was focused on my studies."

"You always say that."

"It's true. And then the next thing I know I'm up here preparing for the canoeing season. Honest."

"You date a lot of other girls this spring?"

"Lisa, honestly, my accounting class was so demanding and my math class had so much homework that I didn't even rent a movie this semester, much less date anyone. Besides, I like you more than any other girl I've met."

"So you said in that card. I should have made you promise to write or call. What am I supposed to think?"

"That I'm busy?"

She noticed his crooked smile, which she returned with a look of disgust.

"Oh, that was the wrong thing to say, wasn't it?" he said.

"I wrote you letters."

"And I treasured every one of them."

"The least you could have done is written 'received' across them and sent them back," she said, clenching her fist in his face.

He folded his hands in front of him and bowed his head. "I have no excuse. God knows I have been faithful to you. I beg your pardon. I failed some classes in high school. It knocked some sense into me. So now I focus on my classes and everything else slips by the wayside. I don't want to lose my focus in college like I did before."

"You are inconsiderate and really bad at time management. If you care about me so much, I should be worth a twenty-minute telephone call." She grabbed his folded hands in hers and jerked them. "But for some stupid reason I like you. It's just a good thing Helga vouched for your integrity."

"She grew up with my mother. They talk. I have no place to hide."

"All right, forgiven one, I am ready for the kiss you should have run right over here and given me when you got out of the van with those four gorgeous, well-endowed, braless German girls. And don't you dare say you didn't notice."

Troy got up, came to Lisa's side of the table, and gave her a deep, prolonged forgiveness kiss. "I don't speak their language. I took Spanish in high school." He hugged her and kissed her again. This time she responded. As he came up for breath, the four German girls came out of the bunkhouse, fresh from their showers with clean clothes and too much makeup. They saw the kiss and cheered.

Lisa smiled at him. "Don't speak their language, huh?"

"Come on." He hugged her to his side. "Let's load that canoe and get you someplace private. It's too crowded around here."

A half hour later, Lisa was packed in the van, the green canoe loaded on top, and they started driving. They talked about school, parents, and siblings and then changed the subject to canoeing skills, moose behavior, and what the bears might be doing this summer, including where they were likely to be concentrated. When he turned onto the gravel road that led to the landing, they could no longer hear each other.

She was going to her secret campsite and hoped that no one had discovered it in her absence. They put the canoe in the water, and she added her pack to the bow. He brought two paddles, put one in the bottom of the canoe, and gave her the other.

"Make sure I have extra rope," she said. "I am going to try lining the canoe down the cliff at the end of the Wickstead portage."

"You're going that way again? You're crazy, girl!"

She gritted her teeth and glared at him.

"Oops, sorry, I'll get the rope," he said. He pulled extra rope out of the van and tossed it under the seat of the canoe.

"Be careful." He grabbed her and hugged her. "It's just that I get … You are the first girl …"

She wrinkled her brow.

"Excuse me, *woman* who has ever gone over that portage alone, and now you're going to do it again. You're amazing." He kissed her, caressing her neck with his hands. Then he followed the curve of her spine and barely touched her buttocks.

She tightened her gluteal muscles and pulled away. "You're sick." She gave him a jab in the ribs. "See you when I get back. Maybe we can heal this relationship."

"Is that a promise? I love you."

"I think I love you too," she said as she pushed off and waved.

Traversing the meandering stream, out of earshot from anyone, she yelled at the red-winged blackbirds sitting on the cattails along the stream, "That certainly did not go well. I was trying to break up with him." Red-winged blackbirds scattered at her tirade. She saw a few fish swim for the reeds as the shadow of her canoe crossed their vision. *He's so pure and faithful. If he ever finds out what kind of a girl I am, he won't want me. I pick a fight expecting him to get mad, and he apologizes. What kind of man is he?* She stopped paddling and cried. *The kind I would sure like to marry; that's what kind.*

· · ·

It was unseasonably warm. The sweat poured down her face and between her breasts, tickling her belly as she portaged the canoe. There was very little wind, intensifying the heat, but lack of wind was nice for a solo paddle. She made good progress. She saw a few other groups camped along the lake the first night but saw no one the next day, especially after the long portages. The afternoon of the second day she arrived at her secret campsite.

It must still be a secret, she thought, as the wood was stacked exactly as she had left it. Nothing appeared disturbed in the two-year interval. She felt at home. She tipped the canoe over on the flat area of grass and pine needles, set up her cooking utensils, then headed back to use the latrine. More importantly, she searched for tracks and bear scat. None.

When she returned, she made spaghetti and sat on a boulder to enjoy her dinner. When she finished eating, she realized that she had spilled sauce on her shirt. *This is ridiculous. Why am I still wearing clothes? There is no one here, hasn't been anyone for two years.*

She stripped and took her shirt down to the shore to wash. After swimming a few brisk breaststrokes out a few yards, she tread water and washed out the stain. It didn't come out. "Gardening shirt," she said, throwing it with a water-polo move onto the rocks.

The next day she didn't bother with clothes. She felt more at home than in her room in her museum house. She spent the day at the waterfall, basking in the pool she had found in the middle of the falls. The weather held with a gentle, comforting breeze. She climbed to the top of the big, white rock and lay on her towel in the afternoon sun. She felt enveloped by nature, part of the environment, at peace. She was supposed to be here. This was where she belonged.

As she paddled back to her camp, she threw in her jig with a rubber worm dangling behind. She caught two walleyes in less than ten minutes. *I'll add these to my macaroni and cheese.*

Back at camp she cleaned the fish and put the heads in a pot of boiling water. She fried the fillets as she cooked the macaroni and cheese. "I am really acquiring a taste for fish-head soup," she said, thinking of Bidah. She added some dehydrated vegetables and ate her combined lunch and dinner.

Stuffed, she put a towel on the rock shelf and stretched out, arching her spine over the granite. Her vertebrae cracked into alignment. "I have never been so content," she murmured to herself. She drifted off to sleep, awakening as the evening star tumbled into twilight. It was still warm. She was surprised that there were no mosquitoes; a gentle breeze seemed to be enough to keep them from her rocky perch. The earth smells made her delirious.

"God, I need to talk to you right now. Will Troy accept me if he knows my history? Look what's happened to me since I was here last. I have better self-esteem. That's good. I'm still in UMD, and I might even graduate. No, I *will* graduate. I passed that ridiculous biology class, thanks to Heidi. Thank you for sending Heidi into my life. It would have been nice if you had given me the ability to spell. Ran out of spelling genes, didn't you? I shouldn't complain; you provided.

"And my parents, you've improved my relationship with my parents. That's a miracle that I didn't expect. They even come to my basketball games now. Well, sometimes. Did you provoke them to do that? I suppose you won't tell me.

"And thanks for sending that deer when I was almost raped. I owe you big time for that. I'm sorry I fucked so many guys before that. You don't mind the bad words as long as I don't take your name in vain, right, God? Besides, I learned my lesson, didn't I?

"Now about Troy, the one guy I really want to have sex with, because I love him. That's a good reason, right? Or do I have that twisted around? Well, he's so pure and faithful that he's disgusting. I suppose you arranged that too, didn't you? Quite a trick you played on me. Why couldn't someone who is just a little screwed up fall for me?"

She spread out her arms and legs as if she were making an angel on the rock. She took a deep breath of the night air. "He is such a neat guy. How could he like me? Is he sick or deluded or ... in love?

"You know what I'm going to do, God? Oh, I suppose you do; that was a ridiculous theological question. Well, I'm going to tell you anyway. I'm going to tell him the whole thing, about all the guys I've fucked and all the sordid little details about the almost rape, and then see if he still likes me." She sat up on the rock and looked at the moonlight dancing on the water. Two loons swam into the light and began their chorus. "If he still loves me, I'll ..." A pair of singing loons interrupted her vow.

The trip went smoothly. Two days later she crossed the Wickstead portage. Portaging through the swamp, she saw the plant that Bidah had used for insect repellant. As she was smearing it on her arms and face she saw a mother moose and baby. *This makes the whole portage worthwhile,* she thought.

The rope trick worked beautifully. With one rope tied to the bow and the other to the stern and around a tree on the top of the cliff she lowered the canoe gently down the cliff. In fact she was chagrined that she had not thought of it the first time. She paddled out of the swampy pond, crossed the portage that had been such agony the first time, and camped on the same island site where she had washed out her wound.

It would be fun to show other people how to do that. Come to think of it, I've been pretty selfish with my skills. Sure I've learned a lot, but if I die, who have I taught? No one. I've kept it all to myself. She swam a backstroke while scanning her campsite. *Surely it would soothe other people's souls the way it has mine.*

She flipped over and did a fast crawl, then paused to tread water. *I should bring a group up here sometime, maybe a bunch of girls, so we wouldn't have to wear clothes. I don't suppose there is a nude art model association that wants to take a group canoe trip, is there?* She laughed, dove deeply into a colder thermocline, and then swam to the surface, jumping and twisting in the air as she kicked herself out of the water.

The trip back went so easily she worried that she was lost. The lakes looked different without whitecaps smacking her in the face with every stroke. But the landing looked familiar as she paddled toward it, and right on time, there was Troy on the shore to pick her up. His tousled hair sparkled in the sun. His trimmed beard quivered with his smile as he waved to her.

We'll see if he really loves me, she thought. Four strong stokes and she was at the shore. He ran to her and kissed her.

"How was the trip?" he asked.

"Excellent, relaxing. I think I am ready to start my junior year at the university."

Troy loaded the canoe as Lisa put her pack in the back of the van. She climbed in the passenger side and looked out the windshield. *When do I tell him? When should we have our big crisis?* she wondered.

Troy climbed into the driver's seat. "Boy, does Helga have a meal ready for you! She's been cooking all day. We are all excited to have you back."

"Chicken and dumplings, right?"

"How did you know?"

"Women's intuition."

Dinner was congenial, and Helga's chicken and dumplings were delicious. But the conversation did not give Lisa any reason to suspect that Troy was interested in anyone else. She asked several leading questions. She winked at Helga, who tried to get him to talk about "other women you have loved, honey," but there apparently were no others. The conclusion was that he hadn't dated anyone since Christmas or even since last summer.

She wondered again when she should talk to him in private. The timing needed to be perfect. Then they would have it out.

Troy got up from the dinner table. "That was great, Helga. You cook much better than my mother. When she comes home from teaching all day, she is too tired to cook, and my father can burn hamburgers on the grill; that's about all."

"She teaches English, right? You told my mother that," Lisa said.

"Yes, at the high school."

"Ah," said Lisa. She thought, *now I will either solidify this relationship or end it.*

"I have two groups to bring out tomorrow morning, that one at five o'clock in the morning and then those football players from last year. I better get to bed," Troy said. He kissed Lisa and gave her a warm hug. "You're not leaving till morning I hope."

"I plan to leave in the morning after another shower and a good night's rest in the bunkhouse." She turned to Ernie. "May I?"

"Oh, you are welcome anytime," Ernie said. "I won't even charge you. Any woman who has crossed the Wickstead portage twice, by herself, should have free lodging the rest of her natural life."

"Ernie, you're as ridiculous as Troy," Lisa said.

Helga got up from her chair and shifted her apron. "Come on, honey; I'll walk you to the bunkhouse."

They walked silently, Helga with her arm locked in Lisa's. As they approached the door, they stopped. "See, I told you he loved you. Helga's chicken and dumplings make men speak the truth. He's in love with you." She turned to face Lisa and gave her a gentle hug. "And I can tell that you love him too. I know that for a fact."

"That's the problem; if he really knew me, and my past, what kind of a person I really am, I know he wouldn't like me."

"You don't think he knows you well enough?"

Tears formed in Lisa's eyes, and she turned away. "There are certain things I haven't told him."

Helga took Lisa's face gently in her hands and forced her to look into her eyes. "Now that boy has worked for us for going on three years. I think I know him as well as my own son. I think he loves you and can handle anything you tell him. You just try putting your history on him and see if old Helga isn't right."

"I'll do that."

Helga kissed her forehead and brushed her hair off her face. "Soon?"

"Soon."

"Now you go to bed and sleep your pretty little fears away." She turned and headed back to her private quarters, leaving Lisa standing at the door.

Lisa looked up at the stars. It was a clear night. The Milky Way was so brilliant that it lit the yard. In the distance she could hear the frogs croaking to attract mates.

She slept well. In the morning the sunlight between the drapes awakened her. She took another shower just because she could and got dressed. Her gear was already packed in the Jeep, so she wandered outside to listen to the birds.

Helga called her in for pancakes. "Troy has not returned from his early group drop-off, and Ernie left about a half hour ago with another group."

The pancakes were filled with blueberries, and there was pure maple syrup to put on top. Helga added a couple of sausages to Lisa's plate without asking. She poured a cup of coffee and set it in front of her. "You take cream and sugar, right?"

Lisa smiled. "Just cream this time, thank you."

Helga got another cup for herself and sat down. "Did you decide when you are going to tell him your story?"

Lisa took a swallow of coffee. It was exceptionally flavorful. "What kind of coffee is this?"

"It comes from Kenya. Do you like it?"

"It's great."

"Now don't you think you can avoid my question by bragging on my coffee."

Lisa's mouth was full of blueberries and pancakes. Syrup dripped out of the corner of her mouth. She wiped her mouth with her napkin and kept chewing. "Sometime today, then I'm going to leave. If he calls me, he calls me. If he never wants to see me again, I won't blame him."

"Oh, he'll want to see you again; I promise you that."

CHAPTER 28

When I dare to be powerful—to use my strength
in the service of my vision—it becomes less
and less important that I am afraid.
—Audre Lorde

isa thanked Helga for the great breakfast, hugged her, and said
good-bye. She looked around the empty parking lot. *I guess this
will have to wait.* She climbed in the Jeep and fastened her seat
belt. Troy drove up. *Now's the time,* she thought. She climbed out of her
Jeep and walked straight to him.

"Oh, I'm so glad I got back before you left," Troy said. He hugged
her and gave her a long, sweet kiss. "You know I love you, don't you? I've
decided to call you every Saturday, at my expense. I know I was bad at
communicating. I apologize. I'll do much better. I promise. I kept my
other promise; I'll keep this one." He looked in her eyes. She gave him
no response, so he continued, "Have a safe trip home. You certainly look
a lot better than after your last summer trip."

"It's amazing how good a person can look when you don't have a
bear stealing your food and a blinding rainstorm driving you backward."
It sounded idiotic to her even as she said it. Lisa primed herself for the
big disclosure.

Just then a Chevrolet van drove up. Four huge young men jumped out of
the passengers' side. A tall, thin, wiry fellow jumped out of the driver's seat.

"Hey, Troy, how are you, man?" the driver said. "We're here for
another trip."

"Excuse me," Troy said to Lisa. "These guys are part of a football team. They came last year too. They're strong but don't have a clue how to pack, and I think if they went more than one portage they would be totally lost."

Lisa inspected the group, curious to see how Troy would handle them. Four massively muscled guys would probably be the offensive linemen. She quickly surmised that the fifth tall, agile-looking fellow must be the quarterback.

Each guy vigorously shook Troy's hand. One of them said, "We are ready for a great trip. Last year we only made it over one portage and didn't catch any fish, so this year we want a guide."

"Yeah, someone who knows where the fish are," a second linemen chimed in.

"And keep us from getting lost," a third player said.

"We got a bit turned around on that big lake you sent us to last year," the driver said.

Troy stalled. "How did your team do last year?"

"We made it to the playoffs, then lost. We could have won, but I threw a bad pass," the driver said.

"We protected him," one of the linemen said, motioning to the others. "He'll do better this year. He's been working all summer with the receivers."

"I wish you success." Troy smiled. "But I have bad news for you. I don't have a guide for you. You have to request a guide when you make a reservation."

One of the linemen, a black-haired fellow in a red muscle shirt and green shorts that were too tight for his quadriceps, responded, "Oh, man, I told you Philip."

"Don't worry, Roger; Troy will take care of us," Philip, the quarterback, said.

"Seriously, I have no one to guide you," Troy said. "Why don't you unpack your van, and I will get your canoes ready. We will go over the map and find something you can handle. Do you want one canoe for two and one three-man canoe, or does one of you want to solo?"

From behind Troy Lisa said, "They need three canoes if I'm going to guide them." Troy turned. His face was red.

Lisa stepped up to Philip and extended her hand. "I'm Lisa Zuccerelli."

"Philip Anderson. I think we need—"

"I'll guide you with a couple of conditions," she said.

"A chick. I'm not going on a trip guided by a chick," one of the lineman said.

"Oh, babe, you don't know what you're getting into," another said.

Lisa gave them a disdainful look. "The first condition is that you address me as 'guide' or 'Lisa.' You will not address me as 'chick' or 'babe.'"

"Yeah, Greg, Billy, show some respect," the more reserved fellow said. He held out his hand and formally introduced himself. "I'm Roger Thomas. Please excuse my rude friends."

"Nice to meet you, Roger," Lisa said.

The sulking duo, Greg and Billy, in cutoff jeans and white T-shirts, approached Lisa. Greg ran his hand through his disheveled blond hair and then offered it in a handshake. "Glad to meet you, Miss Zuccerelli. I'm Greg Nelson. I didn't mean to be rude, sorry." Lisa noted his multitude of red freckles.

The other, who had dark, curly hair, offered his hand as well. "I'm Billy Gagner. I just never heard of a girl, ah, female, woman canoe guide, sorry."

"Steve Flynn." The final lineman extended his hand to Lisa.

"He's the shy one," said Philip, "but he blocks like a wall."

All five looked at Troy like sick puppies. Troy said, "Don't worry; she can handle you. She just came back from a ten-day trip, and last year she canoed without food over the roughest trails in this part of Canada and came back alive. There is no one who knows this area better than Lisa."

"That's a pretty strong recommendation," said Philip. "Shall we take her, guys?"

"Yes," rang the chorus from the offensive line.

"There are some more conditions," Lisa said.

"Don't worry; we'll be respectful," said Billy.

"That's one," Lisa said.

There was a unanimous groan as they all asked, "What else?"

"I need to go through your packs, and you must leave everything"— she watched their eyes—"that I decide you don't need." She saw them look at one another. "I promise that you will thank me by the sixth or seventh portage."

"What? How many portages did you have on the trip you just came back from?" Philip said, sounding threatening.

Lisa counted in her head. "Thirty-two, I believe."

"Wow, where did you go?" Philip asked.

"If you want to get to lakes that haven't been fished … You're not too weak for that, are you?"

"We want fish," said Roger.

"Do we look weak?" asked Greg, flexing his biceps.

"We can handle anything," said Billy.

"All right, any other conditions?" Philip asked.

"Two more," she said, noticing their rapt attention. "You can make the decisions about where we go and when we camp. I will tell you where the best fishing is, but it will still be your decision. However, if the decisions are a matter of safety, I will decide, and I expect absolute obedience, no questions asked. And last condition, you can't complain."

She knew that they thought they understood the conditions but expected the experience they were about to embark on would demonstrate otherwise. But to her relief they each agreed.

Lisa glanced at Troy behind her. He shook his head in disbelief and said, "I'll go get three canoes."

"Well, men, let's get repacking," Lisa said. "Unpack all your clothes and gear in five piles. I'll get three packs. Philip, do you mind packing with me?"

"Fine with me."

As Lisa walked away to get the packs, she heard Billy say to Philip, "You're going to have girl's underwear in your pack." Lisa turned and stared at Billy. He said, "Oh, I'm sorry. Was that disrespectful?"

Lisa turned without comment and went for the packs. She heard the team unloading the van behind her. She returned with three medium and one large Duluth packs.

"You're going to let us have four packs?" asked Billy.

"Yes. This one," she said holding up the largest, "is for your food."

"All our food? We had two packs like that last year and still had to carry some extra stuff."

"Remember: nothing you don't need, one of the conditions."

"Impossible," five men said in unison.

"Possible," Lisa said.

Lisa had them pack two sleeping bags into each medium pack and then sorted through their piles of clothes, cutting the piles to about one-quarter of what the guys had packed. From inside the large Duluth pack she pulled out three plastic bags and instructed them to put their clothes in the bags and squeeze them on top of the sleeping bags.

"Pull out your food," she said. "Let's go through that next."

She went to her Jeep and pulled out her bag of clothes. It was miniature compared to the guys' bags. *I hope I know what I'm getting into*, Lisa thought.

"I can't let you do this," Troy said as he walked up behind her. "You're a girl." He shook his head. "I'm sorry, a young woman, whom I love, and ... Things could happen!"

"Oh, you love me. I could rehash your problem with calling and writing to the young woman to tell her that you love her, but I won't. Besides, I thought I would take them on a few difficult portages to wear them out."

"No, no, no. I won't let you do it."

"Listen, Troy Vogel. What good are my skills if I don't share them?"

"These guys are crude and nasty."

"That will change if I take them up to Argo Lake. There is good fishing along the way and lots of difficult portages, tough as goat trails, straight up and straight down. That will gain their respect."

"Aah," said Troy, "those portages could kill them, or they could kill you."

"You're really worried about me, aren't you?" she said as she winked at him.

"Yes."

She smiled. "I like that."

She returned to find the crew putting their rejected gear back into the van. Roger was sorting out the food on the picnic table. When he saw her, he gave a desperate look. "How can all this food fit into that one pack?"

"Troy, do you have a roll of plastic bags?" she asked.

"I'll get them," he said.

To Roger, Lisa said, "So let's go over each day's menu."

Roger pulled out a sheet of paper showing Lisa what he had planned.

Lisa went through the menu, first breakfasts and then suppers, removing the packaging and placing each meal in a separate plastic bag. Then she said, "Now lunches. What you have planned requires a fire. Are you sure you want to build a fire every day at noon? How about some of these snacks for lunches and then no need for a fire? We can eat lunch almost anywhere that way."

"All right." Roger hesitated but seemed to understand. The others gathered around the table. She arranged their snacks into five piles. "We need five lunches, correct?" She handed a plastic bag to each. "Pack up the lunches men." Each packed one of the piles. A huge assortment of excluded food remained on the table. They looked like hungry puppies.

"You won't need it," said Lisa. "And you will appreciate not having to carry it. Look, you'll have treats for the way home."

"If I get hungry, I get cranky," said Roger.

"You will get real cranky carrying all that stuff over a mile-long portage," promised Lisa.

"What! A mile-long portage?" asked Billy.

Roger looked to his companions. "What about my M&M's and all my candy bars and my Cheetos and my ..."

"Pack it in the van," said Philip. "We agreed."

Lisa slung the food pack on her shoulders and took it to a scale in the outfitter shack. Billy and Roger followed in her wake. "Ninety-five pounds," she said. "Think you can carry it?" Billy looked at Roger, but neither answered.

Next, Lisa asked about their tents.

"We have two ripstop nylon tents. They're real light," said Philip.

"Great," said Lisa as they handed them to her. "These are nice. Pack them in the food pack or on top of two of the clothes packs."

"If we get separated, I want the tent with me," Roger said.

"That's good thinking." Lisa smiled. "Pack the tents on top of two of the clothes packs, then."

Lisa heard mumbling. "All right, what's the discussion about?"

Philip asked, "Which tent are you sleeping in?"

"I'll sleep under one of the canoes, like I always do." They looked at one another, not understanding.

Troy appeared in the van with three canoes on the trailer. He opened the back of the van and threw the personal packs in the back as Lisa fastened the straps on the food pack.

"One more thing," she said. "Make sure all your fishing gear can be tied inside the canoe." She turned to Troy. "Do you have any of those tubes for the rods and reels?"

"I'll get one for each canoe, commander." He turned to the group. "It will only take one day for you to appreciate what Lisa has done for you. Remember to leave your car keys with the cashier, and we will park your van in a secure place."

The four linemen seemed dispirited as they climbed into the van. Philip ran his car keys to the office and climbed in the back as well. Lisa sat in the front passenger seat with her hands folded in her lap. She stared out the window, ignoring Troy's frequent looks in her direction.

Forty minutes later they turned down a gravel road. "I remember getting to the landing much quicker last year," said Philip.

"But Lisa wants to take you to a place that has good fishing," Troy responded. He shifted into a lower gear to climb a steep grade. The pines scraped the canoes as he turned around a narrow corner and stopped at a stream that cascaded over the rocks and then flowed into a swamp.

"Where are we?" asked Billy.

"This is called Forty Moose Trail," said Troy.

"Now that explains everything," Billy said, gaping at the landing. "Has anyone used this landing before? And I don't see any moose."

"I feel lost already," said Roger. "I'm sure glad we have a guide."

"Let's get loaded up, men," Lisa commanded.

Troy and Lisa took the canoes off the trailer and set them in the water. Roger, Billy, and Philip grabbed their clothes packs and set them in the mud on the bank. Greg grabbed the food pack. "This pack is a killer."

"It will take someone pretty strong to carry it. Are you up to that?" asked Lisa.

"I can handle it. It's not that heavy."

"Now a little instruction," Lisa said to get their attention. "I don't want the packs set in the mud. If we had put them in the canoe instead of where they are, they would not get muddy. Getting into the canoes is easy here because of the sandy bank, but many of our portages are rocky, so I want one person sitting on the stern while the other person loads the packs. It is embarrassing to flip your canoe with the packs at the landings."

She took one of the canoes and motioned for Steve to sit on the stern. She then grabbed one of the packs by the sides. "These are called the ears of the pack. Lift them by the ears, not by the straps. A broken strap ten miles from the nearest civilization is no fun to carry." As she stepped in the canoe to load the pack, she wobbled the canoe. "See how Steve stabilizes the canoe so it won't tip?"

She got back out of the canoe as the guys nodded.

"All right, load up," she said.

One person sat on each stern while another loaded the canoe. "This is a lot easier than the way we did it last year," said Roger.

When all was loaded, she motioned for them to get in position. She walked up to the van. Troy had turned it around but was watching out the open window.

"Are you sure about this?" he asked. "This is crazy, Lisa."

"What good are my skills if I'm not sharing them?"

"Will you be safe with five guys?"

"You think they'll take advantage of me?"

He swallowed hard. "I don't know what to think. I'm very fond of you. I would come along for a day if Ernie could give me the time, but we have lots of pickups tomorrow."

"You're jealous?"

"I guess so. I haven't gone on a canoe trip with you."

Lisa was formulating a plan in her mind. *We could go on a trip together like Helga suggested. It would give us a chance to have it out. Either he will love me or hate me after that.* "Troy, why don't you set up a trip for us to go on alone together when I come back? Will Ernie give you time off then?"

"You would do that?"

"Yes, it's a promise."

"Thanks. Be safe. I love you. I'll convince Ernie that I need a vacation. And I'm going to worry about you all week." He shifted into gear and drove off.

Lisa stood in the dust from the vehicle. *What kind of a proposal was that?*

She turned to her crew. "Ready for some adventure?"

"And some fish to eat," Roger said.

Philip was alone in the stern of one canoe, so Lisa climbed in the bow. They all took off down the stream. She observed how each paddled in the stern and who ran into the bank. It would be important on the big lake or in a storm. Philip was adequate but switched sides all the time. She was most impressed with Steve, who had his canoe under control. In the third canoe Greg managed to avoid disaster by his strength, not his skill.

An hour later they came to a short, rocky portage into a lake of the same name as the river. The lake seemed to invigorate them, but they were less focused. "The next portage is near that large, white rock on the other side of the lake," she said.

Steve set a course and didn't veer from it. Greg's canoe sashayed back and forth. Philip was better but used a lot of extra energy to stay on course.

The next portage was steep but less than sixty rods. She held them up at the landing. "Let's switch around, Billy and Roger in the stern." She turned to Philip. "Do you want me to take the stern for a while?"

"Please."

The next lake had several islands that required maneuvering around. Roger struggled, but Billy seemed to do all right. "You don't like the stern do you, Roger?" Lisa said.

"It's just too much work. I'd rather be the engine, not the driver."

"We'll switch at that island," she said. "Billy, you're doing well."

"Steve and I went canoeing as Boy Scouts," Billy said.

"You both have some impressive skills," she said.

Philip turned from his position in the bow. "I have to tell you I'm impressed, Lisa. You paddle with no effort at all. If you can find fish for us, I'll be even more impressed."

They stopped at the island so Roger could get back in the bow. Greg returned to the stern.

"The next portage is three-quarters of a mile, two hundred forty rods. But there's good fishing in the next lake. This portage keeps the wimpy people out. But I know you can handle it. There is a nice campsite on an island offshore. If it's empty, we'll camp there. Sound good?"

"Great, Miss Lisa guide. I'm ready for some fishing," said Roger.

At the portage, Lisa put on her and Philip's clothes pack and swung the canoe on her shoulders. As she marched off down the portage, she said "See you on the other side." As soon as she was out of sight, she started trotting, finishing the portage in less than twenty minutes, despite its length and steep hills. She set the canoe down in the water and put her pack into the center and pushed it back to anchor it among the rocks. She took a deep breath and stretched her hamstring muscles. *Time to check on the crew.*

She found Steve and Billy resting against a tree. Steve was carrying the canoe. "You're almost there. You're looking good," she said.

"This is exhausting," said Billy. "The fishing better be good."

"When you get there, put your canoe in the water and the pack in the canoe, not on the ground. I'm going to check on the others." She trotted down the trail. She found Roger, his face flushed, panting with the food pack. He was leaning over ninety degrees resting in an awkward position.

"Do you want me to take that pack so you can rest?" Lisa asked.

He didn't answer, so Lisa relieved him of the pack. He collapsed. "Thanks. This is sure a long trail. Are you sure there really is a lake on the other side? We didn't do anything like this last year. How did you do it so fast? How much does this stupid pack weigh?"

"About ninety-five pounds," Lisa said. "You were there when we weighed it. And I assure you there is a lake on the other side. I've been there," she said.

"It seems heavier now."

When he caught his breath, Lisa helped him put on his pack. "You'll make it; you're over halfway. I'll check on you, but I need to see how Philip and Greg are doing."

"See you at the end of the trail," Roger said as he took off with renewed energy.

Lisa found Greg and Philip at the bottom of a steep hill. Philip was carrying the pack and Greg the canoe, but Greg was tired, and Philip did not want to switch. She had Greg rest the canoe against a pine tree.

"How much farther is it?" asked Greg.

"You're almost halfway."

"You've already been to the end and back?" Philip asked.

"And you had a pack and a canoe. I'm impressed," said Greg.

"Do you need me to take the canoe the rest of the way?" Lisa asked.

"No girl—I'm sorry, woman—is going to show me up," said Greg.

"I just like to take my time," said Philip. "I'll make it just fine."

"Let's get going then. We don't want to wait till dark to get to our campsite." She helped Greg put the canoe back on his shoulders and then trooped behind them as they finished the course. Philip plodded along without much enthusiasm.

They all assembled at the end of the portage. "See that island ahead?" Lisa pointed across the lake. They nodded. "There's a beautiful campsite there. I don't see any canoes, so let's head for that spot."

With fresh determination they sped to the campsite. It was unoccupied, and they collapsed on the bank after landing their canoes. A large rock face led to a perfect fire pit. There were two very flat areas to put the tents, with dense forest behind for firewood.

"I'm going fishing," said Roger.

"Wait. First we need the tents up and need to decide who is fixing supper, and then the fishing begins," Lisa said.

"Yeah, Roger, you got to do your part," said Philip.

They unloaded the canoes and split into two crews to set up the tents. While the guys were busy, Lisa found a latrine and relieved herself. *Now this is going to be interesting*, she thought. *I hope I did the right thing taking this group. Troy sure didn't think so. Let him worry. But I need to get over some of my fear, and what better way to do that? I wish Heidi was here to sing to me. Still, I need to be careful; there is a lot of testosterone here.*

"Who's the cooking crew?" she asked as she returned to camp. Philip and Greg volunteered to make supper while the others went fishing.

Roger had a pasta meal planned with beef jerky cut up in the spaghetti sauce. It smelled great as it cooked. There was pudding for dessert and corn for a vegetable. The coffeepot was boiling with just water, and there was a variety of drinks: coffee, hot chocolate, tea, and orange drink. Lisa felt like a queen. Her solo trips had never allowed such luxury of choice.

The rest of the group didn't catch any fish, and everyone was tired after eating supper. Lisa overturned one of the canoes for her shelter, stuffed her personal bag under the canoe, and rolled out her sleeping bag.

"Are you really sleeping under the canoe?" asked Roger. "There's room for you in our tent."

"I'll be fine, but thanks for the offer. I've slept under a canoe for weeks at a time."

"How far have you canoed?" asked Steve.

"Over a thousand miles."

"Wow."

Greg said, "We canoed farther today than our whole trip last year. And last year we went over our one portage at least three times. Troy was right. I'm thankful you made us thin down. I never would have made that last portage with all the junk we had last year."

Billy said, "She still hasn't caught us any fish."

Lisa saw the defiance in his face. "Get up at sunrise," she said, pointing across the lake, "and go over to where that river flows into the lake, and you'll catch fish."

"Is that a promise?" Billy asked.

"No promises; fish are fickle. But if you don't catch anything, I will personally make breakfast for everyone."

"That's a deal," he shouted. "I like it when a girl—"

"Careful, Billy," said Steve.

Billy hesitated. "When our guide fixes breakfast for us."

"See this large white pine, fellows?" Lisa said pointing to the tree. "We are going to hang our food pack from that outstretched limb."

It became quite an operation as they took turns tying a rock to a rope and trying to toss it over the limb. Finally they turned to Philip, who was standing watching.

"You throw it; you're the quarterback," said Roger.

Philip threw a perfect pass over the limb with the rock tied to the rope, and the others held up the pack as they hoisted it above reach.

"Nice job," said Lisa. She thought, *There's no bear scat around here, so we should be fine, but this was still a good team-building exercise.*

As the fire turned to embers, the loons began to sing, and the Milky Way spread across the sky. Small talk around the fire slowed to a whisper. "I'm a strong guy," said Greg, "but for short bursts of energy. Those portages were killers." All agreed.

By the time the moon was glancing over the trees, they had all said good night and gone to bed, leaving Lisa alone by the fire. "I'm not tired," she whispered to herself. "But I suppose I should get up early." She stripped to her bikini and climbed into her sleeping bag. The melodies of loons and frogs put her to sleep. Her first day as a canoe guide had been successful. She prayed that the fish would not disappoint her in the morning.

CHAPTER 29

The first rays of light over the eastern trees woke Lisa up from her nest under the canoe. She squirmed out and pulled on a T-shirt and shorts. Her bladder was full, so she headed to the latrine. As she passed the tents, no one seemed to be moving.

Upon her return, the men were urinating in the bushes. Lisa decided it was a male behavior that needed no comment. "You ready for some fishing?" she asked.

"Right, we need a hearty breakfast," said Billy.

"All right, I like that enthusiasm. Paddle to where I showed you. Rubber worms on a jig, no fancy lures. Drop the jig till it hits the bottom; then let the current from the river swing the canoe into the lake. Fish are lazy; they like their food brought to them."

"Men like their food brought to them too," said Greg with a smile.

"You be the hunters; I'll be the gatherer. Catch some fish, and I'll have a nice fire prepared when you return."

The guys gathered their gear and headed for the canoes, three in one, two in the other. They left the third canoe, which was still overturned as Lisa's shelter.

She picked her way through the brush and forest behind the camp. She found a fallen tree and easily snapped off the brittle branches. With one arm loaded with kindling and the other dragging a larger branch, she wound her way back to camp. She heard shrieks as soon as she climbed the large granite rock to their campsite.

Lisa laughed at her charges as the jubilant troupe hauled in fish after fish. They were casting into the turbulent water where the stream entered the lake just as she had instructed. She broke up her kindling for the fire. A few well-placed hatchet strokes and she had split wood.

She yelled across the bay, "Just bring what we need to eat. The fire's ready." Her voice echoed across the lake.

As if by a magic spell, the fish stopped biting. The guys headed back to camp with their prizes. She met them at the shore. "Who knows how to fillet fish?" Of course no one claimed to know the first thing about cleaning the catch, so Lisa had them gather around her to watch. The skills she'd developed at Heidi's place came into quick use. The football players stood like cheerleaders awed by her performance. Six clean fillets were ready for the frypan. She handed Greg the guts on the canoe paddle. "Here, go bury these."

"Me?"

"Aren't you strong enough?"

"Yeah."

"Then do it."

"Who's the chef in this group?" she asked, turning to the others.

Philip volunteered, but the others followed like an entourage of *sous-chefs* giving consultation. Despite the fish negating any obligation, Lisa did not want her breakfast ruined by ineptitude, so she helped. The football players exaggerated their stories of the morning catch as everyone pitched in, mixing orange juice, setting out plates, and frying the fillets.

Problems began after breakfast. Everyone was too stuffed to start packing. "Who's going to do what here?" Lisa folded her arms across her chest. "We have fifteen miles to paddle to our next campsite." She gazed at her satisfied customers.

"Do we have to leave? This is a great spot. Let's just stay here all week," whined Roger.

"Our pickup is at the end of a chain of lakes. We need to paddle every day. At most we can take one day off. Do you want it to be today?"

"Do we really have to paddle every day?" asked Billy. "We should have gone over this before we left. I don't like to work this hard every day."

"Yeah, we need to paddle pretty much every day," said Lisa.

Greg jumped to his feet and flexed his muscles. "I'm ready. What should I do?"

"Take down the tents." With no tents, Lisa reasoned, they might get the urge to pack.

She turned to pack her own gear. She flipped over the canoe and brought it down to the water's edge. In ten minutes she'd rolled her sleeping bag and packed her personal items. She stood ready to add Philip's sleeping bag to their pack.

"I'm packing with Roger today," Philip said, sipping the last of his cup of morning coffee.

"I'm packing with you," Steve said as if he had just been expelled from a private club. "I'd be honored to paddle with you today as well." He scurried like a squirrel recovering his stash and returned with his personal gear and sleeping bag.

The others stacked their belongings in piles outside the fallen tents. Greg pulled gear out as he tried to roll up one of the tents. He gave up, grabbed the floor of the tent, and shook it to remove pine needles, flashlights, socks, and two candy bars.

Lisa was there in a flash. "What are these candy bars doing in your tent?" she asked.

Greg, Billy, and Roger stood stunned.

"Leave them alone," said Philip. "What's wrong with a late-night snack?"

"First, it attracts bears, and second, it attracts rodents. Believe me; you do not want either in your tent." Her demeanor softened. "Please, fellows, I've learned from bitter experience. Keep food out of the tent." She turned to Philip, who maintained a bellicose posture. "I'm not opposed to late-night snacks. Just eat it all before you go to sleep. Do not keep any food in your tent. I am only thinking of your safety."

He shifted his weight. "All right, do what the lady says."

Lisa picked up the two candy bars and gave them to Steve. "Let's get the food pack put together." Steve and Lisa washed the breakfast dishes, packed the food, and finished cleaning up the campfire area. Lisa handed him the lunch. "Put this on the top of the food pack so we can get to it quickly."

He stuck the lunch under the flap and carried the pack to the canoe. Steve and Lisa packed their canoe and pushed it out in the water. Lisa took the stern, and Steve sat on the bow, ready to push off.

Twenty minutes later the other two canoes were packed and ready. "There's a very beautiful campsite three lakes away that I think you'll really like. Ready to go?"

"Yes," sang the chorus, but it lacked enthusiasm.

With a few dozen strokes, Lisa and Steve were way ahead of the others. Steve found a rhythm and was lost in the wonder of the environment. "Hold up, Steve," Lisa said. "They're way behind."

Steve stopped and turned around. "Come on, guys."

"We're coming," yelled Philip. He was in the stern. Greg was paddling in the bow with as much enthusiasm as a slug discovering a leaf. Billy and Roger were even farther behind.

Lisa wondered what would stimulate them. They had just had fish for breakfast, so lunch wouldn't do it, and as soon as they crossed this lake, there was a two-hundred-rod portage to the next lake. The others caught up to her and Steve's motionless canoe.

Steve said, "This is why we lost that game to the Tigers. We had no enthusiasm, no sense that we wanted to win or needed to win. We could have beaten them. We were better players. Instead we lost thirty-five to ten. You guys are acting the same way right now. Are your bellies too full? You're paddling like old women." He turned to Lisa and whispered, "Sorry, no offense."

"None taken."

Greg responded, "You really think we could have won that game?"

"I sure do. But we plodded along. Remember, Philip? You said in the huddle after that bad play, 'Don't worry, we'll make yardage next possession.' But it never happened, did it? We have to give it our best each possession. Now are you with me or not?"

"I'm with you," said Roger.

"Count me in," said Billy.

"Me too," said Greg.

Philip said nothing. Greg turned to him. "We can't do anything without our quarterback."

"All right, I'm the one that was dragging," said Philip. He saw his teammates' stern looks. "I'm sorry. It was my fault. All right, let's do some paddling, men."

The pace quickened as they headed toward the portage.

"This portage is two hundred rods," Lisa said as she put on her and Steve's personal pack and flipped the canoe on her shoulders. "See you on the other side." She was tired of how they had to be prodded into doing everything. *Why can't they see how privileged they are to be in this Canadian wilderness? Why aren't they filled with awe?* Lisa crossed the portage at a gallop and sat down for some solitude. She calculated how long it would take them to finish the portage. But no sooner had she sat down than Steve came bounding down the last hill. "Here's the food pack. I'm going back to spur them on." He ran back up the portage.

Lisa didn't follow, so she wasn't sure what happened, but she heard mumblings around the campfire that night. Steve had helped one with his pack, another with the canoe, and had walked behind Philip, prodding him on. It hadn't just happened on that portage; it had happened all day long. Steve, the quiet center on the football team, had become the team leader.

The next morning Lisa went for a swim and then made a small fire of hot coals as the men rolled out of their tents. Pancakes were on the menu, and Steve coordinated making batter and syrup. Billy and Greg sliced and fried summer sausage. Then Philip and Roger added the batter to the griddle. Each took a turn flipping pancakes. Lisa praised them for their skills despite finding a pine needle embedded in her pancake. She flicked it out without comment. She was glad to have any breakfast at all.

Slow in packing, they still broke camp in half the time of the previous morning. Lisa reviewed the map with them when they were packed. "There are several campsites on this lake. Which one should we aim for?"

"I sort of like the one on this peninsula jutting out from the north shore," said Philip.

"Looks good. Let's aim for that and check it out," she said. She rolled up the map and stuck it in her pocket. "Now, that lake has entrances from several different portages, so we might see other groups there. So let's get going and be there early enough that we have our choice."

With a goal they paddled with new vigor. Across a series of lakes and as many portages they maintained their stamina. In the afternoon, the wind picked up, and they had to paddle against whitecaps. Lisa was delighted to be paddling against the wind. She knew it would have been almost impossible for her to paddle against it by herself, but Steve's consistent strength and weight in the bow kept them on course, and they made steady progress. What a difference another person in the canoe made. After the next portage they switched. Steve was not as good in the stern, but his skills were developing. Besides, Lisa was thrilled by the roller-coaster ride of surfing the whitecaps from the bow.

After hours of paddling into the wind, Lisa felt invigorated, but the football players were close to exhaustion when they arrived at their chosen site. A flat rock shelf was very welcoming. A pile of stones made for a well-used fire pit. They were enthralled with the place. It was a great site, but there was something too good about it. Lisa hiked along the trails behind the camp, sensing that they were too well used for the usual campsite. At a fork in the trail she found what she was looking for: bear scat. She looked down an offshoot, more bear scat. She hurried back to the camp.

"Pack up, guys; we can't stay here."

Five astonished, tired, hungry voices said, "What?"

"Pack up. It isn't safe. Let's head over to that island across the way. I don't see any canoes there yet."

"I'm tired and hungry. I don't want to paddle anymore against this stupid wind. I'm not going. This is a great campsite. We're staying," said Philip. "Aren't we, guys?" He looked belligerent.

"You promised to let me decide if it was a matter of safety; now let's go." There was a silent standoff. "I'm not asking. I'm telling."

"We promised," said Steve.

"I don't like this," said Billy. "I don't see any safety problem."

"There has been a bear here in the recent past. That is the safety problem," Lisa said.

"I'm not scared of no bear," said Billy.

"If it's a safety thing," Roger said, looking at Lisa, "then it's important to do what she says." He turned to Philip and Billy. "Come on; don't be so stubborn."

Philip was the last to get back into a canoe. They had no choice but to paddle with all their strength as they headed straight into the whitecaps. The wind was so loud that they couldn't hear themselves talk without shouting. Conversation ceased for forty-five minutes until they landed on the island shore.

It was a pleasant site, with tall white pines protecting their campsite cove from the wind. The crew looked exhausted and discouraged. As they disembarked, Philip said, "This isn't half as good as that other campsite." He grabbed Lisa. "What was the big deal? Did you see a bear?"

"Scat," she said as she pushed him aside to scout the site. She followed the trails leading from the camp and found no bear scat. She returned to the camp to find places to put their tents. It was a smaller site and not as picturesque, but it had plenty of firewood. A gradual granite slope led into the water. By the time tents were up it was quite nice.

As he opened the food pack, Roger noticed canoes crossing the lake. He pointed to the peninsula. "They're camping in our spot."

"Now we'll see about bears," Philip said as he picked up the hatchet and split a piece of pine.

Just before dusk the wind died down. Lisa encouraged them to go fishing. Philip gathered his fishing gear and said, "Why don't you stay here, Steve, since you're teacher's pet? You can do kitchen chores. We'll go bring in the meat." Philip and the other three climbed in the canoes, leaving Steve baffled on the shore as they paddled off to fish. Billy and Roger went to the other side of the island, and Greg and Philip headed toward the previous campsite.

Steve climbed the rock to the fire pit. "I guess I'm the chosen one for camp chores." Lisa showed him how to make the pudding while she got the kindling ready for the fire. It was another pasta night, so she cooked the pasta, tenderized the jerky, and added the jerky to the stroganoff cream sauce, mixing it all together. *Wow, I've never had stroganoff on my trips before,* Lisa thought. *Roger sure knows how to make the food interesting.*

After Steve had the pudding ready, she handed him the vegetables, and he cooked them. When everything was prepared, she pulled him aside. "Do you see that spit of rocks and gravel sticking out from our island?" She pointed him in the right direction. "Do you know why it is shaped like that?"

Steve pondered for a moment, then said, "No, why?"

"Because this is not really a lake. It's a wide spot in a river system, and the current formed that curved formation."

"Oh."

"Now if we just paddle over there, I suspect it is deep on one side and shallow on the other. The walleyes will be sitting on the deep side just waiting for the current to bring them food. Dinner is all ready, so push everything to the side so it stays warm, and let's give fishing a try. What do you say?"

"Sure."

Lisa banked the coals and set the supper pots close enough to stay warm but not close enough to burn or continue cooking. She got in the stern and paddled while Steve sorted out his tackle. "Put on a simple jig with a rubber worm," she instructed. "Now throw it out. How deep is it?"

Steve cast about ten feet away from the canoe. His line instantly went limp. "Only three or four feet deep."

"Good, just let your jig drag." She oriented the canoe and paddled across the gravel spit. Five strokes later, Steve had a fish.

He brought it in and said, "What a nice walleye! Let's try it again." Steve was exhilarated. They followed the same procedure and caught another walleye.

"One more time, and we'll have fish for supper," he said.

She paddled the same pattern with the same result.

Steve pulled in a third walleye. "We have enough for supper, but can we do it again? I'll release it. I promise."

She laughed at his puerile response and obliged. She paddled the same pattern four more times, which resulted in three more fish, which he released. When she saw Philip and Greg returning, she and Steve paddled back to camp. Lisa had fillets in the frypan by the time Philip landed the canoe. Billy and Roger were just coming around the point.

"Any luck?" Steve asked.

"Not even a nibble. I don't think there are any fish in this lake. Those guys that took our campsite have two big pike hanging on a stringer. They said they caught them in a lake south of here. Maybe we should go there tomorrow," Philip said. He and Greg grabbed their gear and climbed the bank as the third canoe docked.

"We had a strike but lost it," Billy mumbled.

Steve turned the fillets in the skillet to brown the other side.

"What's this?" Philip asked, startled.

"Oh, just a couple of walleyes I caught." Steve winked at Lisa and moved the fillets around in the oil. The aroma of fresh fried fish overwhelmed them.

Greg and Billy ran up from the shore. Greg said, "Wow, who caught those?"

"I did," Steve said.

"Where?" Billy asked.

"Little place that Lisa showed me." He checked the other side. "They're done too; grab a plate."

"Man, Steve, I didn't know you could cook so well," Roger said.

"Definitely the chef of the week; these are great," Billy said.

"Can I fish with you tomorrow?" asked Greg.

Philip was silent, his mouth full of fish and pasta.

When supper was over, Lisa let the dynamics evolve. From their present position they had only a good day and a half of paddling to get to the landing, but she was fairly certain that her troupe had no concept of the distance or what was required to make their connection. She also wanted to see if they would decide among themselves if they would keep pushing, how they would delegate chores, and what role each would play.

"That was excellent," said Greg as he licked his lips.

"Outstanding." Billy was scraping the last of the pasta from the pot.

"This was even healthy," Roger said, spearing the last green bean from the vegetable pot.

"Well, Steve, you made the mess, so you clean it up." Philip stood and walked up to the tent.

Greg ran up the incline of the rock and stepped in front of him. Billy and Roger grabbed him from behind. "Someone who makes such a stupid remark should do the dishes by himself. Who do you think you are?" Greg asked. "On the football field you're the one who gets all the glory, but we each have skills that contribute to winning. Why can't you be a leader? Do you need the praise of the crowd to do your part?"

Lisa undressed down to her bikini, stuffed her soap into her top, and went for a swim. This was a conflict they needed to resolve among themselves; besides, the water felt refreshing. In the stillness of the evening she swam far enough away that she couldn't hear them. Standing on a submerged rock, she washed up. Stuffing the soap back in her top, she rinsed off and then floated on her back, watching the sunset paint the clouds red, orange, and purple.

As the stars twinkled into position, she swam back. She found the dishes done and the food pack hung on a tree limb. She pulled the canoes up on the bank and overturned two of them. She took the third farther up the bank, turned it over, and rolled out her sleeping bag underneath.

All five were sitting around the campfire laughing as Lisa approached. She put on a T-shirt and went to the fire to dry.

"Have a good swim?" asked Greg, scratching a pimple on his chin.

"Refreshing."

"Aren't you cold?" he asked.

"A bit." She turned her back to the fire for warmth and to speed the drying process. "You did a great job of putting the food pack away. Very neat. I'm impressed."

Billy put another split log in the fire. "I think we're getting the hang of this. I certainly feel like I've developed some new skills on this trip, in spite of being a know-it-all Boy Scout."

Steve poked the fire with a green stick, and sparks flew up. "We certainly have seen a lot more geography this way."

"There is a big waterfall we're portaging tomorrow. It's spectacular." Lisa turned to dry her front. Her damp swimsuit had made her T-shirt translucent. Only Philip seemed to notice. Another ten minutes and she was dry enough to put on a sweatshirt and pants. Besides, the mosquitoes were discovering them, although they seldom bothered Lisa.

The loons started their musical etude, which hushed the conversation.

"Are you all seniors?" Lisa asked.

"We are," said Steve. "This is our most important football season coming up. If we do well, maybe we can get football scholarships.

There were scouts at several of our games last year. Philip made three spectacular passes for touchdowns during one game. And he was never sacked the whole season."

"You must have a great coach," Lisa said.

"He's very strict," said Billy, "but Philip has done well."

Philip got up. "I'm tired. I'm going to bed."

Not much more was said except "Good night" to Lisa as the fire turned to embers and they headed for their tents. Lisa sat alone. She banked the coals and lay lengthwise on a log. The stars spilled across the sky as they painted the Milky Way. She took off her sweatshirt and pants and crawled into her canoe shelter.

• • •

It was still dark when she awoke. She decided that she was starting to enjoy the football players. They had picked up the pace and kept their promise not to complain—well, most of the time. They were now proficient at packing and delegating chores among themselves. Lisa had expected that she might have to do all the work, but right from the start they had shared camp chores. Lisa lay in her sleeping bag under the canoe looking out over the still water. Moonlight and stars glinted off the surface. She listened. There was no sound except the loons' cries and the gentle snoring of the guys in the tents.

I need a swim, she thought, *without a swimsuit. Do I dare risk it?*

She crawled out of her sleeping bag, having slept in her bikini. She pulled her towel out of the pack and headed for the water. She listened and heard nothing but snoring. The loons had stopped. She set her towel on a boulder near the shore and kept her eyes focused on the tents as she swam out to deeper water. She stood on a submerged rock and, after another good look around, stripped, looping her bikini over her arm. It felt so good to be naked, swimming like a playful otter. Even the bikini felt restrictive.

She dove deep into the crystal clear water, twisting and twirling. When she surfaced, she swam breaststroke out into the bay. She scanned the camp but saw no stirring on the shore. The water felt like silk streaming along her skin. She spun just to enjoy the sensation across her breasts and bare buttocks. She turned on her back and paddled her feet. The cry of the loons harmonized with the enchantment of the cold water streaming across her skin.

A streak of light across the horizon warned of dawn. She started to chill. A vigorous swim brought her to the shore. The dawn light scintillated across her wet, smooth form. She picked up her towel to dry herself when she heard a twig snap. In the soft light she picked out Philip's face peering at her from the shadows at the top of the ridge.

"Have you seen what you wanted to see, Philip?" she called.

He stepped out from behind the tree and said, "Yes."

In the confines of her towel she slipped back into her bikini. *Was his answer timid or presumptuous?* Lisa couldn't tell. He took a few steps toward her, down the rock face.

"Why don't you go back to bed, then?" Lisa said. "I have nothing more to show you."

Philip turned and headed back to his tent. Lisa finished drying off. *I guess I'll have to be more careful.* She laughed as she sat on a large boulder and watched the full sun peek over the horizon.

She turned when she heard rustling in the tents. *Maybe they're going to get ready early enough that we can get over to the waterfall for some swimming.* Out of the corner of her eye she saw Steve grab the communal toilet paper and head for the latrine. The others followed Philip down to the water's edge. She was surrounded before she suspected anything.

"So why don't you take off your swimsuit for all of us?" Philip said. "Show the guys how cute you look naked." Philip stood in front of her, hands on his hips, trapping her against the shore. Greg, Roger, and Billy stood in back of him. "Come on; we all want to see your lovely curves," Philip taunted.

Lisa felt defiant, angry, and disappointed. *What should I do? I can swim faster than all of them. I could just take off my suit. What difference does it make? I pose naked for the art class. But this isn't art class.* Fear, remembering the near rape, streaked though her mind. *I could fight them off.* She felt guilty. *I shouldn't have gone skinny-dipping. It was too risky. Now I've compromised my leadership.* She stared into each of their eyes. "You really want to see me naked?" she asked.

"Of course. We are red-blooded American boys," said Philip. "Come on, Lisa; take your suit off, like you did for me this morning."

"I was just going for a swim. I didn't think anyone was up yet. I did not take off my suit for you, Philip. You caught me putting it back on."

"I thought you wanted to show everyone your lovely tits." He turned to the others. "And she has a nice cunt too, guys."

The others backed up at Philip's profanity.

"Hey, what's going on?" Steve yelled from the top of the hill. Lisa froze.

Philip yelled back, "Lisa's going to do a striptease. We want to see her naked."

Steve ran down the bank and stood in front of Lisa facing his friends. "Can't a guy even take a crap around here without you guys hitting on the guide? Did you forget the conditions? This isn't respect! Do you want her to leave us here? We can't make it back by ourselves. What is wrong with you guys? She's helped us catch fish, found us campsites, and kept us from getting lost, not to mention showing us how to pack. Is this how we show our appreciation? What are you trying to do?"

Greg, Billy, and Roger backed up the bank. Billy said, "We weren't going to do anything."

Philip smiled and said, "She looks good naked. I just wanted to share what I got to see this morning. You don't mind, do you, Lisa?" Philip grabbed Steve's shirt. "What's wrong with *you*? I'm the quarterback, remember? Or are you taking over this fall?"

"If this is how you lead, I'm not sure I want to be your center. You can get sacked every play if this is the way you're going to treat people."

Two gunshot blasts sounded. Everyone turned to hear yelling at the other campsite.

Greg said, "Someone might need help; let's go." He and Billy took off in one canoe.

Steve grabbed Philip and shook him by his shoulders. "Now be a leader, Philip. Let's go." They set out in the second canoe.

Roger looked at Lisa as she slipped on her T-shirt. He said, "I apologize. You do have a great body, and Philip told us that you wanted to striptease for us. That was really crude. I'm sorry."

"Apology accepted. Now let's go see what those gunshots are all about." They scrambled into the last canoe. Roger was frantic, and with Lisa's strength they overtook the others and arrived at the site first.

"What's going on?" Lisa asked.

A petite teenage girl with short, black hair appeared in her scant bikini, gesticulating down the path. She was hyperventilating too much to talk.

Lisa noted their stringer hanging on a white pine with only a fish head remaining. There were parallel marks of bear paws down the tree trunk. Another girl, lanky with long, blonde hair, was desperately trying to cover herself with a towel as she climbed out of a pile of shredded ripstop nylon that had been a tent. "Is it gone?" she screamed at the other girl.

"Is anyone hurt?" yelled Lisa as the other two canoes arrived.

"No. Just scared shitless," said the girl in the towel. "He ruined our tent."

"What happened?" Philip asked, his eyes switching from one girl to the other.

Two late-teenaged boys came running into camp. One was tall with short, mousy hair and was carrying a rifle. He was dressed in loose boxer shorts he was holding with one hand. A shorter, dark-complexioned youth was running behind. He asked, "Are you girls all right?"

The blonde adjusted her towel over her breasts and groin. "Yes, we're all right. I just wish I had dressed better for company." She stared at the fellows climbing up the bank to their camp.

Philip stepped close to the blonde. "We heard the shots and thought someone might be hurt."

The rifle carrier imposed himself between Philip and the blonde girl and said, "Well, thanks, but the crisis is over."

Steve climbed up the bank. "But what happened?"

The rifleman looked at Philip. "You're the one who came by here last night, aren't you? Well, you can have this damn campsite if you want it. That bear ruined everything." Philip didn't answer. Greg hung his head and blushed.

Billy and Roger stood near the campfire. "There was a bear?" Billy asked.

"Yes," screamed the black-haired girl. "I was asleep, and the bear slashed right through the tent. Ken and I yelled. It grabbed our food pack and ran right over the other tent."

"We were trying to have an intimate moment." The blonde twisted her towel. "So much for peace and quiet in the wilderness."

"I chased it down that trail, but it was too fast for me," the one with the rifle said. "I shot two warning shots, but it only ran faster."

"So you had the food pack in the tent? What about the other tent?" asked Lisa, noticing that both were ripped.

"Yeah, the food pack was in our tent," the petite girl answered.

"Just some candy bars in ours," said the blonde.

"Where did you put your fish guts?" Lisa asked.

The blonde, pointing at the guy holding the gun, said, "Oh, wise one here forgot about the fish. They hung in the tree all night."

"Do you have any more food?" Lisa asked.

"Yeah, we have another food pack hanging in the tree over there," said the shorter guy, "but the bear got the good stuff."

"Your problems aren't over then; the bear will come back."

The guy with the gun looked at Lisa. "So who are you, T-shirt girl?"

Philip said, "She's our guide and a damn good one too." He turned to Lisa. "Hey, I'm sorry what I said to you last night." He looked back at the group of four. "She wouldn't let us camp here. She said it was too dangerous because she found bear scat on the trail behind your camp. I was miffed, but it turns out she was right." He looked down at the ground and kicked a pinecone.

Lisa took command. "We're leaving our site in an hour. We have a long way to paddle today. If you are staying on this lake, I suggest you leave this site and stay on the island where we were. Do you have enough food to get by?"

"If we catch some fish," said the shorter guy.

Steve said, "You pack up; meet us at our site before we leave, and I will show you where the fish are."

The two girls gave each other a look. The blonde said, "Sounds good to us." They looked at their partners defiantly.

The dark-haired girl added, "Because we are not staying here."

"See you in an hour," Lisa said.

As she and the football players headed for their canoes, Lisa saw Philip look back at the blonde as she dropped her towel and crawled into the partially collapsed tent to find some clothes.

The three canoes stayed together as they paddled back. There was lively talk recalling what they had just seen. Lisa thought they had seen a little too much. But the animation ceased as they reached the shore. All five guys stopped paddling and turned to Lisa, who set down her paddle. Silence.

Philip swallowed so hard Lisa heard it. "Lisa, what I did was totally wrong. I'm sorry. You have been a great guide, better than any of us expected, and we treated you like … a slut this morning. When I watched you come out of the lake, you were just trying to swim in private. That wasn't what I told the guys. I'm sorry."

"Yeah, I'm sorry too; I want you to be able to trust me," said Roger, slipping his hand through his waves of black hair.

"You have a great body." Billy wiped the sweat off his forehead. "I was just getting carried away. I'm sorry; it won't happen again. If you want to go skinny-dipping, that is your right as a free American. I just wanted to watch. I did it again. I'll never get this right. Let me start over. You have been a great guide. I didn't think a woman could guide a group of guys, but you've been excellent."

Greg flexed his muscles. "If they gang up on you, I'll beat them off."

"That didn't sound like much of an apology, Greg. As I recall, you wanted to see her naked too," said Philip.

"All right. I did," he said as he hung his head. "I apologize, Lisa."

Lisa stepped out of the canoe and straightened to her full six-foot length. "I've enjoyed guiding you, and I've enjoyed getting to know you, not in a biblical sense of course." They all laughed. "Come on now; we're a team, and we need to clear out of this campsite for our neighbors."

"I apologize too," said Steve.

"What are you apologizing for, you knucklehead?" said Billy.

"For taking a crap at the wrong time?" Steve wrinkled his forehead. They all bumped his shoulders as if he had just made a touchdown.

"Let's get to work, men," Lisa said.

"Right, guide," said the team.

• • •

Four hours later they were frolicking at the waterfall. Lisa showed them how to jump safely into the torrent at the base of the falls and, after a waterslide course down the rapids, swim into the eddy current. They were all awed by how the powerful eddy current swirled them back up to the base of the falls.

"This is better than a water park, and I've been to a lot of them," Greg said as he regained his footing on a rock.

"I almost lost my swimming trunks," yelled Roger. He was standing on a rock in the middle of the rapids holding his trunks up.

Philip was standing on the bank with Lisa watching the excitement. He turned to her. "There's no chance that you could go down one more time and lose certain items …?"

Lisa smiled. "No chance."

"Just teasing," he said.

"Just hoping is more like it."

Exhausted from their swim, they perched on rocks to dry. Lisa had planned on paddling a few more hours but did not want to break the serenity. Awed by the majesty of the falls, each member of her trip sat in silent contemplation amid the roar of the cascade, alone with the creator.

Lisa thought about her charges. *They've learned to work together as a team. They've even become efficient on the portages. Paddling has become second nature. And then there's Philip. I hope he has given up coercive power management for better leadership and given up that intolerable arrogance. I suspect that their football season is going to be impressive this coming fall.* She chuckled to herself as she imagined the headlines: *"Team Wins Division; Attributes Success to Canoe Trip."*

• • •

The last morning of the trip Lisa felt melancholy. She had put so much of herself into her group, and they were now proficient canoeists. As they approached the landing, she thought, *Only the portage to the parking lot, and the trip will be over too soon.* She was in the bow allowing Roger the stern. He had improved so much. He was no longer muscling his way to keep the canoe on course. He had developed a nice J-stroke, and his C-stroke was coming along as well.

"Two hundred rods to the parking lot, men," she said as they arrived at the landing. Nothing was said; each knew his job. Lisa lingered, watching. They took off so fast down the portage that she found herself with nothing to carry. Not quite knowing what to do, she searched to make sure no gear was left behind and ambled up the steep bank that led to the parking lot. Hopefully Troy would be there.

With the football players safely returned to civilization she thought about what she would say to him. *Do I love him? What a switch from all the guys at the university. I'm the one who wants what I can't have. Can he accept my past? I'm going to be honest, tell him everything. It isn't fair for him to think that I'm a lily-white virgin. There must be a chink in his armor. He sure is bad at calling and writing, but that isn't immoral.* She concluded with an outburst at the trees, "I'll do it today. He will break up with me, and then I can cry my way home." Her eyes swelled with tears, and her throat choked up.

An empty-handed group of football players ran over the top of the hill. Lisa blinked away her tears. "You didn't forget anything," Lisa said. "I checked."

"Yes, we did," said Steve.

"Something real important too," Philip said, smiling.

"But we don't have to go all the way back," said Billy.

"Will the load be too heavy, guys?" asked Roger.

"After what we've carried, no way." Greg flexed his muscles.

They hoisted Lisa up on their shoulders, each taking a limb. "She's heavier than I thought," mocked Philip.

"All muscle," said Billy.

"We can handle it," said Greg.

"Let's pick up the pace," said Steve.

They were jogging as they carried a screaming, writhing Lisa aloft to the parking lot. When Troy saw the entourage, he laughed so hard he tripped on the bank and fell seat first on the gravel. "Ouch," he said, grasping his sides.

"We're returning your guide, Troy," Steve said. "Where should we put her?"

"In the front seat," Troy said as he got up off the ground and hurried to open the passenger door. They ran right past him and circled the van twice before finally depositing her in the seat.

"Little trouble finding the seat. We get lost easily when we're not following our guide," said Roger.

The team climbed in the back and started singing their school song. Troy climbed in the driver's seat after securing the canoes. He leaned over and kissed her. "You seem to have charmed them. I'm impressed."

Lisa was still giggling at her unexpected portage carry, but Troy's kiss made her turn away to look out the window. Sadness filled her soul as she thought about what she was going to do and what she was going to say. *I have to tell him everything; I've made my decision.*

CHAPTER 30

In the nineteenth century, an African American lyricist said
that God put the rainbow in the clouds themselves, not just
in the sky. But if the rainbow is in the clouds themselves,
that means that in the darkest times, in the dreariest, and the
most threatening of times, there's a possibility of hope.
—Dr. Maya Angelou, May 6, 2005

Lots of hugs and a tearful good-bye saw the team climb into the
van and head out of the parking lot. Troy put his arm around
Lisa, squeezing her to his side. As the dust settled at the end of
the driveway, he said, "I have never seen a group so transformed. They
were obnoxious, arrogant know-it-alls, and they return appreciative and
competent outdoorsmen. What did you do to whip them into shape?"

"The wilderness has its own strict code, to quote Robert Service,"
she said.

"They came back from the wilderness just as nasty as they went in
last year. I dreaded their arrival when I saw them on the schedule."

"And you let me take them out? You threw this timid sheep among
the wolves?"

"I tried to stop you, but you were too stubborn," he said and squeezed
her shoulder. "But you're hardly a timid sheep. You've got tenacity. Now
I realize you've got charisma as well." Troy took her hand. "Come, timid
sheep; Helga has lunch ready. Tell us the whole story."

As they walked into the Svensons' private quarters, Helga was
pulling a baked chicken out of the oven. Ernie was sitting at the table

but took off his hat and stood as Lisa entered. He said, "So you did survive. Summer help was pretty worried. He never worries about the other guides. I couldn't figure it out."

Troy pulled out a chair for Lisa and then sat beside her.

"That poor boy was on his knees before God all week, praying for your deliverance," said Helga. Troy blushed. She continued, "Now, don't you start telling any stories till I get all this grub on the table."

"The food sure smells good," Lisa said. "After a week in the wilderness with a bunch of football players, a girl gets pretty hungry."

Helga put the chicken next to the mashed potatoes. She said, "That was terrible—these men of mine sending a nice girl like you out with that pack of wolves. I hope you taught them a thing or two."

"They were totally transformed, Helga," Troy said. "When I picked them up, I hardly recognized the group I dropped off."

"It was still a horrible thing to do to someone you're in love with."

Lisa stared at Helga.

Helga said, "Oh, yes, he's in love with you. Don't let him tell you anything different."

"He's been moping around like a sick puppy all week. Couldn't even get the wood split right," added Ernie.

Troy whipped his hat at the table. "Come on; that's not true."

Ernie smiled. "Pathetic, just pathetic. I couldn't get an hour of honest work out of him without him asking, 'Do you think she's all right?' So I'm glad you're back. Maybe his work performance will improve."

Lisa laughed. They all laughed.

Helga sat down as she put the last of the vegetables on the table and nodded at Ernie to say grace. Troy grabbed Lisa's hand as everyone closed their eyes. Ernie seemed to be prolonging the prayer, to Lisa's impatience. When he finished, all the food was handed to her first. Then the questions began. Lisa told the whole story, except the part about Philip desiring a striptease.

The chicken tasted as if she had never had such succulent meat in her mouth before. She rolled each mouthful, extracting the flavor. When the apple pie appeared out of the pantry, she already felt satiated, but the smell was so intense and the flavor so delicious she ate all her pie as well.

Ernie even smiled when he heard about the bear. Helga just kept saying, "Oh, honey." Troy took every opportunity to grasp her hand.

As she was finishing the story, Troy interrupted, "And then they carried her on their shoulders all the way to the parking lot. It was quite a parade."

She pushed her chair back and stood to pat her stomach. She was so full. Troy bolted from his chair and grasped her in a frantic hug. He kissed her to Ernie's and Helga's cheers.

She had no choice but to return his affection. It felt great to be caressed by his strong arms. *I'm going to miss this if he gives up on me*, she thought.

To change the focus of the conversation, she asked, "Did you call my parents?"

"Yes, I did. Now come out back; I want to talk to you about that." Troy nodded at Ernie and Helga. "May I have this moment in private, please?"

"Yes," Helga said between muffled chuckles.

As Troy led Lisa out back, she asked, "So what did my mother say?"

"I spoke to your father. He was quite impressed that you were guiding a group. I failed to mention that they were all guys from a football team."

"He sounded pleased?"

"Yes."

She walked to her Jeep and grabbed clean clothes. "May I use the showers?"

"Certainly."

"Great." She shut the Jeep door and headed for the bunkhouse.

He stood in her way. "There is one more thing."

She faced him. "What?"

"I told your parents that you wouldn't be heading home until next week."

She wrinkled her brow. "Now we are going on a canoe trip?"

"I know you have just spent two, almost three, weeks in the wilderness."

"That's common knowledge, at least around here."

"I was sort of hoping that …"

"Spit it out, Troy. You're exasperating sometimes."

"I talked Ernie into giving me time off so we could canoe out to Stuart Lake together. Just like you suggested."

"May I take a shower first? Or do you like your women smoky and smelly?"

"Be my guest. You can use the men's or the women's since we don't have any pickups or arrivals today."

"I think I'll use the women's. I wouldn't want someone to mistakenly barge in on me." She turned and headed for the shower.

Troy stood with his hands limp at his sides. "So it's a go?"

"Yes. We talked about it. Now, may I take a shower?"

The hot water felt glorious. *There is nothing like a hot shower after a week in the wilderness to release endorphins into a girl's brain*, she thought. She twisted and turned, focusing the spray on every part. Her ecstasy made her feel faint. She cooled the water down and sprayed it across her face and chest.

She turned the hot water up and shampooed her hair. *Now what am I going to do?* she wondered. *If I go with Troy on this trip, I just know it will be all over. Am I leading him on? That kiss was great.*

The water was so soft the shampoo billowed like whipped cream over her head. As she massaged her scalp, she laughed, picturing Troy talking to her father. *He should have talked to my mother. That would have been more challenging.*

She rinsed her hair, squeezed it out, and directed the spray on her back. *The question is, should I spend the week with Troy? It will give me an opportunity to be honest. I can tell him all the gory facts. He can get angry with me, and then I'll go home.*

She noticed that her feet were still dirty, so she took the soap and wedged it between each toe and rinsed them again. *Maybe I can have sex with him before he never wants to see me again.* She stepped out of the shower, towel-dried, and put on the clothes she had taken out of the Jeep. *All my clothes are dirty except these. Well, he'll just have to see me in dirty clothes or no clothes at all.* She smiled at the thought.

The sunlight was so bright when she walked out of the bunkhouse that she covered her eyes. Troy was sitting on a bench under a tree. "Only clean clothes I got," she said as she walked over to him.

"Helga is washing your dirty clothes now. Would it be all right if we left tomorrow morning? I haven't finished packing our food. Besides, there is a good movie showing at the theater in town. Would you like to see it?" He took her hand and encouraged her to sit on the bench beside him. "All expenses paid for a night on the town. But I should warn you it isn't much of a town, and it is over thirty miles away."

Lisa agreed. She insisted on driving her Jeep, and they left for the town. The evening did not help matters. The movie theater was showing a travelogue of Alaska. It was interesting, but except for another couple that left early, they were the only ones in the theater. Troy's embrace felt soothing, but she kept him at bay.

The town consisted of a general store that was also a gas station, the theater, and the combined post office and volunteer fire department. When they walked out of the theater, the lights in the atrium were shut off already, and the general store had been closed for over an hour. The other building had been dark since the postmaster closed at four o'clock. One streetlight led to Lisa's Jeep.

When they got back to the outfitter, Troy said, "Do you want to stay at Roger Leland's house? Your bed has clean sheets."

"No, I'd rather stay here at the bunkhouse. You're coming back to get the canoe and food pack, aren't you?"

"Yes, Ernie is taking us to the landing."

"All right, see you in the morning." Lisa climbed out of the Jeep.

Troy ran around and hugged her and gave her a kiss. "I love you very much."

"I love you too, but I am really tired."

"See you in the morning." Troy waved as he headed for his car.

"You won't love me tomorrow," Lisa whispered. She closed the bunkhouse door behind her. After she heard his car leave, she went into the bathroom to urinate and brush her teeth. She took the first bunk as she came out. As she collapsed on the bed, she felt a lump in the pillow. She switched on the light. There was a chocolate kiss on her pillow. "He's ridiculous. How did he know I would pick this bunk?" she said as she popped the candy in her mouth. "This is not making things easier."

• • •

Morning came with a gentle tap on the door. "I'll be right there," Lisa said. She dressed and headed outside to put her gear together. Her clothes were clean and sorted on the picnic table. A large new plastic bag was beside them. Even her swimsuit had been washed and dried. She selected what she wanted to wear and told Troy, "I'll be right back. I'm changing into my canoeing clothes."

"You look nice this morning."

"Oh, stop. This is what I wore last night."

"You looked nice then too."

"Get the canoe on the trailer and the food pack ready. Here's the gear I need. When are we coming back?"

"Next week sometime. Ernie gave me the whole week off."

She returned to the bunkhouse with her clothes and put on her bikini. Her blouse and shorts went over the suit. She put on stockings and boots, rolled up her long-sleeved shirt, donned a new raincoat Helga had given her, and walked out the door with the rest of her clean clothes in the plastic bag. "I'm ready."

"Me too." Troy climbed in the back of the van. Ernie had the engine started, and the canoe was on top.

Lisa thought about climbing in the passenger seat next to Ernie but decided that would disappoint Troy, so she climbed in after the poor fellow.

. . .

After four hours down a meandering stream with a few small portages and then a mile-long portage, they paddled into Stuart Lake from the south. It was almost a perfect circle with a large island in the middle. It reminded Lisa of a medieval castle with a large moat. The banks rose several hundred feet on each side, which was why the portage had been so steep and the lake free of campers, not to mention a mile-long portage from the north was the only other access.

"I've been here several times, and I have never met another group here," Troy said. "But there are three campsites. Which would you like? There is one over on that eastern peninsula, one on the north near the other portage, and one on the island."

"After my bear experiences, I prefer the island."

"So be it."

They crossed to the island with Lisa in the bow. She was tired of guiding and wanted Troy to make the decisions, at least for this trip. She was impressed with how smooth he was in the stern. The canoe barely wavered in its course. In fact, she didn't even feel him correct their direction. *What a contrast to my football players*, she thought.

Once on the island, she was pleased with her selection. It was a lovely site with a nice flat place for the tent. She wondered whether she would be sleeping in the tent with Troy or under the canoe. Time would tell.

They were a good team as they set up camp together—two seasoned campers who anticipated the other's actions. Everything in order, Troy looked the place over. "A nice home," he said and turned to Lisa. "You ready to go fishing?"

"Why? Didn't you pack any supper?"

"Just grease, breading, and some freeze-dried vegetables. Off to the north, a stream cascades out of this lake; let's check it out." He paused and added, "Unless you've decided to be a vegetarian."

"Sorry, I'm mostly a carnivore, so let's get some fish."

They headed straight for the portage and pulled the canoe up the bank. "Follow me," he said. She anticipated following the portage, but instead he broke through the brush and followed the streambed. He hushed her when they got to a clearing. The stream cascaded through large boulders and flowed into several small pools.

He stepped only on the rocks, avoiding any brush. She followed. He gave her a lure and put one on his own line. He had a modified fly rod. She had her spin cast. He whipped the rod and dropped the fly on top of the water. She had to use an awkward technique, as the fly had no weight, but she still managed to get the fly in the pond. Hers floated around in the eddy current. He pulled his back and reset it.

It was tedious, but soon they had four substantial brook trout for supper. Several others, they "treated and released" as Troy, the emergency department orderly, said.

"Time to go," he said, his first spoken words in hours. "Even I would have trouble finding my way out of here in the dark." He picked up the fish. "Wasn't that fun?"

"This was great. I've never been trout fishing before. It sure is a quiet sport, isn't it?"

"Almost any noise or vibration will scare the fish. I've caught something every time I've come here. Everyone takes the portage. The few groups that do come through here don't even know this place exists." He held up his trout. "Ready for supper?"

"You didn't even have the decency to serve me lunch. Some guide you are. Yes, I'm very ready for supper."

"I figured someone who went three days with no food wouldn't need lunch."

"That was last year. And if you recall, I had crayfish pasta and arrow plant and cattail roots. I did not go three days with no food. Oh, and a perch."

"I stand corrected." He took the fish, and she grabbed the fishing rods. They made their way back through the brush to the canoe. It was magic hour, so the lake was smooth as glass. They paddled in silence. Neither was willing to break the tranquility.

When they arrived at camp, she announced that she needed to swim before supper. She went down to the shore and took off her shorts and blouse. He went to the tent to change into his swimsuit. She stood waiting for him in her bikini.

There's no one here. I think I should go skinny-dipping. I hate to get my suit wet. Besides … She grabbed the straps to pull off her top. She saw an image of Philip standing in front of her telling her to strip. The memory shocked her. *I can't do this. Not yet.* She closed her eyes to get rid of the vision and pulled her straps back up.

She felt a hand on her shoulder. "Ready for a swim?" Troy asked. He dove into the deep water. "I've checked it out before. The water is almost twenty feet deep here. Go ahead and dive."

She dove. The cold, crystal clear water felt great. They swam out from shore. She outdistanced him quickly. When he caught up to her, he dove. She followed. Under the water, he captured her and put a breath into her mouth as he kissed her. He caressed her as they surfaced.

"Nice kiss," she said. "Do you do that to all the girls?"

"I've never brought anyone else here. You're the first."

"I mean the kiss, not the campsite."

"You're the first to get a kiss like that." He smiled, swimming on his back and kicking water in her face.

She raced after him. He swam as fast as he could, but she caught him and dunked him under the water.

He came up gasping. "I need mouth-to-mouth resuscitation, or I'm going to die."

She kissed him. "Does that help, dying one?"

They splashed around till both were tired. Troy had to breaststroke back to camp. Lisa still had the energy to swim freestyle.

As she climbed up on the rock, she thought of stripping. *What would he do? What would he think?* She turned, still considering stripping, but he had just made it to the rock. "A little help please; I'm beat."

She reached down to help him up, and he pulled her back in the water.

"You rascal, last time I ever help you out of the water," she said.

They both scampered up on the rock laughing. Recovering from his mischief, she pushed him back in the water and said, "You deserve that."

She went to the tent to change into her clothes. She slipped off her wet swimsuit and threw it out of the tent onto a rock. She took her time drying off, wondering what she would say if he came in the tent. She heard the fire crackling, put on warm clothes, and crawled out of the tent. He had changed and was frying the trout on the griddle.

Her stomach ached with the smell of spices, hot oil, and fish frying as she whipped up the chocolate pudding. In short order they were ready to eat. She teased him about trying to divide up the food exactly in half, but there was more than enough. They were stuffed by the time she plopped the last morsel of her fish into his mouth.

It grew dark as they finished the dishes. They sat by the fire. Lisa poked the embers with a green stick and watched the sparks fly upward. She paused to listen to the mournful song of the neighborhood loons. She turned to see a pair swimming together in the moonlight.

"Have you known many women?" she asked.

"I've dated a few. Most of the girls I've dated were pretty wimpy, and none of them were interested in canoeing."

There was a loud snap as a pitch blister on a stick of pine exploded. "No, I mean known them in a biblical sense—you know, sex."

"No. I never met anyone that I was that serious about. Girls that are interested in the latest fashions and what kind of eye makeup they need to go to the next campus party turn me off. I'm looking for someone with strength of character and tenacity. Someone who gets all bent out of shape when their patent leather shoes get scuffed just doesn't have the same priorities I have."

"Oh," she said, "you're weird." She hoped he couldn't see her flushed face in the light of the campfire.

"True," Troy said. "You're not like the other girls I've dated. You've canoed solo, fought a bear for food, lived off the land, and guided football players on a canoe trip. You've even fallen down the Wickstead-portage cliff and survived. You are exactly the kind of woman I've searched for all my life, as short as that may be."

Lisa exploded. "Quit gushing over me, Troy, just quit. I'm not the clean, nice girl you think I am." She got up from the fire and walked over to the edge of the lake. Soft tears rolled down her cheeks. She snapped, "And don't promise me anything."

"Lisa, I love you. I love your courage, your strength, your persistence." He tried to hug her.

She snarled and pushed him away. "But I've had sex with half the basketball team and some of the starters on the football team. Is that the kind of girl you want? Do you love me or just some fantasy in your head?" She swallowed hard, wiping some of her tears away. "I'm messed up, okay? One of the plant supervisors at the factory tried to rape me. Stripped off my blouse and cut off my bra with a box knife, then stuck a pistol into my breast. I'm not sure I can trust … men," she spat. She took a deep breath, exhausted from trying to keep everything inside.

"But you just came back from a canoe trip with a bunch of football players."

"They treated me as a guide, not a woman. Well, most of the time. And no, I did not have sex with any of them, to stop your little fantasy." She shifted her feet, twisting her toes into the water. "I might as well spill all my crap," she continued. "I model for art classes at my university. I am bare-ass naked when I model, without even a well-placed towel. Almost every art student at the university has drawn pictures of me naked, pubic hair and bare boobs." She sobbed. "I'm not good enough for you. You haven't even had sex with anyone. You need a nice, pure virgin, someone much better than me, someone who hasn't had a dozen fucking cocks up her vagina." Lisa was breathless from her tirade.

"Is that what's been bothering you all day?" Troy asked. "I knew it was something. You've been holding this crap inside of you?" He held his hands out to her. "Just because I haven't had sex means I'm not allowed to love you? Do you want me to have sex with some girls in Madison and then come back to you? That's ridiculous. I love you the way you are." He motioned to a large boulder. "Sit down."

She stood her ground. His voice was gentle as he said, "Sit down, please? Tell me everything you think will offend me. Tell me about all the guys you have had sex with and the supervisor who tried to rape you. I'll listen."

"You won't like me anymore." Tears streamed down her cheeks. She looked away at two loons. *Probably mated for life,* she thought. She yearned for what they had.

"You won't even let me hug you now. Can it get worse? Try me." He took the initiative and sat on the boulder. She sobbed, looked out over the lake, and then covered her face in her hands. Blinded by her tears, she backed up to the rock and sat down next to him but facing the lake. She couldn't look at him.

The moon traversed the night sky as they sat in silence on the rock. He slid around so that they were both dangling their feet in the water. She let him touch the bottom of her feet with his toes without pulling away. Starting with the guy in high school who had fondled her breasts and how she had jumped out of the car to run home, she told him about each guy. She was graphic and profane.

He remained calm. "Keep going," he said. Except for an occasional question, he did not interrupt her. She talked incessantly as the boil of guilt, anger, and humiliation burst open. The purulence of emotional anguish poured out of her soul.

The moon was behind them before she let him touch her shoulder. She asked, "So what do you think of me now?" Defiance peppered her voice. "Pretty ugly, huh? Not the kind of fucked-up girl you want, am I?" She left him and stepped in the water. "And as for your English-teacher mother, I can't spell either. I know she won't accept me."

"Lisa." He touched her arm, and she didn't pull away. "I can't imagine what courage it required for you to be so honest. I choose to love you. You are not my fantasy." He laughed. "Darn close but not quite. You are a flesh-and-blood woman that I have chosen to love. Just because I haven't had sex doesn't make me an angel. I just haven't lived the life you've had to live. Give me a chance to love you."

"I don't care about your problems," she said. "I need to know if you can forgive and accept me." She searched his eyes.

"One condition."

She heaved a sigh of despair and wondered what he was going to ask. Did she have to have a pelvic exam and be certified free of sexually transmitted diseases? Did she have to promise never to screw up again? *I'm sure the condition will be too heavy, but I've got nothing to lose.* She sobbed. "What? I know I can't meet your expectations."

"Forgive yourself? I can't do that for you. Nothing you have told me has any effect on my love for you. But you have to forgive yourself before you will let me love you."

"So if I promise to forgive myself, then you'll love and have sex with me?"

"Lisa, if you forgive yourself, you'll be free to love a caring, edifying, enriching love of which you are very capable." He paused. "Right now you're not allowing me to love you. I think you need someone to love you, someone who knows what you've been through. I selfishly want to be that person. Please let me."

She collapsed into his arms, sobbing on his shoulder as he hugged her. For the first time in years she felt the load of insecurity, guilt, and hating herself fall off her back. "Do you really love me as I am?"

For a long time they were silent. "Yes," Troy said. His strong arms surrounded her. In her mind she could hear Heidi's song healing her soul. The loons were singing the melody to Heidi's words as the stars danced in their galaxies, and shooting stars added the light show. The Milky Way reflected off the water, dancing on the miniature waves lapping on the shore.

"I'll be faithful to you," she said during a pause in the loons' song. "I need to work at forgiving myself, unloading my crap, but faithfulness is a good first step, don't you think?"

"I will be faithful to you as well."

"Troy, your faithfulness has never been in question." She watched a fish jump after a fly on the surface of the water. The circular waves from the fish intercepted the shoreline. "Do I have to give up modeling? I really enjoy it, being nude, in a socially acceptable environment, of course."

"Any good art come out of the class?"

"Nothing marketable, well, except for one professional artist from the Caribbean. I could show you the oil painting she did of me. The rest are just students. Most of their drawings don't even look like me. The professor has a hard time finding models, and she is so professional that I really like modeling for her. Art saved her life."

"If you enjoy it, keep right on. But I do feel a sudden urge to transfer to UMD and major in art."

"Should I take my clothes off right now and show you how I pose for the class?" She got up and started unbuttoning her blouse.

"No, save it. I'm feeling incredibly excited about you right now. You know ..." He swallowed hard. "Aroused. I'm not sure I could handle seeing you naked."

She hugged him. "You are special. I was sort of ... testing you. I've never met a guy who would pass on the opportunity. You really turn me on. I'm learning to love you, I guess."

He grabbed her waist and turned her to face the lake. He slipped his hands across her belly. Her abdominal muscles resisted his touch.

"Do you see that tree on the point over there?" he asked.

"Yes."

"That tree has lots of pinecones on it." He slid his hands along her sides. "But it had to have good roots before it could bear fruit. Do you know why?"

"Why?"

"Without strong roots it would not handle the storms. We're growing roots, Elizabeth, so we can enjoy the fruit of our relationship."

"How do you know my full name?" She squirmed around to face him, and her breasts touched his chest.

"That's what your father calls you."

"Oh, that's right, when you stormed into my life last Christmas. Did you know I hate you when you're being wise?"

"I love you too, Elizabeth."

"I'm glad." She laid her head on his shoulder as he caressed her.

Oh, God, I do love him. I dropped all that shit on him, and nothing bad happened. All right, I'm willing to be patient for the sex part; just please, God, don't make me wait too long. "Amen," she whispered under her breath

"Were you praying?"

"Yes. And don't ask what I was praying about. It's between me and God. I've already shared too much tonight."

She lifted her head and looked him in the eyes. "One more thing: no matter how much you love me, I still can't spell."

"I promise never to tell my mother. I don't spell well enough for her either."

A wolf stilled the calls of the loons with a long, mournful cry. Then there was only the buzz of morning insects. She put her hands on top of his and pressed them deep into her belly. Under his hands, she could feel what she had yearned for with every man she ever had sex with but never experienced: joy.

Her stomach growled. "Staying up all night with a guy makes a girl hungry. Can you make pancakes as well as you make omelets?"

EPILOGUE
TEN YEARS LATER

Lisa walked in the house, slammed the door behind her, and leaned back against the doorframe. She let out a deep, painful scream.

"Is that you, my beloved?" Troy appeared out of the bathroom with only a towel wrapped around his head. "It didn't go well? I still love you." He kissed her before she could utter a word. He unbuttoned her blouse, reached his hand into her bra, and fondled her breast.

"Stop that," she said.

He froze. "I always do that when you come home."

"But not tonight." She pulled his hand away and buttoned her blouse. "It's not good news. Why don't you cover up?" She plopped on the couch.

"You're the one who runs around the house naked all the time."

"Shut up." Her anger melted. "I'm sorry. I didn't mean to snap at you. Please don't tease me right now."

Troy took his towel off his head and rubbed his hair dry. It stood up like straw in all directions. He wrapped the towel around his waist and sat next to her on the couch. She pushed him away, not letting him touch her. "They did that hysterosalpingogram." She slumped, her face in her hands, and looked at the floor. "The physician said I will probably never be able to get pregnant. My uterus and tubes are full of scars from the gonorrhea and chlamydia infections." She gnashed her teeth, and tears gushed as she turned and laid her head on his bare muscular shoulder.

"That's the x-ray of the inside of your uterus?"

"Yes, and don't ask me to spell it, or I'll punch you."

"I won't. I wouldn't know if you were correct or not anyway."

She jabbed her fist into his ribs. He flinched but didn't say anything. She grunted. "What are we going to do?"

"I doubt if having more sex will do it. After six times Saturday night I was exhausted. And sore I might add."

"Quit joking." She stood and braced his shoulders against the couch, bouncing her forehead into his. "Don't you get it? I can't get pregnant. I'm too screwed up. I wanted children."

He pulled her onto his lap. "I'm not making fun of you. I know you're disappointed. I've known since before we got married that you might not be able to have children. I want children too, but I understood that might be an issue when I chose to marry you. I love you, Elizabeth Tamara Vogel, and we do not have to have children to prove it. Do you want to make an appointment with your physician friend Heidi Barton?"

"I got a letter from her yesterday. She's still in her residency at Hennepin County Hospital. I'm not traveling all the way to Minneapolis to see her. But that's not the point. What are we going to tell my mother? She is just waiting for grandchildren. I feel so guilty about that time at UMD when I was having sex with any jock that was willing to put his cock up my crack."

"Lisa, don't be so crude."

She collapsed. "This is bad," she said. "And it affects you even though it's not your fault. You have millions of mobile sperm according to your lab test." She squirmed in his lap to illustrate. He smiled but kept from laughing. Her face turned angry red. She squeezed her tears onto his shoulder and gritted her teeth.

"Lisa, my sweet, you have brought so much joy into my life. I have never dreamed I could be so happy. You are always doing something I don't expect, even after eight years of marriage. You know these have been the best years of my life, and I hope they have been for you too."

"They have been good years. I do love you." She braced herself against his shoulder. "You know I told God I was willing to be a nun one time, but not being Catholic it was a little difficult."

He hugged her around the waist. He slipped his hands inside her skirt waist and squeezed her buttocks. "Think about the wonderful life we've had. We have a successful business. The Outdoor Sports Shop is doing better financially than we ever imagined. We've gotten to go on lots of canoe trips, even down the Yukon River. We hiked the glaciers in Alaska for our honeymoon. We go to St. Martin on vacation every winter so you can skinny-dip in public. We go scuba diving and take a trip to the Rockies or the Alps to go skiing every year." He slipped his hands out of her skirt and held her face, forcing her to look him in the eye. "And you have a husband that loves you very much."

"But Mother and grandchildren."

"What does your mother know about your promiscuous past?"

"I'm not sure. Linden seemed to know everything, but I never told my parents anything, and I was too upset to find out what they already knew."

"So let's either decide that children are not for us or adopt. What about that?"

"Do you want to adopt? I'm not sure that's what I want to do." She grabbed her groin and screamed, "I want my genitals to work right and get pregnant myself and have my own children."

"What if we had children and they turned out like you?"

She relaxed. "I was hoping that your genes would protect them."

"Oh, don't count on that. As I remember, a certain woman that I married clearly enumerated all my faults for me, on paper no less."

"I was mad at you, though I can't remember why now. I only enumerated your faults so you wouldn't get a big head. Best defense is a good offense."

"They were all true. Look how I've improved after eight years of marriage. I kept that list, so I know what to work on."

She jumped off his lap. "You still have that list?"

"Yes, Mrs. Vogel, in the back of my sock drawer. I can't say I have met all the goals, but I have improved on seven out of ten."

"According to whom?" she asked.

He stood, notched his towel around his waist, and walked her to the back door. "Let's go for a walk."

"Aren't you going to get dressed?"

"I'm not in the mood, and there are no neighbors for five miles. Come on. It's a nice, warm day."

She kicked off her shoes, bent, and pulled off her pantyhose. "I hate these things."

They walked out the back door and around the Olympic-length pool, then down the path between the roses. The path was sand. Troy had hauled several truckloads of sand, one wheelbarrow at a time, from the driveway to the path because Lisa had wanted a path she could walk without shoes. The sand felt good between her toes and comforted her soul. They walked past the tennis court that had been a gift from Lisa's parents for their first anniversary.

Troy asked, "You want to hit a few tennis balls to get rid of your anger?"

"No. I'm not angry; I'm upset."

"Tennis won't help?"

"Your towel would fall off."

"So? We've played tennis nude before."

"With shoes on," she said and kept walking.

The doves were singing their evening song as Lisa and Troy followed the smooth stepping-stones through the more undeveloped part of their property. They came to a pond. The pond was natural, and many would have called it a swamp. Crickets and frogs echoed each other's songs. Cattails and arrow plants populated the marshy edges. A red-winged blackbird took off to join its mate in the nest. Whirling dragonflies kept the mosquitoes at bay.

On the other side of the marsh, behind the cedar trees, they had built a gazebo together. It had been a challenge, since neither knew the first thing about carpentry. It had taken almost a full day just to haul the boards back behind the marsh. They had worked together and done a lot of reading, and despite a few boards that they'd sawed too short and had to replace, the gazebo had gone up. Since it was so far from any electricity they'd had to use hand tools for much of it. Lisa said that it had made them stronger. The gazebo looked good, the mistakes well hidden. They sat on the wooden bench and watched the sun scintillate along the tree line.

"Back to your mother," he said. "Can't we just tell her that the doctor said your uterus is abnormal and you can't have children and that we're thinking of adopting? Infertility is pretty common. We don't have to tell her any more than that. Or we could lie and tell her it is my fault. I have abnormal sperm or something. How about that?"

"We can't lie. You're the one who made me promise when we married never to lie."

"I was testing your integrity."

"You know that I've kept my promise. Besides, somehow she would find out, if Linden hasn't already told her. Do you know what Linden said at our wedding? Just before he played that dance number on the piano, he asked me, 'Are you going to be faithful to Troy or screw around?' On my wedding night. Can you imagine? I slugged him right in the gut."

"I know. He told me later; he thought it was pretty funny. I rather enjoy Linden. He's different. But that runs in your family."

She kicked his ankle.

"Ouch," he said.

"I'm not sorry."

As they sat there a blue jay landed on the side of the gazebo. A moment later a second jay joined it. The birds, probably mates, arched their necks, peering at the humans, as if to analyze the unusual creatures seated in front of them.

"Do you remember why I married you?" Troy asked.

"Yes, but tell me again." The blue jays flew off together.

"I married you because you have tenacity and endurance. If you never get pregnant, you still possess those qualities that I cherish." He put his arm around her and gave her a gentle hug. She resisted but not enough for him to release his grasp. They sat resting together, enjoying the music of the evening creatures.

She slid away and pushed his arm off her shoulder. "Tell me how you forgave me for fucking a whole bunch of guys before we were married. I need to hear that part again."

"We've been over this ..." She glared at him. "All right," he continued, "you were honest and told me all about that part of your life. I chose to marry you in spite of your past. You told me all about your liaisons, and I still chose to love you."

349

"Right. I love to hear you tell me that, but the consequences aren't over." She covered her face as tears dripped through her fingers.

He held her shoulders till she quit shaking and then stood her up. "You're loved. You're forgiven. Most people never have that. You're special, Elizabeth. Isn't that enough? The women's basketball team has had a winning season since you've been coaching them. You have good rapport with the girls. When they were here for that party, I saw the influence you have on them. Each owes you for the personal growth you provoke in them. You not only coach but also teach them how to live.

"You guided five canoe trips this summer. Those teenagers will never be the same after what you taught them. You embarrass the guys on the trip with your strength and stamina, and the girls give up the excuse that they can't do something just because they're women. Aren't those your children? Those are consequences of the choices you've made too." He laughed. "And then Steve Flynn became an NFL center. You had a lot to do with that. You heard him say on national television that it was a canoe trip that turned his life around."

She let him grasp her hand as they walked back toward the house in silence. She scratched her leg on one of the rosebushes. He knelt and kissed the scratch, wiping away the single drop of blood with his tongue. As they walked past the pool, she asked him, "Did you clean the pool today and check the chemicals and the temperature?"

"Yes. The pool is all taken care of."

"Did you wash the dishes and clear off the counters?"

"Yes, and I made a cold pasta salad with pepperoni for supper. It's in the refrigerator whenever you're ready to eat."

They walked into the living room, and she said, "You vacuumed too, didn't you? I didn't ask you to do that. Vacuuming is my job."

"I had a few minutes, so I did it."

They sat on the couch like mannequins in a store display. The telephone rang. Lisa jumped to pick it up. "Hello."

"It's Amy. Barak is sick again, and I just can't miss school tomorrow. Eric has clients from Florida that he has to meet with. Can you take care of Barak? After what he did to the last babysitter, it is hard to find anyone." Amy, Lisa's schoolteacher friend, paused and took a deep breath. "Sorry to call at the last moment. Oh no, he just vomited all over the living room carpet."

"And he has a fever," Eric said in the background.

Amy added in desperation, "Could you be here when Jason comes home from school too?"

"Don't worry," Lisa said. "You know I'm glad to take care of your children, even when they're sick. Troy can handle the store, and besides, we hired a new manager, so I'm free. No problem. You know I love your kids."

"Thanks so much. Usual time then?" said Amy.

"Right."

"Got to go," Amy said. "Now he's throwing up on the couch. Thanks, Lisa."

Lisa hung up the telephone and cuddled up next to Troy on the couch. She put her hand on his chest to feel his heart beat against her palm. She twisted a few of his chest hairs between her fingers. "You heard the conversation?"

"Yes, Barak is sick again, so we are parents tomorrow. They sure struggle with that kid, don't they?"

"Yes." She snuggled closer.

Troy said in a quiet whisper, "Eric says the boys are always better behaved when they've spent time with us. When we took care of them that week they went on vacation, Barak apparently didn't get into trouble for almost a week afterward. I guess we're a good influence on the little rascal."

"He's not a rascal; he's just like I was."

They watched the sun set over the tree line through the massive picture window. The house darkened. The solar floodlight over the pool and the underwater pool lights came on. The soft light cast an eerie blue hue that streamed through the sliding glass door and formed a lighted path to the water.

Lisa stood up, unbuttoned her blouse, and unsnapped her bra, dropping them on the floor. She slipped off her skirt and panties and flung them on the chair beside the door. She opened the sliding glass door and stretched in the doorway, arching her back slowly till her hands touched the floor behind her. For a moment she held the arched position. Then with a thrust of her legs she stood straight upside down on her hands. She searched his face. She enjoyed watching his eyes feast on her body even though she knew it was familiar to him. She flipped upright and walked to the pool to feel the nocturnal breeze waft across her skin. She strolled to the deep end and paused to let the pool lights dance across her nakedness.

He followed, dropping his towel along the way. She dove, and he dove after her, surfacing next to her. She pushed him away and swam to the opposite end of the pool. He followed. She skirted his advance and swam the length of the pool again. As he tried to catch her, she dove, swimming the length of the pool underwater. He tried to follow, swimming furiously, but couldn't match her speed. Both surfaced breathless. She grabbed him and held him close. They tread water in the deep end as their naked bodies enveloped.

"You can play with me now," Lisa said. "But be gentle. I've been through a lot today."

"With pleasure."